The Queen of Deceit

BOOKS BY MICHAEL LAIRD

The Chronicles of Tethera

The Forged Prince

The Torc of Tethera

The Queen of Deceit

The Gates of Annwyn (forthcoming)

The Queen of Deceit

Book Three of the Chronicles of Tethera

MICHAEL LAIRD

The Queen of Deceit

By Michael Laird

Copyright @ 2017 Michael Laird

ISBN: 978-0-9966503-5-9

For Wikipedia, keep it up folks.

CONTENTS

Chapter I

Wave-sweeper

Just before the attack began, Prince Llew, acknowledged heir to the kingdom of Gwent, stood alone at the tiller of his ship, exulting in the early morning wind that swept him south towards home.

Given that, until very recently, he had never been aboard a ship, or even a row boat, his seamanship had come a very long way in a very short time. Never mind that this was only by virtue of daily lessons from Helgar and Addfwyn, his best friend and his man-servant, respectively, the fact remained that they now trusted him alone at the helm. Of course, it was his ship, after all, and it had occurred to him on more than occasion that their trust might have less to do with his skills than with them thinking that, if he broke it, at least he had bought it.

Now that Llew was enough of a sailor to take notice, he could see what an extraordinarily lucky find the little ship had been. Especially lucky, he reminded himself, considering the extremely urgent and very specific purpose he had needed it for.

The Wave-Sweeper, as Addfwyn had named her, was Northman built and not especially large, yet she was a robust

1

craft, intended for both open sea and shallower waters. More than that, she was fast. She also did not need a large crew and, right now, on a steady broad reach, all she needed was a firm hand at the helm to allow her to fairly fly across the smooth morning waters.

It was, Llew decided, not quite like flying—he knew of nothing that compared to that—but it was still grand. Sailing had a magic and thrill all its own—especially while his comrades still slept, and the sea and the sky were all his. Even his great steed, Gower, and Helgar's new horse, Gullfaxi, both held securely in their canvas slings amidships, seemed to be drowsing.

That feeling of speed and freedom only made it more surprising when a great bone grapnel hook flew up from the water and found purchase on the starboard bulwark near the stern, followed an instant later by another on the port side.

Llew goggled at them both for a moment before crying out, "To arms! We are under attack!" Two more hooks found purchase on the railings as he did so.

Wave-sweeper did not have any internal cabins or storage spaces. Everyone slept on the multi-leveled deck with the cargo and supplies, uncomfortable as that might be in foul weather. Now it was a life saver for, as his companions threw off their blankets and furs, while snatching up weapons with stunning swiftness, they were almost instantly available where they were needed. Further, they showed the kind of speed and urgency that is only learned and mastered by those who have recently passed through an extended period of danger and uncertainty.

First up was the red-haired Cymri. Her sword was only half drawn before she spotted a port side hook. In a flash she was in position to begin chopping at the slimy tether attached to it. On the third swing this brought her face-to-face with a horror that used the tether to pull itself up out of the sea.

Man-like in form and size, it seemed somehow misshapen. Its pallor was the greyish color of a drowned corpse, while its facial features were even more grotesque; all of them had seemingly been placed almost at random, with no attempt at symmetry. Enormous gills flapped on each side of its neck, and its hands were webbed and clawed. Never hesitating, Cymri shifted her grip on her blade and, with one quick slash, sent the intruder back into the waves.

Unable to leave the tiller, Llew shouted a warning. While she had been dealing with the first, two more of the creatures had come up to the deck. They attacked her at once. Cymri knocked the thrust of the first away with a flick of her sword that seemed too quick and restrained to do the job, yet it did. She pirouetted away and was gone when the other's weapon passed through the space she had occupied. Then she was somehow behind them. What came next was so quick that Llew was never sure if it was one longer stroke or two shorter ones. In either case, both her opponents fell to the deck and did not rise.

Caradog, the young king of Gwynedd, was the next to stand. Just as he reached his feet and began to run towards Llew, a third hook seized upon the starboard side behind him and the boy spun in place, clearly wondering where he could best be effective in whatever was happening.

"Caradog, up here!" Llew called. "Take the tiller and hold it straight. We dare not let the wind blow the bow off at this speed or we will all be in the sea."

Caradog lunged towards him and stretched out a hand for the tiller, leaving Llew free to dive for his sword as soon as he was certain his shield-bearer had the ship. Snatching the hilt with one hand, and the scabbard with the other, he drew instantly and abandoned the sheath, still tied to the railing. With the enchanted blade, Fragaroc, firmly in hand, Llew felt ready to defend Wave-Sweeper against any enemy.

Helgar had arisen, somewhat groggily perhaps, yet he grasped the situation almost at once. As more of the sea creatures came swarming up the lines hooked on the starboard side, they did not get far before meeting the Northman's whirling axe. Those that were still able made high pitched screeches as they fell away from the ship and back into the sea.

The man-like sea creatures stunk like dead fish and wore armor of sorts, evidently taken from the scales and shells of various creatures of the sea. Their weapons were bone-headed harpoons and, to Llew's eyes, looked deadly enough for most purposes.

However effective these attackers might have been in the sea, the speed with which Cymri and Helgar were dispatching them showed they were more than a little ungainly out of the water. Llew himself sent two of them back into the waves and began to feel the day might already be won—just as a dozen more bone grapnels came surging out of the waves to either side of the ship, catching the railing both astern and aft of where he stood.

He yelled in alarm and moved to defend, noting only in passing that his man-servant, Addfwyn, was near, his stout wooden club firmly in hand. That worthy, in turn, looked about wildly and, seeing that an especially large adversary had made it onto the deck behind Llew, leaped across the intervening distance and delivered a fierce clout to the side of the creature's head. The crab carapace it was using as a helmet split wide open with the force, but managed to partially save the thing's skull in the process. The attacker still went down and stayed down.

Oblivious to this, Llew wielded Fragaroc with almost surgical precision and sent three more of their attackers back to the depths before they could even clamber onto the ship. A quick scan showed him that Cymri and Helgar had done their share as well. With no more attackers onboard, he joined them in chopping at the tethers to the grappling hooks. They did not cut easily; each took multiple slashing blows to completely sever.

Surveying the rest of the small open ship, it was clear the attack was over. All the lines were cut and no more of the creatures had managed to get on deck.

With his foot, Addfwyn nudged the one that had fallen to his club. "My lord, after this one failed to stab you in the back, the rest seemed to lose heart. They must have realized they would have no success here today."

Llew regarded the creature on the deck. It lay unmoving but he could see it was not dead. "This may be the sixth most ill-favored creature I have ever laid eyes on," the prince remarked. "Even its animosity towards us barely serves to make it less endearing than it would be already."

Helgar joined them a moment later, "Shall I put it out of its misery, Llew?" he asked, brandishing his axe for emphasis.

"Not just yet, my friend. We need to know more and it might be able to speak. Cymri?"

She did not answer so he looked up and was startled when did not see her immediately. This was alarming on a ship so small as Wave-Sweeper, even though he had seen she was safe and whole just a few moments earlier.

"Up here, Llew," her voice came from behind Gower in the ship's midsection. "Gower got excited and escaped his sling during the fighting. Help me get him back in."

"Escaped his sling? How—never mind. I suppose that is only to be expected of a shifterish horse." Llew strode down to help ease the big horse back into his canvas carrying sling.

"My lord," Addfwyn interjected, "I can do that for you."

"Oh absolutely not; I simply will not hear of it. Besides," Llew grinned evilly, "I need you and Helgar to secure our prisoner, and then do something about these decks. Otherwise I suspect that, as the sun rises further, we will have a fearful stink—worse than it already is, at any rate," he added. He wrinkled his nose in an expression of disgust for emphasis.

A short time later, with Gower once more secured, and the decks at least partially sluiced down with buckets of seawater, two more buckets of seawater were applied to the sea creature's face, if such a misshapen thing could be called a face. It awoke all at once and, rather than just testing its bonds, immediately began struggling to break them. In this it was unsuccessful. Helgar had used enough rope to envelop it in what was almost a cocoon, there at the base of the mast.

"So it awakens," Llew said to it. "Any particular reason you decided to attack us this morning?"

The creature said nothing but the look it returned was poisonous.

"Ah, I see. You want us to think that you cannot understand us. Well, the only reason I would let you go would be to take a message to Dylan, but if you cannot understand me there would be no point in that and Dylan will simply need to overcome his cowardice and come face me himself."

The Fomorii responded with a snarl.

Llew smiled. "So you do understand me. Wonderful. We have things to discuss, you and I. If we can do that . . . well then, perhaps you could even bear my message to your master."

The creature finally spoke and it was a deep voice, much like that of a very large man—if that man also had lungs full of water. "I am Dux Sevasto! I have no master! I bow only before Dylan, son of the waves, and he has no fear of such as you, only hate. You are a dry thing of the land and what few juices you contain will be squeezed out without notice when he steps upon you."

Llew was not at all surprised to hear the creature admit Dylan was behind this attack. Who else could it have been? Even so, it was unsettling to reaffirm that the master of the seas was personally intent on his destruction.

His own response required little consideration; it was best to put a brave face on it. He gave a sardonic grin and said, "I will grant you the benefit of the doubt and suggest that what you just said might sound more frightening if spoken in your native tongue."

"Fool," the Fomorii spat, "this is my native tongue when speaking in air. But you are a greater fool still if you do not already fear the tide that returns. When he comes for you it will be too late to feel fear. It is best you start now."

Helgar bellowed his mirth and said, "Llew has so many enemies that he simply does not have the time for that, Dux. If Dylan desires attention he must place himself in the queue with the rest."

The sea creature's expression was nearly impossible to make out, but Llew suspected it reflected complete incredulity. Then it blinked twice, nictitating membranes snapping over its bulging eyes. "Pfagh, I know this one's type. They come from the dying land across the sea. At Dylan's orders, we sink their ships in great numbers and they do not swim well. They, perhaps above all others, have ample reason to fear the exalted one, but their minds are not so keen as to know this."

Face suddenly hard, Helgar hooked his axe under the Fomorii's chin. "Hold!" demanded Llew. "One death will not avenge all your people, Helgar, and we risk little if we try to find a better use for this one."

Helgar scowled and lowered his axe a few inches.

The prince of Gwent turned his attention fully to the thing calling itself Dux Sevasto. "This is no parley. You will agree to carry my message to the one you call Dylan, regardless of what you believe his response will be. Otherwise, I will give you to Helgar, here and now. By your own words you have established he has a legitimate grievance with you and your kind."

"What message is this," the creature demanded, "what would such as you have to say to such as he?"

"Tell him—" Llew took a moment to gather his thoughts as all present waited for him to speak again. "Tell him that, despite everything, it is not too late. I know of no reason for his hatred of me. If I have given him cause, pray, let him tell me of it and perhaps we may speak together and somehow abate it."

Dux Sevasto sneered. "The son of the wave has no interest in such an offer."

"Fine, tell him anyway. Further, if he will not at least tell me his reasons for behaving so, then tell him I name him a great coward if he fears me so much he can only send his annoying puny proxies. Tell him he is truly a coward if he can neither explain his grievance to me, nor face me in personal combat. Tell him that, too."

The Fomorii licked his lips with an unusually long tongue, one that was very nearly prehensile, then spoke in a subdued voice. "You are either very brave or very foolish. I suspect there is little difference between the two in this case. I will give him your message. Enjoy what life you have left, for there is not much of it."

Llew nodded to Helgar and the great axe came up. Dux Sevasto flinched as it came down, but all that was severed were the ropes binding him to the mast. It took him a moment to realize he was still alive, then he was over the railing with one quick movement, followed immediately by a loud splash.

Chapter II

A Problem with Bards

Two weeks later, Llew found himself explaining that it was becoming increasingly evident that there was something odd going on with Cymri.

"What am I supposed to do, Helgar?" Llew complained. "Do I just walk right up to her and tell her that her behavior of late has been very strange, then demand to know why?"

"Heh," said the enormous Northman, as he studied the bottom of his nearly empty cup of ale. "I think that could be very dangerous, Llew."

"Ah, you are correct. That suggests a plan of action. Did you not once say that, if ever I found myself on dangerous ground with a female, I should refer her to you?"

Helgar looked up sharply. "Is she trying to get you alone so she might work her wiles on you?"

He laughed as he saw Llew's reaction. "Somehow I did not think so, even if she is the only unmarried woman in the kingdom who might not wish to. My answer must be no, my drott. Some things you must truly do for yourself."

"I rather thought you might say that," Llew grumbled. He drained his own mug and set it down upon the rough-hewn table. For this conversation they had chosen the deepest, darkest corner of the great castle Caerleon's ale cellar. Lit by a single candle, it was precisely the perfect spot for a clandestine meeting. As a bonus, there was more ale than even they could drink. Being so well-hidden and remote, it had taken Caradog at least two minutes to find and join them once his training session with Afaggdu was complete.

Despite a hasty coronation when he had turned fourteen, Caradog still appeared to be well short of that age. He was an awkward young man, certainly, but those that knew him had all developed, however grudgingly, an appreciation for his intellect and education. "You really need to run through it all again, Llew," suggested the young king of Gwynedd.

Llew quirked his mouth. "Wonderful idea, perhaps you could summarize for us."

Without any hesitation, Caradog began listing them. "One, she took your damaged armor to be repaired, but she did not take a horse. Two, there are no unruined villages within a day's walk of where we were. Three, it is very unlikely any village blacksmith would have had the skill to even attempt to repair such fine armor. Four, that armor was enchanted—probably by Moriganna herself—so no ordinary blacksmith could have possibly repaired it."

"That last part is the one that worries at me most," said Helgar, stroking his beard with one hand. "Other than Moriganna herself, I have heard of no mortal in this land who might be able to perform such a feat other than maybe King Govannon of Dyfyd. He is rumored to be such a smith as to rival the dwarf masters themselves."

"Some few of the Fae are reputed to be astounding smiths as well," Caradog offered.

Llew gave him a sharp look. "And how likely that any would have been close by and willing to do it for her? Especially after she turned Queen Mab into a black bird?"

"It makes the most sense if this Moriganna was nearby and Cymri knew it. Then Cymri might have taken the armor to her to be repaired," said Helgar. "Could not this witch have been that close? From what you have said, she could shape-change as easily as you can. Following us so we would not see her would have been simple for such a one. When you yourself turn into a wren, no one notices you at all."

"Aye," agreed Llew, "but Cymri knowing that she was following us, and even working with her, makes no sense. Those two hated each other. Neither of you saw how bad it was, but I had to deal with being in the middle of it for years. I cannot imagine anything bringing the two of them together."

"Perhaps she was replaced by a changeling, as you once were yourself," suggested Helgar.

Llew snorted. "Generally, if the Fae wish to enchant one of their half-breeds so it can be left in place of a human babe, they start with folk a little bit younger than a grown woman."

"Speaking of changelings," said Caradog, "what did King Pendaran say when you told him that his own great-grandfather said you that you could not be of their line?"

Llew winced. The memories of that conversation were still fresh. "He told me that, if the man we spoke with in Avalon was truly his great grandfather, why then, he was wrong. He also said that if it just happened that if that man really was Bran the Blessed, and he was also not wrong, then I just might as well consider myself adopted. 'Oh, no,' says he, 'you are not getting out of this that easily.' I would worry he might be planning to marry me to Llewellyn except that, either way, she is still my sister, either by birth or adoption. Likewise, he reminded me that even if it was Bran, and even if he was correct in saying that I was not of his line, then he was probably also correct when he told me I am Boudicca's heir, and that the throne of Gwent, and even that of Tethera itself, is mine by right."

"King Bran deduced all that because you were wearing the Torc of Tethera," Caradog reminded him. "We know that just wearing it is not proof of anything. Consider that you took it from Goll One-Eye's neck. That would mean the great war chief of the Picts is the rightful high king of all Tethera."

Helgar slapped his knee and barked a short laugh at this. "He is going to be a rightful dead Pict when next we see each other."

Llew spared him a sharp glance. "Save it for your usurping uncle first, Helgar. Goll can wait until you take Lindenjal back. Besides which, Goll One-eye pretty much vanished off the face of the earth after we upset his invasion plans."

"He will be back," Helgar declared, his tone now ominous. "His kind always comes back."

Llew turned his attention back to Caradog's question. "If we follow Bran's explanation of the torc it does not matter that Goll One-Eye was wearing it. According to Bran, the only reason Goll could even hang on to it, let alone wear it, was because the torc was somehow using him to get itself to me. It certainly did not allow him to shape-shift."

"It may be," suggested Helgar, " that Moriganna took possession of one of her Pwacca and used it to shape-shift into Cymri's likeness? Recall how she did that with Addfwyn that time at Caer Einionault? Wait . . . no, I am sorry, that would not account for it either. Cymri would have just told us she had no memory of taking the armor to be repaired if that were true. Instead, it must be that she is covering for Moriganna."

"If Moriganna was even involved," corrected Llew. "We are making a number of assumptions here."

"So, ultimately," Caradog said, "it comes down to how much you trust Cymri."

Helgar snorted. "Well, when you put it like that—"

Llew frowned. "Put like that there can be no question that we trust her. All three of us would be dead many times over were it not for her bravery and skill, her deep stores of knowledge, and her wisdom and calm in applying them. As for skill—"

Caradog sat up. "What about skill, Llew?"

"It is her swordplay. As we all saw, she is quite proficient with a blade. Perhaps she is not quite in Llewellyn's league but perhaps she is. If she is not, then she is not so far off. She can certainly pull her own weight, even with us."

The king of Gwynedd looked perplexed. "What of it? You seem to be a lodestone for women who are skilled at arms. Even that treacherous Meirion, Cai's lieutenant and leman, was no neophyte with a blade—may the road rise up to kick her in her treacherous backside wherever she now roams."

"Um, yes," said Llew uneasily. It was extremely uncomfortable to hear Caradog insulting the woman that was his own birth mother in such a fashion, despite, or perhaps because of, the fact Llew had not yet shared that news with him. That Llew had inadvertently adopted Caradog in the process of learning about it himself, and had thus far neglected to inform the young king of this, merely served to make the subject that much harder to approach.

"The issue is that Cymri and I have been together nearly every day since I was a boy. In all that time I never saw her draw a blade. Granted, Taliesin and Afaggdu may have taught her some things when she was young but, after not touching a sword for seven years, she suddenly reveals herself as someone whose skill is equal to that of those that were actively training all that time? No, it is neither credible or explainable."

"Well," Helgar remarked phlegmatically, "we know she is Taliesin's daughter. We also know that she has not been replaced by a shape-shifter using her form; the hounds that patrol all of Caerleon are always looking for the sneaky creatures. For that matter, Gower, faithful steed that he is, would probably have stamped her into red mist by now were she a shape-shifter."

Llew scowled. "We have come full cycle. It still seems I must just walk right up to her and tell her that her behavior of late has been very strange. Then I will demand to know why. And if she gets angry, or just walks away and refuses to answer, what can I do then? Nothing, that is what."

Furrowing his brows, Helgar said, "Ya, perhaps you should do it somewhere she cannot merely walk away."

"That—" Llew paused in midsentence to consider this. "Actually, that is not a bad idea. All the same, I would still rather not do it at all."

"Better you than us," said Caradog, and held up his cup to knock against Helgar's. The two of them took a big swig of ale before Llew relieved Caradog of his cup. "That is probably enough at your age," he cautioned.

Caradog bristled for a moment. "What? Who made you my father?" he objected.

"You might be surprised," Llew replied quietly.

Helgar sprayed ale a short distance, then wiped it from his beard with the back of his sleeve. "Apologies," he muttered, and got up to leave.

Caradog watched him go before saying, "If strange behavior is cause for suspicion I would suspect Helgar of something as well."

Neither of the two royals laughed.

Chapter III

Cymri's End

It was the next day before Llew found time to ask Cymri for an excursion. They met in the stables at mid-afternoon. Llew had exercised Gower earlier, and he was in the process of grooming him when she arrived.

"It looks to me like you two already went for a ride without me," she observed at once.

"Yes, well, Gower is not always good on waiting and I was down here early—" Llew stopped speaking and regarded her for a moment before starting over. "Actually, it was in my mind to take a small boat out on the lake. I have already had it moored at the postern gate."

Cymri arched one eyebrow. "I hope you are not planning on me to do the rowing?"

"I dare say my feeble arms can handle that chore."

They passed through the postern gate to a ledge that was barely adequate to stand on without falling into the lake. There was no bridge or path, just water. In this way it did not require the heavy defenses that were an absolute necessity for the main gate. As promised, Llew took up the oars and rowed them far out across the lake, very nearly to the other side. It was a singularly private place as the royal barrow grounds were nearby and no ever came near them for any reason other than interments.

"This was a good idea, Llew," she said after a bit. "There are some things I need to tell you and it is best if we do it in private."

"What kind of things?" Llew asked cautiously.

"I think you know I have been keeping some things from you, and from everyone else as well."

Llew ceased rowing and shipped the oars. "I am waiting," he said quietly.

She bit her lip lightly before speaking. "First, I must ask you this. Have I ever been other than a faithful companion to you? I taught you the things you needed to know. I dedicated myself to that singular task for years of my life. I led you to where you could acquire Boudicca's Torc, or else it could acquire you. We rescued Helgar, we evaded the Picts, I led you to Cas-Eiddew where you met Hafgan and gained treasures, as well as learning more of yourself and your sister. I helped you free Llewellyn from King Iolo's tower. And that does not even begin to mention my aid against the worm, defying the queen of the Fae, and in pursuing all of your goals prior to that final meeting with Cai."

Llew drew in a breath to reply. "You also got my impenetrable armor repaired, although I know not how. That is one of several questions I hope you will answer for me. Also, the sword I carry was loaned to me by your father. Yes, Cymri, of all my companions no one has done more for me. I freely admit I would be dead many times over were it not for you."

Llew paused as he considered. This was not precisely the way he had expected this conversation to turn, but his questions could wait. He was sensing an opportunity that might not present itself again.

Throwing away caution, he said, "Yet none of that is why I value you and your friendship above all others." He took another deep breath before making the final, irrevocable plunge. "This is not how I imagined telling you, nor even something I had intended to discuss today, but it seems to me to be far more important. Since the subject how I feel about you has arisen, I must tell you it is my most fervent desire that I be more than merely a friend to you, and my dearest hope is that you would reciprocate this desire as well."

Cymri looked up sharply, as if struck unexpectedly by an arrow. "Llew! That cannot be! I am much too old for you, and there are other reasons as well. It is as you once said, you merely have eyes for one who was once your teacher and . . . and perhaps you are trying too hard to compensate for having lost Bloddeuwedd."

"No," Llew insisted, "it is not that at all. I have given this a great deal of thought, and this is the truth. I realize now that I have always loved you, even when we were both in captivity and me just a student and you my tutor. Yet I discovered I was affianced and duty compelled. If Bloddeuwedd had been who she should have been then duty, let alone duty coupled with desire, could have let me set it aside and, hopefully, never act on it.

"As for age? You claimed to be sixteen when you were forcibly brought to Caer Mallcoedwig, and I was but nine. That was then and this is now. In the seven years since, you have aged but two years' time while I have somehow managed eight. You are eighteen and I? I am now but a year younger; that is less than the difference between my age and Bloddeuwedd's when first we met."

"Can you set this aside for now and hear me out?" she asked. Her mien was one of considerable concern which, in turn, was raising terrible misgivings in Llew.

"Since you ask it of me then of course I can, for now," he replied.

She folded her hands on her lap and studied his face. "My news is such that it will not matter later."

"Tell me then." He felt his stomach clench with dread.

"A question first, Bloddeuwedd took your trust so that she could betray you, intending only your destruction. Can you accept that another might take your trust so that they might prevent you from being betrayed, intending only your salvation?"

"I do not understand the question," he replied, concern written in his eyes.

"Just this then, if I confess terrible things to you, will you—no matter how terrible they seem—promise to merely sit and listen, then allow me to depart thereafter? That you will make no attempt to follow?"

Llew looked for any signs she was less than serious and found none. Disbelief chased confusion across his face. "I am not sure I—wait, what are you saying? If you ask it I will try, but I would never seek to attack you. Not even if you sought to strike me down where I stand."

Cymri sighed and glanced down for a moment. Her extreme unhappiness was obvious, even to Llew, but it was beyond his imagination as to what she could say that would be that bad. "Then know that I have done more to aid and preserve you than you ever imagined. I took you to a secret place to be healed after you were pierced by Celtchar's Spear. I also arranged for the Pwacca that saved you and Caradog from the hounds of Annwyn in the wilderness, the same Pwacca that continue to protect Caer Mallcoedwig. I even allied with that treacherous snake, Dylan, to get you into the confidences of the royal family of Gwent—and I swear to you no one need have died but for his double-dealing with Arawen."

She looked up into his shocked face then. Her hair—although it stayed the same bright auburn—grew much longer. At the same time, her face changed, although only slightly, becoming somehow different even as her features grew more accentuated . . . but the eyes . . . more than anything else it was the eyes, he realized. They had become wise and knowing and very, very dangerous looking.

"Moriganna," he breathed.

"Moriganna," she agreed.

Chapter IV

The Once and Future Queen

An awful thought came instantly to Llew. "What of Cymri? What have you done with her?" he demanded.

Moriganna smiled sadly. "There is no Cymri or, rather, you have never met her. Cymri is just someone that I used to be. It is the name I was given at birth . . . a very long time ago. I only brought her back, after a fashion, because I needed to place myself in King Pendaran's court and, later, because you needed her."

Llew began to stand up in the small boat, came dangerously close to capsizing it, then sagged and fell back to his seat. "No."

"Yes, Llew, by any name there was only ever me."

He could barely hear her, and only with difficulty could he take meaning from the sound of her voice. "But . . . but I saw the two of you together, many times," he protested.

"You saw us together only at dinners during the year before she became a bird. You already know I can switch my control from my own body to that of a Pwacca, and from there I may take nearly any shape I please. Granted, flipping back and forth constantly for nearly an hour each day is trying, a sort of puppet show, but when the goal is worth winning one does what one must. You obviously never noticed that Cymri and I never both spoke at the same time, or even that there were normally slight gaps when one of us spoke right after the other had."

With some small part of his mind that was left to him, Llew wondered what it was he was feeling. It was almost like grief, but Llew was an expert on grief. This was so much stronger, and somehow different, that it was in another category altogether. "No," he heard himself say aloud, "I cannot accept this. No."

This was a kind of grief, and it was far worse, he suddenly realized, than if Cymri had actually died. At least then he could have remembered her as she was. That was not an option here. Cymri, his beloved Cymri, with her vast reserves of knowledge and calm, his pillar of strength and stability in a hostile world, was not dead. To be dead you had to be a real person, and she had never even existed. During all of this his thoughts twisted ceaselessly in futility as they attempted to find some way in which none of this was true.

Moriganna watched him with an expression that, on anyone else, Llew would have labeled as pity. "I am so very sorry for the deception, Llew. You became fonder of her than I had ever anticipated. I came to you as Cymri because I knew I was putting a lot on you with my evil enchantress guise, and I had no desire to make your life one jot more difficult than it had to be."

"You made my life a living nightmare!"

Moriganna arched her eyebrows. "Cymri made your life a living nightmare?"

"No! You did! As—yourself."

"Did I? We revisited Caer Mallcoedwig together. Was it that awful for you? It seemed to me you were fairly pleased to find it as you remembered. That would seem to indicate you do not find your memories there to be too terribly odious."

She leaned forward towards him and stopped just short of resting her hands on his own. "I kept you safe and gave you everything I could to ensure you would survive," she insisted. "If I had ever been revealed, all could have been undone. The Lord of Death has eyes where you often least expect them. I am frequently called the Queen of Deceit and it is in my nature to know these things. You should also be aware that it was I who arranged for Gower to come to you as your faithful companion and mount. I personally tutored you for seven years. I even gave you my adoptive father's sword. With my own hands I forged and enchanted armor for you that could very well become known as the thirteenth treasure of Tethera and, when it was damaged, I stood at a blistering forge and repaired it myself. I also arranged for Afaggdu to come train you. Whether I am a monster or not, I am not the monster you think I am—the monster I led you to believe I was."

"Why are you telling me all this now?" he asked in a hoarse voice. "You think I will make you my chief advisor and let you run everything? Is that what this is all about?"

Moriganna searched his eyes and appeared saddened at what she saw there. "You are not still fooled by my charade are you? I am sorrier than you could ever imagine that it was necessary, but it was the best way I knew of to keep you safe. I never dared let it slip, for you never know for sure when he is not watching. I so longed to give you the childhood every child deserves, the one that was denied me as well, and for the same reason, but I could not."

"How bad was your childhood, Moriganna, and why should mine have been what it was because of yours?" Llew asked in what was almost a shout.

Moriganna's face grew stony. "My purpose in life was chosen for me before my birth, a bargain with my mother, sealed in blood. I was to pass down through all the ages of Tethera, ready to give myself when the great kingdom was threatened by that which could destroy it. My life was sacrificed for the good of Tethera and I was renounced by my own mother, all before I was even born. Despite all that, even in success, I failed. A second doom came to replace the one which I averted. In you there is a chance, however slight, to undo that failure. This is all about saving Tethera and, as for ruling? I could not care less about ruling. In truth, I would do much to avoid it. I spent longer than you can imagine as the high queen in an unhappy time and have no desire to do that again."

"You are an evil sorceress!" Llew spat. "You kill people for trivial things or even just because it pleases you."

"Really? And who do you know, or even know of, that I have killed? Think hard."

Llew was taken aback by the question. He felt certain he could easily identify a dozen or more, yet no names came to him.

"Reputation was all I needed for the disguise," she continued, "I have never, ever, taken a human life—not one. And I am not a sorceress, well, not primarily, at any rate."

With eyes narrowed, Llew asked, "In that case what are you?"

"I am a Druid, possibly the very last one, selected as suitable to become the chosen vessel of the goddess herself, even before I drew my first breath. When she finally came into me I was changed irrevocably. My name became Moriganna, in her honor, and that was the least of it. It takes twenty years of constant study to become a neophyte Druid—decades more to become a master in the Druidic order. I achieved it all on a single day when I was but seventeen years of age."

Llew stared disbelievingly. "Who are you? You said you were high queen of Tethera once. But there has only ever been one . . ."

"Ah, no, I am not Boudicca—"

"Well, and I am reassured by that admission," said Llew, his voice heavy with sarcasm.

"—I am her third and final daughter."

Again Llew had to pause while his reeling mind tried to absorb another unexpected piece of information. Then he recalled something he had once learned from her and seized on it as a drowning man would grasp at a floating log. "Oh really? Her third daughter you say? She only had two."

"Only two that are well known. My father was the last Roman governor of what we now call Tethera. It was called Prydein then, although the Romans called it Brython. His name was Gaius Suetonius Paulinus. He led the remaining legions when they made their final stand near Caer Urnarc, the capital of Powys before it was moved to Mathrafal. My mother slew him there while I still lay within her, already pledged to the Druids before I was born, in exchange for their alliance."

Llew gaped for a moment, then scowled. "The Queen of Deceit was an inspired name for you. I do not believe you for a moment."

"Be glad that it is my title. I did not choose it; it was given to me by the Lord of Death after he realized I was not the least bit loyal to him or his aims. His loss was all of Tethera's gain."

"You still have not supported your claim of having been high queen of Tethera in the past," Llew reminded her.

"Oh, I was not high queen in your past. I was high queen in my past, which includes a time that has not yet come, starting about three years from today, although that will never happen now."

"What?" Llew asked incredulously.

"Among Druids it is one of our greatest powers, the ability to ride the waves of time, either into times long past, or to times that have not yet come."

"Why would you come back from some future time where you were high queen?" he asked, honestly curious at how she would attempt to answer the question.

She paused and her mien became devoid of all personality. In a voice that was utterly flat, she said, "Because Lord Arawen had won, Annwyn was covering the final bits of free land remaining, the last of my people were dying, and there was naught I could do to save anything or anyone. By traveling back as far as I could, to nearly the time when Lord Arawen first wrenched Tethera into this world, this world of the Wild Growth, I have changed things considerably. It still remains to see if they can be changed enough to prevent Lord Arawen's eventual victory."

Llew just stared at her. "Changed how?" he finally asked.

She smiled at him then, and it was with a warmth that he would formerly have sworn was foreign to her face. "For one thing, in this world, you were born, Llew. Because of that, you are not accounted for in the older prophecies, all of which speak only of doom. Also, I once told you that you will make a very great king, and that is quite true. Finally, you are the most wonderful adopted son I could ever have wished for. That alone gives me hope."

Llew became vaguely aware that his mouth was hanging open and closed it.

Something struck their little boat from below, lifting up the starboard side and dumping both of them from their seats, slamming them against the opposite gunnel. This might have been fortunate, as the higher side was abruptly pierced by dozens of teeth that were each roughly the size of Llew's hands.

Chapter V

An Afanc . . .

His sword was under him and he could not draw it but he looked to Moriganna and cried out, "What evil is this?"

The teeth wrenched free and disappeared while the boat splashed back down, relatively level. This was a situation that could not last. The holes left behind by the teeth were too many to count and most of them were furiously spurting water. As they struggled to right themselves, Moriganna answered him. "It is called an afanc. It is a lake creature with something like the head of a dragon and with a body like a snake. If it takes you in its coils you will be crushed. It should not be here, in times past they lived in great lochs far to the north, beyond where the border of Annwyn is today."

"Then it was sent and we know by whom," Llew replied, finally succeeding in getting his sword out. "Can we kill it?"

"They can be killed—but not here in the water. We cannot stay. It will be back in a moment, once it clears the wood from its teeth. Fly to land and we will draw it there." So saying, she became a black bird and launched herself upwards in a flurry of flapping wings.

Cursing to himself, Llew leaped into the air as immense jaws closed on the boat beneath him and crushed it into shattered wood. In midair he transformed himself into a wren and followed the black bird to the nearest bit of land; it was the same land that was occupied by the royal barrows.

Both of them immediately resumed their own forms as they neared the ground. "Why are we drawing it here to fight?" asked Llew as his feet touched down. "Why do we not simply fly to safety? We know it cannot follow."

"It will take up residence in the lake and begin raiding the surrounding area for food—it has an enormous appetite. Even if your subjects are able to field an effective hunting force and eventually bring it to bay, they will lose many of their number before such a beast succumbs. I would not wish that on my conscience and you should not want it on yours."

Llew stared at her. This did not sound like Moriganna. For Cymri, however, it would have been perfectly in character.

Moriganna walked up to the edge of the lake, bent down, and began slapping the water. "They are not very clever. When it comes it will rush out to attack us if we are anywhere near the water, regardless of the advantages it will lose on land. When it does, I will hold it and you must cut off its head. No other injury is likely to achieve anything other than further enraging it."

"It is fortunate I promised Taliesin I would keep Fragaroc close to me at all times and for as long as he deemed I should carry it," Llew commented.

"It is good he did. Remember what Helgar told you his father said? About leaving your spear behind when all of a sudden you might need it? It is also good that it is Fragaroc and not some lesser blade. Such would be almost useless against a creature of this size."

Llew glanced towards Caerleon, standing massive and magnificent across the lake. From the activity on the walls it was clear their altercation with the lake beast had not gone unnoticed, yet it would still be a considerable time before any help could reach them here. Moriganna was right. They would have to take this creature down themselves.

Moriganna stood up and began to back away from the water's edge. "Take care, Llew, it comes."

Powerful ripples had begun about a hundred paces out, near where some wreckage from the little boat still floated, and were propagating in a direct path towards them.

"Move to the side," the enchantress commanded, "it should come straight to me. As I said, once it is engaged and held, simply rush in and cut off its head. This is not a thing that has any appreciation for subtlety."

Reluctant as he was to do her will, Llew nevertheless did as he was bid. The ripples continued coming closer until they reached the shore. One moment all was quiet and still, in the next a great golden green serpent exploded from the lake. Water splashed outwards from the emergence point and showered everything for fifty paces in all directions. He noticed at once that no serpent had ever had a head quite like that one. Great double ranks of white teeth, more jagged than any carpenter's saw, lined the maw of a head larger than a horse's body. Above the teeth, set far back under scaled, bony ridges, were two colossal eyes the size of small pumpkins and black as the night sky on a moonless night.

The teeth were easily seen. They were difficult to stop looking at, especially when the afanc afforded them a better view by throwing back its head and roaring with a sound that must have shaken the far off walls of Caerleon.

It was cut short abruptly when a fist sized rock bounced off its snout. The creature ceased in mid-roar and looked directly, and perhaps disbelievingly, at Moriganna, for it was she who had just thrown the otherwise ineffectual missile.

"Shut up and come eat me if that is what you are here for, otherwise be so good as to just roll over and die," she called to it.

With a furious hiss, the creature slithered out of the water coming straight at Moriganna. Llew blanched internally when he realized it was slithering faster than a horse could run. Moriganna waved her right arm once and there was motion in the grass. The afanc's forward momentum suddenly ceased. It threw back its head and roared again.

It took Llew a moment to realize what had happened. Roots had emerged from the ground along the entire length of the great beast's snake-like body and were holding it fast. He lifted Fragaroc and started to move just before the head turned towards him, apparently attracted by the movement in its peripheral vision. Gwent's prince found himself staring directly into those enormous dark orbs that were its eyes.

His movement ceased as he forgot his intentions entirely. Instead he just stood there, eyes locked with the beast. It drew in an enormous breath of such extent that Llew could feel the breeze moving past him towards its open maw. Its body began to expand as it sucked in a colossal breath. The roots that held it started bursting apart, unable to constrain its increased girth.

Llew saw all of that, but it did not seem terrible important. While he watched, a small form flew onto the monster's face and, as it landed there, became Moriganna, sword upraised. She swept it down and across the afanc's left eye. Llew shook his head, instantly freed of whatever trance he had been held in.

With an agonized flip of its head, the serpent flung Moriganna away in an arc that would hurdle her into a stand of trees a hundred paces away. Despite the need for immediate action, Llew stared, horrified at what Moriganna's sacrifice had cost her—the impact would certainly be lethal—but there was no impact. When Moriganna reached apogee she became a black bird, turned in midair, and flew down to the ground. Resuming her human form, she once again faced the great dragon-serpent, head on, from fifty paces away. Her stance was already challenging, then she smiled and blew a kiss to the beast with her off hand. The tormented creature fixed its remaining good eye on her and shrieked in fury, obviously readying itself to spring forward.

Fragaroc struck true and the afanc's head fell cleanly away from its body. Moriganna had destroyed the left eye, the one that would otherwise have alerted it to Llew's approach.

Chapter VI

. . . and a Korrigan

The coils of the afanc's body, with nothing left to direct them, went mad and writhed out of control, swatting aside boulders and crushing several small trees. Llew ran towards Moriganna pell-mell to avoid them.

He slowed as he approached her, but she walked past him. She passed by the coils of the afanc, now growing quiescent as the beast's body became aware of its own demise. She continued toward the shoreline and, as Llew fully turned, he saw what she was looking at.

There was a woman in the lake. Only her head and shoulders were visible but her shoulders were bare and it seemed likely she was not wearing any clothing. Llew followed Moriganna down to the water's edge.

The strange woman was also quite beautiful, Llew noted, combining perfect features with hair even blonder than his own. It took him only a moment to realize it was an otherworldly beauty. This was not a mortal.

"And what do you seek, little korrigan?" Moriganna called to her. "If it is your death, why then, you have only to come a bit closer."

"You killed my pet," the Fae woman said in a petulant voice.

"I will kill more than that if I see you again," promised Moriganna. "I have little patience for korrigans that do the dirty work of Lord Arawen."

"I do not think you will see me again," the korrigan said gravely. "It took me a long time to grow my pet and now I must start over. By the time I grow another, my master will have sent others to end you."

"To end me?" Moriganna asked, arching one eyebrow.

"Well of course to end you," the korrigan said hotly. "You know what you have done!"

"Far better than you, apparently," replied Moriganna, seemingly unperturbed. "And what of him?" she asked, gesturing towards Llew.

The korrigan gave Llew but one quick glance. "Your bodyguards are of no concern to anyone. If they get in the way they will die. That is the way of things. If their survival means anything to you then you must send them away."

"I like to keep track of who would wish to kill me," said Moriganna, "since the number is so large it is a good mental exercise. Who are you? Give me your use name."

"I most certainly will not!" exclaimed the korrigan.

"Please tell me your name," said Moriganna, "I have asked nicely."

"It does not matter how nicely you ask, I have no wish to share it with the likes of you," retorted the korrigan.

"Then I command you," Moriganna declared in an ominous voice, "tell me your name, three times I have asked."

"Fine," the korrigan said with a snarl. "I am called Arial. Are you satisfied?"

Moriganna gave her a sardonic smile. "Eminently. You may go. Do not cross my path again, little one. I can always find a use for an errant sprite or river nymph, regardless of its loyalties, and however misguided they may be."

The korrigan dived and was gone. Llew had only a glimpse of her feet as she did so; they seemed quite human. He had halfway expected fins.

Finally turning her full attention to him, Moriganna said, "Do not be deceived, korrigans are very powerful, and can be extremely dangerous under the right circumstances, even to you and me. It is no small thing that this one fled without a fight."

She paused, as if waiting. Llew felt she might be waiting on him to say something but he had no idea what that might be. She finally sighed and seemed to give up. "What scary fellows we be, eh?" she said in a reproving tone.

Llew swayed on his feet. It should not be Moriganna saying that! It should have been Cymri and he should have said it with her—but Cymri was gone, and not just gone, she had never existed at all. It felt like there was a huge hole punched in his very being all over again.

Moriganna gestured toward the enormous decapitated carcass of the afanc and smiled again. "Well done. Is it not amazing what we can do together? I would wager even a small army would have had difficulty accomplishing what we just did and imagine, if you can, the cost had they tried."

Llew was still a bit stunned by their short battle as well, or, more specifically, as to what had just happened during it. "You risked both our lives to save my subjects. You risked your life to save my own." His voiced sounded incredulous, even to himself.

Moriganna regarded him wistfully. "Do you recall that I once told you that if I saw a way to save the kingdoms of mankind by sacrificing you with a ceremonial knife upon a stone altar, then I would do so in an instant?"

"Of course I do," he replied. "That was one of our 'special' moments together. The ones that really stood out in my precious childhood memories."

She grimaced and said, "It saddens me that it would be, but yes. It was the truth, too, so far as it went. What I left unsaid was that if I ever saw the only way to save you was by sacrificing myself with a ceremonial knife upon a stone altar, then I would do so in an instant."

Llew had no ready reply. The Queen of Deceit she might be, but lying in this fashion was not her way.

She wiped away a tear and Llew marveled anew; real or not, he would never have imagined she was capable of shedding one. Then she spoke again. "And we have come to the reason I am telling you this now, rather than later. When Cai struck at you I was able to save you, for a bit longer at least, but the price was high. Perhaps not so high as a human sacrifice, but high enough. I sacrificed some portion of my secrecy and the enemy has surmised my presence for, although he is quite mad, he is anything but stupid. Now I must go away. I always tried so hard to stay close to you, to keep you safe at all costs, even if not always successfully, but that time is at an end and, although I must leave, it frightens me terribly to do so.

"I was trying to protect you, Llew, please understand that, even if I frequently failed in that aim. There were so many failures, too, and oh how each has haunted me! There was King Iolo being controlled by Lord Arawen, then that dreadful worm at the borderlands of Gwynedd, followed by Old Nan, as well as Bloddeuwedd's betrayal, even this attack here upon the lake . . . these are all things that could have easily killed you and I never saw any of them coming. I could not anticipate them and each of them could have ended everything . . . could have ended you," she said softly.

"Each of those would have, I think, except for your own contributions as Cymri," Llew admitted grudgingly.

She nodded. "That is part of why leaving you, even though I know I must, is so very hard for me now."

"And what about all the rest of it?" he asked bitterly. "Was I just going through the motions for you while you pulled my strings?"

"No, Llew, of course not, life does not work that way. There were many things you had to do on your own—and you did them. You did them in your own way and you earned your accomplishments. Could any pampered princeling have slain a dragon serpent such as the afanc on the first attempt and in a single blow? As I once told you, I cannot wave a wand and create a king, I can only provide the opportunity. The rest was always up to you."

Llew looked her in the eye. "I do not think you can leave yet, Moriganna. There are many others who need to hear what you have to say and make their own judgements, I do not entirely trust myself in this matter."

"Do not forget what King Bran told you in his last moments. 'Trust yourself to do what needs doing,' Llew. I wrote it down and it will always be available to you now that you are learning to read."

She noticed she was holding her sword, wet with ichor from the wound she had given the afanc. She wiped it clean on the grass, then sheathed it.

"You heard what that little korrigan, Arial, had to say. For the present, at least, it appears you are no longer our foe's primary target. Although he certainly still desires your death, at the moment, it is mine he wants much more, and all his will and resources will be bent to it now that he knows I live. If I remain here I make it easy for him, and I recklessly endanger many that are dear to both of us.

"No, I am sorry, Llew, but I cannot stay even an hour longer. The Lord of Annwyn has now seen part of my subterfuges ripped away and will be targeting nearly all of his resources solely on my destruction. If I remain, even if linked through a proxy, then I only place you in far greater danger as, even now, he is still at least partly blind to the threat you present. It is only for that reason he has not yet bent all his efforts to your destruction.

"Away from you, I can no longer look after you, but I remain like unto a high place that the lightning will attempt to strike first. In this way I am keeping you safer by drawing his energies away. He will reason that you are young and thus dealing with you can wait while he first deals with me. Whether he succeeds or fails, this is too great an opportunity not to afford you. Use it well."

"No," insisted Llew. "You cannot leave, certainly not yet."

She turned and began to walk away. "I can and I must. I doubt you are ready to strike me down, and you certainly have no way to restrain me. I assure you that, with both of us being shape-shifters, that would only be an exercise in ridiculousness."

Llew watched her go, in a quandary as to what to do. Before she had taken twenty steps he called to her and asked, "Are you my mother?"

Still walking away, Moriganna called back to him. "Dear Llew, I did adopt you, tis true, but I doubt that is what you mean. Though some would not believe it is in my nature, I speak the truth when I say this: I did not give birth to you."

"Oh," he replied, "can you tell me of my real mother then?"

She turned then and regarded him. "Nay, I cannot just yet, there are reasons, which I also cannot share. Should we both survive long enough then I will tell you, when the time is right, and it can do no harm."

Llew shook his head in frustration. "Can you at least tell me the reason you cannot tell me the reasons?"

She gave him a wry smile. "So many questions, always. Very well then. It is because even the reasons would be a hint of who your other mother was, and there are those, and not just Lord Arawen, that, upon learning this, would drop all other pursuits so that they might better focus on putting you into an unmarked barrow. You are strong and able but you are not yet ready to survive that. Even if you did, such a dedicated campaign on your life would hinder you too greatly in what you must yet do. We are trying to circumvent prophecy here, and that is not easily done, even under the most favorable conditions possible."

"Did she have chestnut hair?"

Moriganna's eyes flashed. "Hush! Have you understood nothing of what I just said? I do not know how you could know that but, whatever else you may know, say nothing of it. Your survival, and even that of Tethera's, may depend on your silence. I prophesied you would be wise and clever—among other things. Do not invalidate that seeing."

"Bran said I was Boudicca's heir. You have claimed to be her daughter. What am I to make of that?" he asked.

"Boudicca has had many heirs, Llew. No less than fifteen high kings were each and every one her heir, and all their siblings as well, potentially."

"But only in potential," Llew complained in frustration. "So with Pwyl's death, and the end of primogeniture, it falls to me, some scion of a cadet branch, to take the throne?"

"What you do not know can hurt you, Llew, but in this case it is better, for the present, to know less. Now I must go; your guardsmen will be here very shortly." With that, Moriganna changed into a black bird and winged away through the barrow mounds.

"Wait," he called and ran a few steps after her. "What about the Pwacca?" he shouted, as she disappeared into the trees.

Chapter VII

Alone in the Barrows

Llew hung his head for a moment, then looked about. There was no sign of any guardsmen from the castle, yet they could not be far away now.

He noted the barrow mound he was next to, while not the biggest, appeared as though it might be the newest. Wondering if there was a stone marker or something that identified it, he began to wander over to it.

Llew had taken only a few steps closer to the mound when a wave of dizziness hit him and overwhelmed his senses. He reeled and fell, while his stomach roiled and made threats, but then it all passed away completely, as quickly as it had started.

Perplexed by this attack, he regained his feet and decided it might be prudent if he went back to the body of the slain afanc, there to await the guardsmen. They must surely be getting close. With that thought he realized he did not know what he was going to say to them. He certainly could not tell them the truth. His every instinct told him he needed to buy time to think on this before he attempted to explain all this—even to his closest friends.

With that thought came what almost seemed as though it were a sharp pain in his chest. Cymri was no longer one of his closest friends. She never had been. She had never been at all.

Collecting himself, Llew considered. The easiest way would be to change into a wren again. No one ever noticed the little brown birds except, perhaps, for an occasional cat. Then he could fly to his rooms and, with luck, it would be some time before anyone but Addfwyn thought to look for him there.

Llew leaped into the air while willing himself to change into a wren—and crashed heavily to the ground, skinning an elbow rather badly in the process.

Whoops, Llew thought, refraining from panicking just yet. Silently, he willed himself, in quick succession, into a giant eagle, a fox, a dog, a bear, a horse, and finally even a monkey. Nothing happened on any of his attempts. Now it felt safe to panic. In addition to everything else, his torc, the fabled Torc of Tethera, passed down from high king to high king for more than a dozen generations, was no longer letting him change shape.

Llew narrowly stopped himself from saying out loud: "What else can go wrong?" In his experience, just asking that question could be an extremely efficacious way of learning the answer.

He knew which way his "rescuers" would be coming from. That should make it possible to evade them. He raced off between the barrows, using their bulk to shield him from the view of anyone approaching the lake's edge. Gaining the tree line, he spent the best part of half an hour getting closer to the castle. Most people had to enter the castle either through the great gate, or through the postern gate that he and Cymri— Moriganna he corrected himself—had used. Short of flying, there was another way in, one that he was fairly sure only he knew about. He had found it several months earlier, purely by chance, after changing into a fish to explore the man-made lake that was Caerleon's moat. The problem, of course, was that he was not a fish now and could not become one. This particular entrance would involve swimming a substantial distance underwater in near pitch black conditions.

It was fortunate that he was not wearing armor. Unfortunately, he would have to carry Fragaroc with him. He arranged it, as best he could, so that the enchanted blade was secured on his back, rather than his hip. He could see that there was still a huge commotion at the site of the dead afanc, and even the men still manning the wall had their attention on it. That was probably the only thing that made this doable in broad daylight. Llew walked up to the water's edge and slipped in at the closest point to the underwater entrance. It was only six rods or so to the wall and, again, paddling quietly, he was not seen. *Now the hard part*, he thought to himself.

He took several deep breaths and let them out slowly, then took an especially large one and ducked below the water, using his hands to propel his body down to the tunnel. He found it easily enough. Ignoring the slimy feel of the castles foundation on his hands, he pointed himself in, then began flutter kicking for all he was worth. It quickly grew dark and he had to keep his arms before him to feel for obstacles.

After what felt like an eternity he began to wonder how a long a short swim for a fish really was, especially as compared to a long swim for a man. At some point he started seriously thinking about reversing course, but he had to face the realization that he had probably gone in so far already that he would not make it back out. Then he smacked one of his outstretched hands painfully into a stone wall. At that point he pushed off against the bottom and lunged straight up. The air he emerged into had never tasted so sweet. For a time he just clung to the side of the well and sucked in one gasping breath after another. Then he found the hand holes set into the well's interior wall and climbed up into the well room. As this was part of the castle only intended for use during sieges, there was no one there, nor in the hall outside. Two secret passages later and he was in his own rooms.

All this to gain a little time to think? Llew wondered if he was losing his mind. Certainly he had cause. He sloshed across the floor and was about to throw himself into his favorite chair when he realized he did not want his chair to be as soggy as he was.

One of the nicer things about being a prince, he had long since decided, was that one never had to worry about running out of clothes. He eeled out of his wet jerkin and dropped it on the floor, making sure it was on the stone and well clear of his rug.

The door opened and Addfwyn walked in carrying some freshly folded things to put away. He froze when he saw Llew.

Llew gave him a quizzical look. "Well hullo to you, too. Did I surprise you that much?" he asked.

Addfwyn never hesitated. He snatched out his knife and charged straight at Llew.

Chapter VIII

Faced with a Problem

It was actually well done and might have succeeded had Llew not been trained by Afaggdu, a centuries old warrior who knew everything about weapons there was to know. Afaggdu could also make nearly any ordinary object into an effective weapon as needed, even his bare hands. Snatching a candlestick from a side table, Llew knocked the blade off course and, with the other hand, swept a high backed chair around and into his man-servant's legs.

Addfwyn fell to the floor on hands and knees, but did not lose his grasp on the knife. Llew raised the chair and nearly brained him with it before stopping. With anyone else he would have followed through, but this was Addfwyn. A thought crossed his mind. *Unless it is not.* Could it be that the man was under a spell? Or perhaps he was actually a shape-shifter only disguised as Addfwyn?

A shape-shifter made little sense. If Moriganna, the mistress of shape-shifters, did not seek his death—and she had just gone to considerable effort to save him from death—then that theory was useless. Even so, Llew dropped the chair. A less damaging approach was called for.

He kicked the knife out of his servant's hand and then fell across him before he could rise, achieving an arm lock over Addfwyn's throat as he did so.

"Cease this at once, Addfwyn! You have sworn an oath of fealty to me of your own free will."

Addfwyn instead tried to break the arm lock and throw Llew off. He might as well have been trying to throw off the entire castle. "I . . . have . . . done no such . . . thing!" Addfwyn ceased his straining for a moment before he spoke again. "I swore an oath to Prince Llew. You cannot get away with this, and you cannot get out of here without being captured. Surrender now. My lord is not without the capacity for mercy; perhaps you may receive some."

Llew attempted to process that, then said, "So you think I am not Prince Llew?"

In a tone Llew had heard Addfwyn use once before, when it had then been directed at a certain bandit named Meilyr—now deceased—his man-servant said, "I think you are a great idiot. Do you even have the slightest idea what Prince Llew looks like?"

This thoroughly bewildered Llew. He thrust about through own mind seeking ideas that might make some sense of this, yet he found none. It occurred to him, however, that there was a very nice looking glass above his water basin.

"Slowly now," he cautioned, "stand up with me. I warn you; do not seek advantage in this for you will find none. We are going to have a look in that looking glass together."

Without taking his arm from across Addfwyn's windpipe, the two of them awkwardly rose to their feet. Llew peered over his captive's shoulder and into the looking glass. A stranger's face peered back at him.

It was an impressive enough face as things went, with a well-formed nose, thin lips, and a prominent cleft chin—but it was not Llew's face. The piercing eyes were light brown, not blue, and the hair was dark. It was probably not quite as dark as it appeared because it was still quite wet, but it certainly was not the fair hair he had shared with his sister, Llewellyn, and with their father.

For the second time that day, Llew's mouth fell open in shock. So did the mouth of the face in the looking glass. Feeling his captor's grip slacken, Addfwyn struck. One elbow took Llew in the stomach while a boot came down hard on his left foot. Addfwyn squirmed sideways and used his other arm to break free of the arm lock Llew had on his throat.

Or at least he tried to. With the sudden pain in his solar plexus, Llew's first response—resulting from long training often meant to teach him to do the exact opposite of what instinct dictated—was to clench all his muscles tightly, as well as ignore the pain in his foot. With his breath completely cutoff by Llew's tensing, Addfwyn began thrashing wildly and the two of them fell to the floor. They rolled back and forth while Addfwyn desperately used both hands to try to break the younger man's hold. It was like trying to bend a thick oak branch. His struggles weakened, then ceased.

Llew waited a moment longer before he let go. He quickly checked Addfwyn to ensure his breathing had resumed, then said to the recumbent form, "Sorry, old friend. You made it more than clear that nothing I could say right now would be the least bit convincing. For that matter, I would not have believed anything I said, either."

It was relatively easy to gather the materials he needed to bind Addfwyn's arms and feet and then to gag him. The man was tough and would not be out long. Checking his captive's breathing again, Llew gently maneuvered him into his large wardrobe, then closed and latched the door. Addfwyn would break free but not quickly.

He gave the face in the looking glass another disbelieving look and felt hot fury flood through him. Whoever was responsible for this mischief was going to be made to pay for it!

Who and how was the question. He needed information, he needed a plan to get it, and he was in no mind to think clearly. Even through his anger he recognized this as a bad combination. It was also obvious that time was not in his favor, yet this last part did not trouble him. He had no inclination to delay bringing his wrath to bear on the party responsible. Using this, the calculating part of his mind forced his rage down into a cold, hard thing. It was not easy.

Llew considered, now able to concentrate on his next step. Clearly, he would need to seek help from someone who was expert in illusions, and in seeing through them. He knew several individuals that fit that category, but only one of them was a friend as well as being someone he might be able to make contact with. It also came to him that this was only his second or third priority. The first was simpler but not easier; he would have to escape from Caerleon.

Chapter IX

Escape from Caerleon

His armor was kept in his room on a wooden rack made for that purpose. Originally it had held ceremonial armor, but Llew had successfully made the case that, since all of the human kingdoms were essentially at war with Annwyn, ceremonial armor sent the wrong message. The armor was enchanted—it had once been a gift from Moriganna—and essentially indestructible, although there was at least one exception in that regard, as the wicked scar on his chest, and its mate upon his back, had proven. It was also quite immune to all the wear and tear and scuffs and dents of normal use; it never looked less than new when it was cleaned. This fact had aided him significantly in his campaign to make it his armor for all occasions.

Weapons were next. He gathered sword, spear, an assortment of knives, his great longbow that only he had the strength to draw, and a quiver full of war arrows, along with a few hunting arrows, and piled it all on his bed.

Food? There was no food here in his rooms, he would have to acquire it elsewhere. He tossed two full coin pouches onto the pile. So far as money went, it was good to be the prince. Other things? Giving himself a mental kick he went back to the wardrobe and rooted around under Addfwyn until he found a battered pack. In it he had flint and steel, a few extra garments, and some other items he might need on a journey, whether alone or with others. There was no real reason a prince should have such a bag ready and packed to go, but Llew had grown up in a demanding school that had little patience for the unprepared.

There were two basic problems, the first being that he could not just wear the armor. Everyone would recognize it and would also be able to see enough of him to know he did not look like the owner. Even if the helmet sufficiently covered his face, it would still be passing strange to wear it inside the castle grounds if he was not a guard and on duty.

The other problem was how to get Gower out of the stables and out of the castle.

With a sinking feeling, it came upon him that he could not take Gower. His steed was faithful to him, of that Llew had no doubt, but Gower was not like most horses. If the horse did not recognize his master when he came to get him? Llew shuddered. That would end his escape right there, and his life most likely.

Even without Gower, he still could not use the water tunnel he had traversed to get in. It had been difficult with merely his sword. With the rest of the gear he was taking, he might as well jump into the lake with a millstone tied to his feet. He also could not think of any good and sure way to send his things outside to wait for him.

Of course, he mused to himself, *no one knows the face I now wear.* So long as he did not seem to be attempting to pass himself off as Prince Llew, he might be able to just walk out the gate. Better, if he were a mounted warrior returning to a nearby cantref he could make off with a horse in the process.

That made it simpler. Instead of carrying his armor in a heavy bag, he could wear it, covering the hauberk with a light chain shirt and having only the helmet bagged. The helm was a dead giveaway as absolutely no other mortal wore one with antlers. In truth, they were less than practical and would have been quite impossible in combat save that they, like the helmet itself, were indestructible.

Which did not keep them from being a nuisance when going through doorways and under low trees. The hilt of his sword would need to be covered, as would the head of his spear and the front of his shield, but all of these had covers that had been made for them, none of this would draw too much attention.

As for the stables? No one knew them better than he did. He was confident he could find a good horse and be gone an hour before anyone realized anything was amiss.

Once suited up, he considered the first challenge. If he walked out of the royal quarters he would almost certainly be seen and sharp questions would soon follow. Llew opted to avoid that so he made his way through the hidden passage to the hall near the well room.

It seemed to him that the best way from there was simply to take the most direct route to the stable. Although Caerleon was a big place, most people there were at least familiar with the appearance of most others. Yet there were also new faces being added, or passing through, all the time. One stranger's face should not garner too much attention as long as he stayed to common areas and looked as though he was confident and doing no wrong.

Llew clenched his teeth. He was not doing anything wrong. For a moment his anger at his predicament threatened to overwhelm him again. He kept control and wondered again if this was the right course. He might have gone to his father, King Pendaran and attempted to explain. That worthy might have had the patience to test his knowledge and the wisdom to make the leap of faith required to believe he was still Llew.

Possibly, perhaps, maybe—were he not visiting the kingdom of Dyfyd to the west.

A number of servants came down the hall from the other direction and passed him. None of them gave him more than a glance although they were careful to give him as wide a berth as the narrow passageway permitted. Exiting the keep he passed a pair of warriors guarding the entrance. Llew knew them both by name but neither gave him more than a quick look. He obviously knew his way around and was not doing anything objectionable. He was also not being even the least bit furtive. Despite wearing a sword while carrying a spear and shield, they were all were covered and secured, plus he had on a heavy pack . . . well, it was not like he could possibly be the vanguard of an attacking force all by himself was it?

For a lone individual to present a threat he would have to be a Pwacca, one of the evil sorceress Moriganna's shape-changers, yet the hound they had with them assured them he was not. It was resting on its haunches and did not stir as Llew went by. Clearly he could not be one of those vile beasts. With their canines now on constant watch, the castle denizens knew it was impossible for such vicious monsters as the Pwacca to walk amongst them unknown.

Llew was not quite sure whether to laugh or cry. It had been Cymri's idea to use the hounds for this purpose, She had trained them all, which was ironic because, so far as Llew knew, all Pwacca everywhere were slavishly loyal to Moriganna.

Although—Llew considered something. Had any human ever been harmed by a Pwacca? Despite their evil reputation, with the possible exception of himself, he could not think of any cases where they had hurt anyone. Even he himself had only been attacked, he had not actually been injured.

Llew crossed the central courtyard, rife with activity of people coming and going and trying to do things that could not be done so easily indoors. It was pure chaos. No doubt the comings and goings to examine the dead lake monster, as well as to investigate the mystery of the missing prince, were stirring things up even more than usual. Yet all the usual was going on as well. Children ran and played amid guardsmen shooting arrows into targets, servants butchering goats and cleaning fish, other servants carrying hampers of clothing to and from the laundry, and a hundred other activities, all going on at the same time with no concern for what else was happening around them. No one had any attention left to spare for something so ordinary as a visiting warrior doing nothing of interest.

Caerleon was distinguished from many lesser holdings by having a cobblestoned courtyard and, further, by the fact it was sluiced off every evening and thus not nearly as fragrant or befouled as those that were hard packed dirt or mud. Then, too, the level of activity pretty much demanded it.

As he made his way past the covered well, an especially busy place as everyone wanted water for everything, a thought came to him. Llew gasped and seized on a post next to it to keep from falling. He had not been attacked by a Pwacca. He had simply found himself in close proximity to one and he had attacked it.

He had injured it badly. Small wonder then that it had come after him! Who would not return an attack in those circumstances? But why would an instrument of Moriganna's iron will have tried to kill him? For all of her machinations, Moriganna had never shown the slightest interest in killing him. She could have, he admitted to himself, done it at any point in his life. On many occasions she would only have needed to do nothing but let him die, were that her desire. That did not, he reminded himself, mean she had his best interests at heart. It just meant she had more use for him alive than dead. But the fact remained that he and his friends had killed the Pwacca—*and it may not have initially borne him any ill will!* Llew was no longer any stranger to killing, but this was different. He felt sick.

A cook's assistant, having just drawn two buckets of water before picking them up and heading for the kitchens, noticed him and asked, "Are you alright, warrior? Should I summon a leech?"

Llew forced a fake smile before saying, "Nay, thank you. Just a touch of indigestion, I think. I never should have eaten what that street vendor was calling fresh fish."

"Ah," the young woman nodded. "If you have no experience with strange folk on the street selling you food then it is best not to trust them." She gave him a quick once over before saying, "Come around the kitchens when you are feeling better and ask for Linnet. I can no doubt find you something that you will like."

"I just may do that, Linnet. It is a kind offer and I thank you." Llew straightened up and headed on, taking another dozen paces before it occurred to him to wonder if she had been talking about food. He hid his quick flush by stepping into the relative shelter of the stables.

Having entered the stables he encountered a problem he had not previously considered. He could probably walk out the front gate without issue, as long as there was no hue and cry to accompany his leave taking; no one would attempt to stop it. The problem was that leaving with one of the castle's war horses would be a different issue altogether. He was not a known guardsman or horse handler. At the very least, he would be required to show a writ of some sort, something bearing an official seal.

With annoyance at himself, he realized he was not so clever as he thought, or he would have made such a writ at the desk in his rooms before starting out. He was now loath to return all that way; there was no telling how long it would take for

Addfwyn to wake and break free. The alarm would go up then, and the front gate would cease to be an option when it did.

Considering the problem again, Llew mentally kicked himself. The guardsmen at the gate could not read the writing on a writ, they would only be checking the seal. He held up his hand and ruefully regarded his inheritor's ring. He was lucky, he knew, that no one had noticed it on his way here, for it was certainly distinctive. It was not easy to get it off his finger, but he managed. It went into a coin pouch for safekeeping.

The stables were as quiet as they ever got during the day. Most of the horses were missing, no doubt gone with their riders to rescue their prince from the presumed dragon near the far side of the lake.

Gower was still in his stall, of course. No one would dare take Prince Llew's steed. This was at least as much because the great stallion would allow no one else upon his back without Llew present—and would extract a terrible price for the attempt—as because they respected the prince himself.

Llew gave Gower's stall as wide a margin as he could when he went past it and did not glance at the horse at all. It was eerie in that he could feel Gower's eyes following his every movement.

The problem now was that there just was not much else to choose from. He finally settled for a roan mare. Not so ferocious as a stallion or even a gelding perhaps, but its quieter disposition made it more suitable for stealthy patrols and this was not a trip where he wanted undue notice. With a lifetime, albeit a short lifetime, of horse craft, he had her saddled and equipped in moments.

As he started to lead her out a voice to his left said, "Here now! Where are you taking her?"

Llew reined in his first instinct. Because of this he was able to leave the stable hand alive, trussed and gagged, much as he had left Addfwyn, save that the stable hand was still conscious.

"My apologies, Floyd," Llew told the bound man, "I will try to make this up to you somehow, when I can." Floyd regarded him with frightened eyes as Llew took the mare's leads and departed.

He led his stolen mount to the front gate and, as he expected, the guardsmen had questions for him. One continued to check those coming in to Caerleon, while the other—*is his name Alvin?* Llew wondered—was free to question the escaping prince.

"And who might you be and where do you think you are going with one of the king's horses? Show me your writ," the guardsman demanded.

Llew had to remind himself not to use the man's name. Instead he made a show of looking about cautiously, then took his inheritor's ring from the coin pouch. This earned a frown from the guardsman. He probably thought Llew was getting out coins in an attempt to bribe him.

"The one who bade me take this horse and do a task for him said I was to show you this," Llew said, carefully displaying the ring as he held it in one hand and covered it with the other so those about might not see it.

The response was gratifying. Guardsman Alvin's eyes widened a moment before he brought them back under control. "Right then," he said, in an overly bored-sounding voice, "move along then. Safe travels to you."

Just like that, Llew was out the gate, still leading his stolen steed. He mounted quickly and passed out and across the moat, threading his way between people, both on foot and pushing handcarts, that were making their way in and out. Caerleon was always a hive of activity during daylight hours.

He had just passed the outer barbican when he saw the returning patrol. They were eleven riders, lightly armored and armed, and at their head rode his twin sister, Llewellyn.

Llew started and almost panicked before he realized he had little to be concerned with here. If she recognized him then he had nothing to fear, but if, as seemed almost certain, she did not, why then that was only as according to plan. He would be just another nameless stranger on the road. With his head up, making no attempt to hide, he chose to ride boldly past her, approaching as closely as he could—given that he did not want to run smack into the mounted warriors following her.

The princess had evidently been deep in thought for she only looked up as he was already fairly close. Her eyes widened in shock when she saw him and Llew had a premonition of trouble. She stared a moment longer while he endeavored, as best he could, to hang on to his anonymity, even going so far as to dip his head and tug a forelock at her.

Then she found her voice. "Seize him!" she screamed, and drew her sword. Llew's heart quailed in his chest. Never mind the patrol that accompanied her, there were few things in life he was willing to admit, even to himself, that he was frightened of, but Llewellyn's blade was certainly one of them.

Driving his heels into the mare, they bolted down the road. Nearly inside the walls of Caerleon, tired from their patrol, the mounted warriors simply were not prepared to react quickly enough to interfere with him. Llewellyn did not seem to suffer from the same problems. She was after him like a stone from a sling.

Llew glanced back and saw she was not twenty paces back with her sword out and ready to strike. He dared not let himself come within range of that. She seemed quite ready to kill him and might well be able to do it, even if he had been willing to fight back and risk injuring or killing her.

He felt the mare moving under him and began to take her measure. She was big for a mare, if not for a war horse, but she was agile and quick, as well as responsive and well rested. Then he glanced back once more, this time at Llewellyn's mount, a large gelding. The beast was straining for all it was worth and Llewellyn drove it hard, but it was not closing the gap. *Yes*, he thought to himself, *this might work.*

The field to his right was planted with winter wheat, now being harvested. Crofters moved through the field, cutting and stacking sheaves to dry so they could be threshed in early autumn. Llew veered off the road and then jumped the mare over a low stone wall into the neighboring field. At least he would not do too much damage here.

A cry of anger came from behind as Llewellyn, an extremely competent rider in her own right, was forced to actually travel in the opposite direction before attempting the wall. Her gelding, although carrying slightly less weight and normally a stronger animal, was also a larger animal and it was not fresh from the stables. She needed a longer run for it to jump the wall.

Risking another look behind him, Llew saw her only just landing from her jump while he was already halfway across the wheat field. Around him, startled harvesters looked up from their work and either froze in place or dived for cover. Llew gave them some space in case one of them decided to heave a pitchfork at him. Fortunately, it never even seemed to occur to them.

He reached the far side of the field and jumped the wall. Llew had wanted to ride through the small village there but decided that would be foolhardy—he could not afford to be delayed by wagons or people blocking his route—and he did not see a need to risk the lives of the inhabitants. It would be all too easy to trample a child or two by mistake. Instead he veered around the village and came to a large graveyard. The common people did not build barrows for their dead. Aside from the labor involved, in short order the countryside would have been so covered in the things that there would have been no room for anything else. The commoners' burial spots each had a protruding stone monument, usually about waist high and with carvings on it. For a fast moving horse it was an obstacle course. Best of all, there was no one alive here that he could accidentally hurt. This fit the need nicely.

Llew galloped his mare directly into the graveyard. There were no rows, the stones just arose wherever someone, or several someones, had been laid to rest. The key to this game was in making sharp changes in direction, with minimal decreases in speed, just barely missing one stone after another. Normally this would have been a terrible risk to the rider and the horse, as well as being highly disrespectful of the dead. Now it was a necessity and, despite hating the need for it, Llew was loving it. It was over almost too soon when he raced out of it on the other side.

The graveyard backed onto a rocky hill. Leaving the last stone marker behind him, he drove the mare to continue up the hill and at a sharp angle to the left. The footing was tricky but the mare found the purchase she needed, and Llew knew precisely how to guide her and help maintain their balance. Coming down the hill on the other side he passed through a large open pasture while avoiding the flock of sheep to one side of it. There must have been a shepherd about, too, and possibly a dog, but Llew did not pause to look for them.

A quick check showed that Llewellyn was now a great distance behind them. Llew was mildly surprised she was still close enough for him to see her. Even given that her riding skills were quite good, he knew they were not the equal of his own. All modesty aside, no one's were. So far as he knew, no one else had ever before shape-shifted into a horse and seen and felt exactly how it all worked from both sides of the saddle. Knowing that, and that her mount must be nearly exhausted, she had to be taking some terrible risks. It was time to end this before she got hurt.

The pasture was bordered along the back by a thick wood that spread far wider than the meadow itself. Putting on an extra bit of speed he made straight for it. As he raced into the trees, he slowed only slightly, despite the fact that he was now jumping tree roots, dodging tree trunks and boulders, and evading low-hanging branches.

After proceeding a goodly distance into the forest he stopped for a moment to listen. His sense of hearing was another great gift. The Spriggan king, Hafgan, had once told him it was because one of his ancestors had been a Coraniaid, a type of Fae with such keen hearing that they could detect any approaching danger and evade it, but there were no more Coraniaid in the world. It seemed they had not been well-liked, and their incredible hearing had been useless for detecting poison.

Llew waited, motionless on the unmoving mare. As he concentrated on his hearing, it made him aware of more and more about him and at greater removes. It felt almost like he was extending an expanding and strengthening net over all the surrounding countryside and, in the process, gaining an almost visual experience of it. He could hear the sheep he had passed, still baaing at having their grazing disturbed by the excitement. He almost thought he could Llewellyn's exhausted gelding, panting as though its heart would explode, but perhaps that was his imagination. There were no hoof beats. There was no longer any horse pursuing him.

The silence was abruptly broken by an exhausted scream of frustration. "Pox take you!" Llewellyn's voice cried. "I have no idea what you were after here, but you will not profit by it! I will hunt you to the ends of the world if I must, but you will pay for what you have done! I, Llewellyn, daughter of Pendaran and Arianrod, brother of Llew, and descendant of Bran the Blessed, so swear it!"

Llew waited but nothing more was said. After a time he dismounted and led the tired mare deeper into the forest, greatly troubled.

Who did she think he was?

Chapter X

On the Road Again

Caerleon would certainly send out pursuit. Llew was not terribly worried by that. He was confident he could escape detection. The Wild Growth was a name that those who had considered the matter tended to use in discussing the fact that, in Tethera, the land was steadily expanding in size. It never occurred where anyone could see it and thus it almost never occurred in well-traveled places, such as villages and towns. Yet, in any place that was empty, there was a chance that, when next someone returned there, they would find that the land had grown larger. A stand of trees, for example, might be present between two fields that had formerly been adjacent to each other. The added area could be almost anything and it would look as though it had always been there. This was more than frightening as, sometimes, these new bits of land came with their own inhabitants. These creatures were never people, but sometimes they were things that preyed upon people.

This had the net effect of moving all towns and villages further apart, extending the existing wildernesses between them, and even creating new areas of wilderness. It also made it much easier for a lone traveler like Llew to slip through these spaces and around those that might seek to stop him—unless he encountered some of those strange new inhabitants, of course.

He still had no food, and that was a problem. Fortunately, he had his bow and game seemed fairly abundant. It also did not seem overly fearful of him. Even so, trying to keep an eye and an ear out for both food and enemies, while traveling as swiftly as possible, turned out to a bit of a strain. After a bit it dawned on him that he was missing Cilgwri. He had spent considerable time and effort in training the clever black bird to scout out hidden dangers for him. Cilgwri, for his part, was always finding Llew and then wandering off again, never for terribly long. Now his feathered friend must be half frantic from trying to find a man he would not recognize even if he did find him.

It was a depressing thought. He hoped Cilgwri would not wander off and go feral. It occurred to Llew that Cymri had been responsible for bringing the two of them together, like so many other good things in his life. Now that, he decided, was a truly depressing thought. Then it began to rain.

He solved his food problem the next morning when, while skirting another town, he passed a shepherd driving his flock down the road. Not caring to butcher a sheep, Llew appropriated the man's bag of provisions. Seeing how disconsolate the fellow was over the loss—it was probably his rations for a full week in the field—Llew dug out a silver coin and flipped it to him.

It was probably the most valuable coin the poor man had ever held in his life. After a few moments of shocked silence the shepherd made an awkward bow and tugged his forelock. Llew rode on with the man's effusive thanks and blessings still following him.

In the days that followed he was never quite sure when he left Gwent behind and entered the wilds of fallen Powys, but at some point he knew he was no longer in Gwent.

It might have been when he was sitting at his campfire one night. Something came out of the trees and sat down opposite him. He could not be too sure what it was save that it was large and somewhat man-like. This was because its body seemed wreathed in shadows, even in the firelight. The part he could see clearly was two malevolent red eyes that regarded him throughout the night. Shortly before dawn the massive figure stirred itself and departed as silently as it had come.

Or perhaps it had been when a trio of bears, walking on their hind legs, and wearing jewelry and leather harnesses, crossed the road in front of him. Two carried outsized axes and the third a huge mace. As Llew and the mare stood stock still, one of the bears looked in his direction and appeared to give him a curt nod. They passed into the trees on the other side of the road without incident and Llew gave them a substantial head start before proceeding.

After nearly a week and a half, he finally reached Cas-Eiddew. The sprawling ruins of the once great structure were little more than ivy-covered foundations, although they stretched across two adjacent hilltops. It was already late in the afternoon and the moon was clearly visible in the sky. The prince shuddered involuntarily. Tonight would not be a good time to approach the ruins. He was, he decided, too close already. Retreating a couple of furlongs, he made his simple camp.

Nonetheless, when night fell his curiosity got the better of him and he edged up to a point where he could see Cas-Eiddew again. A thrill of fear ran through him when he realized what he saw matched what Moriganna, then Cymri, had once described to him.

The ruins were gone. In their place was a mighty fortress unlike anything he had ever seen. For one thing, it was several times the size of Caerleon and the walls were at least twice as high and deep. For another, something about it proclaimed it had not been built by the hands of men. Banners and flags were visible on the towers and parapets, though in the dark he could not make out what was on them. Eerie lights that were not flames moved within.

Llew stared for few moments longer, then decided discretion might be better than valor, at least for the current situation, and retreated to his little camp.

He waited until nearly terce the next morning, midway between dawn and noon, but there was no reason for concern. Cas-Eiddew now held nothing more than crumbling stone and ancient ivy. He made his way in to the center and then up to the top of the southernmost hill, where he and his companions had camped upon their only previous visit.

Of course, there was nothing like a door to knock upon or a bell to ring for admittance. "Hafgan?" he called, tentatively. He waited a moment but there was no response. Truthfully, Llew was not even sure it was possible to gain the attention of the Spriggans by day, although Hafgan had never seemed to have a problem with being out in broad daylight.

"Hafgan?" he tried again and, again, he was not surprised when there was no response. Third time for the charm it was always said. "Hafgan, it is me, Llew. I need very much to speak with you."

"Hafgan is not here right now," came a voice near his left elbow. "Did you wish to leave a message?"

Llew gave his heart a few beats to settle down before turning to the dwarf-like figure behind him. "You are not Hafgan," he accused.

"Right, I believe I just said that. You can call me Morcar. Are all princes as perceptive as you?"

"Ha," replied Llew. "Wait, can you see me?"

No Spriggan had ever been able to see Llew. As far as they were concerned, he was invisible. Hafgan had claimed this was Llew's fault, given that he appeared to know next to nothing about himself. According to Hafgan, Spriggans only saw things as those things saw themselves, rather than seeing them as they were, or as they appeared to be. For this reason, he said, it only stood to reason that no self-respecting Spriggan could see Llew. On the other hand, Llew had learned to take what Spriggans said, or at least what one particular Spriggan said, with a large grain of salt.

Morcar looked him up and down. "Eh, you look to have not even so much substance as a shadow, just a slight discoloration in the air. I cannot even discern your shape, and you fade in and out a bit, but yes, I can tell something is going on where you are standing."

"That is progress is it not?" Llew demanded. "I must be learning something about who I am."

"Possibly, possibly," the Spriggan admitted. "That is not to say you do not have a long way to go yet, but have you had any recent epiphanies that would account for what little improvement there is?"

"Had any what?" Llew asked.

"Any big discoveries about who you are," Morcar elaborated.

"Aye," said Llew, thinking back to his brief discussion with Moriganna. "Perhaps I have. Look here—this is terribly important to me—I have come a long way for a purpose that is far more urgent. Is King Hafgan really not here? If he is here may I speak with him?"

"I am sorry but King Hafgan is not here right now. Would you care to leave a message?"

Llew shook his head in frustration. Some things never changed, such as the ability of Spriggans to annoy people. "That really sounded rather rote. I urgently need to speak with him directly. Do you know when he might return?"

Morcar shook his head, "We do not expect to see him for a couple of days more. It is alright, Prince Llew, we are a somewhat trustworthy group. I will ensure he gets your message."

Llew looked at him incredulously. "I just traveled a week and a half to see him and the whole world is after my head. Is it not acceptable that I wait until his return?"

The Spriggan pursed his lips. "Well, you cannot wait up here. The moon will be out again tonight and tomorrow night, too."

Wait up here? The idea was so strange that Llew had to take a moment to absorb that thought before he blanched. "Well no, I certainly did not intend to wait up here. I was hoping you could offer me hospitality."

"What?" exclaimed Morcar. "We do not just take in every nearly invisible traveling prince that wanders by. Our lives would be in chaos."

"There are so many of us then? What about the rule of reciprocity?" demanded Llew.

Now it was the Spriggan's turn to look confused. "I cannot say that I have ever heard of such thing." Appearing suddenly suspicious, he asked, "Are you just making that up?"

Actually, Llew was, but he saw no reason why Morcar needed to be told that. "You can think of it like the rule of hospitality," said Llew, sidestepping the question. "When someone receives hospitality he has an obligation to reciprocate should the host ever come calling. You really have not ever heard of it?"

"Living under Cas-Eiddew, we are not exactly what you would call the crossroads of the universe for travelers," Morcar explained. He gave Llew a wary eye again. "And what would such a rule have to do with the here and now of things?"

Llew tsked. "You do not know? Hafgan was a guest of mine for a couple of months. How could you not know this? If you did know it, did you really think to violate the rule of reciprocity?"

Unpleasant fates seemed to find people that violated the rules of hospitality. If the rule of reciprocity was anything like that, Morcar had every reason to look concerned when he said, "Well, put like that—of course we do not—but you have to realize we have never had a mortal guest and you might find things a bit . . . odd."

"Odder than up here during a moonlit night?" Llew challenged.

"Ah," said the Spriggan, "perhaps you will find it no less odder, but you should make out better down below than out here. Welcome to Cas-Eiddew, Prince Llew; hospitality is offered. I am more or less in charge here whenever Hafgan is away, but it is not really a formal thing as there is little formal about the way we manage things. Spriggans are an independent lot . . . as you may have already begun to realize."

Llew snorted. "I think perhaps I had, friend Morcar."

"Aye, well then," said Morcar, "you will not be surprised when I tell you that you must make your own bed and wash your own bed clothes. We have no menials to do such things and would not allow ourselves to be so coddled if we did. Yet, you need not worry about our cooking. Although we have no women folk, we do have our ways."

"Oh, this should all be rather fascinating," remarked Llew.

Chapter XI

Dinner at Hafgan's

"I was surprised to see you here, lad. The truth being is that it has been a very long time since I had a visitor," Hafgan said to Llew. "More to the point, I do not believe I have ever had one. Have they been treating you well?"

"Hafgan?" exclaimed Llew. "Where did you come from? They told me you were away." He looked around, suddenly even further confused. "And where are we?"

While he waited for the answer, Llew inspected their surroundings. Multicolored rock formations flowed from the ceiling towards the floor, while others rose from the floor. In many cases they met. All the stone was rippled and smooth and glistened with a fine sheen of moisture, much as though the entire place was formed of flowing stone that had hardened in the process of dripping, like icicles after a freezing rain. There was plenty of light to see by. It all came from floating motes in the air, wispy things that had no substance. "This is the same cavern where we first met," he observed.

Hafgan shrugged, "Or one much like it. These caves run for many miles in all directions, including down to the Firvulag realms. It is handy for us that it is so—except when neighbors like knockers come calling. So you do not recall my arrival this morning?"

Llew shook his head in the negative. "Not a thing of it. What has happened to me?"

Hafgan showed him a wicked grin. "I thought that might be the way of it. What is the last thing you recall?"

"Morcar told me I was going to have to make my own bed, then he started to lead me to a secret entrance—" Llew stopped. "I do not recall anything after that."

"Well of course not. It would not be much of a secret entrance if we just showed it to the first person to wander up, now would it?" Hafgan clapped him on the shoulder. "Spriggans are a secretive bunch; it is in our nature."

"Morcar said you would not be back for two days," Llew said faintly.

"Ayup, and it took me three weeks, but I had no knowledge you would be waiting for me, else I would have been more inclined to hurry."

"I have been here three weeks?" the prince asked, in a querulous tone.

Hafgan looked puzzled, "Well yes, lad, that only stands to reason. By the way, Morcar says you eat like a horse and snore fit to bring the caverns down, but I would not worry too much about that. He has just never heard his own snoring. He also as much as admitted you more than made up for it when you helped deal with the knockers; may have even saved a few lives. From all accounts you were a regular hero. Stands to reason I suppose."

"Um, the what?"

"Knockers, those dratted things just keep building up their numbers until they spill right over into Spriggan territory and then how is anyone to sleep, I ask you? Not sorry I missed that, I can tell you. With that dreadful knocking all night long and you never know where it is coming from? It is not as though they are not dangerous either—oh no. They get hungry enough and a swarming pack will devour even a full-size Spriggan—boots and all. It is a bit of a miracle they did not devour you. I would say Morcar has naught to complain about on your account. Your snoring was a bargain compared to having you help deal with them. It appears I am in your debt—now what can I be doing for the Prince of Gwent?"

Llew hesitated and actually had to think. Why had he come to talk to Hafgan in the first place? It was easy to get distracted around Cas-Eiddew, certainly, but—

"Aha," said Llew. "It is about me. I have been enchanted to appear as someone else. No one knows my new face and I have even been attacked by my own friends."

Hafgan rubbed his nose. "Really, which ones?"

"Addfwyn for one. He pulled a knife on me."

"In truth? I find that hard to credit. If he did not know your new face then why would he attack? I doubt he wanders about attacking every stranger he sees."

"I was in my rooms when he walked in. Seeing a stranger there it was a natural enough response," Llew said defensively.

"And someone else also attacked you?" the Spriggan King prompted.

"Well, yes, Llewellyn came after me with an entire squad of warriors."

Hafgan furrowed his brow. "In your rooms? Either your rooms have gotten much larger since I was there, or the ones you do have were awfully crowded."

"No, no. She attacked me outside as I had just left the castle."

Hafgan's raised an eyebrow at this. "Is it possible she had some bone to pick with you and saw through your disguise?"

"No, I am most certain she did not," Llew said, growing impatient, "on either account, thank you."

"So, unlike Addfwyn, she does go around attacking strangers?"

"Yes—I mean no. I mean I think she saw me and mistook me for someone else," said Llew, trying to clarify.

"Ah, so you look like someone she does not care for. Did she call you by a name?" Hafgan asked.

"No, unfortunately, and before you ask, Addfwyn did not appear to recognize me as anyone he knew. I was just a stranger in a very wrong place for a stranger to be, so far as he was concerned."

Hafgan grimaced. "So much for getting to the bottom of this quickly. I think you had better go back to when you last looked like you, and recount to me what occurred up until the time you realized you did not look yourself—but hold a moment."

The Spriggan King put a small whistle to his lips and blew once. Llew belatedly covered his ears; the noise had been ear shattering. Hafgan gave him a startled look at his reaction.

"Sorry lad, I forgot you can hear this better than we ourselves do. I have never known a mortal that could hear any trace of it at all, ere now."

A dozen Spriggans entered the cave from half a dozen different directions. Setting down chairs and a table, they also brought food and drink that they put on the table. Then, as abruptly as they had appeared, they were gone.

The mead was mead and very good. The rest of it, the food, was . . . strange.

"What is this?" Llew finally asked.

"Firvulag," replied Hafgan.

Llew put his knife down. "We are eating dark dwarves?" His stomach gave him a preliminary warning of what was coming next if the answer was 'yes.'

Hafgan guffawed at this. "Nay lad, no. I mean to say it is Firvulag food. We Spriggans do not grow our own food, nor do we cook it. Instead we pay to have it brought to us by others, already cooked. Why not? We have coin a plenty and little else to spend it upon."

Llew frowned. "That seems somehow decadent."

Hafgan shrugged. "I doubt it is that much different from what men would do if they could—and if there were no females of the species to chastise them for it."

"But—" Llew stopped to ponder for a moment, sidetracked. "Hafgan, if there are no Spriggan women, where do new Spriggans come from?"

His host grimaced. "Have you seen any new Spriggans?"

"Very well then, where did Spriggans come from?"

Hafgan looked pained, "Ah, please lad, some things are not suitable for discussion at the dinner table. Besides which, you need to tell me about everything leading up to your spot of confusion with your friends."

Llew did so. Surprisingly, Hafgan never blinked at finding out Cymri and Moriganna were one and the same. "I as much as suspected it," he said. "Recall I was once twitting about what a lazy one Moriganna was with her cantrips? It was funny because Cymri was right there, and if I was right, and she was who I thought she might be, she could not even protest."

"You suspected and you never warned me?" Llew expostulated. He continued without waiting for an answer. "And seeing people as they see themselves, how could you not know it was her?"

The Spriggan King held up his hands placatingly. "Now lad, I could have been wrong and that would have done you no favors. She was clearly helping you, and Moriganna does not have a bad reputation among the Fae. A bit harsh, and maybe even scary, but then that applies to a lot of us as well."

Llew recalled a mental image of Hafgan and a few of his subjects, twelve feet tall and tramping an army of barrow warriors into dust. He shuddered. Scary was a fair description.

Hafgan also affected a shudder. "What you did to those knockers, lad? Scary might even be an understatement."

Ignoring that, Llew asked, "Well, and how could you not be sure it was her? You keep telling me how Spriggans see people only as they see themselves. If that is true, would you then not see her as Moriganna, regardless of what illusion cloaked her, much in the way you see changelings as what they are, rather than as who they are meant to be?"

"Try to show some understanding, Llew. This is Moriganna you are talking about. Her enchantments, many of them at least, are not at all like those of the Fae. Against them we often have little more defense than any mortal." He leaned forward and said in an earnest voice, "There are good reasons why she is feared and respected among the Fae. As Cymri, did she not turn Queen Mab into a bird in front of your very eyes?"

"She had stolen Mab's wand," Llew protested, "exchanging it with her own flute."

"Even that would not have been nearly enough against Mab herself in her own stronghold. No, lad, there is that and also, as she said to you, she once was Cymri in her youth, however many ages and worlds ago that was. Apparently she remembers it well enough to be able to see herself that way, at least long enough to fool us poor Spriggans."

"That reminds me," Llew remarked. "What of her claim that she has returned from some time hence?"

Hafgan idly tugged at his beard as he considered his answer. "If she is a full Druid, perhaps even holding some aspect of the goddess herself, as you say she claimed, then she can indeed, under the right circumstances, move through the waves of time, and in any direction she chooses. While some of the Fae have a considerable mastery of time, especially the royalty amongst the Tylwyth Teg, they cannot match that. They can, as you have seen, only slow it down or speed it up, and only within a given area. They cannot step outside of it and reenter wherever they wish.

"This is just another reason why Moriganna makes a better ally than an enemy. Suppose she went back and murdered your grandfather? Where would that leave you, eh?"

Hafgan lifted an eyebrow while looking in Llew's general direction, then took a large gulp of mead. "I would say we have digressed again. We are trying to figure out what happened to your golden head of hair are we not?"

Llew nodded agreement. "Among other things, yes."

"Very well, the initial possibilities would seem to be Moriganna, the afanc, the korrigan, and Addfwyn. Let us begin to see what the likelihood of each is before we look further afield."

The Spriggan drummed his fingers on the table. "Moriganna would certainly have the means to do so but I see no motivation for her. She seems to be on your side, at least for now, and would have little interest in causing you difficulty. The afanc was just a beast, clever for a beast, but a beast, all the same. The korrigan maybe could have done it, but I do not see how she could have gotten away with it in front of Moriganna. And, as for Addfwyn, he has many unusual skills for a simple crofter from the wilds, but I judge enchantment is not amongst them."

"I concur with all of that," Llew agreed.

"Alright then lad, now we must consider it another way. If none of the individuals you came in contact with between your knowing you had one face, and learning you had another—"

"It is more than my face," Llew interrupted. "It is my whole body. Indeed, I am over half a head taller than I was. I am nearly as large as Helgar at this point."

"Interesting enough, but it does not alter what I am about to propose. If no one enchanted you, then perhaps you were disenchanted."

"What are you saying?" Llew asked sharply.

"Just this, lad, as I have already assured you, King Auberon will never tell a lie that anyone will be able to catch him at. It is not the way of the Fae and, as their sovereign, no one is more Fae than he. Yet it was he that told us he took you from your parents and left a changeling, his own queen's son, in your place. He also said that child was by the same father as yourself, making him your own half-brother. The Fae king did it, probably at Moriganna's behest, because they thought you were about to be murdered by Lord Arawen. Given what happened to the changeling, it seems they were right."

"Aye," agreed Llew, "and, in a vision, my real mother, my birth mother, told me that she had been betrayed by those closest to her, such that she would appear to have murdered her own child. She even told me her own father had some hand in helping set this up such that her husband would kill her for it." He released a heavy sigh. "It is not a happy thing to know that your own grandfather was a servant of the Lord of Death."

"Be that as it may, lad," continued Hafgan, "Let us stick to what we have not learned by way of visions. Old Auberon said he had you returned to the lands of men as a changeling for another child. That would mean you were under a changeling's enchantment nearly all of your life, ever since you were but an infant. Since you and Llewellyn were the spitting image of each other, enough so that she spent most of her life pretending to be you, I would say the child you were meant to be a changeling for was the real Llew, Pendaran and Arianrod's boy. So and so, that would mean the way you appeared earlier was the enchantment and, now that it has been removed, people see you in your true form. You say you are bigger. Have you not always been considerably stronger than people expected of your size?"

"But," Llew protested, "the same arguments apply as to culpability. None of the people who did not enchant me would have disenchanted me."

"Ah, you are lucky then, lad. I imagine there are a lot of people that I would find myself disenchanted with."

Llew gave the Spriggan king a sharp look.

Hafgan had the grace to hang his head and pretend to sheepishness, "Sorry, lad, you should not be tossing me lines like that when it seems I just cannot let them pass. But really, 'culpability?' Sounds like you are learning some big words in Caerleon."

Llew decided to press on. "Back to the question, if none of those who were near me could, or would, have enchanted me, who would have disenchanted me, if that is what happened?"

"And there is the thing, young prince. If you were enchanted, someone would have had to do it, yet it is possible to be disenchanted and with no one to do the disenchanting. Consider that this would have been a changeling enchantment on you. Only one thing undoes those. You have to come close to the person you were swapped for. You could have come too close to the original child that you were exchanged for."

"How could that be? I saw no one."

"You said you went over to look at the engraved stone on a newer barrow mound in the royal barrow grounds. Who is interred there? Who was the last royal to pass on?"

Llew thought back. "It would have to be Queen Arianrod, Pendaran's queen and Llewellyn's mother, my supposed mother."

Hafgan nodded solemnly, "And just who else would have been buried with her?"

"In all likelihood? Her dead infant son, the real Llew," Llew said, his voice going flat and toneless, "and there I was in close proximity. That is also when I got dizzy and lost my balance."

Hafgan nodded but said nothing.

It hit Llew hard. For a moment he said nothing, could say nothing. His mind roiled and little facts that had been collecting in the depths came surging to the surface. "It fits," he murmured. "We know King Auberon took me to Caer Wydyr in Tir-Na-Nog and left a changeling in my place in the world of men that was my own half-brother. We know that child was murdered in my stead. We already suspected, too, that the king of the Fae later sent me back as a changeling at the behest of Moriganna. It was done to claim another child which could only have been the real Llew, but we were told he and his mother both were killed before the swap could be made.

"King Bran, the real Prince Llew's great, great grandfather as much as confirmed this when he told me that I was not of his line, and therefore I could not be the real Llew, even though he also told me I was a direct descendant of High Queen Boudicca."

Llew turned his attention on Hafgan. "This but reconfirms everything we have found to date. So if I am not the real Llew, if this is my true face and form, then who am I?"

Chapter XII

In the Wilds of Ergyng

Hafgan shrugged. "Sorry lad, we seem to have quite a few clues on that but I am not the one to put them together. It is a bit difficult for Spriggans to keep up with royal matters in the mortal realm. Problem being, you humans have kings and queens and princes for dozens and dozens of cantrefs, as well as the kingdoms they are in, and even high kings and queens for the late, great kingdom—that all makes it a bit confusing for me, especially given how fast things change hands amongst the mortal kind."

Llew's spirits sank even further. "I cannot let it go. Finding out who I am has got to be the key to unraveling this mess."

Hafgan rose from the table, despite the fact he was taller seated than standing, and walked around to clap Llew on the back, aiming for a spot just above the back of the chair. "Buck up, lad, this is Hafgan. If I cannot do it myself, why, chances are I know someone that can."

"I thought your motto was that if you were not getting the job done with brute force then it just meant you needed to use more," Llew objected.

Ignoring that, Hafgan continued, "I would say a visit to the beautiful Nemain is precisely what will help you most."

"Are you playing matchmaker now, Hafgan?"

"What? Oh, never. Nemain . . . well she is not the marrying sort I should imagine. Even so, I would not trust you anywhere near her were you still betrothed. None of that has anything to do with why you should visit her though. She is a seer, as opposed to me; I am more of a doer."

"Very funny," said Llew. "And what is it this seer does? And do not say 'she sees.' That would not be funny in the least."

Hafgan scratched his head. "That is kind of a hard question to answer then. Seeing is what she does, but unlike you and me, she can see what happens in other places and, sometimes, she can see what might happen in the future. Where she really might be able to help you, though, is that she can also see things that happened in the past. If anyone can find out about your roots, my coins would be on her."

Llew considered. "And you think she will help me?"

"Oh of course, lad. She is as kind and helpful as she is beautiful. She also lives alone in the wilderness along the south coast." Hafgan looked closely at where he probably thought Llew's face was and raised both eyebrows at once. "She is probably starving for some company, too."

"This sounds like a very good idea," said Llew, ignoring Hafgan's innuendos. "Will you give me a letter of introduction or some token to let her know I come from you?"

"Lad, did you not hear what I said? She is a seer. She probably knew I would be sending you to her before you ever left Caerleon."

Llew thought about that for a moment, then decided not to. "Do you think I will have any problems getting there and finding her?"

"How could you, lad? No one knows the land better than I do and I will give you detailed directions."

* * *

Not for the first time that day, Llew wondered if he was still on the right road. At this point, he was halfway certain there were roads out here, in the wilds of Ergyng, that Hafgan had never heard of. The sun and the stars were no help either. The skies were so thickly overcast it was impossible to be sure east was not west. Nor were the roads marked in any way, and this one appeared to be rapidly transitioning from a road to a goat track the further he traveled on it.

Llew reined the mare to a halt and looked about. There was not much to see aside from the surrounding conical evergreens. He pulled his cloak more closely about himself. The day was cool and misty, more like one in early spring rather than high summer.

Again he strained to listen. This was something he had learned was a very good thing for him to do when he traveled alone through the wilds. Although the mist muffled sounds somewhat, and the evergreens to either side even more so, he could, as he concentrated, still extend his coverage a considerable distance up and down the road.

Was there something this time? He tried to concentrate even harder, feeling as though he were a spider at the center of a vast web checking to see if anything was vibrating within his domain. There was. There were hoof beats coming from ahead and approaching.

From his experience, Llew could tell at once it was a single rider, moving briskly at a trot. Not a horse killing speed, by any means, but he was not just ambling either.

Llew debated trying to take cover in the evergreens, but the mare's tracks were too obvious in the soft, muddy earth of the roadway. At any rate, he reasoned, a single rider should not be much of a threat to him, regardless of who it was, other than for a select few, and those few would not be traveling out here in the wilds alone. Even so, and not for the first time since he had left Cas-Eiddew, he reproached himself for not asking

Hafgan if he knew why the Torc of Tethera would no longer let him change his form.

The rider appeared from a turn in the road a short distance away and rode up, stopping only about twenty paces from where Llew still sat astride the mare.

It was Helgar.

Llew suppressed his first instinct, which was to rush forward and embrace his brother at arms. Instead he tried to greet him as one heavily armed stranger on a deserted road might greet another heavily armed stranger. "Greetings, fellow traveler, pardon me, but do you come from anywhere near the south coast, per chance?"

Helgar gave him a once-over. "Nay, come direct from Gwent have I, there is a fork in the road not far behind me, however. Perhaps it is the eastern one you seek to take you to the far south."

"Ah, much obliged. Is there aught I might do for you?" Llew asked politely.

Helgar furrowed his brow as he considered this. "Well, you come from the north, did you come near Lindenjal in your travels?"

"Nay," replied Llew cautiously, "I have never actually been there; I came more from the northwest."

"Ah," said Helgar, nodding slightly. "In that case, I must say my trail rations are growing tiresome, and neglected I did to bring anything to ease the taste. When I was traveling in the northwest I came across a sort of sauce made of mustard seed and vinegar and other herbs. You would not happen to be carrying any you could share, would you? I could pay you well, and a great favor to me it would be just to have you agree to part with some."

This was a most unlikely request to make of a stranger in the wilderness. As unlikely, say, as asking if he had a jar of fig sauce or keg of ale. Now Llew was forced to consider. What game was Helgar playing at? "Nay, I am sorry, stranger, but I can tell you that I have converged upon this road from two separate forks in the past few hours. Possibly one of them leads to this Lindenjal of yours."

"Ah," said Helgar again. "I will have to try that way, bearing to the northeast then. I thank you."

"Indeed, and I you."

Helgar went to continue on his way. *His way to Lindenjal*, Llew thought. The words echoed in his mind. There was only one reason Helgar would be on his way there. This was not something Llew could allow his friend to ride off into alone, no matter what the cost. He half-turned in his saddle to say something, although he was not even sure what it would be. Before he could speak, he was hit by an unreasonably large Northman and borne to the ground.

He landed heavily on his back. Fortunately, Helgar did not come down on top of him with his full weight or it could have crushed his ribcage. He was still partly stunned when Helgar seized him by the top edge of his hauberk and shook him.

"Did you think I would not recognize Prince Llew's armor or did you truly have no idea who I am?" the Northman demanded. He slammed Llew's head against the sodden road to emphasize his words.

Llew's head was clearing a bit, but having it pounded on again was not what it needed, and Helgar's stance was sloppy. Llew pulled his knees up under his attacker, then used his legs to flip Helgar's entire bulk over his head to take his own turn at landing on his back in the road. Before the Northman had even hit the earth, Llew rolled to one side and came to his feet.

Careful to give no impression that he might go for a weapon—he was fairly sure Helgar would not do so himself unless Llew did first—he waited while his opponent clambered to his feet, still swearing at this reversal.

Helgar turned, spotted Llew, and prepared to charge.

In response, Llew remained unmoving in a casual stance, then raised one arm with his palm outward, bidding Helgar to desist. "I know precisely who you are, Helgar Olufson. I was just terribly surprised to see you here, and I was still more surprised to hear you were riding to Lindenjal . . . without me." A hard edge came into Llew's voice. "Had you forgotten that, in the same hour I pulled you from that wicker man, I told you that, when the time came for you return to Lindenjal, I would support you as best I could?"

Helgar's mouth opened but no words came for a moment. Then something seemed to grip him from inside and his face hardened with suspicion. "The bards sing songs of Llew and me, they do. Anyone might know to say such a thing."

"And what would convince you that I am your drott, despite my appearance?"

The Northman snorted. "My drott wore Math's Torc, and I see it upon your neck—which neck I will snap if you have hurt him in the stealing of it—and with it he could change himself into any animal of the field or forest. Show me you can do this and I will believe you, maybe."

Whoops, thought Llew and then, aloud, "I am sorry my friend. This I cannot do. Whatever deprived me of my former appearance has also confounded my ability to use the torc."

To Llew's alarm and frustration, the big man seemed about to attack again. Then Llew saw something that made his eyes widen. "Helgar, do not move, do nothing rash, we are not alone."

Helgar's eyes narrowed. "You are trying to make me think something is behind me? Born yesterday I was not, I will not look."

"Helgar, please, I think it is Gower."

Despite his earlier assertion, Helgar glanced backwards over his shoulder. What he saw startled him so badly he leaped away, turning as he did so in order to face what had come up behind him. This left his back exposed to Llew.

Both of them regarded the creature in horrified amazement. It was Gower, Llew thought, but his hooves were gone, replaced with great clawed pads on thick strong legs. His lips were likewise peeled back in a hostile expression that showed a mouthful of deadly sharp oversized teeth. His mane and tail were long and wild and even the proportions of his body were subtly different. He seemed almost like some gigantic cat-like thing preparing to pounce—no, not cat, Llew realized. Gower looked like nothing so much as some nightmare chimera of horse and wolf.

"Helgar," Llew said urgently. "He saw us fighting and he knows you are a friend of his master. He is prepared to defend you against me. You must convince him that we were not fighting in earnest or this will go very badly, regardless of the outcome."

"Um, ya, I do not wish him to kill you before you tell me what is going on here," Helgar replied.

"You do not want him to kill me at all," said Llew. "Come clap me on the back to show we are not enemies. You must see I would not dare attack you now, regardless of who I am."

"Perhaps," Helgar admitted grudgingly. He began to take a step further backwards towards Llew when the horse-wolf moved, almost too fast to be seen, completely silent on those padded feet, to interpose itself between the two warriors.

Just as surprising to both of them was that Gower was now turned to confront Helgar, fangs bared, and with his back to Llew. Llew tried to understand this for a moment before the facts clicked together.

"Gower, no," he commanded. "No!" And then, "Gower, up!" Gower whipped around and came to stand next to Llew, waiting for him to mount. The padded feet and fangs were gone and so were the strange proportions. This was no wolf-horse creature. This was just a horse, albeit a magnificent one. This was Gower. Llew laughed and stroked the great horse's bare back.

Seeing Llew was not attempting to mount, Gower turned his head back and gave his master a great sloppy lick up one side of his face and was in the middle of a second one when Llew sputtered, "Ack Gower, leave off you great galoot! Leave off!"

Helgar was looking at them both, with wonder evident in his eyes. "Llew?" he asked.

Llew felt a sudden weight on his left shoulder. For all that it was unexpected, it was familiar. He turned his head to see Cilgwri perched there, just as though all was right in the universe.

Chapter XIII

News from Home

Sometime later, Llew asked, "So tell me, Helgar. Before you noticed my armor, what made you suspicious of me?"

The Northman shrugged. "Addfwyn and Llewellyn, as well as one of the stable men, described a man that matches what you now look like. But it was more than that, when we spoke as strangers . . . "

Llew said nothing, giving Helgar time to find the words.

"When you spoke to me as a stranger, it was obvious you were not afraid of me, but you did not insult me, attack me, or even talk down to me. That is not normal for Tetherans, Llew. When Tetherans do not know me then those who fear me are overly respectful, and those who do not fear me are not respectful at all—foolish as that is."

This observation made Llew feel somewhat ashamed of his countrymen, and all he could to think to say was: "Northmen raiding is not soon forgotten, perhaps in time it will be."

He looked for a way to change the subject. "So, aside from Gower and Cilgwri, is anyone else looking for me?"

"Well," Helgar hedged, "Gower disappeared the same day you did. It must be hard to keep something like him in a stable when there is some place else he would rather be. No one knew quite what to make of that since no one but you can ride him. A lot of people thought you had ridden off on him for some reason, after you killed that serpent dragon by the lake."

Helgar tugged at his beard before continuing. "You know, Llew, if you are going to be killing dragons, you really should invite your best friend along. It may be the most fun anyone ever had at Caerleon and where was I? Back at the castle practicing throwing axes; that is where I was."

"Sorry about that," Llew said with a wry smile. "I did not really have a lot of time to send for you once we found it."

"And that is another thing, Llew, Cymri disappeared the same day you did. The guards saw you two go out together in that boat and neither of you ever came back, Thought you were together somewhere. Your father and Taliesin thought . . . ."

Llew directed a sharp look at his friend after his voice had trailed off. "No, do not stop now. What do you think they were thinking?"

The Northman sighed. "They thought what a lot of us were thinking, Llew. It looked like you had packed and taken all of your traveling things, even Gower was gone."

Llew lifted one eyebrow, "Oh, please, do go on."

"Many of Cymri's things were gone as well, things she would not have wanted to leave behind—" he stopped and looked at Llew pleadingly.

"You thought we had eloped?" Llew asked incredulously.

Helgar shrugged. "You are seventeen now. Even if no one quite knows how, everyone knows you are a year older than your twin sister. Strange it is, but Tetherans are made to accept strange. A lot of practice they have had, I would say."

"And we just happened to meet and kill an afanc when we were sneaking away to elope?"

Helgar shrugged. "It is not unlike you."

The prince opened his mouth to speak again, then changed what he was going to say in mid-stride. "Helgar, tell me. How did my father seem about this? How did Taliesin seem? Do you have any idea?"

Helgar clicked his tongue and looked to one side before looking back at Llew. "They started to get upset, then they laughed, clapped each other on the back, and broke a cask together. They were at it the rest of the afternoon. I had a couple of mugs myself. Llew, it was the good stuff, from that little town in Dyfyd."

They rode on in silence after that, with Llew just staring sightlessly ahead. After a time he said, "Well that was a waste."

This drew a puzzled look from Helgar. "Oh no, I assure you, not one drop was wasted, my drott."

In spite of himself, Llew managed a grin at that. "Nay, friend Helgar, I meant the reaction of the parents. Cymri and I did not elope, nor shall we ever. I may have hoped to wed her someday, but that will never happen either."

"We are all young, Llew, she might come around yet. It is difficult to know what goes on in the minds of women—wait!" Helgar's eyes grew wide and his voice lost its normal self-assurance. "Llew, did the dragon eat her?"

With a deep sigh, Llew looked at Helgar and said, "I suppose you need the same tale I related to Hafgan."

* * *

"I almost would rather you not have told me that, my drott." Helgar said at last.

"You? How do you think I feel? I would have had her for my wife if I could have. Indeed, I have been scheming in that direction with nearly all of my ingenuity for quite some time."

Helgar shuddered at this. "That would have been bad. Is Moriganna not your mother since she adopted you? The gods frown on that, Llew."

Holding back a wordless shriek only because it would have panicked the mare, and possibly Helgar's mount as well, Llew said, "She may have adopted me, but she is not my mother. I have somehow met my mother, if only in a vision or a dream, and she is most definitely not Moriganna. Beyond that, I may grant that, if the Queen of Deceit is not deceiving me—listen to how that sounds—then she is still a very distant relation through High Queen Boudicca, and that is quite disturbing enough, thank you. "

Helgar gave a low whistle. "I will have to think on this somewhat, my drott. It grieves me in some strange way to know that our companion is not even dead, but never existed at all. I will say this though, and perhaps I can because I never met Moriganna and my viewpoint is slightly more removed, but if there is a chance she is not an enemy, then I do not believe we can afford to think she is not the ally she claims. We owe her far too much, and she knows far too much about us, about everything, to have her as an enemy. We are already undone if she is against us."

"Very well," said Llew, "I need more time as well. On other matters, what are you doing on your way to Lindenjal? And without me, I might add."

A sheepish look crept into the Northman's face, but there was no guilt in his voice. "Aye, I had not intended to go for another season. I have not got my full growth yet, I think, and I am still learning so much from Afaggdu it would have seemed foolish to rush in now."

Now it was Llew's turn to raise an eyebrow. "Then why are you?"

"It has been over a month since anyone has seen you, Llew. I could not wait any longer. Everyone is doing what they can, but it may not be enough. I have to defeat my uncle so I can raise a Northman force to bring back to the fight. Gwent needs allies now."

Chapter XIV

War is Coming

Llew let that sink in a bit before he responded. "We are openly at war? Surely after what we did in Clwyd, it will be some time before Annwyn can bring its full strength to bear against Tetherans again?"

"Aye, perhaps, but it is complicated, Llew."

"So who is taking the field against us?"

"No one, yet, but your father thinks they will."

"King Pendaran is mobilizing and summoning all of Gwent's allies to repel an invasion?

"Not exactly, no—oh, no one is invading Gwent—put your mind at rest about that."

"So is someone invading somewhere else? Who and where? Or are we invading somewhere? If so, where and who?"

Helgar grimaced. "Yes, and it is complicated, and also yes, and it is complicated."

An exasperated sigh escaped Llew. "Let us try this a different way, what is my father doing—I mean, since he is not looking for his favorite son?"

Helgar's face brightened. "This I can answer, he is calling on Gwynedd to send forces."

"Now we are getting somewhere," said Llew. "Why is he calling for them?"

"It is because Dyfyd has declined to pledge fealty to you as high king. It seems King Govannon is not so eager to accept the rule of another over his own. You would think he could be happy at all the extra time he would get in his smithy. I have heard he likes beating on an iron anvil more than sitting on his iron throne."

"So my father is sending an army from Gwynedd to force them into submission?" Llew asked in disbelief. "Forcing Dyfyd into a reunified Tethera will not give us the kind of support we need for what comes. What happened? Was not the threat of Taliesin reasserting his crown over Ceredigion enough?"

"Nay, Llew, Govannon claims Taliesin has left Ceredigion unattended too long, and it is now fully and forever a part of Dyfyd."

Llew mulled over this a moment. "What is the mood in Ceredigion? Does Taliesin not still hold their hearts? That would be quite a different animal for, if King Govannon finds himself arrayed against the very people of Ceredigion, as well as contesting with forces from Gwynedd and Gwent, even Dyfyd would quickly be compelled to let loose their usurping grip. Once the loss of Ceredigion is a fact, they may very well be brought to reconsider rejoining the great kingdom."

"Taliesin has support, Llew. Who could be more popular anywhere than the chief of all bards? But the forces of Gwent will not be going."

"Uh oh, and why not?"

"Because everything it can spare is being sent to Ergyng."

"Oh, are we attacking them, too?" Llew asked, exasperation in his voice.

"Nay, Llew, they called for support and your father was compelled to send it."

"Why compelled? Ergyng has not agreed to rejoin the great kingdom. We do not even have a treaty with them. And who are they being attacked by?"

Helgar put a hand to the back of his neck and cricked his head to the right with a sharp popping noise. "Do you recall Goll One-Eye, Llew?"

Llew gave Helgar 'the eye.' Whether she had done it to him as Cymri or Moriganna, Llew had experienced enough of it himself to gain some degree of mastery in inflicting it on others.

Visibly chagrined, Helgar looked away and continued on without an answer. "His last invasion fell apart after he was injured, but what we hear is that he is reasserted his control over the tribes and has called them for war—and they have come. Worse, they are coming in numbers we did not imagine they still had."

Llew shook his head dismissively. "The Picts have no siege skills, nor several other things they would need to overrun an entire kingdom. Why is Ergyng frightened enough to call for aid from Gwent? They must know King Pendaran will extract concessions."

"They are not alone, Llew. The forces of Annwyn augment them, apparently to provide exactly those things which the savages lack. Siege engines, supply wagons, and the knowledge to hurt a kingdom precisely where it will do the most damage."

"All things he has in plenty because they were not harmed or disarmed when we drove them from Clwyd," the prince mused. "Unfortunately, that was actually very clever of Lord Arawen, but I would ask why he is in such a hurry to move on us now, when the majority of his forces cannot be ready for a full onslaught?"

A low whistle escaped his own lips when it came to him. "They want to hit us now because the crops are beginning to come in. Many of our men will not be available for military service because they must be harvesting. The crops give the siege forces all the food they need and leave the people of Ergyng to starve. Even should the invasion fail, there is no time left in the season to grow more, and winter is coming. So, even should the Picts fail, Ergyng will be badly weakened next year when Lord Arawen might be ready to send his own forces to attack."

"You are saying what your father said," Helgar agreed.

"Good. I imagine Afaggdu is an enormous help to him in this, as well. Come to think of it, he probably trained us both in strategy. For all I know he has trained every heir to Gwent for hundreds of years."

"Afaggdu is no longer at Caerleon, Llew. He has gone to Ergyng with Llewellyn."

"Llewellyn?" Llew asked in surprise. "Why did she go to Ergyng?"

Your father wanted someone he could trust in charge of so many of Gwent's warriors. He also wanted someone of such standing that would not let themselves be pushed around by the Ergyngling kings."

"Are you serious Helgar? She is what she is and she is surely up to the task. I know our own warriors will give her no difficulties but, at the end of the day, even with Afaggdu there to advise and assist, the Ergynglings will see her as a sixteen year old girl and that will create problems."

Unhappy with this line of thought, Llew nevertheless continued. "They will attempt to avoid taking even so much as simple advice from her, let alone direction. Even if she were male, the kings would surely try to treat her like one of their own subordinate commanders."

"Kings?" Helgar asked.

"Two brothers, Nynnio and Peibio, rule together. You might think two heads would be better than one but, for all that they are distant kin of his, I know my father has very little regard for either of them. They will not be able to bully Llewellyn but, from what little I have heard of them, they will most certainly try."

"Llew, it may not be quite so bad as you might think," Helgar ventured.

Llew looked up sharply from his thoughts, "Oh? And why not?"

Helgar shook his head mildly. "So far as anyone knows, save for a special few, Llewellyn is not in command."

"What! She is reduced to using a proxy? There are any number of reasons why that cannot go well."

"No, Llew. For some odd reason you shaved your moustache, it was maybe something to do with a wager, and then you led the warriors to Ergyng."

For a moment, Llew just gaped at his old friend before it came to him. Shaving the moustache was the clue. As it was, it still took him a moment to put it together. "Ha! You are saying she has disguised herself as me again, are you not?"

Helgar nodded. "She did. If these sharing kings you speak of are as you say, they may still make things more difficult than they should be, even though they should now tread more carefully than ever—beggars should never seek to choose how help is given to them. After the battles in Clwyd, and your defeat of King Gronw, you have developed a fearsome reputation, my drott. That could help keep them in line."

"Hmm," mused Llew, "despite all the madness, everything seems so well in hand. It all makes me feel rather unnecessary. So why are you so keen to take on your uncle now? Is it just so you can bring more men to the fight at Ergyng? Or is to bring them to Dyfyd to support Taliesin?"

Helgar's voice became darkly serious as he replied, "I always said I would take up another discussion with my uncle when two things happened, Llew. One was when I could swing a great axe with each hand as readily as most men can handle one.

The other was when I should have a reputation such as would frighten my opponents at even a rumor that I might be approaching. Your fame has gone wide, my drott, and mine with it. Even in Lindenjal they will have heard of us now. My uncle and his cronies have had much time to realize they are doomed, so now is a good time, although next year would have been better, I think."

"So why not next year, my friend? To understate the obvious, things are rather busy right now."

Helgar pressed his lips tightly together for a moment before speaking. "We need more men, Llew. Gwynedd is refusing to aid Taliesin in reclaiming Ceredigion. Your father said that Queen Enid would do so if she could but, with a reigning king, her power alone is not enough. The nobles there say that, since Caradog was crowned, and swore fealty directly to you, only you or he can rightfully command them to send men. As for Llewellyn, already departed to Ergyng she had, or King Pendaran might have sent her to Gwynedd. I think that would not have worked because you spent some time there and did many great deeds. Well known is a weak way to describe what you are in Gwynedd."

"I will go and kick the hindquarters of every last warrior and ruler in Gwynedd if they will not get off their seats and do their sworn duty," Llew said angrily.

"Not to give offense, my drott, but while they would accept that from a Prince Llew they knew and, for all I know, even enjoy it, they will not be so happy if some stranger with a face like yours attempts it."

"So why does not Caradog merely issue the order himself? He is king, even though Queen Enid still manages things day to day while he is training with Afaggdu." As he said this, a door was thrust open in Llew's mind and he said, half to himself, "He has gone with Afaggdu to continue his training, and Afaggdu went with Llewellyn to Ergyng."

Helgar nodded affirmatively.

"Well, by all that is—tell me something Helgar. Is anyone even looking for me at all? Which is to say, anyone aside from Gower and Cilgwri who, to their credit, seem to be the only ones that have achieved some measure of success?"

"Ya, of course, Llew. After Addfwyn said he would try to find you, your father equipped him and sent him out. Except—" Helgar furrowed his brow and scratched the side of his head, then looked back up at Llew. "I think he headed toward Dyfyd."

"That is it?" said Llew in disbelief. "The crown prince goes missing and all I rate is a man-servant who, it seems, has gone off in the opposite direction?"

Helgar shrugged. "Well, when you say it like that, Llew . . ."

Llew gave a heavy sigh. "Months of boredom, heavily mixed with the mundane and then everything happens at once. It seems our course is set. Assuming your uncle is no match for your mighty thews, how long do you think it might take for us to install you as king of the Northmen in Tethera, Jarl Helgar?"

Chapter XV

Lindenjal

After being told of its wonders so many times by Helgar, it seemed rather unreal to Llew that he was actually looking upon this place. It was also a bit of a shock. This was no tiny settlement of Northmen that had carved a small place for themselves in the wilderness of a far off land.

Lindenjal was a vast collection of buildings of all shapes and sizes, all made from wood with steeply sloped shingled roofs. They crowded each other as far as the eye could see. All of them were behind a high wooden palisade, and resting in the harbor were at least a score or more of ships, loading and unloading, coming and going. The entire place was a riot of activity.

It was also, with only the exception of Caerwent, the biggest town Llew had ever seen. For a time, he continued to regard it with nothing short of amazement. "Helgar?" he asked. "You said there were more settlements like this one?"

Helgar gazed on the settlement himself, a jumble of emotions evident on his face, although none of them seemed to be amazement. "Not like this one, Llew, Lindenjal is the grandest. There are eleven others that approach it in size, some few are only slightly smaller while others? Maybe only a quarter of her size they are. There is no way to count how many smaller steadings and settlements are out there. There would be even more but for the wretched Picts. They are always a problem until the place gets strong enough to drive them away. Even then they often come back to raid."

Llew played with the numbers in his mind. Afaggdu had started him on this form of mental exercise. The ugliest warrior in the world claimed the closest thing to an absolute in warfare was the need to understand what size and strength your own forces were, relative to your enemy's.

"Helgar, based on what you say, there are certainly more Northmen living in Tethera than there are Tetherans in the kingdoms of Clwyd and Ergyng combined." Llew felt a kind of despair at this realization, then realized this was only because it had not been completely clear to him, until that moment, that it really would be almost impossible to drive them all out, even for a true high king—and even if that high king were not already completely focused on the coming doom that was Annwyn. Yet had he not already decided that was not the way he would try to go? Hafgan had suggested he would be better off accepting the Northmen as subjects and putting their numbers to good use. Helgar, of his own volition, had come up with the idea that could make that happen.

"Do not worry so much about numbers, Llew," Helgar said, perhaps sensing something of his thoughts. "You are my drott. Once I have beaten my uncle, and reclaimed my birthright, I will announce this to all and also that you are my drott. Others are tired of having to fight ourselves, as well as the Picts. Their jarls will join if you let them have Tetheran titles, too. You would name them as cantref kings would you not?"

Llew idly smoothed the corners of his moustache while he considered this. "I believe I would. You think they will all swear fealty then?"

"They are Northmen, Llew. They can barely all agree on which end of the axe to hold when they swing it. But enough will come that the others will feel left out and worry about what that might cost them. Then they will join. The smaller and newer settlements will have no choice when we get all twelve of the jarldoms behind us."

The prince considered this, then made a wry grin. "I think we are counting our geese before they hatch. Lindenjal first. You know these people and have had some time to think on this. What is the plan?"

Helgar blinked. "I go to the great hall and call for him to come out and face me. Then we fight to the death."

Llew blanched. "That is all there is to it? Kill the jarl and move up? How does anyone rule for more than a week or two before they meet their own match?"

"You have not seen my uncle or you might not ask that. No, I jest, it is not enough to be the more powerful warrior. The challenger must also have grounds upon which to challenge. If they do not suffice then everyone will grab him up and dunk him in the harbor to cool off. If he persists after that, sterner measures are in order."

Llew considered. "That seems surprisingly lenient for an offense against a ruler, even if it is a first offense."

Helgar snorted and replied, "Coming from a cold clime we are a very hot-blooded people, Llew. If we destroyed everyone that ever lost their temper then there would soon be few of us left."

"I take it," said Llew, "that I am not permitted to help you in this fight?"

"No, of course not, my drott. Still, I am glad you are here. My uncle will not be an easy opponent and all my attention will be fully on cutting him down to size. If you enter separately from me, no one will know we are together. Then you will be free to watch for his trickery."

"Enter separately?" Llew was nonplussed. "I am unlikely to be mistaken for a Northman no matter how well disguised I am. Will not the guards and townspeople set upon me immediately?"

Helgar shook his head. "You are thinking as though you were a Northman going into a Tetheran town alone. The Northmen that have settled here, they are not raiders—not anymore, at least. Tetherans are welcome in Lindenjal. We do much trade with them. Certainly no Northman would openly attack someone just because he is not a Northman. It would be bad for business and the one who did so would likely face the jarl's justice, if there is still such a thing under my uncle."

"Ah," said Llew. "The differences a little history can make. I almost start to feel badly for the poor behavior of my people, then I recall the Northmen were never raided in their homeland by fierce Tetherans storming ashore and attacking when they were least expected."

Llew held up his hand as Helgar started to reply. "Peace, my friend, there will be nothing easy about winning acceptance for your people by mine, but we are both committed to the effort and that is the important thing. I suspect you have already done more to change Tetheran views on Northmen than all other Northmen combined—ever."

Helgar shrugged. "That has never been my chief intent, Llew."

"Remember this, 'Never hesitate to take credit for the good you have done, for others will never hesitate to blame you for the bad you have not done,'" Llew quoted. "But Helgar, this is wonderful news. It means I can move freely within a Northman town. That is a boon I did not expect." He gave a brief laugh. "And I need no disguise, even the other Tetherans will not know me, so they cannot give me away." Then he scowled and said, "Unless they think I am whoever Llewellyn thought I was and come howling for my blood."

"Oh, and it is also good," Helgar added, "because you can keep the horses."

Llew frowned. "I get to stand back, stay out of the fight, and mind the horses? Now I am starting to feel like Caradog."

Helgar laughed, then sobered. "Maybe, but Caradog killed his first warrior before he was fourteen. You and me, we cannot claim as much."

Chapter XVI

Helgar's Challenge

They came in through Lindenjal's north gate, with Llew trailing Helgar by several hundred paces, riding Gower, and leading the other two horses. A merchant with a pushcart and two farmers with ox-pulled wagons were ahead of them. All of them were clearly Northmen themselves. Llew found this to be a very strange sight. He had never really thought about Northmen other than as warriors and raiders, and yet here they were, behaving like simple crofters and street vendors.

Two hard-eyed Northman warriors in full battle array stood at the gate and to either side. Occasionally they stopped people who were entering and asked them questions, although Llew saw none that were denied entry.

With one enormous two-handed axe resting on each shoulder, Helgar brazenly strode right up to the gate. The guards' faces when they saw Helgar approaching were a study in shocked surprise. For his own part, Helgar radiated confidence and said something to each of them that looked like a friendly greeting. He then continued between them and into the town. Neither man moved to prevent him from doing so.

Llew noticed with some satisfaction that, although the guards were big men, Helgar, who had not yet seen eighteen summers, was likely a full head taller than either of them. He had grown a lot in the time since he had left Lindenjal and encountered Llew, but it was evident the guards still knew exactly who he was. Also, while bards spread stories and songs, they were not the only ones that did so. If there was any trade with Tetherans going on, it was likely the people living here had also heard tales and songs mentioning Helgar.

An extensive background story that Llew had prepared for himself, all about how he was a lord's second son from Ergyng, come to examine the feasibility of setting up some regular basis for trade, went completely unused. The guards, still distracted by Helgar's passing, just waved Llew in.

This was a good thing, he felt, as his skills in speaking the Northman tongue were still only slightly more than rudimentary. Although he could usually hold up his end of a short conversation, it could quickly become confusing for both parties, depending on the intricacies of the subject at hand. Still, he had to give his sister another mark for thinking ahead.

When Llewellyn remembered to get reading and writing lessons for Llew and Helgar, as well as for herself, it had occurred to her to take advantage of having their own Northman by having him give them language lessons at the same time. None of them had known at the time that Cymri probably already spoke it perfectly. Probably better than Helgar, Llew thought bitterly. As Moriganna, she had certainly lived long enough to learn.

Upon entering the town, Llew tried to keep his eyes on everything at once. The things that struck at him hardest were the similarities to what he knew. Despite the odd, wooden buildings, with their extensive carvings, and the preponderance of large, light-haired people, they were all engaged in pretty much the same activities as the people of any Tetheran town. Men and women in simple attire were carrying goods, bartering with merchants, tending their animals, and working in their small gardens. Children ran and played wherever they could.

These were people who worked hard and played hard. The sun and the rain, the seas and the snows, these aged them before their time, but they were not hunched and bowed because of it. One difference Llew did notice was that, in addition to an enormous knife, nearly every adult male, and not a few of the women, also had a hand axe resting on their belt.

Perhaps these people could be brought into the kingdom of Tethera, as he and Helgar hoped. Yet, despite those hopes, he often found himself wavering back and forth on whether such a thing was really practical. At the moment it not only seemed eminently feasible but absolutely essential—depending, of course, on Helgar winning his duel.

Helgar, despite his size and attitude, was not indestructible. Many people thought otherwise, but Llew knew better. Helgar would have undoubtedly been slain earlier that very year had Llew not intervened and personally slain the rogue cantref king, Gronw, who had also secretly been the infamous mercenary known as Cai. Although, to give Helgar his due it was worth remembering that he had already been wounded several times, first in the process of single-handedly slaying four of Gronw's warriors and then, a day or two later, wounded again when he simultaneously defeated three more. Even so, King Gronw had been an extremely dangerous foe. There were no guarantees he would have lost a fight against even an uninjured Helgar.

Above all else, Llew watched the crowds for anyone making a move against his friend as he strode toward the center of Lindenjal. This was made a bit easier by the fact that, as Helgar approached and strolled passed them, the people, alerted by the spreading silence of those that had already seen him, stopped whatever they were doing and turned and gaped at the passing warrior. Helgar smiled and waved genially to all and sundry as he strode along.

Llew worried that, by staying in motion and continuing to follow behind Helgar, he was making himself stand out too much from the crowd, but that was only a momentary concern. Within moments of his passing, the people, by unanimous consent, began to follow their former jarl's youngest son. Llew pressed his lips together tightly as he considered this. There was a large open area at the center of Lindenjal and he could see that it was going to be packed.

He took a moment to tie off the horses, they would only slow him in this crowd and he did not want Gower interfering in the coming fight, especially if he might change form in the middle of all those people. Gower he left untethered. There was no way to hold Gower anywhere if he did not choose to remain there. He also would serve as a very effective guard for the other horses.

Word traveled fast. When Helgar came to the town center a great many of Lindenjal's inhabitants were already there. They gave him plenty of room to proceed to an area near a stone well in the center that had a conical shingled roof over it. Seeing Helgar next to it, Llew realized again how big his friend was, even by Northmen standards. If Helgar had attempted to go to the edge of the well without stooping, the roof line would have caught him right in the forehead. For that matter, in this new form I could probably say the same, he thought to himself.

Helgar stood in front of the well and took a dominant stance facing an exceedingly large, multi-story wooden building with, if anything, an even higher and more sharply angled roof than the ones around it.

"Yoohoo, uncle," Helgar boomed, "it is I, Helgar Olufson, no doubt your favorite nephew." In a harder voice, "Come out now and cease your hiding. I name you kinslayer, and I name this day your last."

The crowds now filled the open areas to capacity, save only a wide strip of ground between and around Helgar and the jarl's hall. Llew pushed closer to where Helgar stood.

An eerie quiet had descended. The talking and even the whispering had fallen off and stopped. All waited silently for what came next. They did not wait long. One of the double doors at the front of the hall slammed open and four warriors emerged. They were the best equipped Northmen that Llew had ever seen. All wore heavy armor and carried ready weapons.

"Who is it who calls on us in such a disrespectful manner?" the lead one demanded.

Helgar curled his upper lip. "Skora, wait your turn. I called for a mange-ridden cur, not for one of his fleas."

"That is no way to speak of family, boy, nor of friends of the family. Your uncle has worked hard for Lindenjal while you were off running about having your fun."

"Ya, he was working hard to enjoy the fruits of stabbing my father in the back, and of killing and driving out those of our line that would not support him. You know full well he is a murderer and a kinslayer. Enough! Send him out. Helgar has grown a bit since last he saw me. It is time he saw me again. Tell him to bring his axe. It will not help him, but it is meet that he should have it when we greet each other."

Skora favored him with a sardonic expression. "Alas, your uncle has lost the use of his voice, but do not worry. He is hail enough for all of that. Still, if you wish it, I will take whatever message you have for him and give you the answer he would."

Helgar lifted up the two-handed axe that lay across his right shoulder and twirled it with one hand. Then he looked sharply at Skora. "You are willing to accept my message to my uncle yourself?"

"It is now Lendmann Skora, Helgar. Remember that when you address me."

Taken aback, Helgar blurted, "You? A lendmann? To what king? What king would have such as you in his service?"

"I serve King Hrungnir, Helgar."

This statement earned a scornful look. "King? I think someone has far outgrown his own trousers, eh?"

"I think not. We have only just made common cause with the Picts and with the kingdom of Annwyn. As our victories grow, all of our brethren in this land will join and we will carve our own kingdom. One that will replace what we lost in the old land and make it seem a small, petty thing by comparison. It is not too late, even now, for you to share in it, Helgar. There will be plenty for all. The kingdoms of the Tetherans are weak pathetic things. Their rulers huddle and hide, too afraid to venture forth against such as us."

Helgar regarded the self-acclaimed Lendmann Skora calmly. Then it slipped a bit and he chuckled. The chuckling grew into a full-throated laugh that went on and on. A few of the spectators laughed a bit, tentatively, as if not sure what the joke was. When they began to notice that Skora was not smiling, the laughing died out except for Helgar.

He finally wiped at his eyes with his sleeves. "Ah Skora, so funny you are. Are you sure you are a lendmann and not the court fool?" Then his expression hardened. "You know the rules. I have cause. Send out my uncle to answer for his crimes and to defend himself, if he can. He does not need to be able to speak in order to do that."

Skora sneered. "You think a king has nothing better to do than deal with every idiot with an axe that wanders by? Only one of equal station may challenge a king directly and you are not one. I have heard you call yourself a jarl now, but we do not even know what you are jarl of. No, the king will not waste time with you. You may wish to challenge me instead."

"Very well," said Helgar. "I challenge you Skora, for being in the way of my vengeance and for interfering in a matter of justice. I will now remove your head from your shoulders."

"Ah," said Skora, "I am above your station, too, but you have threatened me and that is a matter for my guards." To the men behind him he ordered, "Take him."

The three of them had already readied their weapons. Now they approached Helgar slowly, moving across the clear expanse of earth separating them. They were cautious and kept their shields up and their weapons poised to strike or defend as they came nearer.

Helgar watched them come with a glint in his eye. At fifteen paces away he drew up both of the two-handed axes he was carrying, one in each hand, and took a cautious defensive position, slightly crouched and waiting. Emboldened by his wariness, Skora's guards moved in. They came in five more paces before Helgar made his move. He spun about and shifted his grip on both axes until he held the very end of the hafts. He closed with the foes in a leaping spin and the axes came down again in a blinding rain of cleaving steel. They shattered shields and knocked aside all other attempts to block his blows. There was simply no defense that could be mounted and, with the increased range he enjoyed by dint of his own size, as well as the length of axes that were normally meant to be wielded with two hands, his foes could not get close enough to return his attacks.

All the same, it was reckless and dangerous. Llew pushed his way through the crowd. People gave cries of surprise or yelped with outrage when he pushed his way past them. Doubtless he would have started a few fights himself on a normal day—but this not a normal day. He finally came to the front and had an unobstructed view.

Helgar, it seemed, had already dispatched all three of Skora's warriors. He stood not twenty paces from Lendmann

Skora, his axes still red from his short fight. For his part, Skora had been joined by five new guardsmen. Even Helgar was not capable of mowing through endless numbers of such men. If nothing else, his method of fighting through multiple opponents, which Llew had not really seen before, had to be fairly tiring, even for him.

The Prince of Gwent strode out into the contested area. "Hold, please," Llew announced, so very glad he could speak Northman at least as well as he could. "This is getting rather silly and it is my turn."

Chapter XVII

The Kuningaz in Waiting

Skora directed a withering look of disdain toward him. "This is not your affair, Tetheran, we tolerate such as you because you are sometimes useful. By definition, meddlers are less than useful to us. Be off with you."

"Be off with yourself," Llew remarked in a deadly calm voice. "You just said your jumped up usurper jarl has reappointed himself to a higher imaginary title and that your true jarl has insufficient status to deal with him. If this Hrungnir of yours wishes to hide behind the skirts of his warriors with such a thin lie, then so be it. Now, however, it is I that challenges him. Send the coward out to face my blade. He has personally wronged me and I have issue."

Skora gave a snort of disbelief. "You have neither issue nor sufficient status. How could you think otherwise? When I have you thrown in the harbor you will still be wearing all your armor and your hands and feet will be bound for good measure."

"You have asked two questions," Llew replied. "I can answer them both with one. Jarl Helgar, who am I?"

Although he looked no happier than Skora to see Llew challenging Hrungnir, Helgar turned slightly and raised his voice so all could hear. "You are Prince Llew of Gwent, heir to the combined kingdoms of Gwent and Glywysing, rightful liege lord of the kings of Gwynedd, Clwyd, and Ceredigion. In short, you already rule, or will rule, every kingdom in Tethera save only Dyfyd and Ergyng. You are the kuningaz in waiting, their future high king and," Helgar continued, "you are my drott."

There was a collective gasp from the crowd at this. Llew turned and gave Skora a grim smile. With his limited vocabulary, he had to pick his next words carefully. "Now that this has been established, my status should be quite sufficient, even were your kinslayer usurper now claiming himself to be lord of the world's oceans as well. As for cause? He has wronged one who calls me his drott.

"Take note that I am not the one huddling in fear behind a throne. Tell the great coward to get out here or stand revealed as the weak clay he is. If he chooses the latter, he had best take ship and depart these shores forever." Llew's eyes narrowed, "And it would be better for you, I think, if you were on that ship with him." Llew was stumbling on some of the longer words but, judging by the crowd's reactions, it seemed he was getting on well enough to make himself understood.

Skora seemed as taken aback by these revelations as anyone else, but he rallied swiftly. "Maunderings of a lost Tetheran mercenary," he declared. To his men, he said, "Take them both."

The guards hesitated. One took a tentative step forward. In response, the crowd rippled and rose, seeming to press forward and making an ugly sound as it did so. The guard retreated back to his original position.

Llew clapped Helgar on the shoulder. "What scary fellows we be, eh?" he said in a low voice that did not travel far.

Skora, taking in the situation, calmly raised his hand to his men, palm out, as though it was only by his own will that they were prevented from going forward. "Very well, little prince. We will presume you have the status and the right. Neither will mean much to you in a few minutes time. King Hrungnir will grind your bones to make his bread." At his command, one of the guards rushed back into the jarl's great hall.

The crowd was not far away on either side. The prince wondered how well the people could overhear when he was not yelling, and if those who could hear them would understand his own language.

In Tetheran, Llew said, "It sounds as though someone has been telling him our bedtime stories for small children. I should think my bones would make very poor flour."

Helgar did not smile. Indeed, his scrambled sentences gave evidence of his internal consternation. "Llew, is not your fight this one. Is my uncle and it is me and mine betrayed. Falls on me it does to face him."

Llew chose his next words carefully. "I am sorry, my friend, I would not deprive you of this, not for anything. I know what it means to you, yet it is clear they are not going to allow you to do it. It still must be done and it is equally important to both of us that it be done. Come, let me do this for you and then you can kill Goll One-eye for me when we meet at the walls of Erg. Share and share alike, eh? Is that not what friends do for each other?"

This got a grudging grin from Helgar, but just barely. "Llew," he said urgently, "it is not just the joy of killing him that I fear you will deprive me of. My uncle is dangerous—truly dangerous. He can wield a great axe in each hand as I now do and he has much experience doing it. In battle he is like a wild animal—and that is before the madness comes upon him and he becomes a berserker. You do not have the kind of experience for this fight. Your shield? You may as well toss it aside; it cannot help you. If he hits you, even once, it is all over with you, for no shield will block his blows. He has shattered men's shield arms as they tried to block his axes. Those men are all dead now."

That gave Llew pause, but only for a moment. "That is good to know, but Afaggdu taught me the proper use of shields, and perhaps a few improper uses as well. I will keep it for this fight and it may even do me some good. Just do not ask me for weregild should I hurt your uncle too severely."

Helgar did not smile. "Do not joke, Llew. You have never faced anything like him before."

Llew gave him an appraising look. "All this talk about 'status' is not fooling either one of us. Regardless of what he says about it, the reason he is not letting you fight your uncle is because he thinks you might actually have some chance to at least do some injury. As for me? Skora sees me as a puny Tetheran, obviously too weak to present any real threat to his puppet king."

In other circumstances, Helgar would have found it a great joke that Llew was calling himself puny, but at the present his attention seized on something else.

"Puppet king?" Helgar asked incredulously. "You think my uncle would take orders from the likes of Skora? Llew, that is not possible. Never would he do that."

"Then we have a mystery, but I think we will get to the bottom of it shortly. You realize our roles are reversed now? Suppose I begin winning but cannot destroy him quickly? Skora will have time to become desperate as he sees several years' worth of planning all on their way to the trash heap. Nothing is more unpredictable than a desperate man, and I do not know what he will do, but you will have my back."

"Llew," Helgar rumbled gravely, "I will always have your back. If Skora attempts any mischief, I will crush him underfoot."

The crowd around them grew completely silent again, and Helgar's lips compressed together tightly as he stared at something over Llew's shoulder. Llew turned and looked. King Hrungnir had emerged.

Chapter XVIII

Meeting with Hrungnir

Neither Helgar nor Llew, especially with his new appearance, were small men. In point of fact, they were very large men who each stood a head taller than most of the Northmen around them, who, in turn, were probably half a head taller than most Tetheran men. King Hrungnir made them both look small. Standing at least a full head taller than either of them, he held a two-handed axe in each hand as though they were no more than hand axes. His hair was wild and untamed, running halfway down his back in a greasy cascade. He wore scale mail much like Helgar's and his eyes were full of madness. Upon seeing Llew he gave a roar which was clearly a wordless challenge—or a warning.

Llew gaped in amazement, fear came and went and was replaced with something that blended it with annoyance. "Truly Helgar? Truly? You came to fight this alone? What were you thinking?"

There were no preliminaries. Hrungnir simply charged at him. There was none of the curiously elegant, almost dance-like spinning that Llew had expected after seeing Helgar fight with his double-axes earlier. Indeed there was no sign of any sort of style or grace at all. The king of the Northmen did not need either, most men would die easily enough as it was. Hrungnir was an unstoppable juggernaut bearing down on him at high speed.

Llew's sword and shield suddenly seemed wholly inadequate to deal with what was coming. He himself felt less than adequate and he almost froze—almost.

Hrungnir's roar was still reverberating as he came within melee range of Llew—and stumbled. Llew's shield, thrown with near perfect timing and all of the prince's strength, had caught the giant squarely across his ankles. Regardless of strength, there was a question of balance that strength alone could not resolve.

The king began to fall face-first into the muddy ground—but Llew was already in motion and moving in before the shield struck. Unexpectedly, he was nearly undone when he caught the scent of the big man and almost gagged. Even people that never bathed could not produce an odor like that. *Surely*, he thought, *their king cannot be wearing untreated hides?*

Using his now free hand, Llew caught Hrungnir's left arm. It was still holding a great axe but was now flailing in a futile attempt to regain balance. Using it, Llew spun himself around to the other side of his opponent.

Swords were not meant for thrusting and the center of Hrungnir's hauberk, front or back, was the most heavily armored location on his person. On the other hand, Llew had once driven Fragaroc deep into solid stone. This was not as difficult.

Pushing off of Hrungnir's torso as it was still crashing to the ground, Llew managed to land in a standing position that, for a moment or two, was only precariously balanced. Once he was certain he was not about to fall into the mud himself—hardly a fit way to appear to the locals when he needed them to be impressed—he gave the stunned crowd a quick nod before he turned to regard his fallen enemy—just in time to see the massive Hrungnir climb back to his feet, despite Fragaroc still driven clear through the center of his back and emerging from his chest on the opposite side.

The muddy visage turned towards Llew and a long growl began that might as easily have come from an enormous bear. Hrungnir had lost one axe but now held the other in a two-handed grip. There was no doubt in Llew's mind what he intended to do with it.

Out of ideas, he floundered for some explanation and a possibility emerged. He had seen wild boars, a spear transfixing their vitals, continue to fight on for up to a minute before they recognized they were mortally wounded. Surely this was something similar? All he had to do was stall and time would take care of things for him—would it not? Still, he felt some other thought was gnawing at him, but he had no time to think.

Hrungnir lunged for him and Llew leaped to one side, then stayed in motion to avoid the axe. He did not look but he could hear it pass through the air behind him. He raced around the well looking for anything he could use and grabbed a heavy oaken bucket without slowing. By contrast, the bigger man was not nearly nimble enough to chase him around the well without slowing somewhat. Heartened, Llew slowed as well and flung the bucket under the giant's feet before continuing on his way. Hrungnir, unable to see below the roof without bending over, failed to glimpse the bucket before it was underfoot. He stumbled on it and crushed it flat, but not before losing his balance again. His entire body slammed hard upon the earth. *That*, thought Llew, *should about do it*. He turned to look and then had to dance back as massive hands reached for him and barely missed.

Incredibly, with Fragaroc still piercing him through and through, Hrungnir was scrambling back to his feet, his zeal for killing all things Tetheran apparently undiminished. Even the greatest of wild boars would be down at this point and, Llew realized, something else had to be at work here.

The thought that had been gnawing at him suddenly bit down hard.

The inability to speak, that horrendous rotting smell, the inhuman look in the eyes, and the sword thrust cleanly through the heart . . . most especially the sword thrust through the heart. It came to Llew that he was not fighting a man but, instead, he was engaged with something more akin to a barrow warrior.

That changed things substantially. Running until his opponent dropped was not a viable tactic, yet his only weapons remaining were knives, and they were clearly not going to be of much use either. Was there something he could do with the remaining bucket? It had a rope tied to it, perhaps he could— no, that was just grasping for straws.

Hrungnir only had one axe now and apparently did not have the wit to bother retrieving the other—Llew looked about and spotted it. Another trip around the well, with Hrungnir still in close pursuit, and he had the lead he needed to grab it up as he passed. They were now similarly armed. Llew could use even a two-handed axe well enough, yet it seemed a poor idea to go toe-to-toe with his opponent's weapon of choice. He had no doubt he would be the underdog in such a competition.

Yet, Llew reasoned, if Hrungnir was as mindless as he appeared, he might just do the same thing each time he was presented with the same choice. Once more Llew made another lap around the well. Predictably, the king followed. This time however, Llew continued around again. His pursuer did the same. A third orbit followed, and then a fourth. Llew knew he was gaining ground because he could see Hrungnir under the well's roofline. Hrungnir could not do the same because he was too tall. Another lap and Llew found himself—still running— looking at Hrungnir's back. Even with the well's roof blocking his field of vision, no thinking man would allow himself to be lapped like this without noticing what Llew was doing and turning to face him.

Afaggdu had once asked him if he truly thought there was any virtue in fighting fairly and honorably against creatures that had no concept of such ideals and never would. Llew had taken this to heart and it made him feel a lot better about doing what came next. Llew swung, and Hrungnir never saw it coming. It was a solid blow but, in this case, as Llew had known it would be, it was not enough. He swung several more times before he was satisfied. Then he planted the head of the axe upon the ground and leaned upon the haft to catch his breath while the Northmen of Lindenjal cheered enthusiastically.

At length he straightened and walked over to Helgar. The reinstated Jarl was standing over the prostate form of Skora, one foot planted firmly on the back of the lendmann's neck.

A group of Northmen from the crowd made as if to also approach and Helgar held up one hand, palm out, with only the first two fingers and the thumb raised, seemingly a request that they bide for a time. They complied.

Skora's guards were nowhere in sight. *They must have run off*, Llew thought to himself and greeted his friend with another: "What scary fellows we be, eh?"

Helgar regarded him thoughtfully as he approached. "How did you know he would be so stupid as not to turn around when you got so far ahead you started to catch up?"

"Actually," confessed Llew, "my idea was to get around the curve from him, so the roof of the well would hide me, then drop below the stone rim and roll back so I could use the long handle on the axe to jam between his legs and trip him. After that I was going to grab his ankles and dump him down the well. This was better, I did not have to foul the water."

His friend remained silent, still giving him an intense look, and Llew shrugged. "Yes, I know, it was too complicated and it might not have worked."

"I do not think it would have worked either, Llew. What would make even the attempt worthwhile?"

"I was trying to avoid making such a terrible mess at the end. Did you already know your uncle was some sort of barrow warrior?"

Helgar shook his head in mute denial.

"It is a bad sign," said Llew, "that Lord Arawen can now create such a thing from a man that has not even lain in a barrow. Moriganna once told me it would make for a much more powerful barrow warrior, but its creation would require prohibitive amounts of power from its maker. Enough power that, to create even one, the caster must expend the same effort as he would for many thousands that have lain long beneath the earth. This is why he raids barrows and seeks out the long dead; it is because anything . . . fresher, is just too costly for him. She said this was the only reason Lord Arawen has not overwhelmed us long since, slaughtering whole populations to create an ever-expanding army that would soon outnumber the living."

His expression grim, Helgar nodded toward the man under his foot. "I think this one has some explaining to do."

"Not that it is not a good place for him, but why is he on the ground?" Llew asked.

Helgar smiled unpleasantly. "He decided he had someplace else to be when you were cutting Hrungnir's hair—along with the rest of him—but I thought stay here a bit longer he should." He gave Skora a kick. "What about it, flea? Why was your dog already dead when we got here?"

Skora remained silent. Helgar shook his head. "Oh Skora, that will not work. You need to tell me and Llew everything. This is especially true because it occurs to me, it does, that if you had already killed him, and had him made into a barrow warrior before he killed my father, well then, this would explain much about his betrayal."

With a start, it came to Llew that this was something even he had not yet considered. Many Tetherans thought Helgar was a bit on the slow side. This was probably because of the way Northmen tended to talk when speaking in Tetheran, but they could not have been more wrong.

"Do not worry, Skora," Helgar continued, "if you do not care to speak to us. I will merely tell all this to the folc of Lindenjal, explain what you have done, and offer you to them. Sadly, they will no doubt have their own questions. You know our people. They might make it a kind of community project to find out the rest of the story. Poor Skora! That would probably be hard on you. Tell my drott what he wishes to know and I will not offer you to them. Speaking for both of us, we will let you go unharmed so long as you agree to leave Lindenjal immediately. This is your decision, but you had best make it quickly."

Skora talked; it did not take long. After a nod of agreement from Llew, Helgar reached down and picked him up off the ground by the back of his neck and set him on his feet. Then he gave him a kick that propelled him in the general direction of the northern gate.

Helgar turned to the assembled crowd and pointed to the departing Skora. "There goes the man who murdered my uncle so he could be made into a barrow warrior, and who also killed Jarl Oluf and most of my family, just so he could turn you all into another army to serve the Lord of Death. But do not think too harshly of him. He was told he would get a kingdom for doing this and he actually believed it."

* * *

A few minutes later, after things were settling down, Llew asked, still shaken by what he had just witnessed, "I thought you said you were not going to offer him to the people of Lindenjal?"

Helgar affected astonishment. "I did not offer him to the folc, they took him without invitation."

"After you told them what he had done and why," Llew said drily.

Helgar shrugged, "I only promised Skora that you and I would let him go. I did not promise to keep his secrets. Why it would not be right of me to keep such important news from my own people. What they did after that was up to them. Northmen are free men, and I had little right to prevent it unless doing so was somehow important. After all, there is no honor in leading a people enslaved through fear and subject to your every whim, even if you are like my uncle and are scary enough to do this."

Helgar raised his arm in a sweep as he indicated all of Lindenjal, "Welcome to Lindenjal, my drott." His gaze fell upon the cluster of Northmen, again waiting to approach and he turned back to Llew. "I am sorry, I have forgotten my manners."

Helgar gestured towards the men standing before the crowd, "Please come, I will make introductions to my thegns and tonight we will have a feast so you may become better known to the folc. They will be your folc now as well."

Chapter XIX

The Crone's Complaints

Llew regarded the salt marsh without enthusiasm. Endless chest high grass and reeds, broken only by varying sized patches of still water and mud flats, did not fit his ideas concerning pleasant travel conditions. Picking a path through it was going to be tedious in the extreme, not to mention muddy and buggy as well. This woman was supposed to be a seer? Could not she see that living in a salt marsh was a very bad idea?

The tide was out so it did not seem likely it was going to get any easier if he waited. Llew sighed and began his slog.

He left his gear tied in a tree with Gower running free and the mare hobbled. A salt marsh was no place for horses and they could use the time to graze and rest. As usual, he trusted Gower could protect both himself and the mare, as well as keep everything else safe.

After about two hours he was covered in mud nearly to his waist, and he had insect bites in every location the unpleasant things could reach. He was beginning to worry he might have gotten turned around in this trackless waste of briny water and hardy grasses when he saw the wooden construction. Someone had set up an enormous stump at the center of a circle of massive wooden posts.

This had been no minor undertaking. Trees this size had not grown anywhere nearby and getting the trunks through the same muddy paths he had taken to get here would be an incredibly difficult thing to do. The posts were old, very old, so old it was difficult to understand how they had not yet rotted away.

Llew considered the matter. There were collections of standing stones everywhere across the land, but to make such a construction out of wood was peculiar, to say the least. Forced at last to shrug it off, he continued on his way, it was hardly his area of expertise and there certainly were not any Druids around to ask.

The only sound was that of buzzing insects, some after his blood, a few more determined to get into his eyes and ears. This made him consider that it might be time to stop and listen more carefully. Doing so, he discerned that, somewhere to the south, waves were breaking on a beach. Apparently there was an end to the salt marshes, but where was this Nemain hiding out?

He nearly missed it. In fact, it was only a short distance from the circle of posts, but he had already passed the peculiar little hummock of earth, sprinkled with broken tree limbs, drift wood, and large clumps of reeds, when something about it registered in his mind and he turned to regard it again. From this side he could see the rude excuse for a door, mere broken planks, probably drift wood, tied together with bits of rope and twine.

It might very well have been abandoned for many years. It was difficult to imagine anyone wretched enough to build and live in such a thing in such an unpleasant place. Still, hermits and the like were known to be highly peculiar and often all uncaring about the things that most sane people insisted upon. Perhaps this fellow, if not too far gone, could tell him where to find Nemain. He retraced his steps to stand about twenty paces from the pile, checked to make sure his sword was loose in its sheath, then called in a loud voice, "Hail the house."

There was no response. Llew was hardly surprised. What would anyone even live on out here? He walked forward to the door, such as it were, and was preparing to push it aside with his boot when it abruptly opened.

Llew found himself almost face to face with the most appalling harridan he had ever seen. Her face was nearly too dreadful to look upon. One eye was bloodshot and staring while the other was covered by a rude squarish eye patch. Likewise, her appearance was hardly helped by the shapeless gray garment she wore that appeared as though it might have been borrowed from a barrow warrior. Although he was nearly startled out of his skin, she gave no evidence of surprise at all.

"So it is like that, eh?" she screeched. "A poor old woman is a bit slow to get to her door and the rich young dandy just decides to kick it in without the slightest bit of invitation? Ah, that the world has become such a terrible place."

"My apologies," stammered Llew, "you see I thought the place vacant and—"

"—and then it occurred to you a bit of random destruction might be fun, never mind if the poor person living there might be down at the seashore trying to find something to sustain her sad little existence yet another day."

"Well no," replied Llew, "actually, I am—"

"I know full well who you are! I am a seer am I not? No, do not bother to answer. You already knew that before you even left the home of those little thugs that call themselves Spriggans." The old woman gave a deep sigh of displeasure. "The new prophecies said you were to be fairly clever. I see I should not be putting too much stock into prophecies anymore."

"Now just a minute," Llew interrupted, "I think—wait, you are Nemain?"

"Maybe that is the problem," she muttered to herself. "He is trying to think. Mayhap that is the source of many of his problems."

This time Llew, merely glared at her, determined not to give her anything to interrupt.

She cocked her head a bit to one side and looked up at him. Llew almost thought he saw the beginning of what could have been a wicked smile, but on the wrinkled wasteland of her face it was nearly impossible to tell. He did note that, if she had more than two teeth, they were kept in some place other than her mouth.

"I know all about your problem and of course I saw you coming, Prince Llew, or should I say Lleu? Tea is already on. May as well come in and have a cup before we get started—unless you would as lief stand there looking silly while I have mine."

Llew's heart quailed at the thought of consuming anything that came from such a noisome place and brewed by such a disgusting server, but the rules of hospitality were clear. Ducking his head as low as he could manage, he stepped into her lair.

"Um, so you know Hafgan then," Llew ventured, looking for a place clean enough and sturdy enough for him to sit down. "I am presuming it has been some time since you have seen him?"

The old woman snorted. In a voice like a metal file being used to shape the hardest of stones, she answered, "Ridiculous question, I am a seer. But if you mean to imply it has been a considerable time since Hafgan and I have met with each other, then the answer would be that it has only been a couple of centuries. Is he still as handsome a rogue as ever?"

Thinking back on Hafgan's recollections of 'the beautiful Nemain,' Llew wondered if even a couple of centuries might be long enough to account for the differences he was noting.

Nemain gave him a poke in the shoulder to regain his attention. "A bit slow are you? It seems I must ask again. Is Hafgan still the handsome rogue I remember?"

Llew gave himself a mental kick as he tried to find something both politic and truthful to say. "Ah, I have not known him nearly so long but, in all honesty, I must say it would be difficult to imagine him one bit better looking that he is today."

"My," she said, smacking her lips, "that certainly is good to hear. Perhaps I should pay him a visit sometime soon."

Llew choked back his first response and instead, again somewhat truthfully he felt, replied, "I am fairly certain there is little that might excite him more than were you to unexpectedly show up for a visit."

Once inside, his hurried inspection only confirmed that the hut's interior was precisely the way he had pictured it. This meant it was somewhere between staggeringly horrendous and horrendously awful. He wondered if he could become ill just by sitting in the rickety woven reed chair she gestured for him to take. The roof over it apparently leaked, and part of it was damp and mildewed. He settled for sitting on its edge so that he might be better able to jump to his feet should it begin to collapse or he discovered there was something living in it.

There was no chimney, the smoke just went up through what served as a sort of thatched roof. It was not a terribly efficient method for letting smoke pass and some of it did not seem able to find the way out on its own.

The tea was bubbling in a pot over the tiny central fire. It looked and smelled like boiled weeds. All Tetheran tea was made from weeds steeped in hot water—but they had to be the *right* weeds, and you did not boil the water after the weeds were put in it. Llew hoped Hafgan was right about this woman's abilities as a seer; she was certainly not a cook.

After carefully ladling some of the liquid, which Llew could not bring himself to think of as tea, into a wooden cup of uncertain hygiene and questionable provenance, she passed it to him and he regarded it unhappily. Nemain, in turn, poured another cup and promptly quaffed it, despite the fact it had been boiling just seconds earlier.

While he waited for his own cup to cool he thought he might ask some questions. "So you already know of me and are willing to help me?" he inquired.

"Dear me, no," she replied. "It is not my purpose to help you. I have no idea why Hafgan would you give the impression that I would."

Llew was not sure he had heard correctly. "But—"

"No," she declared, "I am here to help me and me alone. It is you who are here to help me. If it happens that this also aids you then that is simply your good fortune. It is certainly not because I am willing to help you."

The prince took a moment to digest that. "So will helping you also help me? If you are a seer then you should know the answer."

"Silly boy," Nemain admonished, "seers are like anyone else in at least one way. We can only see what we look at. Even more important than talent is to know when and where to look. That is what you will help me with."

"And how can I do that?" he asked, caught between anger and curiosity.

"You saw the great circle on your way here." It was a statement, not a question. "That circle, buried in peat for most of its existence, has endured for over twenty centuries."

"Twenty centuries?" Llew exclaimed. "That is rubbish. There were no Tetherans then."

Surprisingly, the crone did not reply with an insult. "Nay, there were not. Perhaps you are a clever boy. It is true that Tetherans have been here only half as long as that, but did you think that we were the first? It is likely we will not even be the last, unless, of course, the Lord of Death succeeds in his aim to destroy all that lives. Even so, there were Picts before the Tetherans. Before the Picts there were other peoples, and still other peoples before them. Go back far enough and there were . . . others, not men but something else altogether. Nor were they the first; it continues for thousands of centuries before them. Indeed, the history of mankind in these lands is only a tiny fraction of that enormous span in which they have been claimed by other than simple animals."

It was hot and smoky in Nemain's hut, but Llew shuddered involuntarily.

"There is," she continued, "another great circle on the beach, just to the south. You would not see it if you walked there for it is buried below the sand and surrounded by peat. Nonetheless, it is there, and it has been for twenty-six centuries. My simple abode, in which we rest, is half way between them. Do you see the significance? Do you?"

Moving only his eyes, Llew glanced right, then left, and then looked directly at her. "No," he announced.

"Pfagh," she said in disgust. "Were you taught nothing by your betters? It is simply obvious. The two are linked across six hundred and sixteen years of history. Using the younger ring we can effect a window into the past, to see what the older ring could have seen in its own time. I will hold open that window to six hundred and sixteen years past and you will look through it so that we may both learn what can be seen. This is why you are here, on this very day, and at this very time, to help me."

"Then, returning to my original question, will helping you help me?" Llew demanded.

She gave him a suspicious look. "Of course it will . . . probably. Why else would you be here? It certainly is not for your health."

He eyed the cup of liquid she had given him. "You are most correct on that account."

"You have not drunk yours yet? Toss it down boy. It is meant to be hot and it does not stay good long, even then. I have already had mine. Quickly now, they are meant to be consumed at the same time."

The rules of hospitality were unyielding. He had to partake of what the host offered. Llew steeled himself for what was coming, and then put the wooden cup to his lips. The tea was nearly scalding and quite painful yet, in a way, that was a blessing. The pain at least helped prevent him from being able to get the full taste, As it was, what he got of it nearly caused him to convulse, but he resisted and choked it all down.

Nemain favored him with what might have been a wicked smile. "Ah, good, just sit still and do not try to move. It should take effect quickly, especially given that you have never had it before."

Llew looked up sharply at this. "Take effect? Wait, what is in this? What have you given me?"

She clucked gently. "Now, now, as I said, it is for my own good."

He tried to say something more but found his tongue was strangely unresponsive. He then tried to rise but his legs were not obeying him either. Before he could reach full panic, everything else seemed to stop working as well.

Chapter XX

Chariots in the Dark

"Your job," the woman said to him, "is to guard my person and drive my chariot. You will not ask questions save only when you truly need more guidance to do whatever else I may assign. You will not caution me against anything I seek to do. You most especially will not prevent me from doing anything I seek to do. This war belongs to all of us, but this is my army and my battle and I will not be coddled. Do you understand?"

"I do understand, my queen," Llew heard himself say. "Your will be done."

"It had better be." She gave him a hard look. "I do not expect you will do half so well as my former driver, but I expect you to try, or else to die . . . as he so bravely did this morning. If you would rather not make the attempt, or feel you may have any difficulty taking orders from a warrior that also happens to be your queen, tell me now and I will select another."

"My queen, I have no reservations. I am entirely at your command," Llew answered.

"Remember that. Also remember that, in proximity to me, you will hear things, and that you are sworn never, ever, to share any of my secrets that you might overhear. Now, bring my chariot. It is time. Rome's legions await, although we may be a bit earlier than they expect."

Taking that as license to leave, Llew turned and got his first view of the woman he had just identified as his queen. More than anything, she looked like Moriganna. She was somewhat shorter, and her hair was an even deeper shade of red, despite the silver threads running through it. Although she was probably somewhere between thirty and forty years of age, she looked as though it had been a difficult life. Yet her eyes clearly proclaimed she had met and defeated all challenges thus far, however much they had left their mark on her. She looked tough and rangy and had the bearing of a warrior. The axe thonged onto her belt bore no ornamentation and had clearly seen much use, although not for hewing wood. Around her neck—Llew almost stopped, motionless in his shock, although somewhere deep inside him he knew that he should not have been surprised at all. He managed to take a closer look before he passed by her and confirmed what he already knew. There could be no doubt; she was wearing his torc, the Torc of Tethera.

Seeing that he was in a large tent, Llew continued turning and saw the exit, then headed for it. Outside it was dark. The night was moonless. The only light there was came from numerous open fires and torches in what appeared to be a vast military camp. He stopped to take stock of the situation. Nemain had merely told him he would be able to witness past events. She had never intimated he would be a part of them. He glanced down at himself and saw a crude mixture of Roman armor and furs. He had a short sword, sometimes called a gladius, at his side and he felt, rather than saw, a whip upon the other side.

The elements were clear. A massive army, under the command of a red-haired warrior queen wearing the Torc of Tethera, marshalling for a night attack against Roman legions?

Clearly, this was Boudicca, preparing her finishing blow against the hated Roman occupiers. It would be the final act before declaring herself high queen and founding the great kingdom of Tethera—precisely six hundred years before his own birth.

Yet why was he here? What could this possibly have to do with him in modern times? This was all ancient history from long before he was even born.

Fortunately, he did not have to go looking for a chariot; two young men brought it to him, an ornate red and white machine with wicked spinning blades extending from the wheel hubs and pulled by two fine white horses. These equines were somewhat smaller than the warhorses of his time, and were clearly not quite up to Caer Mallcoedwig standards, but what else was? He climbed up onto the charioteer's position, a thick net of ropes connecting the horses to the chariot itself, and made a mental note to himself not to fall off while the chariot was in motion. One of the men offered him a large shield, while the other offered him the reins.

Well this should be interesting, Llew thought to himself. He had never driven anything remotely like a chariot before. A major battle against Roman legions could be a very bad time to learn. Yet, as he took the reins, he realized he knew exactly how to handle a chariot—indeed, there might be no man of Prydein who could drive one better, and he knew it was largely for this reason that the queen had selected him.

More chariots, too many to count, rumbled up behind him and to his sides. The low hills above the camp were covered with warriors on foot. It was too dark to estimate their numbers but, judging by the torches they carried, Llew estimated it must be thousands. Then he upped that by an order of magnitude, tens of thousands. Could it be tens of ten thousands? What an army! Something was wrong with his eyes and he wiped distractedly at them to find wetness. It dawned on him that it was tears, tears of joy and pride, pride that his people had once been able to come together as one and demonstrate a united strength that must be unmatched in all the world. Could he and his father ever command such a force, Annwyn would surely fall in a week and Lord Arawen, the self-proclaimed Lord of Death, would be no more.

The queen emerged from her tent and held up a spear while the torches and campfires around her made her visible to all. It came low and deep, a vast rumbling sound that unnerved him for a second until he knew what it was. "Boudic-ca, Boudic-ca, Boudic-ca . . ." came from the combined voices of all the warriors in all their numbers. Llew joined in without hesitation, astounded at how eerie and frightening it was, even when he was part of it.

At length, Queen Boudicca lowered the spear with a sudden flourish. Llew recognized that flourish, it was the same motion he had used when facing King Gronw with the legendary Spear of Celtchar, the weapon of the gods that never missed and always slew. The chanting tapered off and she strode forward and stepped into the chariot. At her shouted command the chariots all began to move. Llew knew they were heading for a low flat place in the line of hills where the troops waited. It was not a great distance and, within a small part of an hour, the chariots had all taken up their positions in the line. Before them was a wide plain. Although the starlight gave little enough illumination, Llew could see no sign of an enemy upon it.

From a nearby chariot, a woman called, "Well, mother? They are all abed in their camp like good little soldiers. We will not require anything save the chariots alone. Let us wait for the barest light of day and charge them while they still wipe the sleep from their eyes."

Boudicca waved one hand dismissively at her daughter. "Peace, Aeron, they are all ensconced in a gorge on the far side, and with a forest at their back. They have chosen the place such that they are thoroughly protected, and we make enough noise they cannot but become aware of us well before we would reach their camp. Worse, the Druids have told us that, although we outnumber them by as many as fifteen to one, we shall surely lose if we let them play their game as they choose, while we play it with them. Is the Unseelie Court ready?"

"I am," a voice spoke out of the darkness next to them. Somehow the torches had conspired to leave a shadowed place that thoroughly hid whatever stood there.

Llew tensed, he knew that voice.

Boudicca confirmed this herself a moment later when she said, "Very well, Queen Mab, if you would be so good?"

Mab's voice came again. "Tell all your people to put out their torches, every one of them."

Queen Boudicca relayed this to her commanders and the word went out. Darkness began growing outwards from her as the nearest torches went out first, followed successively by those further and further away. At last they were all out and only starlight remained.

The queen of the Fae began chanting in some strange tongue and, ever so slowly, Llew became able to see her, as well as all the rest of the vast army, in varying shades of dark blue. Even the hills and the plain surrounding them appeared in shades of dark blue and black. Glancing to the men and women closest to him he realized their eyes had all began to glow with a faint phosphorescence. Presumably his own were as well—and it was letting him see in the dark. Night became a strange sort of day and Llew knew the Romans were already in serious trouble, even if the numbers alone were not stacked so badly against them.

But Queen Boudicca was not done. "King Hafgan," she called, "are you present?"

Startled, Llew looked about wildly and saw Hafgan was indeed nearby. It was surreal. This had to be over six hundred years earlier than when Llew had first met the gruff Spriggan, and yet here he was, not looking one whit differently than he did in Llew's time.

"Aye, lass, and my folk are ready. I spoke with them and they are quite convinced that you have, without a doubt, been lied to and mistreated by ones who thus broke their oaths to you and yours. These fools will soon learn what a bad idea that is in a land where Spriggans dwell. The lesser ones serving those fools will find that is not a good idea, either.

"Recall our little agreement though. There is to be no wholesale slaughter. If the lesser ones surrender and lay down their arms, then you will put them safely on their little ships and bid them goodbye for good."

"All save one," Boudicca declared, almost hungrily.

Hafgan nodded. "Ayup, what is more is we have also decided that anyone above the rank of what they call a centurion is all yours."

"You are still too soft by far, Hafgan," Mab declared.

The Spriggan king grinned at her. "You think so, Mab? You did not used to."

Mab turned and strode away, saying nothing as she went.

Plainly able to see him, Hafgan glanced at Llew without recognition, then turned his attention back to Queen Boudicca. "New driver I see. I warned you about these lightweight chariots did I not? Think you will be able to hold your lads in check long enough for them to do some good this time?"

Boudicca gave him a sour look. "Aye, they will hold until I tell them not to, and I will not tell them not to until the circumstances are favorable. You were right and I was wrong and it cost us. Who would have believed such a one as yourself, who cannot even see over the front of a chariot, would know so much about their use?"

Hafgan shrugged. "I have had a lot of time to learn things, lass and, unlike my brethren, I do not even charge for sharing them. One of the things I have learned, however, is that while experience remains a cruel teacher, most mortals will accept no other."

The Spriggan stretched and added, "I will go tell the lads to begin. You should start hearing the screams in about ten minutes. After that, they are all yours."

Once Hafgan left, Aeron spoke again. "Honestly, mother, why do you let that stumpy little thing speak to you so?"

"Because he is a Spriggan, because he is useful, because I like him, and most of all because, unlike all the rest of the Fae, I trust him. You must learn not to judge by appearances only, dear daughter. Now go find your sister and be sure you cover each other's backs. I will be fine."

As Aeron had her driver move her chariot down the line to be nearer her sister, Llew heard Queen Boudicca mutter to herself, "Whoever her nameless Roman soldier was, he had better have been a brilliant fellow. The child will need that for balance at the very least." Then slightly louder, to Llew, "I said that aloud. That is another one of those things you will not discuss with anyone."

"Certainly not, my queen," Llew replied, fascinated by the implications of what he had just heard. Boudicca must have gotten her wish. Aeron's only son was—or would be—High King Mathonwy and, by all accounts, he had been—or would be—second in mental acuity only to his own son, High King Math. So some nameless Roman soldier was the founding father of the royal line of Tethera? This was not something anyone would ever believe, even if Llew should ever become sufficiently short of wit so as to attempt to reveal it.

At a word from their queen, her armies began to move forward at a leisurely pace that made it quite easy to maintain formation. The entrance to the gorge at the other end of the flat plain had just barely come in view when Llew realized he could hear screaming and other loud sounds emanating from it.

"Ware, my queen," Llew said, forgetting he was not supposed to issue any cautions to her. "There is screaming in the gorge as King Hafgan predicted."

Fortunately, she did not take his announcement as a breach of orders but, instead, called for a halt. They sat and waited as a trickle of men began to emerge, running, from the gorge. Soon the trickle developed into a steady flow before becoming a veritable flood of Roman legionnaires. Most were not wearing full armor, some were not even armed. They poured forth, thousands of them, fleeing from something terrifying, and ran out onto the plain. There was not even the slightest trace of anything resembling the dreaded Roman formations that made them so dangerous in battle. Instead, they all ran directly at the massed forces of what would someday soon, Llew guessed, be the combined forces of a unified Tethera.

They were mad, thought Llew, then recalled the Romans had not had their eyes enchanted by Queen Mab. They had no idea what was before them on that dark plain. It was all pitch black to them. They just desperately wanted to escape whatever had come upon them from out of the woods behind that gorge. A moment later and Llew could see what it was himself. Dark giants were at the mouth of the gorge—many of them. The giants were swinging a variety of weapons, all of them the size of small trees. The slower legionnaires should have had no chance whatsoever. Llew had seen these dark giants before and so he knew now that they were going very easy on the Romans, seeking only to herd them out rather than to actually do them any harm.

These were Spriggans in their other form, perhaps the last word in physical force. Although Hafgan was as cagey and clever as anyone Llew had ever met, and was quite willing to use those attributes to work his will, the Spriggan king also liked to joke that, when raw force failed one, it was only because one was not using enough of it. Perhaps he was only half-joking. The Romans clearly thought the Spriggans were using enough of it.

In actuality, it seemed most unlikely to Llew that Hafgan's subjects were using any lethal force at all. Hafgan had once told him that Spriggans were not allowed to kill humans. Somehow that made this more impressive, rather than less. The Spriggans were driving ten thousand men before them, yet probably had not killed a single one of them. *Although*, thought Llew, *they likely do not count it as their fault if some of the Romans get trampled to death by their own side.* Predictably, given what he knew of their nature, the Spriggans did not leave the gorge to pursue.

Boudicca issued a single command and her armies started forward. The men on foot went first, leaving broad channels that the chariots and horsemen then used to race past them as they drew closer to the first Romans. The legionnaires, almost blind in the darkness, never even saw them coming.

Despite Hafgan's admonitions to take as many prisoners among the rank and file as they could, it was slaughter. Too many of Boudicca's people had lost too much to the Roman conquerors. Yet it took hours to reduce the entire Roman contingent to nothingness. There were just so many of them and, when the moon finally rose, it allowed them to see somewhat better than they had.

Time and again Boudicca led the chariots through the Romans, never slowing except to regroup on the far side and charge again. And that was the way of it, Llew realized. If the chariots did not slash through and emerge free on the far side to regroup before another charge, then they were doomed. That made them nearly worthless against massed and disciplined troops. He was beginning to see why they were no longer used in modern times. The conditions for their effective use were just too constrictive, they required specific terrain and they would be relatively easy for a prepared enemy to thwart, but they were made for this situation and took a frightful toll on the unorganized and unprepared foe.

Yet the legions of Rome were tough and experienced and, above all else, exceedingly well trained. Where they could, they still managed to come together in small box-like formations, the breaking of which inflicted heavy losses on the warriors attempting it. Toward what had to be near the end of things, Boudicca's forces had just broken a large square when a captured chariot sped out of what had been its protected center.

Two Romans rode upon it while a third clung to the net in front and drove it. Boudicca gave a scream of rage. "Get them!" she cried to Llew. "Catch them!"

The other chariot had a wobbling wheel, an inexpert driver, and was carrying three men rather than two. Llew's considerable charioteer skills—he still had no clue why he had them—served to bring them alongside in less than a minute. The two Romans in the chariot had their short swords out and were prepared, but they were not prepared for Boudicca.

The nearest wheel was the wobbling one. It had lost the round armored plate from its axle that would have covered it from the side. As they closed, the queen thrust her spear between its unshielded spokes. The effect was instantaneous. The wheel locked and the entire chariot twisted sideways, then leaped into the air and flipped repeatedly while the panicked horses tried to continue on their way. It was suddenly raining legionnaires.

"Stop!" Boudicca ordered, but as Llew pulled on the reins to comply, she did not wait, opting instead to tuck herself up and roll off the back. In an instant she was up and running towards the downed men. Llew kept the horses in motion and turned the chariot to follow her, then came to a full stop when they were close.

She was astride one that was lying on his back. It was an older man that had lost his helmet. Her short dagger was buried deeply in his chest. "A gift, dear governor" she told the dead man, "from all of us Iceni." She looked over to Llew, "You are my witness. Gaius Suetonius Paulinus died more cleanly than he deserved, in battle and by my own hand."

Llew glanced at the other two Romans but they were not moving. What little remained of the battle had moved on and they were alone, except, he observed, for two old men in white robes that were approaching on foot. They were armed only with rough walking staves.

Llew still held his shield, although it had not yet seen any use. He jumped down and sprinted to get between them and Queen Boudicca with his shield up and his short sword drawn and ready.

The men stopped then and one of them called out, "Queen Boudicca? A word?"

That got her attention. "You two again? Fine, what is it now?" Llew lowered his sword slightly and spared her a glance. She rose and stood, then nodded slightly in his direction and he lowered his blade further.

"Congratulations on your victory. It seems to be very complete," the second stranger said.

The queen looked down at the dead man at her feet. "Aye, quite complete, but I am somehow certain you did not come here merely to tell me that."

"No, of course not," said the first man. "We just wanted to confirm that the full terms of our agreement have been met and that you will honor it."

She glared at him with lowered eyebrows. "You thought to question my honor?"

Both men eyed the dead Roman, then looked about at the battlefield covered in Roman bodies before the first man spoke again. "Er, no, most definitely not, your highness, rest assured we would never do that. We just wish to confirm that you are satisfied with the outcome, although we already know it is substantially better than it would have been without our, ah, intervention."

The queen nodded. "True enough, I did not like what you showed me, but I do not question it is what we would have been stupid enough to do, save for your warnings. You also convinced the Fae to do their part, and so I shall do mine. I remind you that you swore to allow no use of her in plots against the succession. You also promised no sacrifice. Will you have a man ready to receive her? What about a wet nurse?"

"She will be no threat to you or yours and she will not be sacrificed. We will have one of ours ready to receive her, your highness. As for the last, no nurse will be needed; we will name her Cymri, and she will be highly honored amongst us, indeed, the only milk she shall have will be from otherworld cows."

Queen Boudicca appeared ready to snarl. "Did I ask what her name would be? Very well, when this child is born, she is yours." She gave the dead Roman a vicious kick and added, "As if I would ever want to keep anything that came from this one."

Chapter XXI

On the Run

Llew woke with a yell and promptly slid off the rotting reed chair onto the floor. He looked about wildly and saw the crone watching him from a stool that looked too poorly made to support even her slight weight.

He gasped for air and said, "Cymri, Boudicca—"

Nemain scowled at him. "Cease your yelling at me. It is more excitement than my old heart can take. I saw. Through you I saw it all. Am I not a seer?"

Her expression suddenly brightened. "You missed your calling, boy. It seems you were meant to be a charioteer."

"I—" Llew paused and regarded her. "Was that me? How did I know how to do that?"

"It was not you." She snorted in derision. "You were just looking out of another man's eyes—one who has doubtless been dead for more than five hundred years."

"No," he argued, "it was me. Everything I did was me."

"No, boy, it was not. You merely experienced everything he did. Your mind tries to explain away the impossible by telling you it was you and that the decisions were yours, but it is only justifying things after the event. You were not there. You could not have been there because all you had was a window, not a door. What you saw occurred when Tethera was in another world, before it was brought here and the Wild Growth began. Were I able to send you back through a door, you would only emerge in this world six hundred years ago. Tethera would not be here yet and there would be naught but whatever there was before Tethera was brought here."

Llew shook his head in a vain attempt to settle his mind and better order his thoughts. "Why did you show me that? It does not tell me who I am."

"Silly boy, I told you I was helping myself. There were things I needed to see. If you saw anything that helped you then that is just a bonus, and you are welcome. Not that I have heard any thanks yet," she grumbled.

"I do not think I heard anything that helps me," he said slowly. "Unless it was . . . she was giving away her unborn daughter to those men in exchange for some help in winning the battle. What she said at the end . . . it was a child the Roman leader had forced on her." He looked up at Nemain, stricken. "They said her name would be Cymri."

Nemain shrugged. "Should that mean something to me? Doubtless she is long dead as well."

"Cymri was Moriganna or, rather, Moriganna claims she was Cymri when she was young." Llew remained sitting on the floor, unsure if his legs would hold him were he to attempt to rise. "I knew Moriganna was old, but I had no idea. Over six hundred years! Who could have imagined?" Another thought came to him. "And she really is Boudicca's daughter. Would that not make her rightful high queen of all Tethera?"

An old sack had found its way into Nemain's hands and she was stuffing it with bits of trash from around her hovel. Clearly he did not have her full attention, but she showed she was still listening when she spoke. "Do not be ridiculous. Aeron was the senior daughter, the crown went to her son, Mathonwy, and all royalty since are descended through that line."

"And Mathonwy was a son forced upon her by some nameless Roman soldier," Llew marveled.

Nemain stopped what she was doing and gave him a hard look. "As a seer of some experience I will tell you something, boy. That is not something you ever want to tell just anyone. People only believe what a seer says she sees when they are ready to believe. No one will want to believe that, and it will damage whatever standing you have with them."

A thought came to Llew. "Who were those men who were going to take Cymri when she was born? I think you probably know."

Without looking at him, she grunted and said, "Of course I do. They were Druids. It goes without question they wanted her because of something they had foreseen,"

"Druids were seers, too?" Llew asked.

She gave a sour laugh at that. "Of course they were. Druids had three orders, the first two are required stages on the way to becoming a full Druid. Before you ask, I will tell you. Members of the second order are called orates—what people nowadays call seers."

Llew had to stop and consider that. "So you are a Druid?"

"Oh dear," she clucked to herself, "and just when he was beginning to sound a wee bit more clever than he looks, though that is not saying much. No, I told you, there are no Druids left. I am an orate, the very last one left. Orates were members of a Druidic order, but orates were not yet Druids, even though some used to eventually become such. Being an orate was a necessary step on the way to becoming a Druid."

He mulled that over for a moment, then asked the obvious question. "So what were members of the first order called?"

"First order?" she echoed. "Of those you still have plenty. We call them bards."

Nemain had gone back to work stuffing things into her bag and it was sometime later before Llew thought to ask what she was doing.

"What? Did you think I might be stuffing a pillow for my bed? This is just a bit of last minute packing. There are some things I just do not leave home without."

"Why?" he asked.

"Why does anyone pack anything before they go anywhere? Because if I was away from home and needed them then what would I do? I ask you, what would I do?"

Llew made a sound of exasperation. "I meant why are you leaving home? Why ever would you do that? Could it be that your parents have arranged a marriage for you that you want no part of?"

Nemain grimaced. "If that was your idea of wit, do not give up your throne if you intend to keep on eating. You and I are going sight-seeing together into the wilds of Tethera. Or did you think that one simple window was all I was good for? Hardly answers your questions about anything by itself, does it? It certainly does not answer all of mine. We will need much more than that and we cannot get it here. Even if we could, we must move now. Mucking about with time the way I do—well, it can attract things we would rather not meet."

The flame of the fire seemed to die down a bit and something passed over the hut with an accompanying noise that Llew told himself could not possibly be the sound of wings beating. It was much too loud for that.

"Get up," she ordered. "It is time and past time to go."

She led him out and it was evident that he had been inside far longer than he had thought, for it was the dead of night. There was total stillness everywhere. Without hesitation, Nemain found a muddy path through the reeds. It was a different one than that which Llew had used earlier. The moon was a sliver, and misty clouds kept passing before it interminably so that their trek varied between dark and very dark. Without the old woman guiding his steps, Llew was quite certain he would have gotten nowhere. It was almost as though she could see in the dark and she knew the trail, such as it was, perfectly.

With Llew's eyes of so little use to him, he fell back on the use of his hearing. He was listening with as much concentration as he could spare while still walking and, with so little to distract his eyes, the results were incredible. He felt, as he sometimes had before, that he could almost see his surroundings in all directions at once, and in a way his eyes never could have.

A question came to him then that he felt he had to ask. "Nemain, my torc is not letting me shape-shift. Why is that? Can we change that?" he whispered.

She replied in a quiet voice, "Use your wits, boy. How long did you wear it before you first began to be able to change form?"

"Nearly a year, but—"

"And were there times in that year where changing form could have helped you? Certainly there were and we both know that. You could not shape-change because the torc does not simply grant your wish when you try to take on a new form. It has to know you, study you, and learn everything about you, body and mind, before it can even begin to adapt itself completely to you."

Llew felt hope blossom. "Does that mean that it will work again for me, once it has adapted itself to my new form?"

Nemain chuckled quietly. "Do not count your geese before they hatch. It may yet be a long time before it does. You could still be months in the grave before it was to happen. Do keep trying it occasionally, though, for one never knows, does one?"

It was as they were passing between two small bodies of open water over a causeway of silt and rotting vegetable matter that Llew sensed the small sound of something quietly emerging from the water to their right—just before it abandoned all attempts at subtlety and charged them. He took two steps towards it to block it from Nemain, his sword out and ready before the second step was complete. He could not see his target as anything other than a shape, vaguely human-like in form, but larger.

Given that he could not clearly see its attacks, he abandoned defense and instead made three heavy slashing passes against it. Each connected and the damage must have been substantial. He was rewarded with a rising whistling shriek that came from nothing remotely human and what was left of his foe staggered backward and into the water, leaving pieces of itself behind.

The constant reek of effluvia had somehow increased by an order of magnitude during the attack and Llew very nearly grew ill. He still managed to hold himself ready for a long moment, sword raised, but nothing reemerged from the water.

"Well? Let us get a move on," Nemain grumbled. "Standing here all night is a poor plan indeed."

Stung by the ingratitude, Llew commented, "Far be it be from me to suggest I just saved your life."

In the darkness Llew felt, rather than saw, Nemain's crooked smile. "How sweet. Is that what you think? Does it not occur to you that I live here? If little nuisances like that were a threat to me then I assure you I would not."

Llew kept his reply to himself and they pressed on. Once out of the marsh it took another hour or two, hiking in near total darkness, to reach where he had left Gower and the mare.

With what little light the stars granted, Nemain eyed the mare skeptically. "Could you not at least have had the decency to bring me a smaller animal to ride?"

Chapter XXII

The Cythrawl

A short rest and they were on their way again by mid-morning. The horses were well rested and Llew had rigged a saddle, of sorts, on the mare for Nemain. Despite her protestations on how the animal was too large for her, Llew noticed that, despite her advanced age, she had little difficulty in mounting and she rode with practiced ease for one of her advanced age.

Llew clamped his tongue between his teeth to avoid commenting on the fact she apparently just liked to complain. He had dealt with old people like this before. Unfortunately, in this case he could not merely escape from it. It was something he would have to put up with.

Onerous as it was, their association was not proving to be without rewards. The experience of actually riding with High Queen Boudicca in the last battle of Caer Urnarc was beyond price. He scowled inwardly. Of course, it might not be an unmitigated blessing if it delayed him in finding out what had happened to his appearance and in undoing it or, possibly, in getting his people to accept him as he was. There were things that needed doing and he seemed to be only one that could do them.

Afaggdu had once told him that no man was indispensable but, after Llew had later experienced a revelation at the edge of death, he was no longer sure he believed this. Discovering the possibility he might be indispensable did not make him feel powerful and important. Instead it had made him feel overwhelmed and afraid, inadequate and, occasionally, insecure. He had also learned the fear was not primarily the fear of his own death; it was the fear of failure. When personally faced with death he had found that dying, while a bitter blow in itself, was made far worse when it would be the cause for ultimate failure. In that respect, this change to his physical appearance was very nearly as bad. Being unable to do the things that needed doing because no one recognized him? Like death, this theft of his identity was only another cause for failure, the primary difference between the two being that, so long as he yet lived, he might, at least, steal back his identity.

To do this he needed information and, as Hafgan had said, a seer seemed just the thing for that. Unfortunately, Llew had not reckoned that the seer might be Nemain.

He gradually collected his thoughts. "So, if Moriganna is a goddess, why does she not simply—"

"Stop right there," Nemain commanded. "She most certainly is not a goddess. Where would even a foolish youth such as yourself get such an idea?"

"She said that she was the chosen vessel of the goddess," Llew reminded her. "What else could that mean?"

Nemain made a rude noise. "That? Just that she is the current vessel of the goddess. To understand that you must understand a bit more of what the goddess is and, most especially, what she is not."

Nemain still wore the tattered garments from when they had first met. At the moment, however, they somehow looked less worn and shoddy, almost regal. "Listen carefully, for I have no wish to repeat myself, particularly when it is most likely just going in one ear and out the other. The goddess is not a person, not even a very powerful person. The goddess has no body, no face, and neither hands nor feet. The goddess has no emotions either, no love, no hate, no envy, no joy, for she does not even have the ability to think.

"Now you are wondering what is left for the goddess to be? Yes, you are, do not deny it. The goddess is purpose and power and both of these are conveyed through a single attribute, and that attribute is memory. The goddess exists only as memory. She does not grant advice nor suggest strategy; she does not even grant all of her memory, only what the vessel needs. The goddess is the memory of every vessel she ever existed in, yet the vessels are only mortals and so can hold but a tiny fraction of all that memory within their conscious minds. Yet that memory is knowledge, and knowledge leverages their power, with the caveat that the memory also directs and channels their thinking, such that the bulk of this power is devoted to a single purpose."

Nemain paused then and, as the silence grew long, Llew tired of waiting. "You have not said what that purpose was," he reminded her.

"Ah, so you are paying attention. That purpose is creation, nothing more and nothing less."

Llew approached this cautiously, trying to make sure she was saying what the thought she was saying. "So you are saying Moriganna is the vessel of the power of all creation? Moriganna?"

Nemain glanced sideways at him and gave him a reproving look. "She is dedicated to the purpose of creation. She has access to some small part of the great store of knowledge that is the goddess, and all that she does, all that she conjectures, and all that she learns is added to that store."

"Even so," Llew continued doggedly, "how is it that this is not sufficient to bring about the undoing of Annwyn and Lord Arawen?"

"It is the way of all things to be destroyed in time so that more may be created. Destruction is thus not only desirable. It is a fundamental part of the world at its deepest levels and every bit as important as creation. Together they create the sacred balance. Neither can be destroyed but the balance can be tilted and it is only the balance, resting in near equilibrium, that allows the world to persist."

"Lord Arawen, our self-appointed Lord of Death, would probably disagree with that," Llew pointed out.

Nemain gave a deep sigh and Llew braced himself for the expected pithy rejoinder, but it never came. "That is because he is imbalanced, and he seeks to project that imbalance upon the world, heedless of the natural order of things, uncaring of the damage he does to the balance of the entire world. He has appointed himself the enemy of creation itself, in direct opposition to what we mortals refer to as the goddess."

Llew considered that. "If he places himself directly against the goddess he is certainly overreaching; is he not? And if Moriganna is the very vessel of the goddess and his mortal foe, is he not already doomed?"

"Perhaps not," Nemain answered in a heavy voice. "You may not realize that Arawen of Annwyn does not merely worship destruction, he is the living vessel of the Cythrawl, what we would call the force of destruction. It remains to be seen if the Cythrawl is, or is not, equal in power to the goddess herself."

Llew felt himself grow cold at these words. Aghast, he asked, "Lord Arawen of Annwyn? How are we to destroy destruction itself?"

"Have you never learned anything? Not even the tiniest bit of wisdom? We cannot destroy destruction. The Cythrawl is not our enemy any more than the goddess is. Destruction is as crucial for the proper functioning of the universe as creation. Consider; how could you possibly create anything without something being destroyed in the process? How could you destroy something without it first being created? The two are equally important and it is that fact that creates and maintains the sacred balance. Thus both are absolutely essential to the existence of all we know, but both can be misused."

"But Moriganna and Lord Arawen are deadly enemies," Llew objected. "You make it sound like they should be partners in all things."

"It is as I said," continued Nemain, "destruction and creation are meant to form the sacred balance and exist in perfect synergy—"

"Synergy?" Llew asked.

"A word borrowed from the long departed Romans. It refers to a state in which one or more things are working together," answered Nemain, uncharacteristically saying nothing of the fact he had interrupted her.

"Why does the Cythrawl not abandon him and find a new vessel if he is so perverting its proper purpose?"

Another sigh escaped Nemain's lips before she replied. "Like the goddess, the Cythrawl is not a creature. It does not think, it does not make assessments, and it will not pass judgement. It simply is. I do not think it will leave Lord Arawen until the day he dies."

"Then what drives him? What made him decide to destroy everything?" Llew persisted, still trying to understand.

"Know this, Lleu. Something hurt Lord Arawen and, rather than grieve and go on, as most would, he chose to become overly focused on revenge, and doing this caused him further damage. In this way, he became vulnerable to the blandishments of those that have no world and are forever clawing at the walls of those they can find, eternally seeking egress from their non-existence."

Llew was not ready to even begin to think about what she was talking about now. Instead he asked, "What will happen if the balance is not restored and one side does triumph over the other?"

"Fool boy," exclaimed Nemain. "Were you not paying attention? Neither side can win. If the balance is not restored, the only outcome can be our world shattering from the stress. Then those without will find their way within to feast on the wreckage. It will make even the worst of the horrors unleashed upon us by the Wild Growth seem pale and few by comparison."

For a number of reasons, Llew did not like the turn this conversation was taking and chose to change the subject. "So where to now, all knowing one?" he asked. "You obviously have some destination in mind to advance our little quest."

"Indeed I do. We are going to—well what am I saying?—the name would be meaningless to you. Call it the wooden ring. That should be simple enough for you."

"The wooden ring," Llew intoned, "as a name, it is informative and descriptive, too."

"Confronted with his own ignorance, he resorts to low sarcasm," said Nemain. "I could give him allowances for being very young, but I will not."

"Were not these sea circles of yours also made of wood?" asked Llew.

"They were for a special purpose and, for us, they have served that purpose. The place we are going to now was once the seat of all faith in the lands now known as Tethera. Enormous and amazingly intricate, it was an astounding work that strained the skills and the resources of all who once dwelt here, yet it was a marvel and, to them, it was a bargain. Alas, it was made of wood and no peat bed protected and preserved it. It is quite gone."

"If it is gone then what is the purpose of our going to where it was? We may as well stop at the next place we rest the horses," Llew said.

"Ah, the wisdom of youth! On your lips it sounds much like the reverse."

Llew pressed his lips together tightly and waited.

"Alright then, you would hear the truth, boy? Nothing that is destroyed is ever completely gone so long as it once existed."

Except for those things that never actually existed, Llew thought unhappily, his mind on Cymri still.

"Permit me to ask again, just why it is that we are on our way to something that was destroyed?"

The crone favored him with what might have been half a smile, even though it revealed but a single yellow tooth. "Everything that ever exists leaves its mark upon the world, boy, even when it has long since passed on. In this case, although that remnant of its mark will be a far trickier thing to work with, I believe enough trace of the original may still be drawn forth for our use."

Llew considered that for a moment. "So we are going to a place you would have me call the wooden ring, a place that has long since been destroyed. Yet I still know nothing of where it is or for what purpose we travel to it."

Nemain arched a lone eyebrow at him. "Whose fault is that? You never asked."

* * *

When they arrived, the wooden ring looked like any other grass covered lea. Looking at it, Llew made a note to himself that if he ever intended to leave any lasting structures to future generations, he would need to have them built from stone.

They made camp in the center and Nemain brewed some of the odious mixture she called tea. "I have little idea where this will take you. If it turns out you have anything resembling free will, then try to use more wisdom than I have seen you employ thus far. Remember that your purpose is to learn events of the past, not change them."

"Another window rather than a door?" Llew asked.

"Perhaps," mused Nemain, "if windows could die and rot away, leaving only a twisted phantasm of their former selves behind."

Chapter XXIII

The Wooden Ring

All was darkness and Llew feared he had lost his senses. Gradually his perception adjusted and he was able to make out that he stood in a place surrounded by barrow mounds. Aside from the number of them, it was especially odd in that they were all freshly dug.

In fact, despite it clearly being the middle of a moonless night, he could perceive teams of men still working on them, even while new ones were still being built.

Was this what he was here to see? He looked down at himself and could see nothing but dark leather armor covering every part of his body. His hands were covered in thick leather gauntlets and one held a coiled whip. Memory kicked in and he raised his hands to his face. It, too, was covered in a leather face guard. Part of him wanted to strip off a gauntlet and reach a bare hand under that faceguard to check his suspicion. He overruled this impulse. There was nothing to be gained and he already had a good idea of what he was.

Cyhyraeths were, as someone named Cymri had once told him, a race of men in ancient times who feared death far beyond what any rational being should. In seeking immortality, they had made a bargain for eternal life and vigor.

Unfortunately for them, they had apparently never thought to specify true immortality. Although they would never die of old age, or its ailments, they could still be slain by violence like any other man. Far worse, they also had not received eternal youth. While still possessing the strength and agility of young men, they continued to age, and those still alive had been doing just that for thousands of years. It was no mystery why such as they covered every inch of their bodies with black leather armor. They probably could not stand to even look at themselves, yet alone at each other. Rotting corpses, although horrible in their own way, at least looked natural. Cyhyraeths looked much, much worse.

Cyhyraeths had also, according to legend, lost their place at the table, with regard to mankind. It had something to do with how they had fulfilled their end of the dark bargain that had made them thus. So far as Llew knew, they were all now in the service of Lord Arawen of Annwyn. It was a kind of ultimate irony that men so afraid of death should have become the minions of the Lord of Death.

Llew fitted the clues together in an instant. Cyhyraeths were clever and highly skilled in most things. Dozens of centuries of life experience made sure of that. They were also highly placed in the ranks of the enemy because of this. Together with the whip, and the nearby work crews, this seemed to indicate he was an overseer of some sort.

A cloud passed from in front of the moon, releasing the lunar light it had blocked, and Llew could abruptly see he was standing upon a vast plain, and that the orderly ranks of endless barrow mounds extended as far as the eye could see.

He moved closer to the nearest until he could clearly see the workers laboring to build the new mound. They were all barrow warriors. Llew had faced barrow warriors in battle and, horrible as it was to fight a dead man, he did not fear them on a physical level. Yet the very idea—the reality—that lay before him, of dead men digging more burial mounds for the dead, was frightening on an entirely different level.

This could only be somewhere deep in Annwyn, the land of the dead, domain of Lord Arawen. Yet the Lord of Death drew his warriors forth from barrows, he did not put them in barrows. What was the purpose of this?

The barrow before him was still in an early stage. A rough wooden enclosure had been constructed, and enough earth was placed around it so that it was now a rectangular hole in the ground. Corpses would be placed inside, and the top would be roofed. Then enormous quantities of additional dirt would be placed on top to complete the barrow mound.

A creaking noise that had gone almost unnoticed by him was now becoming much louder. He turned to see a cart was nearly upon him. It was drawn, not by animals, but by more barrow warriors.

Why not? asked some part of his mind that was not recoiling in horror at all of this. They did not need rest or sustenance. Why not use them for drawing carts if they were not needed for fighting at that moment?

Another Cyhyraeth walked alongside it. Another faceless form covered in leather, it approached him and there were no greetings. Llew somehow knew that Cyhyraeth no longer used them. Eons of familiarity with an ever diminishing group of individuals, in which there were never any new additions, had gradually ended the custom. This one was named Craeus, not that it mattered. They almost never used names, either.

They seldom even spoke except to exchange information. They had no use for small talk or pleasantries. Llew looked in the cart. "Why only one?" he heard himself asking. "My instructions were no less than three score per mound."

Craeus shrugged. "This is a special one. The fool actually agreed to let the master wear his body for four seasons. Of course, he did not even make it quite the full year before his fellows rose up and killed him for the things they thought he had done."

This elicited a dry chuckle from Llew. "There is no end to the foolishness of mortals. What could have persuaded even the greatest of idiots that this would be a good idea?"

"The usual. The master promised him vengeance on the one who had killed his only heir."

"Which wretches were in the employ of the master, I am certain. Too bad for them. They should have negotiated better," Llew remarked. "What made this one worth so much effort in the first place?" Llew realized he was asking a lot of questions but Craeus did not seem to think it odd. If not for a little gratuitous gossip once in a while, how else would they while away the ages?

"He was their last high king," answered Craeus, "as you surmised, the master had already taken care of his only heir. The great kingdom is now destroyed. It only remains to pick up the pieces when the harvest is ready."

Llew waved an arm to indicate the endless rows of barrow mounds. "It will be a fine harvest, too; I can barely wait."

Craeus shrugged again. "It is only a little over a century hence, nearly six score years if I heard correctly. It will be here before we can blink."

* * *

Llew awoke gasping. What he had seen was still all too clear in his head.

"Peace," said Nemain. "What we saw must have occurred over one hundred years ago. Only a child would panic this very instant."

"A hundred years," repeated Llew, "ah, yes, because they were interring High King Pwyl and that is when he passed, nearly a full century before I was even born."

"Exactly a century before you were born," said Nemain, apparently because she could not resist correcting him in even the smallest of details, "and he did not merely 'pass.' His best friend in the world, King Bran, whom you actually met and respected, put him down like a mad dog to stop the atrocities he was committing against his own people. That put an end to the great kingdom of Tethera. Everything since is just dogs fighting over the scraps."

"It was hardly Pwyl's fault," Llew said defensively, "you heard them say he was possessed by Lord Arawen himself."

"And," she remarked caustically, "I heard them say he had put himself in that position voluntarily."

"He was manipulated, driven into madness by the murder of his son," Llew reminded her.

"That is no excuse!" she shouted.

Her vehemence startled him. "He was not insane, not initially at least; he was weak. Understand that. Because he was weak he could not face his own grief and deal with it, and so he allowed grief to fall on every living soul in Tethera. We all have grief, boy. What we do not have is the right to expand it by our own selfish actions until there is enough for everyone . . . and most especially not for those we are sworn to care for."

Silence ruled for a time. Llew realized that the night was nearly over when he began to hear bird song amongst the trees.

"You are a seer so answer me this. I am of his bloodline; will not his flaws manifest in me? Am I weak?"

Nemain remained quiet for so long that Llew grew increasingly uneasy at what the answer might be if she was so reluctant to speak on it. "Tell me," she finally said, "King Gronw was an evil, self-centered man. Are you concerned his son might be the same? You chose to let him become king of Gwynedd."

Llew thought of Caradog. "Point taken."

Then a terrible thought came to him. "Nemain, they were planting corpses in those barrows, sixty to a mound and the barrows went on in all directions, as far as the eye could see. They also spoke of harvesting them. That can only mean bringing out those within as barrow warriors—endless numbers of barrow warriors—and the harvest they spoke of in six score years . . . it is about to begin if it has not already."

"Oh, and you just worked that out have you? Get some sleep, boy, we have far to go today and, at the end of it, we will probably have to see how well you can use that pretty sword of yours."

Chapter XXIV

Caer Caradoc

Again, they got far too little rest and were on the way by midmorning. Llew soon discovered he did not feel as bad as he was expecting, and wondered if the time he spent embedded in the past somehow counted as sleep, at least so far as his body was concerned.

"Where to now?" he asked, once they were a short distance from the wooden circle.

Nemain favored him with an expression that did not look very favorable at all. "There are a few small things we need to purchase. We will make a brief stop at Caer Caradoc and then proceed to—oh, you can call it the stone ring."

"Another place that has long since been destroyed?" Llew inquired.

"Oh yes, of course, because stone has such an unfortunate tendency to quickly rot away," she said unpleasantly. "No, of course not. Are you daft? It is made out of stone. It has been there for ages already, and will be there for ages more. Stone is strong, it endures."

"And this one will tell me what I need to know of my own past? Something that may actually be useful to the problem at hand?"

She made an exasperated noise. "You ask that as though the past two seeings were not useful to you. It is scarcely a reason to rail at me if you have not the wit to understand them."

"How is that?" he demanded. "How does either one of those help tell me who I am and help with what has been done to me?"

"You have some excellent clues, boy. Less talking, more thinking, and you might already know. If it is too much for you then bide a bit, with another piece of the puzzle it may be easier for you."

Changing his tack, he said, "You mentioned I would have some sword work this day?"

"I said," she corrected, "that you might. If you are unwilling to take a gentle hint to be quiet for a time and do some thinking, then take a rather stronger hint and be quiet for a time so I may do some thinking."

Llew did think for a time and decided that being treated like Caradog was not all fun and games, nor did he much care for casting himself in that role.

They came to a road, barely more than a game trail, and Nemain had them turn on to it and continue moving south and west. Trees became more scarce and, after a time, they came across a rise and there, on a gentle flattened hill, sat a walled town. It was an imposing place, the high walls sat atop an enormous earthen fortification and in the center could be seen a second such earthen moat and embankment, with a stone fortress sitting atop it.

The entrance was directly before them on the east side, but they did not get much closer before Llew began to feel uneasy. The reason for this was not at all mysterious. It was plain to see that the great gates had been torn down and there were wagons and carts, some smashed, and some merely flipped over, that were partially blocking the approach. Bones of the creatures that had pulled them were scattered about in the roadway. Not all the bones were those of animals. Likewise, no smoke was in evidence from the chimneys and hearth fires of the town. In short, the place was deserted and destroyed, not necessarily in that order. The stone fort in the center showed considerable amounts of damage as well.

"Picts?" Llew suggested.

Nemain continued on her way to the entrance. "I do not think so," was all she said.

Llew checked to make sure Fragaroc was loose in his scabbard as they passed the destroyed gates.

"Not a bad idea," remarked Nemain. "Whatever did this, it happened months ago, but do keep an eye out for lesser threats come to feed on the spoils."

What they found inside was no longer a surprise. The houses and buildings were all damaged, some with entire walls knocked flat and all of them with parts of the roof destroyed, There was no sign of any living being.

Llew took a look about. The strange state of destruction was making him profoundly uneasy. "I do not know if it is empty because the survivors fled, or because there were no survivors."

"If anyone survived," said Nemain, "it is because they hid successfully during the attack. Afterwards they would not have remained long enough to even bury the dead. Come, boy, you have not yet had your daily ration of thinking. Tell me what did this."

He ignored the insulting way she had demanded an answer and applied himself to the problem. She had already ruled out Picts. They were not a good choice, in any case, as they had no siege equipment ... although ... they were supposed to have advisors from Annwyn now. Could this little town have been something in the way of practice for assaulting Erg?

No, he decided, the damage was not consistent with siege weapons, despite the power that must have been needed.

Whatever had attacked had just torn down the gates and entered, crushing and scattering everything in its path. And then there was the way each roof had been partially removed . . . .

Llew paled inwardly. This had not been done by a 'them.' This had not been done by anything that could be referred to in plural form. "Giant," he whispered. "I did not think there were any left."

Nemain quirked her mouth and gave him a suspicious look. "And how do you know it was not just your Spriggan friends attacking at night?"

Llew gave her a disbelieving look. "Even in their giant forms they are not big enough by half for some of this. Also," he said," his voice hardening, "Spriggans do not kill humans. That is a secret but I think you know it already."

"Ah, and you are right boy, well done. And here I was beginning to give up on you. Yes, a giant is the right answer. A big one, too, as you noted, at least four man heights. Even Spriggans would have little chance against such a behemoth; its weight alone could well be greater than thirty of them glued together—or three or four hundred men, take your pick. Good thing you have your sword handy."

The prince looked about with disbelief at the damage to what had evidently been a well-defended and prosperous community. "I somehow doubt even Fragaroc would make much of an impression on such a creature, provided I could even approach close enough to score upon it. Possibly with siege weapons something might be possible, provided it held still. Have you had any seeings of me fighting such a thing?"

"Nay, boy, my seeings are usually of a different nature. Do not be overly concerned. I am certain, you will acquit yourself well, should it come to that," said Nemain.

"I appreciate your confidence in my prowess but—" Llew began.

"Say nothing of it. I simply reason that, handicapped in so many other areas, you must be good in something and this just could be it. You do show something of a proclivity for destruction. And what is the worst that could happen? It steps on you and I have to find some other way to the stone ring?"

Llew started to make a snappy retort, but words failed him. Then he had a thought. "Wait, you think this thing is an obstacle on the way to the stone ring?"

"Very good. That is probably the entire reason it cleaned out this town. It is extending a clear zone around the stone ring and intends to keep it free of anyone that gets too close."

"Prowess or not, how am I to defeat such a monstrosity?" he demanded.

"That is not my area of concern," Nemain replied. "Think of something, make it chase you around until it falls off a cliff. Or else do what you usually do with opponents that are beyond you; roll something heavy down on it."

"We are in the middle of a grassy plain," Llew objected, "and besides which, I have only resorted to that method on two occasions . . . and not for that reason on either. How would you even know—wait—do not bother answering, you are a seer, of course."

"Why that is exactly right. He does learn. I am so pleased."

Llew sighed and made no reply.

"Keep an eye out. Instead of buying the things I wanted I shall have to loot them, and there may be unpleasant things living amongst the ruins. Fortunately, the things I want are unlikely to have been looted."

A hour of probing around through houses and shops followed. Most of what she gathered was clothing and personal items There were also a few other things of a less obvious nature, along with a pair of saddles and other accoutrements for riding.

"We only have one horse that lacks those things," he pointed out, after she assigned him the dubious honor of carrying them.

"Yes, I was hoping to acquire another horse or two here, but that will have to wait. We may as well be ready, however."

They spent the night in a small guard house that Llew felt offered sufficient protection for him to hold off several potential attackers at once, providing none of them were giants. The next morning they were on their way, having never seen another denizen in the ruins larger than a pigeon.

Riding out the open eastern gate, they circled around to the north side, and then proceeded in a generally northern direction.

After an hour or two, Nemain called a halt. "There, ahead of us, boy, you see the stones? We have to go there and we will need some time once we do. I believe there are forces arrayed against us that will seek to prevent that."

Llew regarded the distant upright stones. They were bigger than most and most were connected by lintel stones laid between them, It was indeed a stone circle. More disturbing was all the barrow mounds he could see.

"There are lines of barrows all over the place. Will barrow warriors be a problem?"

"Pray they will not be, boy, but any you encounter will not be from these mounds. This is a sacred place. If the enemy has grown so strong he can raise barrow warriors here, then we have already lost."

"Do you think the creature that destroyed Caer Caradoc is allied with this enemy?"

Nemain hesitated a moment before saying, "I believe that creature was sent by the forces arrayed against us. Specifically, it was sent to prevent me and you from doing precisely what we seek to do."

"That town was destroyed months ago. Long before we set out," Llew observed.

The crone turned in her saddle to look directly at him. "Do not believe separation in time provides absolution from causality. Our beginning this trek, even though it was but a few days ago, is the reason that town is dead. It falls on us to ensure it was not for aught."

"The enemy can determine what we will do before we have done it?" Llew shook his head at this. "I find that more than a little disturbing."

"I can sometimes determine what the enemy will do beforehand. The enemy can only make informed guesses from a limited number of probable futures and attempt to act on those guesses. Because there is not one possible future, he is forced to split his forces to cover as many possibilities as he can. It is for this reason that he cannot bring an overwhelming force to bear on any of them. In this case, it seems he sent a giant."

"Is that not an overwhelming force? How are we going to overcome a giant?"

Nemain scowled. "We? I am a seer, you are the hero. You must take care of it. I am not concerned with how you do it. If I am correct, however, it will attack before you reach the ring. Go forth now to the stones. If you reach them without incident then I will join you. If something tries to prevent that, convince it not to interfere with us. Do not be overly concerned; for all their size and their very long legs, giants are not especially fleet of foot. Part of that is because it takes a long time for their brain to communicate with their legs, but the larger reason is that they are deathly afraid of falling. Their own enormous weight works to their detriment in such a mishap, and a hard fall can kill them."

"So I will try to find a good place to trip it then."

Nemain gave a short, harsh laugh. "Perhaps you can tie its bootlaces together."

It was with enormous trepidation that Llew set out to cover the distance to the stone circle. He was so tense that it was almost an anticlimax when the giant appeared.

Chapter XXV

Once there was a Giant

One moment, the countryside was clear and relatively flat, and there did not seem to be anywhere a giant could even hope to hide. In the next, the creature was rising above a relatively nearby stand of trees. Something deep in his mind told Llew there must be a low place, perhaps a ravine, behind those trees or the giant could not have hidden its entire bulk. Yet most of his conscious thought was on the appearance of the giant itself.

Llew had somehow been expecting something along the lines of a colossal man, possibly wearing clothes or at least a loincloth. This was ... different. It was man-like in form but wore only long brown hair in place of clothing and, while its face could have been taken for that of a man were it reduced to human proportions, it could only have been a horrendously deformed man with symmetrical but extremely coarse features dominated by a long sharp nose.

Standing at least four or five times the height of a man, it came striding directly towards them brandishing a tree as a crude club. It seemed to Llew he could feel the ground shake as each foot struck it. "Hoo-ah, hoo-ah," the giant called in a voice deeper than the great horn at Caerleon. Llew watched it approach for only a moment before he turned Gower and they raced away. For once, the great horse seemed disinclined to object to retreating from a fight.

Llew was thinking frantically as they fled. There simply was not much in the way of local terrain that he could take advantage of. The area was entirely too level, and the small stands of trees would provide no barrier at all to a creature of that size and strength. Remembering the well at Lindenjal, he led the giant in a wide arc around the stone circle while he attempted to find a working strategy. It continued to pursue and it occurred to Llew to wonder which would tire first, Gower or the giant.

His sword, despite the fact it was the fabled Fragaroc, would be useless here. At best he might hamstring the brute, but only if it did not knock him into the next kingdom with that club, or else simply stamp on him. His bow would probably drive arrows deeply into it, but he would get off only a few shots before it closed with him and chances were that none of them would be debilitating, let alone fatal, against a thing of its size. Llew knew he was certainly not such an archer that he could, say, shoot for the eyes and hope to hit one, let alone both, in such rushed conditions.

In the tales of ancient heroes, they usually killed such things by delaying them with a game of riddles until the sun rose and turned them to stone. That was of little use here, for the sun was already up and did not seem to inconvenience the monster in the least. This giant also did not appear to be nearly intelligent or intelligible enough to exchange riddles with.

The other way ancient heroes killed giants was getting them to kill each other, usually by hitting one with a rock from a place of hiding so they would quarrel amongst themselves. Llew spared a glance back. There was still just one giant pursuing them. Also arguing against this strategy was the fact that he and Gower were most definitely not in hiding.

Occasionally, a hero was purported to have spitted a giant or dragon with a lance, but the sheer scale of this giant made that a ridiculous proposition. Or did it? His eyes widened with realization that, in his case, it might indeed be the way to victory.

He tossed aside his shield and turned Gower to face the seemingly unstoppable juggernaut. Then he took his spear and dismounted. Bidding Gower to stay put, he began to run straight at the oncoming giant.

Sensing the chase was over, the giant chuffed out its strange cry again, "Hoo-ah, hoo-ah."

Llew had his entire being focused on the narrowing interval between them. The spacing had to be just right . . . and then it was. Llew came to a halt, drew back, and threw his spear with every fiber of muscle he could command. The spear flashed through the air like a bolt of lightning and with a crack of thunder, buried its entire length in the giant's chest.

The giant gave one last cry that seemed to shake the ground itself, then began to fall. Llew dove and rolled to the side as thousands of stones of giant, still moving forward at great speed, struck the ground and continued forward, carried along by its own mass and momentum.

Unable to believe that it had actually worked, Llew stood and regarded the enormous body that lay before him. Never before had it ever occurred to him that the price he had paid for his spear might ever have been a fair one. Now he had to wonder if it had not been a bargain.

Then he gritted his teeth as he realized what he must do next. Drawing Fragaroc, he advanced upon the slain giant to recover the Spear of Celtchar, the spear that always hit and always killed—one of the twelve great treasures of Tethera.

Retrieving the weapon took some time. It had buried itself deeply, but he was of little mind to leave it; certainly no one had ever have paid a steeper price to wield it than he had. It still boggled him that even Celtchar's Spear could have killed such a foe in a single cast, yet such was its nature. As he worked to dig it out, he wondered again who Celtchar had been and what budding contest in ages past could have compelled the gods to place such a weapon in the hands of a mortal man.

Llew finally mounted Gower and rode to the stone ring, his gory spear in hand and held out well away from Gower and himself until he could clean it. Nemain was already there waiting for him. She looked up at his approach and gave him an annoyed frown. "It is certainly about time. What kept you?"

Chapter XVI

The Reign Falls

Llew and the cloaked figure ahead of him moved silently down the narrow stone corridor. As they did, Llew was careful to keep the infant held tightly in his arms. The place was confining, unpleasant, and far too strange for one like himself. Why would men build such a place?

Even while thinking this, Llew recognized where he was. Since joining the court at Caerleon he had been here twice. This was Caer Cardiff, once the royal seat of Glywysing when it had been an independent kingdom. The marriage of his putative parents, King Pendaran and Queen Arianrod, had merged its lands into those of Gwent.

It seemed odd that his immediate impression was that this place was little grander than a rabbit burrow. Possibly because he was a somewhat seasoned viewer of past events, Llew suspected this attitude he felt was due to the influence of whoever's eyes he was seeing this through.

Pausing before an ornately carved door, the figure ahead of him turned in profile and Llew saw it was King Auberon, King of the Fae and Lord of the Seelie Court. Here? In a human castle? The monarch moved his fingers in a silent cantrip. Then he opened the door and bid Llew enter.

A lady's maid and another servant, that Llew guessed to be a nursemaid, were here in a small but well-appointed anteroom. Both were sound asleep due to the king's enchantment. Without further instruction, Llew went to the cradle and carefully deposited the sleeping infant he held. Then he took up the one that was already there. This required a certain amount of caution, as the two infants were almost completely identical, despite the fact he could see right through the changeling's illusion that made them absolutely indistinguishable from each other so far as mortals were concerned.

Llew took one last look at the infant in the cradle. Then turned to his king and said, "Queen Mab will be infuriated. Surely even you cannot be comforted by such a thought? She may even try to kill you . . . again."

The King of the Fae chuckled. "That is old territory, long familiar to us both. Do not fear for me, my dear. Mab and I are too perfect for each other, Her attempts will not be whole-hearted and, whether it takes years or even centuries, we always reconcile."

Llew scowled. "It still seems wrong to place the Queen's own son with mortals."

"It is all part of the beauty of this plan, dear Drysi. Even should this mortal king find out about our little substitution, the child will still be quite safe."

Llew was so startled at being called Drysi that he almost missed what came next. He was a Fae-woman? Still holding the babe with one arm, he discretely moved one hand to check and froze with astonishment at what he found.

Not noticing where Llew's hand was, the king apparently misread his expression. "Clearly you cannot conceive of any reason why King Pwyl would quietly raise another man's son. See if you can figure it out."

Another vision featuring the mad King Pwyl? And Llew was holding his heir? Everyone knew Pwyl's heir was murdered.

What he and King Auberon were doing here, by replacing him with Mab's own child, would make that a lie. If nothing else changed, it would be the changeling that died in the heir's stead. This put all of Llew's thoughts into a whirl.

King Bran himself had once told Llew he was not of his own line, yet he had insisted Llew was also the rightful high king of Tethera. This meant he could not be King Pendaran's son. That son had been the real Llew, murdered as an infant, along with his mother, by a sickness sent by Lord Arawen.

Yet before Llew and Bran had ever even met, King Auberon of the Fae had already told him, straight out, that Llew had been taken from his original parents and a changeling left in his place. Further, that changeling had been a son of Mab and was later murdered after the exchange. This child he had just placed in the crib was also a son of Mab and quite likely, it seemed, to die in place of Pwyl's heir. How many sons did Mab have? Did it matter? It still seemed impossibly unlikely this set of shared circumstances could ever have occurred more than once. Could it be that he, himself, was Pwyl's son, as well as heir?

There was still a problem with this, Llew realized. Even though Llew was not Pendaran's son, Pwyl's heir had been born, and presumably died, a century before Llew himself could possibly have entered the world. Yet a potential solution was already occurring to him.

It was well known that, within their own domains, the Fae could control the passage of time, delaying or hastening it as they pleased. Even Hafgan and Moriganna, as Cymri, had confirmed this. Indeed, many of the old tales included someone that slept within a Fae tumulus and only awoke after decades, or even centuries, had passed in the world of men. Llew knew that as an infant he had been taken through a tumulus into Tir-Na-Nog. King Auberon had never said when he had emerged. He could very well have emerged a century later . . . but not a day older. In point of fact, this was necessary if he was slated to have been substituted for King Pendaran's son, the real Llew.

Llew ran through all the trails of logic repeatedly, desperately seeking something he had overlooked. Yet they all fit; there were no disconnects. Even with the wildest of coincidences possible, it seemed there simply could not be any other way.

There was one more fact King Auberon had given him when Llew visited him fortress of glass. Llew, and the changeling that was left for him, shared the same father. If his theory was right—

All of this had taken only seconds, but King Auberon had evidently tired of waiting for a response. "The reason he would is because—"

"—because both babes are his own sons, one by his mortal queen and one by Queen Mab," Llew finished.

The king's eyebrows arched in surprise. "Truly, Drysi, that was such a remarkable leap of intuition that I will overlook the fact you interrupted me. You must really show me how your devious mind deduced that, but not now, later."

Slowly, inexorably, Llew's gaze lowered to the child he was holding. There could be no mistake. This was why he was here. It was to see something he never would have believed otherwise, regardless of who had told him. The infant in his arms, the one he was looking down upon, could only be himself, seventeen years younger—and one hundred and sixteen years earlier.

He lifted Drysi's face to look back at King Auberon. Despite Llew's own growing sense of dismay at the situation, Drysi smiled appreciatively. "You are still the most devious of us all, my king."

"Such is my nature," the Fae King said drolly. "Still, I would leave nothing to chance. I will take the boy back to Caer Wydyr and you will remain here to observe his mother's reaction. It is unlikely she will detect the exchange, yet those birds of hers are of unknown capability and so we must be cautious. I will change you into a wren to keep watch from the rafters. If all seems well, come to me and report. If it does not, then you are to ensure the child's safety, whatever it takes. Come to me then, and we will adjust our plans accordingly."

Llew was reluctant to pass the child over to King Auberon, not least of all because it was his own younger self. Yet had not Nemain cautioned him on not interfering with events? Indeed, was there any way that he could? Then he recalled touching himself when he had learned he might be in a woman's body. Surely the real Drysi would never have done that? Perhaps this vision was more of a door into the past than a window?

Yet changing things could be immensely dangerous. Suppose he dropped his infant self onto the hard stone floor? Would he himself simply cease to exist if that happened? The world might then reshape itself as one where he had died as an infant. That might be possible. Moriganna herself claimed she had remade the world into one where she never became high queen; did she not? Of course, this only begged the question of how she could have memories of having been the high queen if she had changed the history that saw her become high queen.

Regardless, Llew decided he was obligated to see if he could affect the unfolding of past events. Then he cautioned himself; this power, if he truly possessed it, must be used very cautiously indeed. He was thus extremely careful as he handed over the child. Then, in Llew's last moment of existence as Llew, he asked, "Pardon me, my king, the identity the changeling is to take on—what is his name? You said he was King Pwyl's son, but just who is this child you are taking back to Tir-Na-Nog?"

The Fae king eyed his subject quizzically. "Did I not tell you? His name is Lleu, trueborn son of High King Pwyl and High Queen Rhiannon, she of the three birds. If they should learn of our substitution, your first order is to protect this changeling, particularly from her for, if we cannot leave him here, then Mab will certainly want him back—particularly since I cannot let her have the real one in his place." With that he waved his hand casually and turned his the Fae woman into a wren.

The tiny bird flew up into the rafters immediately, perching out of sight of those below. When it looked down, King Auberon and the babe were gone, only the changeling and the servants remained.

Lleu. His name was Lleu, not Llew. Llew was Llewellyn's birth brother and he was dead and gone these past sixteen years. The names were very similar, to be sure, but they sounded slightly different and he knew he would have trouble getting used to the new one.

With a thud, he realized that this also explained why the Fae kept calling him that name instead of Llew. They knew full well who he was because they knew his past. Nemain had also called him by that name but, in her case, it was more likely because she knew something of his future.

Lleu forced himself back to the situation at hand and considered. King Auberon had charged him, believing him to be this Fae woman named Drysi, with the changeling's safety until it was clear the mother could not perceive the exchange or, at the least, would not harm the child. Yet, if history was any guide, the changeling was doomed. It was a well-known 'fact' that Pwyl's only heir was murdered as an infant. As Lleu had attempted no significant changes yet, and had remained merely an observer, this babe was bound to die in the real heir's stead—in his own stead.

Once upon a time, Lleu had received a vision when he was very close to death. In it, his mother came to him and told him that even she had believed her child was murdered and thrown into the sea to die. She also told him that her own servants had made it seem that she had murdered the child, forcing her to flee the wrath of his father who, in his fury, would have killed her. Realization and knowing can be two quite different things. Realization now came over him. His mother was Rhiannon of the three birds, last high queen of Tethera!

Her vision had said nothing of where she had fled, or what had become of her. Lleu found himself desperately hoping she had found a new and better life for herself somewhere. *Perhaps she even remarried and had more children*, he thought. By now even her grandchildren might have children of their own. This meant that somewhere in the world there might be people he could claim kinship with—maybe even a lot of them. This was a heady thought for an orphan. It was the sound of a door slamming below that brought him out of his reverie.

The changeling was gone! One of the women, the lady's maid, was missing as well. While he had been daydreaming on the rafter she must have picked up the infant and taken it into its—his—mother's chambers. While he was trying to decide what to do, the doorway to the corridor opened and another lady's maid entered holding a tankard with a lid upon it.

"Did you get it?" demanded the nursemaid.

"Aye, I had luck in the kitchens, they already had the geese plucked and in the pot but then they slaughtered a young pig. Careful, this is nearly full and we will not want it anywhere save on her."

The two opened the door to the high queen's chambers and both went in. Neither noticed the small bird that wheeled in behind them before they could close the door.

Lleu scanned the room in an instant. There she was! The woman from his vision, the one with the chestnut hair and the sad story that had claimed to be his mother. She was asleep in her bed and the activity had not awoken her yet. Drugged, Lleu recalled, she had told him she was drugged when they came for her child. He flitted around the room looking for the infant and caring little if the servants saw him now. There was no infant.

Lleu was confused. Had someone else altogether have come into the front room and taken the changeling out through the corridor? He landed on a rafter to reassess. The treacherous maids were sprinkling he contents of the tankard over High Queen Rhiannon's gown and bedclothes. It was blood.

"What did you do with it?" asked the lady's maid that had brought the tankard.

"Why, straight out the window, of course, even on water the fall is quite sufficient. The tide will take away the evidence," came the reply.

Lleu's stomach roiled. He was too late. The changeling had been murdered, just as, if not for Auberon and Moriganna's covert actions, he would have been.

Another lady's maid charged into the room. "Hurry," she cried. "He is coming fast. Give her the antidote!"

A vial was quickly produced and waved under the high queen's nose. She immediately began coughing and her eyes fluttered open.

"Oh, my queen," exclaimed one, pointing at the blood stains on her gown, "what have you done?"

Another gave a little scream and cried out, "How could you have done this? And he just a wee babe!"

The nursemaid exclaimed, "Dark forest gods forfend, she has murdered her own child!"

The last lady's maid said nothing but simple wailed in pretended grief.

High Queen Rhiannon looked about confusedly as she got over her coughing. Her eyes widened in horror as their words began to make sense to her. "What are you saying? Where is my baby?"

"Oh, you have gone and killed him, your Highness, how could you?" replied one of the maids.

There was the sound of a large sword being drawn. The room grew instantly silent and all eyes flashed to the doorway. A big man in fine clothing, with long dark hair and a thick moustache framing his mouth and chin, stood there, eyes wide, a look of horror on his face. In his hand he held a naked sword.

Then he spoke in a voice like heavy iron being dragged over rough stone. "We have had our differences, Rhiannon, but for this there can be no forgiveness.

"You . . . have . . . killed . . . my . . . son!" He started forward toward her, raising his sword as he came. From his perch overhead, Lleu was frozen by the realization that this was his father, High King Pwyl . . . also known as Pwyl the Mad.

"Enough!" cried Rhiannon. The room filled with bird song and the attacking man, along with all four servants, collapsed to the floor, unmoving. She held up her arm and from various perches around the room came three birds to land upon it. These were not natural birds. By appearance each was cunningly crafted of precious metals and gems. Then she looked up at Lleu, still resting almost invisibly on a rafter far above her.

"Come down at once," she commanded. "I want some explanations and I want them now."

Not sure if he was being compelled or not, Llew fluttered down and changed out of wren form. It simply seemed the thing to do.

"Fae?" The high queen said, visibly surprised. "Very well, what do you know about this? Better yet, where is my son?"

"Your son was taken by King Auberon to a place of safety, your Majesty," Lleu said without hesitation. "A changeling was left in his place. That is who these creatures," Lleu indicated the nursemaid and lady's maids on the floor, "actually murdered."

High Queen Rhiannon looked down at the blood upon her gown with visible distress.

"Pig's blood, your Highness," Lleu hastened to say. "It is only pig's blood from the kitchens."

Rhiannon gave him a hard look. "A changeling you say? At the instigation of what mortal? There must be one for I know full well Auberon would not risk breaking the covenant so willfully."

Lleu nodded. "I was not told, but I believe it was at Queen Moriganna's bidding."

"What? That old meddler is once again interfering with me and mine? Never mind. You say your people have my son and he is safe? Can you also get me out of here and to some sort of safety?"

The Fae woman smiled, but that was Drysi's doing; Lleu was still too horrified by his failure to preserve the changeling. "My king's instructions did not cover this, but it would be my pleasure, your Highness. There are several small ships at this castle's docks. We have merely to borrow one."

Chapter XXVII

The Declaration

Lleu awoke and pushed himself off a cold slab of solid rock. It was the middle of the night and he was in the center of the stone circle. His body was chilled but his mind seemed to be on fire. Did he truly have all the pieces now?

Nemain crowed aloud and seized him by both shoulders. "Tell me, boy! You have all you need. Put it together in your own words, all of it! Leave nothing out so that old Nemain knows that you understand. Do it now, while it is fresh in your mind!"

He struggled to put it all in place. "I am Prince Lleu of Tethera. I am the son and heir of High King Pwyl and High Queen Rhiannon. Soon after I was born, fearing for my safety, Queen Moriganna, with the aid of King Auberon of the Fae, Lord of the Seelie Court, arranged to leave a changeling in my place. That changeling child was also my father's son, although his mother was Queen Mab, Lady of the Unseelie Court."

There was a small fire nearby that he and Nemain had made earlier, before his world was turned upside down—again. He struggled to his unsteady feet with the aim of getting closer to its beckoning warmth. He stumbled and nearly fell, but

Nemain caught his right arm with surprising strength and helped him towards where he wanted to go.

"Continue, boy! All of it, now, while it is still fresh."

Memories were coming at him from all directions, making it even harder to even stay upright. "As Moriganna and King Auberon both feared and suspected would happen, there was a plot to kill me. The changeling was murdered instead, and the body thrown into the sea. My mother's own servants then made it appear as though she had killed her own child. My father went mad and tried to kill her, but she escaped his wrath and fled."

From another dream, with its own memories, what was it the Cyhyraeths in the barrowlands had said to each other? It was connected.

"My father then made a bargain with Lord Arawen that allowed that villain the use of his own body for a year's time, in exchange for vengeance upon the killers. The Lord of Death used that year to commit such atrocities on the peoples of Tethera that King Bran was forced to slay him, still believing him to be my father. Thus ended the reign of the High Kings and Queens of Tethera."

"Good, good," Nemain clucked. "And what of the babe that was stolen, the babe that was you?"

Multiple memories, things that had been said to him in person, as well as in his strange dream-like excursions through the rings, merged with guesses and deductions he had been making, some of which he had not realized until this moment, all came to him now.

"I was taken to the Fae King's Fortress of Glass, Caer Wydyr, in Tir-Na-Nog and, although I suspect Queen Moriganna and High Queen Rhiannon must have each demanded me back, the Fae kept me for a century. Despite this, only a single day and night passed for me within their otherworldly halls. Moriganna must have eventually assumed I had grown old and died in their service. Meanwhile, a prophecy arose that proclaimed the Great Kingdom of Tethera would only be restored when High King Pwyl's heir took up his crown. Since this was clearly impossible, Queen Moriganna sought a way to circumvent the prophecy."

Picking up strength now, he continued of his own volition. "No doubt prodded by her machinations, King Pendaran's father plotted a series of marriages and subterfuges that would eventually make one of his own line into the high king of a new great kingdom. Queen Moriganna probably worked behind the scenes to help make this happen. Determined to foil this new plan, the Lord of Death decided to kill off King Pendaran's line, as he believed he had with King Pwyl's.

"As before, Queen Moriganna must have learned Lord Arawen was planning to take the life of the infant heir, in this case Prince Llew. To forestall this, she tried to do as before and requested another changeling from the Fae, but this time she insisted she be the one to make the swap, presumably so that the Fae could not keep the child, as they had before.

"King Auberon, playing his own game, gave her the changeling she requested, enchanted to look precisely the same as the infant Prince Llew, but the changeling was no Fae half-breed this time. It was me. This time, however, she was unsuccessful in getting the exchange made before the Lord of Death placed a sickness upon the real Prince Llew that killed both him and his mother, Queen Arianrod, as well.

"Queen Moriganna had naught for her efforts but a changeling that no longer had any value, or so she thought. In actuality she had the original heir, the one she had sought to keep safe a century past. Ignorant of this, and apparently unwilling to kill even a changeling, she gave it to her stable master and his wife, to raise as could best be managed.

"It was after this that King Pendaran fooled everyone. No one had anticipated that, rather than admit the death of his only male heir, he would let it be known that it was his daughter that had died, while secretly raising her disguised as her dead brother."

Queen Moriganna had not expected this, but it is hard to deceive a deceiver. She must have seen through it and realized the daughter's disguise, because she did not immediately substitute me as she had originally planned. Knowing this, she could not. For obvious reasons, the substitution of an infant boy for a girl would have been immediately obvious to Pendaran and whoever else was in on the conspiracy. Yet, in that case, I am not certain why she did not simply approach King Pendaran and prevaricate, falsely telling him that she had succeeded in saving his son via the use of a changeling."

"Bah, it should be obvious even to you," Nemain exclaimed. "Would he trust the word of one known as the Queen of Deceit? He would have tested her story by having you taken near the barrow of his dead son and thus revealed you as a changeling."

"Ah, of course, so she could not substitute me as an infant or child. Neither could she give me to him—even if she trusted him with my safety. Instead, she knew she would have to wait until we were old enough that we could bathe and dress unassisted by those few who knew of the disguise. This meant she had to ensure I was educated and trained in order to facilitate the eventual swap as an uneducated stable worker in royal finery would have fooled no one."

A chilling awe came over him as he realized what he was saying.

"The changeling spell, which is what made me into the semblance of Prince Llew, as he would have looked had he survived, is broken. I now appear as the man I was born to be and, for over a century, prophecy has foretold my coming, the sixteenth in an unbroken line of direct descent from High Queen Boudicca herself. I am not just some changeling trying to evade that prophecy and seize power, regardless of how well-intentioned.

"I am, and have always been, the rightful High King of all Tethera."

* * *

"Well it is certainly about time you figured that one out," said Nemain, sometime later. "I was not sure we would ever get this far but we have. Glorious day, there may yet be an end in sight to all this traipsing about."

"I am still," Lleu admitted, "a bit uncertain as to how to proceed. The kings of Tethera will never willingly accept an actual son of High King Pwyl as their high king. Arawen poisoned Pwyl's reputation far too badly for that."

"What do you mean by that?" demanded Nemain. "Have not all but Ergyng and Dyfyd agreed to bow to you?"

"They agreed to be ruled by Llew, son of Pendaran, not Lleu, son of Pwyl."

Nemain dismissed that with a wave of her hand. "They agreed to be ruled by you. So first convince them you are the same person they swore to serve. Only then need you worry about acquainting them with your actual ancestry. The prophecy will not care."

Lleu eyed her dubiously. "I may have to try that, but I do not especially like it."

"It hardly matters, boy. Now give me your hand, I will need to borrow some of your young strength for what must be done next."

He tentatively extended his hand and she seized it. It felt rather as though it was caught in the cleft of a bark-covered tree branch.

"Now," she said, "this particular circle of stone is more than a mere window. Aligned with the land around it and the sky above, it has many purposes but, foremost amongst these, it is also a key that will unlock a door we shall shortly open. There is a storm gathering in the waves of time but, with a tool such as this, the way may still be opened, if only just a bit."

She raised both her hands, including the one that held his. Through their linked hands he could somehow feel her throwing their perception and strength outwards. Their combined will flashed across the world and seized upon a standing stone buried beneath the earth. Quick as a wink, she extended their will further, from that stone to a second, and then to another, leapfrogging down a chain of hundreds of them. Somehow Nemain's will, and through her, Lleu's as well, was holding all of them locked in an iron grip, and a kind of pressure began to build within the vault of his mind. The power exhilarated him even as he worried over the rapidity with which it increased. It was also extremely tiring.

Then the pressure eased, and all was as it was before, save that Lleu could still feel all of those standing stones—even their positions relative to each other—as a kind of awareness in his head that he could not completely ignore. It was, he thought, not entirely dissimilar to what a Fae stone had once done to him when he had sought to travel to the isle of Avalon.

"What have you done to me?" he demanded.

"Hush your complaining. It is nothing I have not also done to myself. I have but turned the key and unlocked the door. What you feel will pass once we have opened it . . . if we can."

Lleu put one hand to his temple. His head felt strange to him but there was nothing on the outside to account for it. "I see," he said, although he did not, "and when will we attempt to open it?"

"That is difficult to say as there is no longer any direct road, and the Wild Growth has at least doubled the distance, but I would say the final destination we will reach together is perhaps two days from here."

Lleu released a deep sigh and went to see if he could find enough wood to build up the fire.

Chapter XXVIII

The Raising

Traveling north across the grasslands, they had the best part of two fairly quiet days. Nemain seemed to be too deeply in thought to do much of her usual complaining, or even to make many digs at Lleu. It was on the afternoon of the second day that the next giant appeared.

This one was nothing like the first. For one thing, it was only nine feet tall and resembled nothing so much as a very large man. Unfortunately, he appeared to be wearing a full suit of extremely thick and well-made armor. Likewise, a sword, scaled to match its owner, depended from his baldric and a round shield of enormous circumference was upon his back.

"Who approaches the hidden circle," the giant bellowed.

Before Lleu could reply, Nemain answered. "I believe you know full well who we are. Please stand aside. We are in a hurry."

"Indeed, I do know who you are, but I wish to let no one pass who has not fairly contested with me," the giant insisted. "Is the prince your champion in this matter?"

"Aye," exclaimed Lleu, "and as Nemain has said, we are in a hurry. As for fairly contested? Well that is a matter of definition is it not?" He brought up the Spear of Celtchar from the sling below his saddle where he carried javelins, when he used them.

"Hold!" shrieked Nemain and drove her mare close to him, grabbing his forearm with an outstretched hand.

"Are you mad?" asked an amazed Lleu. "We have no time for this and he is in our way."

"I never stated the challenge was to be to the death or even with weapons," the giant rumbled.

"What then?" asked Lleu. "You thought perhaps I would agree to wrestle with such as you?"

In silent answer, the giant pointed to a nearby stump. Upon it was a flat board, lovingly polished and decorated with a pattern of some sort. Small carvings were set upon it.

"He is challenging you to a game of gwyddbwyll, you bloodthirsty buffoon," Nemain exclaimed. "You cannot merely ride about the countryside murdering anyone you fancy. What kind of a warrior would do that? What kind of king would do that? If you are to prove you are better than your father and ready to become the high king that Tethera needs, then you must certainly be better than that."

Shamefacedly, Lleu considered the playing board a long moment before speaking. He was familiar with the game; some called it fidchell. Afaggdu had played it with him many times in order to teach him the importance of thinking ahead and of planning. That he had done so little of either before drawing a weapon, let alone the terrible Spear of Celtchar, just made this all the worse.

"So be it then," Lleu said in a quiet voice, "what are the terms? What stakes do we play for?"

The giant's body language conveyed confusion. "Terms?" he asked. "I merely challenge you for a game before you pass by. Whether you win or lose, you are still free to go on."

Lleu experienced a fervent desire for the earth itself to open up and swallow him whole. Could this get any worse?

Nemain spoke to the giant in a kindly voice that Lleu had never heard from her before. "We cannot spare the time right now as our business is truly urgent. I am sure the boy will agree to give you a game someday, should he survive what is coming."

"Very well," said the giant. "I hold you both to be persons of honor, and I will let you pass. I would have, of course, in any case." And to Lleu, "I look forward to our game together on some other day, young prince."

Yes, Lleu decided, his shame could not only get worse, it just had.

Nemain eyed the expanse of tall summer growth ahead of them. Interspersed with small yellow and blue flowers, the grass gently swayed in the afternoon breeze. "We are very nearly upon the edge of the hidden circle and we dare not be within it when we call it forth," she declared. "Let us dismount and leave our horses here with our friend. I am certain they are safe with him—you might say that I have foreseen it."

Numbly, Lleu dismounted and followed her about a hundred and fifty paces further before she stopped. "Now it is time to get some use of all that power we accumulated while looking through windows. Indeed, it is fortunate we were so successful because we will need every bit of it. The hidden circle will try us both. Give me your hand again."

Lleu held out his hand and Nemain took it in a rough grip. Once more the pattern of giant stones became foremost in his head. He quite literally could think of almost nothing else. Then she exerted an enormous power that, for all its strength, was somehow being leveraged by the use of the stone ring to the south as a kind of fulcrum. In some way he could not have described, he could feel it in both his mind and body, yet he was without even a frame of reference to describe what he felt. A moment passed and then, slowly, ever so slowly, the many hundreds of standing stones begin to rise from their subterranean resting places.

The stones came up in a long arc that seemed to go on forever in both directions. Towards the center of the arc something else was sinking. It was all too much, the pressure he had felt earlier at the stone ring increased a hundred-fold and pain ripped through him for a brief moment; then it was over, leaving only a terrible fatigue so complete that he was sure his own heart would lose the strength to continue beating. Yet the stones were still rising; somehow, what the two of them had started was still pushing them up. At length it was done, and they both fell to the ground, beyond exhaustion.

Time crept by and Lleu forced himself up to a sitting position. In a passing glance he could see Nemain was ahead of him and already beginning to stand up. The old crone's vitality was incredible. Then he forgot his weakness and looked again, momentarily disbelieving what he was seeing, yet there was no mistaking her. The woman climbing to her feet was not Nemain. It was Moriganna.

"Oh, no," said Lleu.

"What is the matter with you now, boy?" Moriganna asked, in a voice that was a near perfect impersonation of Nemain. "Cat got your tongue?"

She gave Lleu a wry smile and offered a hand to help him to his feet. He ignored it and, somewhat shakily, managed to clamber up unaided. "Are you going to tell me Nemain was never real either?" Lleu demanded.

Moriganna seemed quite unaffected by his angry glare. "No, Lleu, she was as real as anything in this world. The goddess has more than one aspect and, as her chosen vessel, they are as much me as I was once Cymri."

"What was the point?" Lleu cried out in a near shout. "Another game you can play with me? Is that what this is all about for you?"

Moriganna remained the essence of calm. "I told you my existence as Cymri was compromised and that neither I nor

Cymri could remain near you. It would have been disastrous for us to travel together with me undisguised. As it was, several of the Pwacca have worn my appearance hither and yon, all while they led the Lord of Death's minions on a merry chase."

"You still could have told me what you were doing," Lleu said, clenching and unclenching his fists repeatedly.

"Before you get any angrier, did you believe what I told you at Caerleon?"

Lleu scowled, then admitted, "Not all of it."

"And now?"

"I—I believe a lot more of it."

"Seeing is believing, Lleu. You had every right to be skeptical. I knew I would have to show you. There were also certain things I had to know as well and only through our joint seeings could I do that. Finally, with each seeing, we accrued more of the energies of the waves of time. Those energies were necessary for us to do this," and she gestured to the endless line of standing stones.

Lleu regarded them, a bit in awe despite his anger. "And just what have we done?" he asked.

Moriganna favored him with a crooked smile. "Dear Lleu, you would never believe me if I told you."

"Aaargggh!" he yelled, as loudly as he could.

"Feel better?" she asked.

Lleu took a deep breath and expelled it. "Perhaps I do, a little. So, tell me. Is this even your true form or do you have still others?"

"This is as true as my form can be, Lleu. As for other forms? Like the Pwacca, your shape-shifting, and mine as well, is limited to taking the forms of natural creatures—and our own, of course. We may change the size, the age, or even become a hybrid of more than one of our forms, but we only ever appear as a single, unique individual of that type, regardless of what type of creature that form is."

"Now you are lying to me, are you not?" Lleu scowled. "I have seen at least one Pwacca take a human form other than its own. Had you forgotten?"

Unperturbed, she replied, "You saw a Pwacca take a form that you know was not its own because it was my form. You overlook that it had willingly permitted me control of its mind and, I emphasize again, the form I took was my own."

"And also that of Addfwyn! Had you forgotten?"

Still serene, she replied, "That was not him shifting. That was merely a beguilement. An enchantment cast upon you was causing you, and you alone, to see him as someone you trusted. It had nothing to do with shape-shifting."

After mulling this over, Lleu could not find a flaw in the logic, so far as it went.

"Satisfied? Then let us get our horses and we will ride to the center. There I will show you something that I expect you will more readily believe through your eyes than through my words."

"I am not so certain I dare believe either when you are about," Lleu said, giving her a dark look.

"This then first, as a gesture of the Queen of Deceit's good will, if not her honesty. When did you last attempt to change shape?" she asked.

Lleu thought on that. "I do not believe I have done so since you departed and left me at the royal barrows. The first time it took nearly a year for the torc to align itself with me. Do you mean to say it might have already learned my new form?"

She said nothing and simply regarded him silently.

His eyes widened. A moment later he disappeared and a wren streaked through the air, circling Moriganna half a dozen times before becoming a man again.

"My thanks?" he said, feeling somewhat sheepish. "I guess I just quit trying and I am uncertain as to why. It certainly would have cost nothing to check once or twice each day."

"Indeed. Now to our horses, we could fly ahead but there is no reason to leave them here."

As they turned and walked back, Lleu noticed that the giant was gone. All that remained where he had met them was Gower, Nemain's mare, the stump, and another horse, a smaller stallion. There were also pieces of the giant's armor and equipment scattered all over the ground.

Nonplussed, Lleu looked at the debris for several moments before turning to Moriganna. "Do you realize what this means?" he asked her.

"Pray, enlighten me," she replied.

"It means," said Lleu, "that there must be a naked giant running around somewhere."

Chapter XXIX

An Orphan's Vengeance

Taking the additional horse in tow, they remounted and rode towards the center of the hidden ring, and Lleu found he now had time to put his most immediate question into words. "When you left me at Caerleon, you said it was better for me to know less, but that was then and this is now. Is there any reason why you can no longer tell me more of yourself?"

"I will tell you more," Moriganna agreed, briefly biting her lip before beginning. "When I first entered the waves of time I was seventeen and I emerged on, what felt to me, to be the very same day, although six centuries had passed in the world of men.

"I knew it was my purpose in life to find and marry the next high king of Tethera, my handsome young prince, and produce an heir. The Druids had raised me for that express purpose and I was their creature completely, ready to do precisely as they instructed. Does it surprise that I could ever have been so young and compliant? Yet it was only for this singular task that the Druids bartered me from my mother and sent me into the waves of time."

Lleu thought about that. "To marry a man centuries in their future? One question immediately comes to mind."

"I will answer it. They foresaw, from fourteen generations earlier, that my world's High King Owain, Pwyl's grandson, would be cuckolded by his wife. They also foresaw that, as a result of that, she would give birth to a child that would not be of the line of Boudicca, yet that child would be crowned as high king. So it was that they foresaw the destruction of Tethera for, although it is not common knowledge, Tethera's very existence is contingent upon always having an heir of Boudicca to rule it and, as he shared no blood with his supposed father, this heir was not that."

"I have never heard of any King Owain," Lleu objected.

"Naturally, in this world he was never born, for Pwyl's line never produced a grandson for him. "

"Wait a moment, so this Owain was my son?"

"No, Lleu, in that history, Pwyl married another and you were never born. Instead, Pwyl's heir, and Owain's father, was an ill-tempered brute named Urien.

"Where was I? Ah, but when I emerged from the waves of time, there were no Druids to greet me as there should have been. I was all alone in the hidden circle. My presence there made possible what came next; the goddess had been waiting for a receptive mind for a very long time and, in the span of a single heartbeat, she made me her vessel.

"That was not something I was entirely unprepared for but, then again, you can never really be prepared for such a thing. I also understood at once that the goddess had entered into me because there were no Druids left to do her will."

Perplexed, Lleu asked, "And what had become of them?"

"I did not know. I still do not. Despite all the knowledge I gained, there was nothing that told me where the Druids of that world were, or what had happened to them. I think that might mean there were no Druids left anywhere. For all their powers, they were only men. They certainly failed to foresee the rise of the Lord of Death, or perhaps they did, and Arawen took measures to silence them. It must have happened a long time ago, for I have seen no trace of Druids in this world, either."

"What did you do then?" Lleu asked, intrigued, despite himself, at this story of a history that had never happened.

"I did what I was sent to do. In time, the son of Owain's unfaithful wife and I were married. I produced the required heir, restored the line of Boudicca, and all was right with the world." She sighed.

"That sounds like it brings you grief," Lleu said.

"It does. Arawen emerged from Annwyn in overwhelming force. He killed many, my son and my husband amongst them. As high queen, I fought on alone for nearly a century, but the outcome was never in doubt. Arawen had grown too powerful. For centuries he had been unopposed, and he had spent them all in growing his strength. In the end, he destroyed everything.

"At last I made the only move remaining to me. I retreated into the waves of time. I was determined to make my way back to a past where I might still have a chance to defeat Arawen. Ultimately, I could not travel past the day he brought Tethera into this world of the Wild Growth. To go any further would have placed me in this world before Tethera arrived and thus been worse than useless.

"Hmm," mused Lleu, "you alluded to as much when you were playing at being Nemain, soon after we met."

"Yes Lleu, I thought it would be enough. I thought I knew what I had to do. So I changed my name and went to him, thinking that, somewhat as I had with Pwyl's great-grandson, I could join with him and heal the rift. You know something of how that turned out. A century spent trying to gain his trust and I nearly did not get out alive. It was only my legions of loyal Pwacca that allowed me to escape. But I gained much knowledge of Arawen. I learned his most potent enchantments, I learned of his plans, and I learned of him."

"You learned of him? Then what drives him to do all this? What made him decide to destroy everything?"

"As Nemain, I have already told you. He is damaged, Lleu. This made him receptive to the blandishments of those he should never have listened to, and it further unbalanced him. Now this imbalance is so great he has no qualms at tilting the sacred balance itself. He means to tip those scales in favor of destruction by destroying everything beyond any hope of redemption. In this he is but the pawn of certain things beyond all worlds. He labors only to serve their purposes and will not be swayed."

"But what damaged him?" Lleu persisted.

"It is a sad story. His father was of the Tylwyth Teg, but his mother was not. She and her people are now all gone and he possesses no affinity for the Tylwyth Teg—rightfully so, for they have no love for any of their half-breeds unless they also have human blood. Because of this, however, Lord Arawen feels he is the last of his race. He blames men for killing his mother and her people. He also blames his father's people, the Tylwyth Teg, although not because they have no use for him as a half-breed, but because they were complicit in the extermination of his mother's race."

"Why would he believe such an awful thing of men?"

Moriganna shrugged. "Because it is true."

"We killed his mother's people?"

"Well, not me or you, I was asleep in the waves of time and it occurred centuries before you were born."

Lleu refrained from grinding his teeth together.

Moriganna glanced toward him and raised an eyebrow. "They were apparently a variety of Fae that were incessantly malevolent to all, preying relentlessly on men and other Fae alike. They ignored many warnings, refused to give homage to either King Auberon or Queen Mab and, worst of all, failed to honor Boudicca's Covenant."

"So what happened then?" Lleu demanded, not entirely sure he wanted to know but, by the same token, convinced that he must.

"High King Math happened. He had just beaten the Fae's attempt to renege on the covenant they had made with High Queen Boudicca. In so doing he insisted on, and got, a concordance to put some consequences in place for those that defied the covenant. He apparently felt he had no choice but to make an example out of the first who sought to blatantly disregard it—and he did."

"So he killed them all? He must have thought they richly deserved it and were irredeemable."

"Consider that High King Math was my nephew's son and you are his direct descendant, albeit thirteen generations later. It is natural for us, to want to justify his actions, even now, though we lack sufficient knowledge to either praise or condemn."

Lleu mulled this bit of information for a moment. "So the Lord of Death, the encroachment of Annwyn, the Wild Growth . . . this is all about an orphan's vengeance? Still, if a mortal king did this thing to his mother's people, why does Arawen both blame and hate the Tylwyth Teg for it as well? How were they complicit?"

Moriganna shrugged. "Time and again these rogue Fae proved they were beyond the reach of any force Math would have thought to use, but the Tylwyth Teg showed him what may very well have been the one way they could be harmed. It was a weapon that could only be used once. For that reason it had to be both thorough and final—and it was.

"So he had no choice but to kill them all?"

The Queen of Deceit looked pensive. "We always have choices, Lleu, and even when they are all bad we still have the responsibility to choose those that are least bad. But bad is also relative. What Math may have felt was the best choice of a bad lot was obviously not a position Lord Arawen shared—ah, here we are. We can finish this tale another time. Now we have something rather important to do in this place."

'Here' was a circular depression nearly sixty paces across and three man-heights in depth. Standing stones formed three concentric circles within it. They surrounded an enormous rectangular stone that lay on its side in the center.

"What is this?" Lleu asked.

"This is our doorway," Moriganna replied, "and before you ask, it is a doorway to many places. Where you exit depends on how you enter. It would probably be best if you just referred to it as a portal stone."

"While my puny intellect appreciates your attempts at avoiding circumlocution, it does begin to feel a trifle bit insulted," he remarked, as he dismounted and moved closer to inspect the object in question.

Moriganna rolled her eyes. "I wondered if it was not a mistake to teach you so many words we derive from Latin. Apparently it was."

"I take it we are going to enter it then?"

Moriganna shook her head. "Not we, just you. I must remain here to hold the door open so that you may return to this world and this time."

That got his full attention. Stone forgotten, Lleu turned in her direction. "Perhaps you had best tell me a bit more on what this is about," he suggested.

A brief smile touched Moriganna's face. "That would take all the fun out of it."

Chapter XXX

Somewhere in Time

While Moriganna climbed back up to the lip of the depression, Lleu stood on the portal stone wondering, not for the first time, how he had been persuaded to do this. He was not given long in which to do so.

Once out of the circular hole, Moriganna took a position with her legs together, arms upraised, and began chanting. Lleu found he could not quite make out the words. He was just starting to wonder how long this was going to take when she finished chanting and dropped her arms. Then she disappeared. All of the stones circling the portal stone disappeared as well, along with the sky, the sun, the ground, and everything else that was neither Lleu nor the portal stone.

The nothingness that filled the world around them was, Lleu discovered, more than a little hard to look upon. It was not just that he looked upon empty space, the nothingness all around him was so complete there did not even seem to be any space.

To her credit, Moriganna had tried to tell him how unnerving this would be, but he had waved off her warning. He was not, he had decided, going to be discomfited by minor strangeness. Had he not just killed a vast giant in a single blow?

Yet, that did not seem to matter in the here and now—if here and now were words that even had any meaning in this context.

To help calm himself, Lleu forced himself to look straight down so that his main field of vision was entirely occupied by his feet and the portal stone. At least this way there was something for his eyes to take in.

Typical, he thought. Even within the waves of time themselves, he was expected to hurry up and wait. If he had understood Moriganna correctly, he now had all the time in the world—literally—and he simply had to do nothing until something happened. He spent awhile wondering, if there was no sun, no stars, and no moon, why he was not in total darkness, but this line of thought proved singularly unproductive.

After a time, sheer boredom forced him to look up. He discovered at once that the nothingness was now mitigated, to some degree, by a vast multitude of portal stones. They ran away in a seemingly infinite progression to either side of his own stone. Stranger still, on each of those other portal stones stood another Lleu. Moriganna had not mentioned this to him when she was describing what must happen!

The other versions of himself seemed too far away to speak to, so he waved instead. The one he waved to did not see it for, just as Lleu turned and waved, the other Lleu turned and waved at the Lleu on his far side, respectively, while that Lleu was doing the same to yet another Lleu further on. At this point Lleu was willing to bet that the Lleu behind him had just waved at his back.

It occurred to him to wonder if the Druids had developed a special vocabulary for dealing with this kind of thing. It was clear his own command of language was inadequate to easily speak about any of this.

After an interminable period of whatever it was he referred to as time, Lleu found himself constantly looking about, even though there was nothing to see but an unending series of himself. Moriganna had not warned of the possibility of any sort of attack here, but it had come to him that, if he could get here, something else might. There might be other travelers, or creatures that had somehow become trapped here. There might even be creatures that lived here. *Except*, he pondered, *what would they subsist on?* The only answer that readily presented itself to him was travelers.

Consequently, he was somewhat edgy when an object began approaching from what appeared to be a very long way off. With no visible means of support or propulsion, it moved smoothly and slowly, while hanging in utter emptiness. As it got closer he could see it was a large wooden box, with elaborate carvings on every surface. Lleu calmed somewhat. This was not unexpected.

From his pack, he took out a long rope with a three pronged iron hook. Moriganna had scrounged it from the ruins of Caer Caradoc with just this purpose in mind. He was glad she had, for the box, at its closest approach, would still be well out of reach, and he was not willing to risk stepping off the portal stone for any reason, regardless of how important she said it was for him to retrieve it.

The box would have continued on its odd path and, looping back repeatedly, eventually found its own way onto the portal stone in another three years or so, she had told him, but there simply was no way they could afford to wait that long.

Lleu threw the hook and missed completely on the first attempt. On the second, he hit it, but the hook found no purchase. The box reached its point of closest approach and began to curve away. Starting to panic a bit, he spun the hook around and around, paying out rope until it was rotating about his position at the center of a large circle, then he let it out still farther. After a pass where it almost reached the box, he let out another ten feet. This time, when the rope hit the box, the hook continued to swing around it until it clunked into the opposite side, just past where its rope first began to wrap around. Flicking the rope, he gave it a quick, short snatch and the hook caught the rope. Wary that it might yet slip out of his loop, he carefully dragged it in to where he could grab it and tug it onto the portal stone with him.

Although it had been floating while he brought it near, the box abruptly became very heavy the moment it was over the portal stone. Lleu then spent a few moments hopping about on one foot, convinced he had smashed one of his toes into jelly, despite his heavy boots. Fortunately, once he had the boot off to check, he found it had only caught the tip of his boot and there was no permanent damage.

He spared a glance at his nearest neighbors. One of the two had retrieved his box, while the other had apparently failed. Lleu wondered if that was because it had not come close enough. It was not his problem, he told himself. At least, it was not exactly his problem—was it?

Lleu put that line of thought firmly aside and briefly considered trying to open the box. He just barely managed to resist the temptation. It helped that Moriganna had cautioned him strongly against doing so, and it did not hurt that she had also been the one who, as Cymri, had once told him the story of the Greek maid, Pandora.

More time seemed to pass. In spite of the strangeness, he was getting extremely bored. It did not help that he had no way of telling how much time was elapsing here in the waves of time. It might, he decided, be rather like flying with the wind. He had noticed when flying that, when he matched his own speed to that of the wind, it could no longer be detected. The air became calm and still for, like a boat floating down a placid stream on the current, they both moved at the same rate. Was there a similar principle at work here? Perhaps it was making him unaware of the passage of time in the world at large?

Having followed that line of logic, Lleu now experienced a bit of trepidation—just how fast was time passing outside of the waves on which he rode?

The question answered itself a moment later—or in what seemed like a moment. All around him there was suddenly the comforting feeling of . . . something. Above him was a night sky, studded with stars. Moriganna was standing on the ground directly before him.

"You never realized what a luxury it is to have something around you all the time, did you?" she asked. "Like a traveler in a barren place, whose only food is what he brought with him, so was the portal stone the only space there was and that only because you brought it with you."

"It was . . . strange," said Lleu, not disagreeing.

"I see you had some success, congratulations."

"Thank you, I think," Lleu replied. "Shall I open it for you now?"

"No, I rather think not. The less who know the nature of our new asset, the better, for now." She held up a hand to forestall his response. "Do not be concerned. If this works as I hope, you shall know soon enough, but there are things you must do now."

"What? Yet more seeings?"

"Nay, Lleu, we have run out of time for that. You have been gone nearly a week, regardless of what it may have seemed like to you."

Lleu grimaced. "I was afraid of something like that, I had actually worried it might be considerably more."

It was Moriganna's turn to be surprised. "You anticipated the displacement?"

"It is not," he said, looking directly at her as he lifted one eyebrow, "as if I do not have some experience with waves and winds and travel."

"Intriguing. You will have to explain that some time but the problem now is that the Pictish horde is in Ergyng. Your sister is there with many warriors of Gwent to augment the Ergyngling forces but it will not be enough. There is no sign yet of Helgar, or any of the Northman warriors he might be able to command. Something else will be needed."

"What else is there?" Lleu asked, confused. He thought about it. "Possibly I could raise some men from Clwyd but, with their reprieve from Annwyn, most of King Delwyn's army has probably been released to the harvest. Clwyd is a land in dire need of everything it can get to turn its fortunes about."

Moriganna tsked. "King Delwyn has passed his throne to King Baddon, and what men he could scrape up quickly he has already sent. No, Lleu, have you forgotten the Pwacca?"

Chapter XXXI

Unfound Allies

"Pwacca?" Lleu exclaimed. "I thought they were just clever animals."

One corner of Moriganna's mouth quirked up. "You mean like Gower?"

Lleu momentarily started at that and had to think back. "Ah, yes, you know that I know he is one because you were at the table as Cymri when Oswalt ap Hire told us that," he said slowly, as he thought it through. "Oswalt being the closest thing there is, after you and, of course, the Pwacca themselves, to being an expert on them."

It took a moment before Lleu realized he had thought of Cymri without the accompanying anguish. He was changing inside, as everyone was doing all the time, growing into a different Lleu, one that had come to accept something that could not possibly be changed. This was much like how he had been so badly shaken the first time he had killed in combat but, later, when he had recalled the event, found that it no longer distressed him nearly as much.

He thought also of how much his younger self of a few years earlier, so intent on one day being free and footloose, bound to no one and able to go and do whatever most pleased him, would be horrified. He had willingly, at every step of the way, become a man driven by events, and by his own nature, to give up so much freedom and, correspondingly, take on responsibility for so much more than himself.

Every moment that I live, the old me is destroyed and a new me is created in my place, he thought to himself. Terrible as that seemed, he knew it would be worse if it were not true and, instead, he simply blundered through life, never learning, never finding new understandings.

Truly, it *was* a balance of destruction and creation, and he felt he was beginning to actually understand, at a deeper level, how even something like the Cythrawl, the very essence of destruction, was as necessary as the force of creation itself.

"Lleu?" Moriganna asked, looking concerned. "Stay focused, please, we really do not have much time now."

"Sorry," he mumbled. "What were you saying about Gower?"

"I knew he was Pwacca because his father was Pwacca. I also had him put in a sack and carefully positioned where you would find him and could rescue him. You gave me a bad scare when you bobbled it and you both went down the rapids."

"You—" Lleu stopped. "No, never mind. That sort of thing really should not surprise me at this point."

Moriganna actually laughed at that. "Very well, then you shall not be surprised when I tell you that I created the Pwacca through a mixture of magic and breeding, but it was the breeding of animals only, none of the races of men or Fae were any part of what they sprang from. Now they can shape-shift into men so well that none can tell the difference. This means they cannot be considered as mere animals any longer—nor should they. Suppose there were some of the race of men that could shape-shift into animals. Would you then categorize them as animals?"

"You are referring to the two of us; are you not?"

"Of course I am. The point being that it hardly matters where you start from if you wind up in the same place. A person is as a person does—which is to say that when shapes are mutable, the only way to define a person is by their capability and their behavior."

"Pwacca behave as men?" Lleu shook his head in the negative. "Your Pwacca guards in Caer Mallcoedwig certainly stood out too much to make that claim."

Moriganna acknowledged this with a shrug. "They were meant to. It was part of my misdirection."

"Misdirection? To hide what?"

"Lleu, you spent your whole life in Caer Mallcoedwig up until you were fourteen. Did you ever notice that many of the villagers were themselves Pwacca?"

"You are making that up," he accused.

"I am not. Why would I? I am simply explaining why I can provide you with more Pwacca than you think I can. Perhaps it will even be enough to make a difference."

"Really?" asked Lleu, trying hard to suppress a sarcastic tone. "How many are available to aid me in Ergyng?"

"Hmm," Moriganna said thoughtfully, "I really could not say. Oswalt? Would you have some idea?"

"Yes indeed, my queen," replied Oswalt ap Hire as he stepped out from behind a nearby standing stone. The kennel master of Caer Mallcoedwig was barefoot and wearing a simple woolen robe.

Lleu spun in a full circle trying to see who else might have wandered up unexpectedly. No one else was visible. "You just delight in catching me off balance, do you not?" he complained to Moriganna.

She smirked before replying, "When you are as old as I am it is good to keep things interesting." To Oswalt, she said, "Very good, dear, please do answer his question."

"With pleasure, my queen. Outside of Vandwy, we have—"

"Hold a moment if you would please, Oswalt," Lleu interrupted. "I am very interested in hearing about our allies' numbers, but I have a more pressing question." He looked to Moriganna and briefly bit his lower lip. "Why is our kennel master, of all people, here in the middle of nowhere?" he expostulated, waving his arm at the new arrival.

"Really Lleu, I am right here and my hearing may not be as good as your own but there is no need to shout. I know you must recall my lessons on how a king should not show his emotions until he is certain he is in control of them. However, in answer to your question, Oswalt is here because I asked him to meet us here. Part of his task was to make sure there were not going to be any further sendings of Lord Arawen guarding the hidden ring."

Lleu turned his attention to Oswalt. "Were there?" Lleu demanded.

"Nay, my prince. I was here for nearly a week and found nothing. The greatest challenge I faced was boredom, actually."

"You could have tried a few games of gwyddbwyll against the giant," Lleu suggested. A suspicious thought came to him then. "That is unless—"

"Aye, my prince, that was not an option. Also, do not forget that you promised me a game when this is all over."

Lleu moved his attention to Oswalt's robe and bare feet. "No," he said.

"Yes, your Highness, I am a Pwacca."

Lleu ran through a range of emotions and various states of incredulousness. Finally he said, "All right then, tell us about the Pwacca numbers these days, good sirrah." A thought came to him before Oswalt could draw breath to speak. "Wait! You are the one in charge of not letting the other Pwacca get to the hounds?"

Oswalt winced. "No, my lord, that was just a subterfuge. I was told to tell you nothing terribly useful when it came to

Pwacca. That was also a long time ago and I allowed myself to give in to what was certainly a low sense of humor. We Pwacca reproduce in the same manner as men or wolves, which is to say, with the females of our own kind. They do exist, even though there were none amongst the Caer Mallcoedwig guards."

Moriganna was laughing now. "Lleu did you really–" she paused to try to quell another round of laughter but was only partly successful, "–did you really think Pwacca were the offspring of Pwacca males and female hounds?" Again, she found herself trying to control her obvious amusement with less than total success.

"So," Lleu said in a darker voice, "if that is not the bottleneck it seemed, then tell me good sirrah, just how many may I call on for aid against the Picts? Was it you that once told me they numbered several hundred when your kind left Annwyn, well over a century agone?"

Oswalt shrugged apologetically. "Most are in the realm of Vandwy, they cannot reach us in time. However, we have stripped the forces guarding Caer Mallcoedwig to a minimum, and also called on those members of the village militia that are Pwacca. It is not a lot, of course, but then only one of every ten villagers is apt to be a Pwacca and, as with the human villagers, many of them are not suitable to join the militia. All told I would say we will be able to send one hundred of our number with you to Ergyng."

Lleu wondered what the realm of Vandwy was, then put that question aside to better consider the matter at hand. He had seen shape-shifters in combat. They were nothing short of terrifying and, as Moriganna had hinted, they had many other potential uses than just straight up battle.

"It may be enough to turn events in our favor. Are they nearby?" And then, "Hold on again. Did you just say as many as one in every ten villagers in Caer Mallcoedwig is a Pwacca?"

"Yes, my lord."

Once more, Lleu's world was shaken. "They are indistinguishable from the men that are their own neighbors?"

Moriganna gave a light laugh before she said, "Yes, Lleu, that is exactly what I was aiming for."

"All right, very well, you know what? I surrender. Just tell me where we can meet them. After that, just point us at Ergyng."

"Alas," replied Moriganna, "this is where we part company. You will have to meet them and get to Ergyng on your own. And no, before you ask, I will not be with you, not even in some disguised form. What I have to do will not wait for that."

"So it will be just me and Oswalt then?"

"Nay, Lleu, I need Oswalt's services. He was here to meet me, more than you. It will be just you and Gower, but do not fret. Gower is quite able to take you to the other Pwacca. Further, you were gone a week and I was bored, so he has learned a new trick."

Chapter XXXII

A Plethora of Pwacca

Once Lleu had finally ridden out of sight, Moriganna carefully removed the enchantments sealing the box he had recovered from the waves of time. "That has done it," she announced at last. "Oswalt, would you do the honors, please?"

It took only moments for him to pry the lid loose and shove it aside.

"Carefully," she cautioned, "like me, that box is a thing of great antiquity."

She approached and looked within. "Well, and there you are. I should imagine you have some questions. In your position, I know for a fact I would."

"You?" replied a voice from inside. "What are you doing here? No—that is a rather silly question is it not? Something has clearly gone considerably amiss."

"That," Moriganna replied drily, "would be an understatement, but there is no sense quizzing me about it. Bide a moment and I expect you will know all you need to know—and probably not a bit more."

* * *

On the road again, Lleu thought to himself. It was just him and Gower. He had no objections to that. It was the closest thing to the illusion of freedom he ever seemed likely to know. It had to be enjoyed now, while he had it, because it would only require a three day ride to reach Caer Ergyng and, sooner than that, he would meet the small force of Pwacca coming to meet him along the way.

After Moriganna had shown him Gower's new trick there seemed little excuse for further delay. Despite this, he had lingered as long as possible, hoping to see Moriganna open her mysterious box. She was, of course, far too wily for that and had finally shooed him off.

Only a few hours passed before he heard hoof beats coming from behind. It was a single rider so he merely turned Gower about and waited. It took a few moments before his pursuer came close enough that he could make out who it was. Curiously, it was Moriganna, and she was pushing her mare as hard as she could safely manage in order to catch up to Gower. Once she saw that he had seen her, she slowed considerably, presumably to give the poor animal some rest.

As she came even closer, Lleu froze. It was not Moriganna; it was Cymri.

Damn her, he thought to himself. Why did she have to do this to him?

She reached him and came to a stop.

Lleu said nothing for a long moment. "Well?" he challenged. "Is there some special reason why you changed your mind about accompanying me?" Left unspoken was the greater question: Why had she taken this form before rejoining him?

She regarded him coolly. "Let us pretend for a moment that I am not Moriganna in disguise."

Lleu snorted derisively. "And why would we do that?"

"Because I am not Moriganna. You and I are only just meeting for the first time. Moriganna came from a future that can no longer be ours, whereas I come from a past that belongs to us both. I am this world's Cymri, not Moriganna's."

Thunderstruck, Lleu tried to take this in while she continued, "And thank you for retrieving me from the waves of time. I know I would have come out in only three more years, but six centuries in such confined quarters was already quite long enough."

"What are you getting at? This world's Cymri? What does that even mean?"

"It means Moriganna came from the future, I came from the past. Which is to say, wherever she came from originally, she came to our world from what could have been our future, once upon a time. Now she is just a refugee. Whether it is from a future that no longer exists, or simply one which we can no longer reach, does not really seem to matter. I, on the other hand, have never been to the future, not of this world or any other, but I was born ages ago. For me, this morning started on a day six hundred years ago and, for me, that day is not yet over.

"Wish me a happy birthday, Lleu. Today I am seventeen years old. Contrast that with Moriganna's many centuries. She may have begun as a Cymri, we may even have begun as very nearly, or even precisely, the same Cymri, but she did not begin as the Cymri I have already become. For all that we might have identical origins, we are now different people and always will be."

Lleu felt unwilling to try to make sense of this. "So, the Druids took you from your mother when you were born, raised you on the milk of otherworld cows, and packed you into the waves of time the instant you reached your majority? They must have given you an important task. What is it?"

She regarded him steadily. "The same as that given to Moriganna in her world. Upon emergence from the waves of time I am to seek out the high king's heir, wed myself to him, and produce the next heir."

She let him writhe, speechless, for far too long before she relented. "Oh, cease your worry. I am not some ignorant summoned thing, forced to do the specific wording of whatever is demanded of me. It is clear the situation has changed in ways that make all of that a moot point, even if Moriganna had not already fulfilled that charge in the world she came from."

At long last, he found his voice. "We could not be married in any case. If it is as you say, then you are my own aunt!"

"Fifteen generations removed, Lleu. Do the numbers and you must realize that, after all this time, nearly every man, woman, and child in Tethera is probably, in some way, a descendant of Boudicca and my two older sisters. On that basis I am probably less related to you than anyone in all the land."

Lleu changed his focus, well aware he might simply be practicing avoidance for the moment. "And how much do you know about the situation? Moriganna could not have spent more than a handful of minutes detailing it to you."

"She did not tell me anything. Imagine sleeping six hundred years and having a list of things to do the moment you awaken, but who should be at the side of your bed when you do? I would wager you might be surprised if it was a much older version of yourself."

Lleu chuckled in spite in himself. "Yes, that would certainly be a sign that things had not gone as anticipated. So I am a total stranger to you?"

"Take it a step further, Lleu. Imagine you then discover your older self is the vessel of the goddess and, because she is, you are, too, and you know this because the goddess has placed certain knowledge directly into your head."

"So you know everything Moriganna does now?"

"No, that is just it. I know almost nothing. The goddess only imparts those memories that she believes we need. Almost all I have are the memories of when we, and by we I mean you and me—when Moriganna appeared to be me—were together."

This was testing Lleu's ability to suspend disbelief. "So you can recall when you told me a tale about Greek philosophy or some such but, if you then left the room and went out to do Moriganna things for a bit, you would have no memory of anything until you returned to me?"

"That is precisely the way it is, Lleu."

"So, effectively, you have memories from your future, that is my past, although it did not happen to you, and you only have a carefully chosen selection of those memories?"

"You have described it perfectly."

"Ah," said Lleu. "No, wait, what did I describe? Hold—a better question—are you my Cymri or Moriganna's Cymri?"

"Llewellyn once asked you if you had named your bird Cymri. Do you recall your response?"

"I told her she was not my bird, she was her own bird . . . I see what you are saying. I did not mean to imply ownership."

"I did not believe that you did. I just want to let you know that you cannot apply any of your preconceptions to me. I am me, whatever that means, and I am not someone else's version of something that is either me or not me."

Lleu gave her a hesitant grin. "I think I understand what you are saying, far more that most ever could, in that I sometimes have a similar problem. So what now? Obviously you mean to accompany me to Ergyng. Is that what Moriganna intended you to do as well?"

She glanced away. "Moriganna may be making up many of her so-called plans as this goes along. Surely she cannot anticipate everything, despite the advantage of her years of experience and personal knowledge of at least one future. She has not confided in me, but I do not think she was of any one mind on what to do with another Cymri until she saw just how much the goddess was willing to share with me. Only then did she offer me her mare and send me after you."

"For her own part, what did she appear to be doing when you last saw her?"

"Well, and I thought it was odd. First, that man in the robe turned into a horse, then she put a saddle on him and rode away."

"More peculiar than you may realize," Lleu remarked. "She could have just turned into some flying thing and taken to the sky."

"Really?" Cymri's gaze went unfocused for a moment while her expression became an odd one. "Oh, of course she could. I just realized I can do that now, too."

Startled almost beyond words for a moment, the moment passed and Lleu laughed. "I think you will fit in pretty well with the company I keep."

"Well of course I will. I already know most of them as though I've known them for years." Another funny look crossed her face. "Yet although Taliesin is supposed to be my adoptive father I have fewer memories of him than you would expect, Moriganna first came to him in the form of a nine year old, so they only had about seven years together, during which he also traveled a great deal."

"Nine years old? Did he not realize children start out younger than that?"

"Of course he knew that. Moriganna had his brother tell him that we were his daughter and that our mother had passed on."

"Afaggdu was in on it? That explains many things in and of itself. Although, what of this supposed mother? That seems a weak point, or was the woman really dead?"

Cymri laughed at that. "The chief of all bards travels everywhere, and he practically has to beat women off with a stick when he is not interested in them. Yet he is nearly always interested in them, and he very much dislikes hurting their feelings. My supposed mother could have been one of so many people it would have been impractical to check, even if he could have tracked them all down. He simply took Afaggdu at his word and he is too good a man not to do right by any child he might father. I hope he is not hurt by Moriganna's deception, for he honestly loves her—I mean me—and this may all be too odd for him."

"No worries," Lleu told her. "He spent several years as a tree once. He is as used to odd situations as any of us."

* * *

They sheltered that night in another collection of standing stones and, when midday came, they were still on the plains. Thus it was that they were able to see the approaching eagle long before it could reach them. Bidding Cymri to remain behind, Lleu rode ahead a short distance and dismounted to wait for it. It had not taken long to realize that this was no ordinary eagle. It was far larger than a man, as large as Lleu himself, when he shape-shifted into one.

For this reason, he was not surprised when, just before it landed, it transformed itself into a hulking beast best described as a wolf with a man's form. Even so, the spectacle was such that he failed to note the eagle had been carrying a heavy pack, until it thumped onto the ground beside the wolfish form.

Dozens more of the wolf-like beasts emerged from the high grass around them and quickly formed a full circle around Lleu and Gower, creating what seemed to be an impenetrable wall of fangs and claws. Even knowing precisely what they must be, Lleu found it to be a terrifying sight.

Gower flicked an ear and took a mouthful of grass.

The Pwacca that had been an eagle was visibly larger than the others; now it approached more closely. "So," it said, in a perfectly understandable voice, given that it was somewhat deep in timbre, "our prince finally comes into his own."

Lleu gave the creature a once-over. Even amongst Pwacca, this one managed to look considerably more frightening than the rest. "You have the better of me; we have not been introduced."

"I am called Araf amongst our people. I am pack leader of all Pwacca in this world."

"A pleasure, I am sure," Lleu replied. "Indeed, I am very glad to see you. I understand we have a considerable challenge ahead of us. I take it you will be my lieutenant?"

The pack leader grinned, but it was really more of a display of teeth than anything else. "My prince, we are loyal to you. It is in our blood, as you must well know, but if you are to be our pack-leader and lead us in combat, you must do it in the traditional way."

Lleu sighed and considered the situation. "As if I could not guess, what would that be?"

"You must challenge and defeat the old pack leader. No weapons, no armor. Just us. Teeth, claws, horns, whatever you may shape-shift for yourself, for you may make as much, or as little, use of your shape-shifter powers as you wish."

"Really?" asked Lleu. "I mean, seriously? While I have spent most of my short life training in weapons and fighting on horseback, I am now expected to throw all that out the window and persevere against one who has probably spent every day of a long life practicing for just such a kind of combat? And what's more—"

He gave Araf a suspicious look. "Wait. Your name means slow in the old tongue, does it not? Why would they call you that?"

The pack master shrugged. "You have seen through my little jest; for you there will be no test, for its outcome could change nothing, although I suspect you have shorted yourself and might present far more of a challenge than you think. As for my name? It is something of a joke amongst our kind. I am reputed to be rather quick witted, as well as terribly swift with claw and fang, even for a Pwacca, so it amused the pack to give me a contrasting name."

"And," Lleu continued, his suspicion growing by leaps and bounds, "when you are in human form, do you also take a similar name?"

Araf grinned, and this time Lleu could perceive canine amusement in it, rather than just razor sharp teeth ready to sink into his prey.

"My prince knows me too well." Araf replied. He glanced toward Gower. "I see you have been taking good care of that puppy you found. It is good to see you both again."

Lleu nodded slowly, his surmise confirmed. "It is very good to see you again as well, Slow Tomos."

* * *

How to proceed was the question of the day. Lleu was in favor of all of them taking eagle form and proceeding directly to Ergyng by air, a travel mode that would shorten the trip from days to hours.

"Ah, Prince Lleu, happy as I am to see you and Gower doing so very well together, we do have a problem in that he never learned to fly," Slow Tomos told him.

"The versatility of Math's Torc has also led you to overestimate what most Pwacca may achieve. Lizards, birds, fish, these are not forms most Pwacca may normally take. Only one Pwacca in a hundred is able to shape-shift into the form of any creature that is not furred, as you seem to do easily, without even a thought."

"You just flew in as an eagle," Lleu objected.

Slow Tomos, or Araf, as he was calling himself in Pwacca form, grimaced. "Even at only one in a hundred, there are a great many Pwacca that can do this, but here? I am the one in a hundred here."

"What about bats then?" demanded Lleu. If they can become furred creatures, why not bats?"

"Oh, that they could probably manage, most of them, but as for flying?" Araf shook his massive head regretfully. "Bats see with their ears, not so much their eyes, and this is entirely too difficult and strange for most. Also, there is the problem that men were made for climbing in high places. Wolves? Not so much, I fear."

"You are determined to wreck my nascent plans and ruin my fun, eh?"

Araf lifted vast, furred arms in a shrug. "Perhaps, but it gives me no joy to do so, my prince."

"Let us go as quickly as we may then. On the way I will turn my mind to the problem of how we will get in past the siege lines. I take it everyone can keep up with Gower and myself?"

"Certainly, my prince, although Gower could probably outpace us all were he to work at it, even carrying you in full armor. Further, he could—" Araf broke off in consternation as Cymri rode forward to join them and he got his first impression of her at close range. The other Pwacca all lowered their heads to the ground in subservience.

"My queen!" Araf began, "I had understood you would not be here today."

A quick glance at Cymri showed she was fascinated by the enormous Pwacca. Of course, thought Lleu, she has memories of meeting Pwacca in this form with me, especially when we left Caer Mallcoedwig the first time, but that is probably somewhat different than the actual experience, particularly if they are second-hand memories.

"Ah, no," Lleu said quickly, before Cymri could reply. "This is the Cymri of this world—a real Cymri," he added, realizing that Slow Tomos would certainly have known of Moriganna's deception in portraying herself as Cymri. "You may think of her as a distant cousin of Moriganna. She is our ally in everything, and is not to be harmed."

Araf lifted his nose and took a deep sniff of her. "Have no fear on that account, my prince. She has the scent of the queen's line. So far as she is concerned, no Pwacca alive would seek to do anything but protect and serve."

"My," said Cymri, "how fortunate, then, that I bathed this morning."

Chapter XXXIII

A Town Called Erg

"My mare," Cymri announced, "is simply not up to all of this." So saying, she unsaddled it and set it free. It immediately raced back in the direction from which they had come, more than eager, no doubt, to get away from all the unsettling shape-shifters.

Seeing Lleu frown as he watched the animal race off on its own, she said, "Do not be so worried about its welfare. Moriganna fully understands Pwacca and horses, and she is expecting its return." And that was the end of it.

They traveled swiftly after that. Even surrounded by twenty Pwacca, there were still forty of them to range out before them and forty to run behind. Some of them took turns becoming horses for Cymri to ride. Even in horse form, there was something distinctively wolfish about them. Lleu, for his part, was finding it difficult to believe that, if what Moriganna and Oswalt had said was true, then he would have recognized many of them, had they taken human form.

Nevertheless, this was confirmed when, as one of them was allowing Cymri's saddle to be transferred to its successor, Lleu thanked it for its service. It spoke to him then. Through great sharp teeth the words still came quite clearly. "Ah, no thanks are necessary, my prince. We are all volunteers and hand selected for this mission by our queen. There is nothing we would rather be doing than serving here, this day."

"I appreciate that beyond words," Lleu replied, in his most serious voice. "I will still do my best to see you all well rewarded for this effort."

"My prince, we have waited long and this service is its own reward."

"What were you doing while you waited," Lleu asked, curious as to what the response would be.

His world experienced another small shakeup when the creature replied. "Ah, you do not recognize me in this form, and there is no reason you should, my lord, but I am Yorath. We worked together in the stables for a time, before the queen bade you move into her keep."

* * *

The capital of Ergyng, a very large town with the unimaginative name of Erg, , stood on two large hills, each surrounded by high walls and towers and boasting a very impressive keep at its highest elevation. The two hills were connected by additional walls that flowed down and across to the next, pierced only by a single great gate. The town itself was closely backed by a navigable river. A large bridge ran from the far side of that river, to an island in the river's center, and then continued on to meet the town center itself, at a second gate, opposite the one that faced them.

It was as Moriganna had said. Erg was under siege. Hordes of Picts covered what had been fields and low hills before the town. Save for the remnants of the fields, and the occasional rubble of what must have been a low stone fence, there was little to indicate that the land had been covered with farms not long before. The crofter's cottages, sheds, shelters, and fences must have all been pried apart and dismantled for firewood and other things. The Pict camps themselves were untidy affairs, with only the fires, and the rudest of lean-tos and brush huts, to mark their place.

But the numbers! The land before them was carpeted with armed men, most wearing little else besides ornate patterns of blue paint. Lleu quailed a bit inside as he thought of what the feeding of all those men must be doing to the harvest-ready fields in the rest of the kingdom. He looked for, and found, wagons bringing in provender and more lumber. This had to be the work of Annwyn's assisting forces, but where were they concentrated?

Then he spotted it. It was not difficult to find; an island of relative order and calm sat amidst the seething horde. The Picts themselves were giving the area a wide berth, seemingly unwilling to openly admit their fear of its inhabitants, yet likewise unwilling to approach within a hundred paces of it. The place was toward the center, set well back from the front lines, and was surrounded by a rough palisade. Inside were numerous tents and cavernous wooden buildings, obviously thrown up in great haste and never meant to last. It was also evident a great deal of construction was going on inside, but not on shelters.

Siege engines, Lleu saw, and a great many of them. He looked again at the town. With so many of those towers, catapults, and . . . whatever those other things were, some new deviltry of the Lord of Death, no doubt, the horde would easily be sufficient to overrun and capture the center of the town, the low part between the two hills. But the hill top portions themselves? With their walls atop high cliffs, it was difficult to see how any investment in men and machines would be able to drive a force over or through those walls, so long as any defenders yet remained.

The Picts, Lleu was quite certain, were not the sort who could, or would, maintain a long siege. Lleu tried to treat it as a puzzle. The Picts could decimate the lands of Ergyng, despoil a full-season's crops, even bottle up the kings and their armies and turn to rubble some part of their capital. Yet while Lleu could certainly see that this would be useful to Lord Arawen, what did the Picts think they would ultimately gain from it?

More to the point, where would they be vulnerable? The Picts themselves presented no obvious center or weak points. The palisaded area where Annwyn was making its own, sinister contributions, was the only obvious target, yet even to approach it would involve driving through a large swath of the Pictish horde.

Lleu shook himself from his thoughts. To approach this closely without being seen, he and the others, even Cymri, had all shape-shifted into wolf form, albeit wolves that could speak. Even so, one hundred and two wolves would not remain undetected forever. They had to move.

"I see little we can do from here. Our first step must be to join the defenders inside."

No one had any hands with which to gesture, but the flip of Araf's head toward the Pictish invaders was telling. "Our blue-painted friends may not wish us to do this, Lleu."

A wolfish grin came unbidden to Lleu's mouth. "I do not intend to give them any say in the matter."

* * *

Arval ap Yarwood had taken up his position on the tower beside the river gate at noon. Six hours had passed since then and his boredom was now complete. The savages had closed off the far end of the river bridge and a small encampment of them remained there, ensuring nothing would pass over it in either direction. Likewise, there was no way possible for the Picts to mount a successful attack on the gate across a two hundred foot bridge that was scarcely eight feet wide. Consequently, his level of alertness was flagging badly when something caught his eye at the wharves, just outside the wall by the bridge. Something had moved!

He scrutinized the area but there was nothing—wait, what was that? It dawned on him that he was seeing river otters coming out of the water and disappearing into the broken barrels, collapsing shacks, and other clutter that was always on hand where boat traffic regularly came ashore. It was otters; he could tell that just from how they moved, but there were so many of them—dozens and dozens it seemed. Their coming must have upset the local rat population, for now he saw that a multitude of rodents were emerging from the ruins and debris and disappearing into the holes and burrows along the city walls.

Arval scowled. The filthy things would no doubt find their way into all manner of places they should not be. Thus he was caught by surprise when he looked forward again and noticed there was a red-headed young woman standing outside and before the gate. She wore a formal gown of some archaic style, and she appeared to be without baggage or mount. Flanking her to either side, were two armed and armored men—two very large men. How they had gotten past the Picts he had no idea, but they were clearly Tetherans and would have to be brought inside. The law of the land, almost since before there even were Tetherans in the land, was that no Tetherans were ever enemies when Picts were at hand. It was beyond question that it could be otherwise. Further, the men, at least, would be two more defenders against the menace that whelmed beyond the west gate.

"Look alive," he called down to the squad inside the wall. "Three to enter by the postern gate. Best get them in before the Picts discover they are out there."

Arval turned back to see a dozen more rats scurry into a low place under some stones near the wall. How many rats were out there? What had they all been living on? And just what had been going on with all those otters?

Chapter XXXIV

A Trip to the War Room

The postern gate was a small door set in the wall that opened from the side of a tower adjacent to the gate and perpendicular to it. As soon as several soldiers had used it to rush them in, Cymri took the measure of the men that met them inside. They all appeared to be typical guardsmen, young warriors in somewhat inferior armor, with none of them being of high birth or privileged station.

"I am Princess Cymri ap Taliesin of Ceredigion," she told the one who appeared to be most senior. "I must speak with my friend and companion, Prince Llew of Gwent, at once."

The poor guardsman was so flustered at this that it never occurred to him she had not introduced her personal guards. And after all, why would she? She was not merely a princess; if she was who she said she was then she was a personage of considerable renown. Further, her heroic exploits were nearly as well-known as those of the prince of Gwent himself.

"Y-yes, my lady, at once." Noncompliance was never even an option, so far as he was concerned. Not only was her station incredibly far above his own, the stories, while perhaps not dwelling on it, all seemed to agree that she had a considerable temper, when she chose to exercise it. Although he might personally have some doubts as to whether she actually had, just a few months earlier, turned the queen of the Fae into a bird, he still suspected there had to be some basis to the tale, and he was not the least inclined to find out what it was, most especially not the hard way.

The guards he dispatched for escorts led them swiftly down the narrow streets, despite already being crowded with refugees. Small children attempted to play between entire families and their livestock, all camped in the narrow streets. The odor went beyond intense; feeling almost as if it were a soft wall they had to push their way through by dint of strength alone.

A little girl, perhaps three or four years old, Lleu was not a good judge of such things, was kneeling at the side of a filthy puddle, beating it absently with a stick, heedless of what splashed on to the woebegone sack she was wearing as clothing. His heart ached at the sight and he wondered how he could ever have thought his own childhood, as a stable boy, a difficult one.

Walking behind Cymri, trying to project the image of a guard scanning constantly for threats to his charge, Lleu regarded the packed, miserable masses with considerable angst. This was the low part of the city between the two hills. It was likely every man, woman, and child here would be killed if the Picts were not stopped. As of the moment, he still had no idea how he would manage that feat.

They then ascended a broad cobblestoned ramp to the top of the larger hill and passed through another great gate, still standing open. It was crowded up here, too. Lleu was vaguely aware of a constant throb of conversation as the people took note of Cymri's passage and speculated on what her presence might portend. With his superior hearing he could focus on individual exchanges, and he did so repeatedly, trying to take the gauge of their mood. What they said was all nonsense, of course, but at least it sounded hopeful. At last, their escort brought the three of them to a solid looking keep, and they all passed through its gates to enter a large building inside.

A sudden thought came to Lleu. His antlered helm was bagged, but that would not be enough. He pulled his cloak up and around his armor and then said quietly to Slow Tomos, "Quickly, your helm, I need it. Llewellyn must not attack me on first sight, as she did at Caerleon."

The guards must have thought it odd that he would don a helmet before meeting with royalty, but the princess appeared unperturbed and so they said nothing as he put it on.

Lleu had expected they were being taken to a throne room or some other reception area. Instead they abruptly found themselves in a war room. Dominating the great hall's center was a vast sand table; the centerpiece of which was a highly detailed model of the town, nestled in the midst of the surrounding countryside. Armies of carved wooden men lined the walls of the town and carpeted the plain before it.

The room itself was crowded with warriors in far finer armor than that worn by the guards. *The nobility of Ergyng are here in force*, Lleu thought to himself. He looked about for Llewellyn but did not see her immediately. Then a figure at the sand table, standing between two finely equipped older men, turned to face them. Despite expecting this, Lleu was still caught in surprise. It was like gazing into a looking glass from a month ago, minus his moustache, of course.

It had been a very long time since he had last seen her so disguised. Once they met King Pendaran at Caer Enion, over two years earlier, there had been no reason to continue the deception. He had quite forgotten just how close the resemblance was. Had been, he corrected himself, for he no longer looked like that, and likely never would again.

The disguised Princess had eyes only for Cymri. "Cymri? How are you here? Why did you come? Wait—hold on that—did you bring—"

She had clearly been going to say 'Llew' and then realized that might be awkward, given her disguise. "Ah. do you at least know where you-know-who is?"

"Why, Prince Llew," Cymri exclaimed, "we can swap gossip at length later. For now, will you not introduce me to our hosts?"

Llewellyn appeared a bit surprised at this, but said, "Aye, certainly. This is scarcely a courtly introduction but these are not normal times. To my left is King Peibio ap Erg and to my right is King Nynnio ap Erg, joint rulers of all Ergyng. Your majesties, I bid you greet Princess Cymri ap Taliesin."

Both kings inclined their heads ever so slightly.

"So, Princess Cymri, you have come to us at a most inopportune time," said King Peibio. "Yet I find you quite as radiant as all the tales claim. Were we not under siege I would guest you at my castle and the feasts would last a week."

"Ha," exclaimed King Nynnio, "a week indeed! How very miserly of you, dear brother. For such a beauty, and a much lauded heroine as well, my feasts on her behalf would last a full month."

"Ha yourself," retorted King Peibio. "You are very free with your imaginary feasts, even while it is clear that every day of the year would scarcely be too much whilst such a guest remained, yet she might grow tired of that." To Cymri, "I was only thinking of your own preferences in this matter, dear lady."

"Ah," said Cymri, "think nothing of it. Having just completed a most arduous journey I desire nothing more at present but a bit of rest and perhaps a chance to freshen myself. Sadly, all of my personal effects were lost in getting here. Perhaps the Picts will take some joy in them, as I no longer can."

Neither king spoke up. Llewelyn glanced from one to the other and made a face. "Until our gracious hosts can find you some rooms appropriate to your station, please take my own. I can also offer you some things you will find helpful in replacing what you have lost. I will deliver them personally when I check to see if the accommodations are sufficiently pleasing to you. Would that suffice, my lady?"

Cymri inclined her head in partial agreement, but then locked eyes with Llewellyn. "Truly, I realize you are very busy here, but sooner would be better."

Llewellyn cleared her throat before speaking in a husky voice. "By your leave, your lieges, it seems another duty calls. Perhaps while I am gone the two of you can work out this impasse we have arrived at, and possibly you would be so good as to determine just which of you will supply the archers we need for the south central tower?"

Do I really sound like that, Lleu wondered, and then, *did I really sound like that?*

Striding forward, the impostor Prince Llew offered an armored forearm to Cymri. Closing ranks, Lleu and Slow Tomos followed them out.

Llewellyn took them outside and across another courtyard, then through a door and up a short flight of stone steps to another door, this one guarded by a pair of sentries. Opening it, she spoke in a loud voice, "Welcome, Princess Cymri, it may not be quite what you are used to but it should serve. I can find other accommodations for I surely do not need so much space. Please, come in."

"Why thank you, Prince Llew," Cymri gushed in return. "Of course, my guards, Tomos and, um, the new one, would scarcely be earning their overgenerous wages did I not let them inspect it for my safety."

Something about this caused Llewellyn to look sharply at the two men accompanying Cymri. Fortunately, the guards in the hall were not looking directly at her face when she suddenly appeared to recognize Slow Tomos. Lleu was impressed by this for, although the steward was not wearing a helm and had some distinctive features she had heard described, her only other clue had been the name Cymri had dropped; the two of them had never actually met before. It was only a momentary lapse. Llewellyn immediately transformed her face back into a mask. "By all means, princess, fighting men should always be allowed to earn their keep."

As soon as they were all inside, Llewellyn quickly closed the door behind them, then turned to Cymri and said, "I have no idea what you are doing here, and with the steward of Caer Mallcoedwig, no less! Logic would dictate this other fellow must be a certain missing person, yet he is too tall. You can remove the helmet now, in any case."

"No!" said Cymri. "He most certainly cannot! Not until we have a short chat. You must also pledge to neither draw blade nor raise the alarm when he does."

"What is this? I must pledge not to defend myself, in my own rooms no less, in order to see what lies under that helm? You would need to assure me that this is someone I know and trust before I should agree to that."

"Llewellyn," Cymri said grimly, "I would hope that you know me well enough to trust me when I say that you absolutely need to do this."

"Ah, well," Llewellyn relented. "Now you shame me. Of course I trust you, of all people, but why—oh very well, I agree with your terms. Now is this Llew or not?"

"It is, and it is not," Cymri temporized.

"What—"

"It is the Llew you knew, but he has been the subject of a powerful enchantment. He no longer appears as he once did and, most likely, never will again."

Llewellyn visibly blanched, then steeled herself. "Very well, let us assess the damage then, shall we?" To Lleu: "Remove your helm."

At a short nod from Cymri, Llew cautiously raised his hands to the helm and lifted it off. The change in Llewellyn came with no lead time whatsoever. Her expression instantly flicked from one of trepidation to pure fury and she leaped full onto him, bearing him backwards to the floor. Lleu escaped immediate damage to the back of his head, as its hard stones were covered by a woolen rug, but pushing his torque up high against his chin, she seized him by the throat with both hands.

Fortunately, it was the work of a moment for Cymri to seize one arm and Slow Tomos the other. Between them they were able to break her grip and drag her off. "Llewellyn, you promised me!" Cymri barked in her ear.

Llewellyn, seeing that she was not going to get free to continue her attack, ceased the worst of her thrashing and glared at Cymri. "I said I would not draw blade. For this I do not need it!"

"Who do you think he is?" Tomos asked.

"He is—" Llewellyn paused to cast a hard look on Lleu again.

For his own part, Lleu was massaging his throat with one hand while the other was up, open palm to her as he tried to simultaneously give her a reassuring smile that probably only succeeded in making him look nervous. Reassurance was not an easy emotion to project at the moment.

"I am suddenly less sure," Llewellyn temporized. "Perhaps I do not know. His behavior is—never mind, why would you think he is Llew?"

"I think he is Llew because he is Llew. I have traveled with him for some time now. No impostor could fool me. Nor Gower, for that matter, and you know his loyalty. He escaped and traveled across Tethera until he found his one true master.

He helped carry us here, but he could not enter via the way we came, so he is waiting far out in the country, safely beyond the Picts."

"You can ask me anything," Lleu offered, rising again to his feet. "Do you recall that I once told you I wanted to learn to write because it seemed more useful than learning to read?"

Llewellyn snorted. "Ask you anything? Fine, since you are wearing the Torc of Tethera, I ask you to become a wren."

"Fair enough," he replied. And he was a wren. He made three passes about the room and then returned to the form of a man.

Llewellyn took a deep breath and slowly let it out before speaking. "And still wearing your armor, unlike most other shape-shifters would be. Very well, welcome back, dear brother. This is somewhat frustrating in that I find I am not even permitted to be mad at you, since I helped drive you away myself. I suppose I should have suspected something like this when you escaped at Caerleon by outriding me. I do not know of anyone else that could do that. Indeed, you were not even riding Gower at the time."

Collapsing into a comfortable looking chair near the fire place, she asked, "I take it this may be a rather involved story?"

"Just a bit," agreed Lleu.

"Then, pray, bide a moment. Afaggdu should be done with Caradog's lessons by now. Allow me to summon them so we only have to do this once."

Chapter XXXV

Too Many Kings

Afaggdu's first words on seeing Cymri were less than happy. "Ah, lass, you should not have come. This kingdom is troubled, its rulers are mad, and this is no place for my brother's only daughter. Even should we survive this, he will probably kill us both for imperiling you here."

Cymri's eyes flashed as she retorted, "You may think of him as my father and your brother, but he is also Taliesin, chief of all bards, and I am, by his own admission, a bard. That would be sufficient reason alone for why my travels are, and will remain, my own affair, regardless of where they take me."

"Heh, lass, he may understand that as a bard, but as a father he is likely to box my ears for this, all the same."

"You kept it up until the last," she marveled, "even now you still try. Sadly, the game is up, 'uncle.' You have been a wonderful uncle to me, and Taliesin a wonderful, hmm, tutor. What this warrior," she gestured at Lleu, "is about to say will complicate and change that, and perhaps even make it more real than you thought, but I do hope it will not alter our feelings for one other. I will tell you in advance that, for my part, it will not."

A troubled look came across Afaggdu's fearsome features. "Ah, and I do not like where this is heading. Already it sounds to be uglier than I am." To Lleu: "Proceed, then."

The story took some telling. When Lleu recounted the part about discussing Cymri with Caradog and Helgar in the ale cellar, Caradog came to realize who was telling it, even before Lleu told them. They had to take a break to settle him down before they could continue.

"Look at us," marveled Caradog, "all of us in one place at the same time. Well, all except for Helgar that is. Ooh, I will play his part, too. See how this sounds." He cleared his throat. "So, Llew, about these cursed Picts, vot are we going to be a doing, eh? Ask you I do."

Llewellyn winced at the poor imitation of a Northman's accent. "I think you would be better off voicing Gower."

"But Gower hardly says anything," replied Caradog, looking somewhat perplexed. "And no one but Llew has even heard him do that."

"I rather think that is the point," observed Cymri. "Shall we let Lleu continue his tale?"

"Lleu?" Caradog asked.

Cymri sighed and said, "Please hold such questions until the end."

It was not much further from there before he got to the part where Moriganna revealed herself as having been Cymri in disguise the entire time they had known her. This caused another break in the narrative while Llewellyn cried a bit, and Caradog tried manfully not to. Afaggdu betrayed no surprise at all, only worry mixed with something else. Ah, it was guilt, Lleu realized. After all, the man must have been secretly in league with Moriganna since before they had first met.

Before they could let Lleu go on, Llewellyn and Caradog first repositioned themselves to sit considerably further away from Cymri, apparently having deciding that, since there had been no Cymri, this must be Moriganna, once more in disguise.

At least, thought Lleu, *they are not actively trying to flee the room.* However, despite this, they were frequently casting openly suspicious, almost hostile, glances in her direction. He decided to take it as a positive sign that they were, at least, believing his story, and so saw no need to immediately attempt to straighten them out on that point.

When Lleu mentioned his altercation with Addfwyn in his rooms. Caradog actually snapped his fingers. "Addfwyn! It is not just Helgar and Gower. We are missing Addfwyn. He can go about being unobserved and overlooked, even when he is not present. How remarkable!"

Lleu forbore commenting on the inherent contradictions in that remark and continued.

When he recounted his adventure with Boudicca he took pleasure in noting that even the unflappable Afaggdu sat straight up and seemed to absorb every word, sometimes pausing him to ask for specifics.

Toward the middle of it, Llewellyn called for food and, when it arrived, insisted the servers leave it and depart. This they were slow to do until Afaggdu stood up to show them to the door. At that point they found they almost could not leave quickly enough. Given that they did not know him well enough to realize he was the greatest warrior in the land, it seemed Afaggdu's appearance alone was responsible for their alacrity. By his own admission, he was also the ugliest man in the land. Indeed, when first they met, Lleu had initially mistaken him for some variety of ogre.

Despite his cheerful self-deprecation, Afaggdu also had an extremely fine mind that lent itself most especially to matters of tactics and strategy. It was therefore no surprise that, after hearing Lleu's story, it was he that spoke first. Caradog and

Llewellyn were still stunned into silence, while they tried to make sense of what they had just heard.

"So, lad, you have come into your own and it is a bit more involved that any of us would have expected. So and so, are you of a mind what you must do next?"

Lleu gave it a moment's thought. Was this a trick question? "I thought I might see about sending many thousands of Picts packing for their wilderness. What say you to that?"

That elicited a short chuckle from the hideous warrior. "Ah, and that is good. I was afraid in all these high level machinations you might have lost sight of the—hmm—more immediate concerns, as it were."

"Small chance of that. I am always surrounded by people that seem to believe they know what I should do next, and none of them seem terribly reserved about sharing those beliefs with me."

"I think," said Llewellyn, "you will find that getting rid of the Picts may be more difficult than you might expect—and not for the reasons you might think."

Afaggdu clucked ruefully. "Aye, and she probably has the right of it. The greatest obstacle to breaking this siege has two names, King Peibio and King Nynnio."

"What? How can that be? They are the rulers of this kingdom, why would they wish to prevent us from its rescue?"

Caradog piped up, "Oh that is an easy one, Llew, or rather, Lleu, as I guess I should call you now. They might well want their kingdom preserved, but their main goal in life is preserving their own hides, and they judge they can do that best by staying well inside the town's walls."

"Indeed," added Llewellyn, "and the next dearest goal of each is to undercut the other. So if either one of them could, while ensuring his complete safety, remove his brother from power, why then, after that he might very well be interested in breaking the siege—provided he could still remain completely shielded from harm."

Words failed Lleu. "That is—well it is foolish. Those goals are all in contradiction to each other."

"And there you have the crux of the problem," admitted Caradog. "Somehow the siege must be broken for them, instead of with them."

"Yes, your highness," said Afaggdu, "and just how would you go about it?"

Caradog looked surprised. "Me? You are asking me?"

"Why should he not ask you?" Lleu inquired. "I know he has had you playing his little games of war in your copious free time. As a study in strategy, how would you go about this if we cannot rely on the brother kings for assistance?"

"Oh." Caradog appeared to consider the matter. "I guess I would find the enemy's greatest weakness and seek to exploit it. Given that any part of that Pictish horde is much like any other, that would make our target those siege engines the builders from Annwyn are making for them. They would burn if we could but get close enough."

Afaggdu nodded understandingly. "And what would you gain by so doing?"

"Well," said Caradog, tapping the side of his leg absently, lost in thought as he stared at the ceiling, "they would no longer be completely assured the ability to overrun the lower, central part of the town. In point of fact, even in their numbers, I am not certain they could do it with ladders and grapnels alone, and I doubt they have the patience or the mindset to build a ramp.

"We could buy even more time by shortening their stay. When they run out of food they will have to leave. Along with the siege engines, there are also many wagons that they depend on to bring the provisions they need to sustain the siege. We could burn them along with the siege engines."

"What of Ergyng itself?" Afaggdu pressed.

"Oh, I see. It really only buys us time. The Picts will still despoil everything outside the walls of Erg, including the crops ready for harvest throughout the kingdom. All that survived would be what was in the town and perhaps in any other strongholds that survive, but with starvation and disease, that might not be so many. Certainly the kingdom of Ergyng would be of dubious value to anyone intent on opposing Lord Arawen of Annwyn—possibly it would even be a handicap."

Lleu stood and stretched, stiff from hours of sitting. "I know what Helgar would counsel." Looking about he saw he had everyone's full attention. "He would call out Goll One-eye and challenge him to single combat. Since Helgar is not here I suspect I could get the villain sufficiently incensed to come give me a try. I blinded him and stole his torc. I suspect he can hardly refuse and still expect any respect from his followers.

"Without Goll to bind them, their cohesion will be destroyed as there will be no one that can quickly step into his place, and a good many of them, if not all, will break off and return to their wilderness. If any part of them remains—well, we do have two armies here."

A shake of Afaggdu's head drew Lleu's notice. "Really?" said Lleu, surprised. "I thought you would be on board with this from the start. You do not doubt I can take him, do you?"

The ancient warrior snorted before he said, "Oh, in a fair fight, my coin would be on you, certainly. Why to hear you tell it, you single-handedly slew a giant on the way here. But do not underestimate the Pict's war chieftain. He is not their chief because of his fine table manners. The problem is getting him to agree to fight you one-on-one. For a savage, he is bound to be fairly canny, and I know how Picts like to go about things like revenge. He will want to destroy as much as he can before facing you. He will reckon you might be dispirited by your losses, not a bad thing from his point of view, and it would better demonstrate to his fellows the finality of his victory over you as he crushes not just you, but everything, everything within reach, that you would seek to protect. That will be of overwhelming importance to him."

Lleu made a face. "You think he could refuse a direct challenge? In front of the entire horde?"

"I think the advisors from Annwyn, in some way or another, would give him a face-saving pretext for doing so. Possibly they could threaten to withhold their support if he accepts the challenge, or perhaps they will spread lies about us planning the contest as an opportunity for some treachery. The specifics do not matter. The Picts will not expect their allies from Annwyn to adhere to their own standards of honor. The Lord of Death's minions being opposed to letting the warchief hazard the entire invasion on the outcome of a single risky fight is something they will understand, even as they despise it. The bottom-line, lad, is that, whatever justification is given, he will not fight you until he has already defeated us."

"So," Lleu mused, "it comes back to Caradog's initial thought; we destroy the siege engines to buy time for the town, we destroy the advisors so Goll will have fewer options, and we destroy enough of the wagons that are here so they can no longer supply themselves without staying on the move."

Rising to her feet and stretching, Llewellyn said, "I'll give the orders to prepare for a sortie then, regardless of what Peibio and Nynnio have to say about it. In any case, it will have to be done entirely with our own warriors because those two will not contribute."

"Is it truly so bad that neither will make the effort to save their own kingdom?" asked Lleu.

"Oh, one of them may be eager to send forces to help us— although he would not come himself—but the other will oppose him in this with the result that nothing will happen." She shrugged, "Or it could happen in the reverse order. Either way, nothing gets done and we are on our own. Better that than face this coming 'harvest' of Lord Arawen's with one less kingdom to our strength."

Before leaving, Llewellyn stopped at Cymri, peered at her face from inches away, and said, "I do not know what to make of you, but even if you are not our Cymri, I am so glad you are here. You soften what would have been a very hard blow."

Although well proportioned, Llewellyn was a very large woman. She could never have passed herself off as the old Llew were she not. It occurred to Lleu then, that with the giant Bran as her father's grandfather, it was hardly surprising that she, and the real Llew as well, had he survived, were so very large.

Impulsively, Llewellyn gathered the smaller woman into a great bear hug, nearly lifting her entirely from her feet, then setting her back down and releasing her, saying only: "You and I have much to discuss, when there is time." She left the room quickly, her Llew persona firmly back in place, while Cymri watched her go with a peculiar half smile.

"I have so few memories of her," Cymri remarked, sounding somewhat wistful. "Although she was younger at the time, she spent nearly as many years with Moriganna's Cymri as you did Lleu, but the goddess has passed me few of them. Perhaps because they do not also include you. She looked up sharply at the others. "You need not tell Llewellyn I said that. I want to become her Cymri, too, and I shall, time permitting."

Something had been troubling Lleu and he began to realize what it was. He turned to Afaggdu. "You were far less surprised by my story than all the rest, save possibly Slow Tomos. Indeed, only the parts where I explored the past, and maybe some of the other fights, seemed to hold your interest," he accused.

"Eh, what are you saying lad—your Highness. Just spit it right out."

"You knew! You were in cahoots with Moriganna the entire time. You had to be."

His former mentor regarded him soberly. "I will not ask for forgiveness, I have long known this day would come, if not when, and all I did I still believe necessary. You will either forgive me or not but I expect that you will."

"Tell me what else you have deceived me on, and I might," Lleu responded.

Afaggdu spread his hands, palms up. "Well, and of course, you must already know I have never killed any of her Pwacca, despite that song and dance I gave you at Caerleon. Remember? When I told you what supposedly happened after the ambush that separated us? Likewise, who do you think could have persuaded Taliesin that a nine year old lassie that showed up at Caerleon while he was off on one of his treks was actually an accidental daughter of his? Nay, I have a fair amount to answer to my brother for. Never mind that Moriganna turned him into a tree for several years when he got too close, and I allowed it. All of that is between the two of us, though, and he will know it all in the end. Be not concerned on that account."

Lleu was fascinated in what felt like a horrible sort of way. "Will he not hate you forever for your part in this this?"

Afaggdu laughed. "Ah lad, we are brothers, and have been for ages. If we let the little things get our goat we would have set ourselves against one another long ago. Why, I recall the time he—never mind. Just take it from me; no, he will not hate me."

Chapter XXXVI

Erg Strikes Back

It was not long before Lleu discovered that the only horses within Erg were those brought there by the warriors of Gwent. There were four hundred of them, all told, and Lleu was bitterly unhappy with this. "How is it," he exclaimed to Slow Tomos and Afaggdu, "that the erstwhile kings of this place brought in no mounts for their warriors?"

Afaggdu was phlegmatic. "I doubt very much that they would consider conducting a sortie into that on foot." As they were standing on the ramparts over the western gate, he was able to gesture directly at the mass of Pict encampments. They covered the land before the town all the way to distant hills where the tree line started. "The absence of horses would therefore seem to indicate that both Peibio and Nynnio, whatever their disagreements with each other, had no intention of sortieing at all. It certainly spares them from having to make excuses for not leading the charge themselves."

"It does not bode well for the situation, does it?" asked Slow Tomos. "Bad enough to have two kings that are at odds with one another, that both are terrible cowards as well is just one disaster heaped on top of another."

"You could have your friends supply us with a hundred additional mounts," suggested Afaggdu.

Before his steward could reply, Lleu said, "No. The Pwacca can be especially useful in many ways, but that just makes them too valuable to risk in many of those ways. When I commit them it must be as leverage to get a result far larger than what an incremental increase in numbers would gain me." He glanced at Afaggdu and raised one eyebrow. "Did I get that right, my trainer?"

"Aye, you learned well," admitted Afaggdu. "You always were an exceptional student. Of course, you had an exceptional instructor as well."

Lleu smiled at that. "So I did."

Turning to Slow Tomos, Lleu asked, "And what of our friends? Are they learning anything of value?"

"Perhaps a bit, here and there, your Highness. It is surprising what a hundred clever rats within the walls can learn, when given free rein to do so. I can tell you that this rivalry between Peibio and Nynnio is no act. They really do hate and fear each other even more than they hate and fear the Picts. It is amazing their uneasy truce has lasted long enough for them to live as long as they have, or that their kingdom has survived it."

"It will not survive it much longer, at this rate," muttered Lleu. "Anything else?"

"Nynnio was married, but it looks as though Peibio may have had his queen poisoned not long after she announced she was with child. Peibio, on the other hand, has never married but has three mistresses and each of them has a son. None of those boys are his but he has been led to believe they are. For this reason, he is hiding them from Nynnio, who would likely poison them in retaliation, and to prevent Peibio's line from inheriting.

"In other news, they have both been robbing the common treasury blind and have hidden away considerable fortunes, no doubt each with the intent of purchasing the other's downfall. We believe we have found all the secret locations where they have hidden their stolen funds. In the process we actually found quite a few secret rooms and passages. There is even one tunnel that extends entirely under the river and emerges from a hidden door on the other side. It has not been used in a long time but there is a fresh supply of torches at this end that makes us believe it is intended as a last ditch escape route. That tunnel also embodies some cunning features where it passes under the island that would allow it to be collapsed by someone at either end. That it could be used from this end indicates they are concerned by the possibility of enemies finding the tunnel and seeking to use to get into the city. That using it at the other end would, in addition to collapsing the tunnel, also collapse the bridge supports on the island can only mean someone intends it as a last resort retreat route, and thus seeks to forestall any possible chance of immediate pursuit—"

Slow Tomos stopped as he realized Afaggdu was staring at him, aghast. "Yes, my lord, did you discern something untoward in what I am saying?"

"Only that privacy is dead and buried and the two of you are responsible for that."

"Pish-tosh," replied Slow Tomos. "It behooves us to know as much as we can about the situation we are in, both within and without. Our own security demands it."

"Oh, aye, I will let it pass for now but—" he turned to Lleu. "Do not you forget, this is no way to go about things once the current crisis is over. Dealing with those walking dunghills, Peibio and Nynnio, may justify, and even require, this, but many of the folk who are being observed have done nothing to us and intend nothing against us. Spying on them in this manner is without honor."

Afaggdu immediately raised his open hands in mock surrender before there could be any reply. "I know! I know I frequently downplay honor when supporting it would be stupid, but this is not one of those cases."

Nodding once in understanding, Lleu turned back to Slow Tomos, "Have some of the fellows keep an eye on those hidden troves. If anyone starts making sudden withdrawals, I will want to know who it is and as soon as possible. As for the raid, Llewellyn has named me, Cymri, and Afaggdu to lead this with her, each of us commanding one hundred warriors. Tomos, it will fall to you to keep an eye on things here while we are gone."

Slow Tomos nodded in the affirmative. "I will do my best, Lleu."

To both of them, Lleu said: "Let us see now how Llewellyn is doing and if she saved some horses for us."

* * *

The narrow streets leading to the town's massive front gate had been cleared of refugees to make room for mounted warriors, crowded in even more tightly than the people had been. Horses stamped their feet and rolled their eyes while their riders, nearly all men of Gwent, strove to retain control of the situation. They also had to be constantly enjoined to do it quietly. Lleu wanted no forewarning of their attack until the gate opened.

He was near the front, not far from the gate, when a rider who was not a man of Gwent edged her steed close enough so they could talk somewhat privately.

"I do not like this," Llewelyn said, not for the first time that day. "With you here, I feel strange pretending to be you. You should be leading this attack, not just serving as one of my captains."

"It is nice to know that you have reconciled yourself to my current appearance," replied Lleu, "but others would not be so sanguine. The time will come when we must break it to them, and I am anything but certain when that will be, but I know it is not now."

Lleu knew, as she did, that she did not need to lead the attack herself. As Prince Llew of Gwent, she had many sturdy champions to carry the attack for her, yet she had refused to entertain the idea.

"No doubt you are correct, dear brother, but I do wish you at least had Gower to carry you into this."

"I am pleased you can still call me brother, now that we both know there is no blood tie between us."

"There may be no blood tie, Lleu, but there are many ties. Did my father not tell you that, if you ever discovered you were not his son by birth, you could consider yourself adopted? You will always be my brother in my heart."

"Thank you, dear sister," Lleu winced inwardly as he heard his own words. They might sound sarcastic, but he had not intended them so. Fortunately, Llewellyn understood him precisely.

There was a disturbance in the massed riders behind them, and King Peibio, accompanied by four armed men, pushed his way through until he was within speaking range of Llewellyn.

"Here, here, here," he cried, "who authorized this? We had agreed that no attack was to be made. It threatens the safety of Erg and so cannot be contemplated."

"We agreed on nothing," Llewellyn shot back. "You and King Nynnio decided you could not support this. I maintained it was an imperative. Unless those siege engines are destroyed, as well as the capacity to make more, the very center of this town is doomed."

"Perhaps it is doomed," said King Peibio, emerging from between the riders behind his brother. "But we are not so convinced. In either case it is our decision that we not risk the destruction of us all by the opening of that gate."

"We have been through this," Llewellyn retorted, eyes blazing. "If we do not destroy the siege engines, then what is left of us will be trapped on these two hilltops while they raze the rest of the kingdom."

"Be that as it may, we have stores aplenty and the savages must eventually depart. Our survival is be assured and we can put the rest to rights in good time," insisted Peibio. For once, his brother king did not speak up to disagree with him.

Appalled by their cowardice and their callous disregard for their subjects, Lleu started to snap a reply before remembering that his true identity, and therefore his right to speak to them, was still hidden. It did not matter. Llewellyn was more than ready to reply.

"In good time? With what would you rebuild your kingdom? Save for those that survive on your hilltops here, and a in a few other strongholds, your people would be dead or fled. Their farms and crofts burnt along with their homes and villages. You would never live to be so old as to see this kingdom recovered from that—especially since you would then be helpless at Lord Arawen's eventual coming. Oh, he might save you for last because you would be so little threat, but that buys you next to nothing in time."

"Is that your experienced take on the situation?" King Nynnio demanded. "Because my brother and I believe—"

"A pox on what you the two of you believe! Show a little backbone and you might yet have a chance."

"We—what?" sputtered King Peibio. "You trumped up little prince! We will speak with your father about this insolence, you may be sure. In the meantime, that gate is to remain closed."

The Gwentish subaltern in the doorway to the gate room called down, "Your highness, it is time. The compound's gates are now wide open while they bring in more logs. They cannot close them before you could arrive."

"My apologies, your highnesses," replied Llewellyn, "if their gate is open, then so must ours be. I would suggest you may wish to remove yourself from where you stand else four hundred riders are likely to trample right over you. Your survival would not be so assured were that to occur." She signaled the subaltern in the gate house. Ignoring the king's protestations, he ducked inside and, a moment later, just before the gates began to move, they could all hear the windlass as it began to turn, pulling open the vast doors.

There was no moat or bridge before this gate. Nynnio and Peibio found themselves staring directly out at the vast Pictish horde, only a few hundred paces away. The royal brothers were unmoving, frozen in place by pure terror mingled with disbelief.

"And," added Llewellyn, "you will discuss my insolence directly with me when we return." She drew her sword and shouted a wordless cry as she kicked her horse into a gallop out of the gate, closely followed by nearly four hundred warriors of Gwent.

Nynnio and Peibio did move then, in a most undignified manner, and only just in time.

Out of the gate, Lleu brought his column even with Llewellyn while Cymri and Afaggdu did the same. These were well-trained warriors, Gwent's finest. Less experienced men would have had to halt outside the gates to create the formation in which they would attack. As it was, they did it at a gallop, the lead elements slowing only a bit to let the rest catch up and spread out. This was also Lleu's first chance to try this horse, a somewhat spirited little stallion, at speed. It was not a bad mount, he decided, but it was definitely not Gower.

At a little under four hundred paces from the gate they hit the first Pict camp. With less than thirty seconds to prepare, this went very badly for the Picts, many of which did not even have time to snatch up their weapons. The Picts had no horses, no armor, and no formation or discipline of any sort. They even disdained the use of bows other than for hunting game. They had no chance against the tidal wave of steel and thunder that rolled over them. The mounted riders never slowed down; slashing and stabbing, they just rode into and over the camp, emerging from the other side in mere seconds. Lleu could not even be certain how many men his own sword had struck when it was over.

Then they reached the next camp in mere seconds and did it all over again.

On the fourth camp, most of the Picts had time to at least grab up their spears and clubs. Lleu saw two men struck from their saddles, followed by a third when his horse was speared. Small consolation as it was, he was fairly sure none of the Picts responsible for those successes would live to brag about it to their descendants, or anyone else, for that matter.

And then they were at the enclave. The walls were of stout timber forming a spiked palisade and they were set behind a waist-deep trench which, itself, was set behind a rather rough but imposing spike wall. With the time and forces the raiders had to work with, the place would have been effectively impregnable. Fortunately, the gates were wide open while they were bringing in more logs for their construction. Llewellyn had made sure of this before she had even opened the town gates.

Leaving nothing but death in their wake, their numbers barely undiminished, the four hundred rode in. Men in the service of Annwyn—no one could say where Lord Arawen kept coming up with them for most were neither Tetheran, Pict, nor Northmen—scattered before them. There were a great many of them and it could have gone badly had they the organization and discipline to pick up even their own tools and fight back.

As it was, they fled between the many siege engines in all stages of construction, desperately seeking shelter from men who had no mercy in mind for them. For all these efforts, they fared little better than the Picts in their camps had. Among them, however, were other things.

Lleu recognized them at once. Man-like creatures, covered head to toe in black leather armor, they could only be the Cyhyraeth. It made sense. Who among the Lord of Death's minions would be the best advisors and builders? Those that had the kind of knowledge that was only gained over centuries, of course. He grimaced. As advisors and foremen for Lord Arawen, it kept them off the front lines as well, a very important thing for a creature that is trying to live forever. It would not save them today, Lleu decided. Today they were on the cutting edge of the front line, but it was the wrong side. The cutting edge was a very bad place to be when you were not the blade. He veered to the right and introduced one to the cutting edge of Fragaroc. Then cut down another that was overly concerned with escaping, and insufficiently concerned about selling its life dearly.

Something came over him then, an overwhelming feeling of sickness and corruption. What it felt like he could only describe as great choking clouds of black smoke and ash, pushing out of his interior, perhaps even out of his soul. For a moment he wanted nothing more than to die and be done with everything. He felt the same dread force pass through his horse, as it withered and died in midstride. Then, as suddenly as it had come over him, the feeling was gone, but his horse was still going down. Lleu was young and strong, and he was more at home on a horse's back than on his own feet. It was all that saved him for it never occurred to him to shape-shift. He freed his feet from the stirrups, jumped up to a standing position on his saddle, then leapt far to the right as his dead mount slammed into the ground, twisted sideways and rolled. Trapped in the saddle he would have been lucky to break only a few major bones.

As it was, he landed heavily on his feet, letting the momentum continue to carry him forward to hit the ground on his side, sword kept over his head, and rolled only once before coming back up on his feet, Fragaroc still in hand. His shield was lost. He took a couple of staggering steps forward and found himself no more than ten paces away from a figure in long black robes, its fingers still extended toward him. It was a familiar figure.

"Garl," he snarled. "How you came here I do not know, but you will not have long to regret the path that brought you." Raising Fragaroc, he charged forward.

The sorcerer, a look of disbelief and shock imprinted on his face, perhaps at the fact some unknown warrior had resisted his dark enchantment and now had the temerity to speak to him so boldly, turned and ran, clutching his robes up to keep them from tangling his legs. Lleu followed in close pursuit. Seeing this was not a race he could win, Garl dropped to the ground and wriggled under a wheeled siege tower until he was out of sight.

"Great sorcerer, eh?" jeered Lleu. "I am not certain how you got away from your proper fate, but I do not think you will much care for this one, either."

Llewellyn rode up to him then. "Lleu! We hold the compound and have closed the gates, but the Picts are massing. Soon they will be able to forestall any chance of us escaping and, not long after that, they will have the numbers to break in. We have not the time to set all of this afire."

"In this case, am not entirely without a backup plan," Lleu responded. "Shall we see how well it works?"

"I hope you know what you are doing."

"Surprisingly, this time I think I actually do." Lleu raised a whistle to his mouth and blew, long and hard. Yet, so far as

Llewellyn could tell, it had made no noise, then he dropped it back into a belt pouch. "I need a new mount, anyway."

"What happened to your last one?"

"Garl happened to it."

"Garl? He is here? How did he get away from the Firvulag?"

"He is a very sneaky fellow, but do not worry overmuch, dear sister, he is currently hiding under this very siege tower. He did not plan his line of retreat very well."

Llewellyn's eyes positively gleamed. "I should say not! We are going to burn this one first!" And then, as it belatedly occurred to her, "Lleu, what was that whistle for?"

A shadow passed over them, accompanied by a vast flapping noise. Llewellyn glanced up just in time to see the great scarlet dragon do a wingover and swoop in their direction. It was very clearly a dragon, although she had never seen one in real life. Dragons were just a variety of heraldic beast, they did not actually exist. Like everyone else that could see it, she froze in place, unable to move.

Everyone but one.

"Well, look at that," Lleu said, "it appears I have a mount to replace the one Garl took."

Chapter XXXVII

Departing from Plan

The dragon, easily the size of a large cottage, landed on its feet before them, its long sinewy neck swaying from side to side, and all of it covered in gleaming red scales.

Lleu strode towards it and called out, "Gower, up!"

At this, the great beast turned its left side to Lleu and tilted in that direction sufficiently so as to allow him to clamber up to its back.

That broke Llewellyn's freeze such that she was able to call out, "Lleu—what did you call this thing?"

As he looked for a good position to sit, forward and astride where the neck met the body seemed best, he replied, "Maybe I did not tell you, but Moriganna taught Gower a new trick; naturally it involves shape-shifting for he is, after all, a Pwacca of a sort."

"A dragon?" Llewellyn was not yet ready to accept this. "You said Pwacca could only take the shape of natural creatures," she accused. While they were speaking, a few dozen of the most daring warriors had recovered enough to come towards the great beast, couching spears as makeshift lances, but she waved them off.

"Have you ever seen a dragon?" Lleu countered. "They are all gone now, but apparently they were natural creatures of the world—although perhaps not this world. Who knew, eh?"

"A hundred such creatures would solve everything, Lleu. Everything! Why did Moriganna not teach them all the trick of changing into one as well?" Llewellyn's brow furrowed as a thought came to her. "Or did she?"

"Gower's special, dear sister. Indeed, I have always said that to any that would listen, and it turns out this is more true than even I expected."

Hearing his name, the great horned head on its serpentine neck curved back towards its rider. Massive jaws, hiding teeth as large as the afanc's had been, opened, and a long forked tongue flicked out towards him.

"Ack! Gower, no. No! Leave off you great galoot—leave off!" At this, the dragon reluctantly ceased its attempt to lick Lleu on the face.

Despite everything, Llewellyn briefly chuckled. It was a deep hearty chuckle where another woman might have giggled. From her earliest days, she had been taught never to giggle, the better to serve her disguise as her own dead brother.

"Lleu," Llewellyn's voice had lost none of its wonderment or its concern. "Special in what sense?"

"No one has told me outright, but I surmise he is something of a throwback in his bloodline. That would account for his size and perhaps even his ability to take the form of an creature that no longer exists."

"And the fact he does not change into a man, or speak?"

"He does not speak much," Lleu corrected, "but yes. Enough of this, the men have cleared the compound of our enemies. Get everyone remounted and ready. Gower and I will scatter the Picts massing outside. When that happens, open the gates and return as we came. The Picts will not stay scattered long. On no account can anyone stay in here a moment longer."

He looked up and down the long rows of siege engines, towers, catapults, and whatever those tall things were that looked like a combination of the two. There were also the tents and temporary buildings, the log palisade, and the spike wall. A few small fires were spreading already. "Most especially because this whole place is nothing more than a great tinder box, and we are about to give it a tremendous spark."

"You are going to ride him while he flies? Lleu, no! you have not even a saddle. What if you fall?"

Lleu shrugged. "Then I have to change into something that can fly back aboard, I suppose."

"Oh, certainly, of course you would," said Llewellyn, coloring a bit.

"Go now," he urged.

She nodded and rode off towards the gate. Lleu continued to watch while she paused for a moment along the way. She pulled up her horn and blew a long resounding note on it. This had a galvanizing effect on the warriors of Gwent. Those that had dismounted now quickly regained their saddles. From all throughout the compound they began streaming in to fall in line behind the appropriate standard bearers.

Someone came dashing out of the large tent next to them, surprising him and Gower both. "Hold there, who is that?" Lleu barked.

The smallish figure turned, saw the dragon, and froze.

"Caradog!" exclaimed Lleu. "You are not supposed to be here."

His freeze broken, Caradog raised his eyes to Gower's back, only then spotting Lleu. Caradog unfroze much faster than most others had. "You realize, Lleu, that somehow, for you, this is less surprising than it would be for anyone else," he remarked.

"And you, Caradog, did not answer my question, I know for a fact that Afaggdu decided you were not quite ready to raid with us yet."

"Ah," started Caradog, "you are right in that he said that, but when you see what I have—"

"Enough, we will discuss it later, when there is time. We actually have several things to discuss and I have been putting some of them off for far too long. Now hurry, Llewellyn rallies the warriors and you must ride out immediately, or never."

Gower sensed his desire then and leaped aloft, great wings flapping harder and faster than things that size had any right doing. Getting some altitude—Lleu was no newcomer to flying— he could see the riders from Gwent formed up at the compound's gates. He could also see the hundreds of Picts that had already gathered outside, and thousands more were still coming. They could certainly see Gower, a great many of them were distracted by him, staring upwards, pointing and gesticulating after their initial freeze broke. It slowed their gathering only a little, unfortunately.

This had to be done right the first time, Lleu knew. For the initial surprise would abate, and not even a dragon was immune to everything. With the slightest pressure from his knees, Gower was prompted to dive toward the thickest mass of Picts before the gate. This in itself was too much for many of them. Most scattered, although many did not. Then Gower pulled out of the dive higher, and further aside from where they might have expected his swoop to take him. Sweeping across them only a dozen man-heights above, Gower aimed his head to the side and breathed fire. Dozens of Picts were set ablaze. Packed in amongst their already panicking brethren, the result was predictable. Chaos ruled.

It was at that moment that the compound's gates opened and nearly four hundred riders of Gwent came forth upon them. Lleu gave it only a moment's attention. In the absence of any semblance of united purpose amongst the besiegers, the raiders would have a relatively easy time of it in cutting their way back to the town. He and Gower had something else to take care of.

Gower banked and turned again and they came back at the compound, overflying the length and breadth of it while the fire just continued to pour forth from the dragon's gaping maw.

How, Lleu wondered, could a dragon pour forth such an unending conflagration yet still be a natural creature, rather than some monstrous member of the Fae? How could this not be magic?

Another pass after that satisfied even Lleu. In an attack on the town walls, the siege engines, especially the towers and battering rams, would have been covered with wet hides to protect them from burning, but they had none now. They burned as easily as the hundreds of wagons and supply tents did, many of which had been full of provisions to support the horde's vast numbers. Everything became one continuous bonfire. When it ended, the Picts would find they had nothing left from Annwyn save ashes. Lleu suspected that was all anyone could ever hope to ultimately receive from the Lord of Death. He tried for a moment to identify which siege tower Garl had been hiding under but, with all the flame and smoke, it was impossible to be sure, nor could it matter.

Now he and Gower climbed for altitude. Landing in the walled town was going to be interesting. Lleu grinned inwardly as he thought of the consternation they were likely to engender. To prevent any unfortunate misunderstandings, it would be wise to let Llewellyn proceed him with calming explanations. His amusement promptly vanished when he looked ahead to the town. The raiders had returned, but the gates were not opening, and the riders now appeared to be trapped between the town walls and tens of thousands of angry Picts. Gathering rapidly, they would soon be ready to rush.

Leaving Gower circling, Lleu slipped off his back and dived to the ground, first as an eagle, and then as a large black bird, intending to land on Llewellyn's shoulder to ask what was going on. Before he got that far, it dawned on him what a waste of time that would be. Instead he aimed himself for inside the walls so that he could go immediately to the windlass and open the gates. He winged over the walls and, before he even reached it, it became evident where the real problem lay. The gates had been barred and chained and all manner of beams and debris were blocking them from the inside. The windlass would be useless and, even as a dragon, Gower himself would be unable to rip it all aside in time to do any good. To manage so much in the time available, Peibio and Nynnio must have had crews ready to go to work almost the instant the gates had closed behind the departing raiders.

Lleu kicked himself mentally. Had he suspected the depths of the brother kings' cowardice and perfidy he could have had the Pwacca on guard to prevent this very thing. The men Llewellyn had stationed in the gate house were gone. Probably they had been overpowered and taken away when the kings' men started barring the gates.

Looking around, he suddenly realized there was no one at all in the area of the gate. What had possessed them to abandon the area? Did it matter? He had people trapped outside!

His eyes fell on a heavy door set into the wall beside the gate. It was the inner door for the postern gate. Lleu landed and took his own form, then ran down the short section of steps to the door. Unbolting and unbarring it, it swung open to reveal a short tunnel, only a few paces long, that turned a tight corner into another such door. The outer door was secured in similar fashion to the inner gate. Wrenching it open he was looking into a sea of riders. He could clearly hear the sounds of fighting behind them. Caradog and Llewellyn were both there near the door.

"Llew, we cannot fit the horses through there! Why are the gates still closed?" Llewellyn exclaimed, in her emotion forgetting to use both the false name they had agreed upon for him, as well as his real name that she had only just learned.

"It is sealed, and we will not get it open in time." He steeled himself for what he had to say next. "Dismount and get the men in. There is no hope for the horses."

Aghast, as were all the other warriors, Llewellyn stared at him open-mouthed for a moment, then his words seemed to register and the necessity behind them was evident.

"All of you, dismount, and get yourselves inside, leave the horses, we have no choice. Caradog, get yourself in first, I would have a head-count of all who enter after you." She defied her own orders then, and wheeled her horse away from the gate.

"Where are you going," demanded Lleu, though he was sure he knew.

"We have skirmishers against the outer edges already, I must direct a fighting retreat or too many of us will never make it inside."

Lleu strode forward. "Afaggdu and I can take charge of that, you need to remain here and get your warriors in. We want Caradog's count to be as high as possible and too many will be loath to leave their mounts without you here to steady them."

He did not wait for a response, but changed into a wren and flew up until he saw Afaggdu, fighting against the leading Picts, along with all those riders that were in direct contact with the enemy. Much of their advantage of being mounted was negated by the close press. A rider to the side of Afaggdu was struck from his saddle even as Lleu winged in. Seeing that, he instantly changed back into a man, and half landed, half fell, into the empty saddle of the fallen warrior's horse.

Fragaroc was out of its sheath in a moment and he brought it down with good effect, again and again, until, even pressed forward as they were by their own numbers, the nearest Picts fell back before the death that faced them. Afaggdu, only mere feet away was yelling something. Lleu made himself listen.

"It is bravely done lad, but none of us in the rear guard are going to make it, get yourself inside. Should you fall here with the rest of us then it is all for naught."

A sea of Picts was before them and the tide was coming in. He looked to their rear and saw hundreds of riderless horses. They would probably be roasting over Pict fires in a few hours he realized, with considerable bitterness. Then a shadow passed over him and with it came an idea.

"Nay," he screamed back, "I will stampede the riderless mounts. Take whatever men remain and follow them out, get clear of the Picts." Afaggdu was shaking his head in the negative but another thought had come to Lleu. "Yes, you must. Ride to the northeast and see if Helgar is bringing any Northman forces. They cannot come into this unprepared."

Now a black bird, Lleu flew up to the circling dragon and took his place astride it. After a few words of command, and a nudge from his knees, they swung about and glided down to where the mass of riderless beasts were pressed against the walls. At their point of closest approach, Lleu cried out, "Speak, Gower, speak!"

And Gower roared. The horses below, rolling their eyes in terror at a sound no horse had heard in ages and, with no place to go, they created one. Since they could not pass through stone walls, they pushed towards the Picts. Some of the Picts, all of whom were on foot, might have had a suspicion then, or perhaps not. It was not as if riderless horses could be especially dangerous to them.

Gower let loose a considerable puff of flame. It did not hit anything, but it did not have to. It was the straw that broke the equines calm. They no longer merely pushed against the Picts, they rose and fell, hooves flashing, and forced their way through and over the Picts.

To ensure the momentum would not become stalled, Lleu had Gower glide down across the enemy lines and, with a mighty whoosh, he again breathed flame, dousing a swath two hundred paces long in consuming heat. With the Picts attempting to scatter, the horses would be able to continue their trampling exodus.

Beneath him, Lleu felt Gower's body give a great shuddering lurch. He roared again, but it was a different roar. Lleu slid forward, frantically trying to see if he could find a problem—and there it was, his worst fear confirmed, a wooden haft stood out just above Gower's front right leg. There was blood aplenty as well, although the dragon's shiny blood-red scales served to hide a lot of it.

The town! Lleu knew they had to make it to the town. To set down out here would be death. There was no time to tell anyone they were coming. There was no time to do anything but land inside, if they could. Gower was trying, but he was no longer fully responsive to Lleu's signals. Still, he turned until he was on a direct line for the city gates. Lleu then waited until he was sure before yelling, "Gower, we are not going to clear the wall, and we must, we absolutely must. Can you give one big flap, Gower? Just one, that should do it, just one." Gower roared, weaker this time, Lleu thought, but he made no motion to rise and the walls were coming closer in a hurry.

"Gower, now! You must!" Lleu screamed.

The great beast shuddered, but nothing happened. Then he shuddered again and, finally, there was a single great flap of his wings. It was not much, but it was enough. They only barely cleared the wall, and then the courtyard was beneath them, moving up rapidly. It was a hard landing.

Chapter XXXVIII

A Father's Advice

Lleu stood on the wall above the gate. Before him was the vast encampment of Picts. Despite the many that had died that day, they still seemed as numerous as ever. He could feel his hate for the survivors, yet he was afraid of where it might take him. At that moment, if he could have waved his hand and struck them all dead, he was certain he would have done so. That knowledge made him not like himself very much, either.

Kings Nynnio and Peibio had each taken refuge on their respective hilltops. Doubtless, they would emerge in a few days with more demands for their safety, once they resigned themselves to the fact that he, and most of his warriors, had survived. For now they stayed out of his reach, and that was probably a good thing. Of course, they were not really out of his reach, At a word from him, the Pwacca, currently disguised as rats in their walls could emerge and strike them both down. The truth was that he could not do that. It was not consistent with his own self-image, the person he tried so hard to be. It also would have left doubts as to how the kings of Ergyng had come to their ends, and that would cast suspicion on him. Such would be the death knell of all plans to rebuild the Great Kingdom of Tethera and, because of that, the death knell of all men. Things would be exactly as Moriganna had once told him they might. Grass would grow in the roads and all the land would be a single howling wilderness, an unmarked grave for the dreams of Man, with all the great castles fallen.

He sometimes had nightmares in which he wandered through a land like that, himself a powerless revenant, unable to change anything, but forced to observe it all, forever.

Behind him, someone cleared their throat. Lleu knew it was Slow Tomos. He had heard his steward coming for nearly a minute before he actually arrived.

"Yes?" he asked flatly.

"Your Highness, I believe Gower will live, he was able to retain his form as that of a dragon until we could remove it. As a horse it would have surely killed him. He is a horse again now, and resting, although I would not say comfortably."

"I thank you, Tomos, surely, were it not for you and Cymri, he would have died. I used him foolishly out there. There are good reasons why no real dragons are alive today, and they pretty much all involve large numbers of men with weapons, or so I have been led to understand."

"Do not blame yourself for Gower's injury, your Highness. I assure you, he does not."

"Only because he probably does not understand how foolish I was in making that last pass. It may not even have been necessary."

"Aye, and then again it might have been, your Highness. No one is going to second guess you on that, nor should you try to do so yourself. Also, please bear in mind that, whatever else he is, Gower is a warrior, in his own way, and he is prepared to give his life in your service if that is required. We all are."

"Ah, yes, Pwacca," commented Lleu, annoyed that Slow Tomos was placing so little value on Gower's life. "But what is Gower to the rest of you, really? Compared to you he must be little more than a huge, slow-witted brute."

"Your Highness, we are Pwacca and we are proud of it—all of it. Service and loyalty is a part of who we are and a source from which we derive much of our pride, but that is not all that we are. We are new, so we have more than our share of throwbacks, Pwacca that, in many cases, are more animal than person, and we have a beautiful place for them in Vandwy where they are cared for so long as they live. We do not consider this a burden. Sadly, most do not live so long. They are, after all, more animal than person, and so cannot truly serve, much as they might feel the need."

"And why is Gower not there?" Lleu asked. "Why are you all so eager to let him come to a violent end for a cause he cannot even truly understand?"

Slow Tomos looked pained. "I do believe Gower is more person than animal, he is certainly the most capable throwback we have ever seen. As such, I believed he was worthy of service, and I used all of my influence in prevailing upon Queen Moriganna to find service for him, perhaps against her better judgement."

"Why would you do this?"

"So that he might live his life, however much of it he is given, in happiness. I would like to believe I would do the same for any Pwacca that I could, your Highness. For my own son, I could certainly do no less."

* * *

After that Lleu went down and sat with Gower for a time, although Gower slept deeply, still under the effects of a powerful healing draught Cymri had administered.

After a time, Cymri came. She was moving very slowly and in obvious pain.

Concern blossomed. "Cymri, are you injured?"

"Not precisely." She grimaced. "As I expected, the goddess provided those memories I needed to be a consummate rider and warrior. Where she failed me was in not providing the muscles and ligature, and even callouses, that someone who had acquired their skills in the traditional way would have."

Clarity came to Lleu, coupled with enormous relief. "Ah, you are just sore and blistered then?"

"Do not use the word 'just' in describing my soreness and my blisters. Saying it is 'just' them is completely misstating the situation, or so it feels to me."

"Thank you," he told her. "Thank you for everything, for that matter, but most especially for what you have done for Gower this day."

"Lleu, wild horses could not have kept me from doing this and you know it."

He tried to smile a bit at that and failed. "How bad is it, please, tell me all of it."

She pursed her lips before replying, "Well, he will not be taking anyone for a ride anytime soon—"

"None of us will be taking any, courtesy of Kings Peibio and Nynnio."

She ignored that and continued, "—but I expect a full recovery. I seem to have a considerable amount of Moriganna's knowledge of healing and potion crafting, probably because she herself got much of it from the goddess and thus it is not solely hers."

"Damn Peibio and Nynnio," Lleu said absently, then, with more feeling, "Damn the Picts."

Her expression was vaguely pensive as she appeared to consider her next words. "You may as well curse Lord Arawen as well, Lleu."

"Oh, I most certainly do, every day."

"Ah. Yes, that seems appropriate, but be sure we are cursing everyone for the right reasons."

"Eh?"

"You may certainly blame Peibio and Nynnio for denying us access to the town, and causing us to lose our horses, not to mention the sixty-three men that either rode off with them or were slain. And you may blame the two kings for your having to fly back into the teeth of so many Picts. But you cannot blame the Picts for injuring Gower, much as they would have liked to."

"I suppose you are going to tell me that throwing spears is just in their nature?" Lleu replied, in a somewhat bitter tone.

"That was not a spear I removed from Gower. It was a scorpion bolt."

"But—" It came to him then. A scorpion was a small ballistae, suitable for helping defend a fortified town. It was not a weapon that Picts would be dragging along. Other than spears, they did not use missile weapons of any sort in combat, not even bows and arrows.

There were several scorpions on the hilltop walls of the town. Despite the fact that the Pictish lines were well within their range, Peibio and Nynnio had not been employing them, claiming that they were a surprise better saved for a time when their use might make a decisive difference.

"He was shot from Peibio's hill, I believe, and there are no excuses. You were clearly visible on his back, directing his fire against our enemies. Someone just did not want us to have a dragon's capabilities. The same way someone, or someones, did not want our horses back in town."

"Why would they not want the horses back in?" Lleu demanded. "I thought it just the result of them being too afraid to reopen the gate?"

"Possibly," she shrugged, then winced at the movement, "but unlikely, even for them. I believe they did not want us making any more sorties and possibly further provoking the Picts. What better way to bind our hands in that regard?"

Lleu nodded as understanding came. His eyes narrowed. "And then, even if we got back in, we would be unable to depart, forced to remain and defend their lower town. Doomed to death, perhaps, but we would at least slow the Picts down for them and inflict some losses. They have already accepted the loss of the saddle area between the hills, and the razing of most of the kingdom; their top priority is saving their own worthless hides."

He looked up at the hilltops, first one, then the other. "In order to do this, they have chosen to be our enemies. I do not think we can win, trapped between enemies. Something must be done."

"How so?" Cymri demanded. "Lleu, you cannot kill them or even depose them. It would never be properly understood, and the suspicions would derail all plans for the reunification of Tethera."

"Yes, yes, and then Lord Arawen will come in and eat us all, one at a time. No, I understand this, but the current situation cannot continue, and I will do what I must. Are you going to get some rest now? I need to speak with Caradog before I am too tired, much as I have been dreading this."

"Lleu! He is not that bad."

He grinned tiredly. "That is not what I meant and you know it."

* * *

"Ho, Caradog."

"Yes, Llew, er Lleu? Cymri said you were looking for me?"

"Indeed, it is time we spoke together on a few things."

Caradog's eyes grew wide. "Yes, I should not have come on the raid, but when you see what I have—"

"Hold it there for a moment," Lleu interrupted. "Let us consider first that you should not have come. Why would that be precisely?"

Squirming under Lleu's direct stare, the king of Gwynedd started to reply but words did not come. He tried again. "I could have been killed, I know that. It would have made a proper hash of things, too, if I had been. I did not think about that then. Rather, I thought it was my own risk to take, my own life, and I so wanted to be a part of it all, Lleu. I still do."

He took a deep breath and looked up before saying, as a great king to his high king, "Please forgive me, your Highness. I will not do it again."

Keeping a solemn expression, Lleu tried to hide his surprise. That was exactly what he had wanted to achieve with this discussion: a realization by Caradog that he had done wrong, why it was wrong, and a commitment to do better going forward. By offering them up, freely and sincerely, the young royal had effectively taken all the wind from his sail.

Instead of saying this, Lleu simply nodded sagely, and replied, "As always, you are full of surprises. I am glad you have thought it through and that you plan to be at least a bit more circumspect going forward. The intent certainly counts for a great deal. Very well, we will set this discussion aside and perhaps we will never return to it."

Caradog looked surprised then relieved. "Thank you, your Highness." He reached into a bag he had brought and held up a sheaf of scrolls to the prince of Gwent.

Although he did not take them, Lleu gave them a good hard look. "This is what you found in the compound? And what are these, precisely? Secret notes between Garl and his Cyhyraeth lover, perhaps?"

Caradog made a face. "Ew, I should hope not. I would never be unable to unread them were that the case—and I would certainly desire nothing more than to do so! No, these are the plans for that strange new type of siege engine they were building. The one that looked something like a catapult but stood nearly as tall as a siege tower."

"Um, does it actually say what they are for, somewhere in there?"

"Well, no," Caradog gave him a funny look. "Although the design makes it somewhat obvious. In essence, it is a very large sling, mounted on a very large catapult. Many men are required to draw it back and, depending on its size, they can hurl objects larger than any man can lift and three times as far as the best catapult could hope to send them."

"They could have sped up the capture of the lower part of this town then," Lleu observed.

"Quite definitely, I do not know how well even Caerleon would stand against them, if enough were built and brought against her."

Suppressing a shudder, Lleu responded, "We will not let that happen." A thought came to him. "Is it possible to also build them on the walls or towers? It seems the best thing for keeping them out of range would be to have more of them."

"You saw it at once," Caradog accused. "That is precisely the way to do it—at least, I think it is. What is more, I believe that, in a stationary position, it might be possible to power the things by lifting and securing a heavy weight, then dropping it when we choose, rather than having to keep an entire company of men on the ropes to draw one back and hold it."

"An improvement then," Lleu mused. "Well done. Yet I cannot believe Lord Arawen, or his Cyhyraeth, came up with this out of nothing. I wonder where they stole their plans from."

"Maybe from those Pictish kingdoms that Helgar said were north of Annwyn? He did say they were more advanced than we are, at least in some ways."

"Hmm, possibly, though it is hard to imagine, even so. Caradog, could you build one of these on one of the towers abutting the western gate?"

The young king spread one of the parchments with his fingers, then looked up at Lleu with a bright smile on his face. "I am not certain, but I would like very much to try."

"Good, take whatever you need. You are not certain you can build one and I am not certain how to make the best use of it, yet, but I can already think of several interesting ideas."

"I will begin at once, Lleu."

"Nay, hold up. We are not done here. Now it is time for me to apologize to you. Not—" Lleu swept his hand at the plans, "—not for anything to do with this," he added hastily, seeing Caradog's startled expression.

"Say, rather, that there is information I should have shared with you months ago, but I have been uncertain as to how you should receive it and so have held back. Seeing you, today, in that compound, it came upon me that, much as I have been hesitant to tell you, and much as I would be distressed by your passing, not to mention my own, I would never forgive myself should anything happen to either of us before I told you."

"I confess, I am both mystified and filled with apprehension at what it could be," said Caradog.

"Yes, well, it is this then. Sometime back, your birth mother came to me and—"

"That is not possible. My birth mother is long dead—" His eyes widened as he realized he had interrupted his liege lord in mid-sentence.

Lleu let it slide. "That is what you were told. In point of fact she . . . she abandoned you, and her throne, and everything else that should ever have been of consequence to her and, when she came to me, earlier this summer, she was very much alive."

"Please go on," Caradog whispered.

"This is hard to tell you. She ran away to be with a bandit. In doing so she willingly became a bandit as well and left behind the child she and that bandit had produced."

He could see Caradog was having a difficult time processing this. The young king was, however, possessed of a very keen mind. "Lleu! What are you saying? An outlaw's child cannot inherit. Am I then not a king? And wait, my father was nothing more than a common bandit? Oh, I do not doubt you, but I question this, Lleu, I must."

"Calm yourself. This was nearly two weeks before you reached your fourteenth year. As you had not reached your majority, it was a simple thing to arrange that you be adopted by someone who was not an outlaw."

"Oh, well, and that is a relief—wait—I am adopted? Who adopted me?"

"Would you perhaps care to sit down?" Lleu inquired.

"Yes—no, I cannot sit down, yet I am not sure I can stand. Just tell me; who are my adoptive parents?"

"Not parents," Lleu responded, "parent. You only have a father."

"Who, who?"

Lleu could not resist, it just slipped out. "Now you sound like an owl,"

"Auggggh," Caradog was passing beyond impatience.

"It is I, Caradog, or should I say it is me?"

"What, you?"

"Aye."

"You?"

"Look on the bright side, Caradog. It was a way to preserve your claim to your throne. I do not expect you to call me dadi or bring me presents on my birthday." Again, Lleu could not help himself as an amusing thought came to him: "Besides, this way you now have Moriganna as your grandmother."

It took the young king awhile to wrestle with all these new things at once. Then a sly smile came over his face. "And High Queen Boudicca as my great-grandmother. Thank you, Lleu."

"You are most welcome."

"Are you done stamping on my mind with great hobnailed boots yet?"

Lleu had the decency to look distressed. "Not quite yet, I fear."

Caradog did sit down then. He looked up at his adoptive father, nearly three years his senior. "Alright, I am ready."

"What you assumed earlier was wrong. Your birth father was a bandit, yes, but perhaps not a common one."

"Oh," said Caradog, "I am actually somewhat relieved to hear that. If I am to be of a bandit's blood, better that he not be common, I expect."

"Caradog, forgive me, there is no easy way to tell you this. Your birth father was King Gronw and, as you well know, he is dead by my own hand."

"Lleu," said Caradog, after a bit.

"Yes, Caradog?"

"I believe I expected wrongly. I realize now that common would have been much better."

"Perhaps, but this will make a more interesting tale for your grandchildren when you are in your dotage."

Despite himself, despite everything, Caradog chuckled at that, and Lleu knew then that the young king would be alright. A vision had once challenged Lleu to deliver this information in a way that would not damage the recipient, and he had somehow muddled through and succeeded, despite many sleepless nights in the interim that were spent wondering how he could. He had even been prepared to try to offer the dubious consolation that, bad as Gronw had been, Lleu's own birth father, the Mad King, was hardly an improvement.

Caradog was too clever twice over, however, for it was only another few moments before he deduced another truth. "Meirion? Meirion is my birth mother?"

"Indeed," Lleu answered. "She broke with him at the last and came to tell us everything. It was her idea that I apprentice you and assume all bonds of family while she renounced them. I had to pay her a whole silver for you."

"It is nice to know the degree to which you value me, father."

Lleu winced. "Calling me that is certainly your right, but I would prefer we keep using Llew—I mean Lleu."

"Lleu, in all seriousness, please tell me this: where has she gone?"

"There is no way to know. She told me we would never see her again and, for my part, I believed her."

"So she not only abandoned me, she came back to renounce me as well. I suddenly do not know which side of the family I hope that I take after."

"I am glad you retain yours sense of humor, Caradog. It seems as though in all the stories I have heard, the child immediately wants to seek out its lost parent, in spite of all advice to the contrary, and—"

"And?"

"I was going to advise you not to seek her out."

"Lleu, if your mother, your birth mother, was still alive, would you seek her out, despite everyone telling you not to?"

"Given that she did not renounce me and was trying to find me the last time I saw her? Yes."

"That is not fair, Lleu."

"The situations are different, Caradog. Were I in your boots, I cannot say that I would not, just that I hope you will not. Meirion will not be gladdened by a reunion and, for that reason, neither would you. Besides, we have other things to do at present."

"Agreed. We are caught between our good friends, the kings named Peibio and Nynnio. With friends like these, we do not need enemies, particularly when we already have seventy thousand Picts come to drink our blood and burn us as sacrifices."

"I agree entirely, my young shieldbearer. The twin kings must be dealt with first, before we can hope for any victory over the Picts. Yet, as Cymri pointed out, I cannot be conquering Tetheran kings and seizing their thrones."

"Perhaps not. But what if they abdicated?

Lleu shook his head tiredly. "They will not abdicate."

Fingers drumming on his knees, Caradog rocked back and forth, apparently deep in thought. "Lleu? Everyone knows they are cowards. What about if they just ran away and abandoned their kingdom? You know? The way my birth parents abandoned me?"

Lleu snorted. "That would be a very different matter."

Chapter XXXIX

Where No Man Pursues

King Nynnio was awakened in the middle of the night by loud slamming and banging in his antechamber. He started to shout for the servant on call, then thought to wonder just who it was that was making such a racket. Clawing his way off his bed, he realized he urgently needed to make use of his personal privy; he often did, right after awakening. Even so, he dithered for a moment and decided it could wait a few seconds longer. Now was the time to strike and to find out for himself who was creating such a ruckus as to disrupt his sleep. Then it would be taken care of; oh, yes it would! There would certainly be no reoccurrences after that.

Striding to his bedroom door, nightshirt flapping, he jerked it open. As one, a score of Pictish warriors, busily engaged in looting his antechamber, all looked up at him. They each projected a fierce, animal ruthlessness, further accentuated by the fact they scarcely even appeared human, wearing almost nothing save the strange blue patterns painted upon their faces and bodies with woad. Had the king remained fully cognizant of such things, he would have realized then that he no longer had any need to visit his privy.

He did have the presence of mind, after a moment or so, to dodge back into his room and slam the door. He dropped the locking bar just as the door shook with a mighty impact and the blade of an axe appeared, penetrating the solid wood boards of the door at about the same height as his head. There was no time to delay. He fled through the secret panel behind his bed, even as he heard the door begin receiving multiple heavy blows. By no stretch of the imagination could it possibly last long.

The question was where to go? He could bypass the Picts in his antechamber and get to his front hall, but the Picts must have already overrun that. How else would they have gotten in? Did it even matter at this point? They were already here. He had to concentrate. It went through his head that even the hidden passages might not be safe; some others knew of them and they could have been caught trying to escape into them, revealing their existence to the invaders.

He quickly found a ladder and went down to the tunnels. The secret tunnels penetrating the hill were many. In ancient times there had been a mine and, while whatever ore the miners had sought was long gone, their diggings yet remained.

Nynnio had made contingency plans for this kind of thing, his personal safety was too important not to, but none of his plans had anticipated his enemies getting so close without an alarm being raised. He looked down at his soiled night shirt. First he needed clothing. Armor would be better but he had no practice in wearing it. It dawned on him that it did not matter if he needed clothing or armor, there was no safe place to get either in his keep. Why, the entire hilltop must be overrun. The town between the hills must be gone as well.

There was nothing for it but to get a move on. Yet running down into the tunnels without light would be foolish, no matter what was behind him. Fortunately, he had stocked some torches and fire starters at the base of the ladder. He almost could not make his shaking hands strike the sparks to light one.

Ominous sounds echoing down from above told him the Picts might already be in the hidden passages. Still, he persevered and got one lit, its flickering light doing little to illuminate the many shadows where anything might be hiding. Trotting down the tunnel, away from the entrance and, he hoped, away from the Picts, he knew he still needed somewhere to go.

There was nothing for it. If the Picts had overrun his own hilltop and keep, then he had to hope that idiot brother of his still held his hilltop. It was, after all, both higher and bigger, and it made sense the Picts had expended their energies in taking the easier one. The tunnels would pass down under the low part of the town and take him there eventually. Even so, as he considered the matter, arriving secretly and without his own guards, or anything else for that matter, his status there might be problematic. Certainly he could not trust himself to Peibio's tender mercies, not without some sort of an edge.

King Nynnio stopped to take his bearings. Yes! Just ahead would be a dead end passage to the right. It actually hid an entrance to one of his main treasure rooms, filled with gold and silver purloined from the public vaults over a long period of time. That might serve, although he badly wished now that he had possessed the foresight to hide some clothing and weapons there as well. Next time he certainly would. For now, however, showing up with plenty of gold would help him buy some of Peibio's men right away. He could then leverage that to ensure his faithless brother did not just do away with him quietly. It would be dangerous and dicey, but less so than the certainty of what his fate would be with the Picts!

He reached the curving passage to his treasure chamber and trotted down and around the first curve before realizing there was a light ahead of him. Something at that light saw his own torchlight as well, for deep voices called to each other in no language he understood. Shadows appeared, flickering on the tunnel walls, showing man-like forms rapidly getting larger as they ran toward him. It never even occurred to Nynnio to ask how the Picts had found their way here; he just turned and ran for all he was worth.

Sobbing with fear, he made his way down and under the central part of the town. It took a long time, as he kept stopping to see if he could sense anything approaching from either behind or ahead. The stone and rubble covered floor was distinctly unfriendly to his soft feet and they were were cut and bruised in many places, while his rush torch, made to last for an hour, was nearly exhausted. He still had a long way to go to get up into Peibio's keep and he would, he knew, need another torch. Fortunately, there was a source near at hand. There were always several in the chamber by the east tunnel, the one that went under the river. Keeping a supply there was one of the few things he and Peibio had ever agreed upon, and only because there was no telling which of them it might one day benefit. Yes, he would make his way there and get a fresh torch or two.

Then he would sneak up to Peibio's and see what he could do to get a bit of the place for his own. Peibio had long had the better hilltop, it was time he shared. Perhaps it might even be possible to get more than just a share of it. King Nynnio scowled to himself. It would be harder without any gold but he might be able to do it, if he could get a few words to the right people before Peibio knew he was there.

The torch was guttering when he finally made his way to the chamber before the great tunnel. This was not really out of his way as three tunnels met here. One being the great tunnel under the river, another the one he had just come down, while the third would lead across and up into Peibio's territory, precisely where he was going.

He found the box of torches easily enough, and had just lit a fresh one with the flickering remains of the old, when he became aware that another lit torch had entered the chamber while he was distracted.

Terrified, he jumped to his feet, torch held before him as a weapon. There appeared to be only one man, perhaps he could be bluffed. He squinted into the gloom as the figure came closer. "Brother?" he asked, with growing incredulity.

For it was King Peibio that stood before him, also dressed in a nightshirt, albeit a somewhat less stained one, and holding a nearly expired torch.

Realization dawned on both men at the same time. "Pfaugh," cried Nynnio, "you have lost your hill to the Picts, where shall we go now? I ask you!"

"Me?" replied Peibio. "You ask me? I had meant to come to you, but apparently you are no bulwark against anything. At least I had the presence of mind to escape in a fresh nightshirt. You, on the other hand, are truly pathetic."

"I will show you pathetic," snarled Nynnio, starting forward.

"Wait," said Peibio, holding up a single finger for silence, a look of dread replacing the anger on his face.

"What—" began Nynnio, confused. Then he heard it. Excited voices, again in that strange tongue, and the slapping of feet on stone, were coming from the tunnel behind him. He glanced back and saw light and shadows becoming visible within it.

"You fool," Peibio hissed, "you have led them straight to us!"

Speechless, Nynnio pointed a finger to the tunnel the other had come from. Now it was Peibio's turn to look back. Light and shadows were visible from that tunnel as well. More of the deep voices could also be heard.

Peibio reacted instantly. He pushed Nynnio down and snatched his torch, then ran pell-mell down the eastern tunnel that led under the river. Down, but not out, Nynnio jumped back up in an instant and, with no choice in the matter, pursued his brother. If nothing else, he knew he had to stay in range of the last light source they had between them.

The brothers had no sooner passed out of sight before a dozen Picts came trotting out of each passage. They met before the entrance to the eastern tunnel. The flickering torches they carried made their blue patterns less distinct in the semi-darkness but, somehow, even more frightening in appearance.

One of them spoke in Tetheran. "Shall I collapse the tunnel once they are through, your Highness?"

"Nay, replied Lleu, "let them do it from the other end. Done from there it will also take out part of the bridge, will it not? I think there is small chance of them deciding to return anytime soon, but I would prefer we reduce those odds to zero."

"Aye, done from the other end it will indeed collapse part of the bridge, your Highness, but they might be too frightened to stop to trigger it as they flee."

"I think," said Lleu, "that they are too frightened not to."

A moment later, the noise of massive amounts of falling rock, and a bit of dust, emerged from the eastern tunnel.

"Besides which," Lleu continued, once his voice could be heard again, "We cleared the Picts guarding the other end for a reason as, whatever fate these cowards find, I would have it be as much of their own devising as possible. Come what may, they at least have a chance."

He turned and favored his Pwacca with a smile. "Speaking of chances, we still have a siege to break, and now we might have a chance to do so. We certainly no longer need rats in the walls. In Peibio's keep we will join the rest. Our friends should have what we need to clean off this woad before anyone sees us, also there are armor and weapons, too, just in case the Ergynglings need to be reminded of who is now in charge, but we must hurry."

The Picts vanished, torches and weapons dropping to the ground, and two dozen wolves raced up the dark northern passage.

Chapter XL

The Inner Circle

After a very short night's sleep, Lleu met with his friends on one of the northern hilltop's towers. It offered a magnificent view of the vast Pictish encampment, and it also looked down on the main gate to the town. The top of one of the towers flanking that gate was covered in carpenters and soldiers, already at work on Caradog's giant sling catapult.

Lleu was in disguise only in that he was still representing himself as Prince Llew, rather than Prince Lleu, to anyone outside of his closest confidants. Backed by royal friends, a demonstration of his shape-shifting abilities, and the still hidden strength of the Pwacca, he had deemed it time to reassert at least a part of his identity. His fears of doing so had been partially allayed when no one, neither the warriors of Gwent and Clwyd, nor any of the Ergynglings, had shown the slightest desire to question Llewellyn's announcement that both King Peibio and Nynnio had fled their kingdom. They had not been well loved, and the crumbled segment in the eastern bridge lent additional veracity to her words.

Nor did anyone show any signs of questioning Llewellyn's declaration that Prince Llew's appearance was now magically altered, perhaps permanently. Beyond stating that it had been changed by enchantment, they had neither given, nor needed to give, any further explanation. The complete acceptance of the nobility was obvious when, shortly after he was revealed as the true prince, a contingent of them approached him and demanded he promise he would crown a new ruler to fill the vacuum in Ergyng.

As for their former lieges, no one evidenced any concern whatsoever. Part of that, no doubt, was their bemusement in seeing Llewellyn reveal herself as the Princess of Gwent. Somehow, that had created far more of a stir than learning that their kings had abandoned them to the Picts, or that the Prince of Gwent now had a new face.

With him on the tower was Llewellyn, no longer disguised as Llew and resplendent in her own armor, Cymri, Caradog, and Slow Tomos.

Also with them was a friend they had made earlier that summer. Ian was attending a meeting some might have thought to be far beyond his station, but the former king of Clwyd had declared Ian's father, who was already a cantref king, to be the heir to his kingdom. Further, it had not been long, after the last battle against the forces of Annwyn in Clwyd, before his health began growing worse with each passing day and, though he still lived, he had passed his crown to his successor. So it was that the former Subaltern Ian was now Prince Ian.

Lleu had been momentarily bewildered to see Ian when, the night before, he and Llewellyn had emerged from King Peibio's stronghold. It was true that Moriganna had made a point of mentioning that Clwyd had already sent what help it could, but Lleu had completely forgotten this, and his surprise was nearly total at finding that a contingent of warriors from that long suffering kingdom had already arrived, nearly two weeks earlier.

"Well," Lleu began, "We have reduced all of our problems here to just one."

Slow Tomos looked out over the tens of thousands of Picts covering the nearby country-side. "I think that is still sufficient to keep us busy, Lleu."

Caradog could not resist adopting Helgar's accent again and said, "Aye, and that is vell and goot for today, but vot shall ve occupy ourselves vith tomorrow? Ask you I do."

"I do not doubt we can stay busy," Lleu remarked in a dry tone, "but you do raise an interesting question, um, Helgar. We do not know if Helgar and his Northmen are coming tomorrow, next month, or never."

Llewellyn considered this and asked, "Do you think he will have success in establishing his primacy and raising an army?"

"He was clearly in charge of Lindenjal when I left him," Lleu replied, "but I cannot speak for how well the other Northmen settlements will fall in line. My coin would be on Helgar, certainly, but it may take more time than we can delay."

"Our besiegers outnumber our own warriors by thirty to one. For all of their lack of discipline, armor, arrows, or fortifications of any sort, those are not the kind of odds which should cause us to attack, especially without any mounted warriors whatsoever, and the first frost of winter will be upon the land before Gower can fly again," observed Slow Tomos. "So, we cannot hope to overwhelm them by land, by air, or even from the waters of the river."

"Right," said Lleu, "and all of those are things they could expect at this point, if they do not simply trust us to sit tight and let them destroy the kingdom. Yet if I learned anything regarding strategy from Afaggdu, it was this: other than with overwhelming superiority, decisive victories are never achieved without use of the unexpected. Accordingly, I have decided we will do the unexpected."

"And how do you intend to do that, Prince Llew, or should I call you Lleu?" inquired Prince Ian.

"Lleu is fine, Ian. Anyone that overhears will just assume you pronounced it badly. I intend to apply our greatest strength against their greatest weakness. They will never see it coming. Caradog?"

"I could wish we could test it first, Lleu. If it works at all, it should be ready in perhaps three days' time."

"We do not have that luxury. There is no way to test it such that the Picts could not observe us doing so and adjust accordingly. Three days hence? We will need it ready to fire just before dawn."

"Forgive me, your Highness," said Slow Tomos, "but I must hope that this is not the entirety of your plan, a single giant sling catapult, untried in actual combat?"

"Certainly not. You and the rest of the Pwacca did a fine job with our cowardly kings, but the reward for doing a good job is most often another job, and I have a particularly dirty one for you and the rest of the fellows." So saying, Lleu passed a rolled up parchment to him. "That should detail exactly what I have in mind."

Slow Tomos unrolled the scroll and spent a moment absorbing it before he looked up. "Yes, I believe we can do this in the time available, but it may be close."

"Caradog and Slow Tomos? What about the rest of us, Lleu?" asked Llewellyn.

"Nothing overwhelming. I leave it to you and Ian to reorganize all of our forces into a single, cohesive, military structure under a single chain of command."

Llewellyn nodded gravely. "In three days?"

"Heh, I know it is ridiculous, still, do what you can."

"It may not be even that easy. The men of Ergyng might not be in a hurry to fully comply with a woman's commands, Lleu."

"They will for you. After the coronation this evening you will be their queen. We will fudge on your age a little bit, but I expect no objections on that account."

She looked startled and tried to object, but Lleu held up a hand to forestall her. "It is the logical choice, your line is kin to the previous ruling family and, besides, you are the only one of us present, other than Slow Tomos, that is not already ruler or heir to their own kingdom."

Slow Tomos cleared his throat uncomfortably and Lleu gave him a sharp look. "Oh, no. Tomos, are you trying to tell me that you—"

"Yes, your Highness, Queen Moriganna has already declared me, as Araf, heir to the kingdom of Vandwy."

"Vandwy?" Caradog asked in sudden confusion. "What is Vandwy?"

"Yes, I have heard you speak of it before," Lleu said slowly. "But there has never been time to ask you about it."

"It is, perhaps, a subject best saved for another time, your Highness, but suffice it to say that it is the secret kingdom of the Pwacca. After your injury from King Gronw, you spent a year and a day there while you were recovering and being trained in the use of your shape-shifting power, but you do not consciously remember it."

"There is a secret kingdom? Of Pwacca?" Caradog demanded.

"I only remember bits and pieces," mused Lleu, in answer to Slow Tomos, "as if in a dream. It seemed a very nice place."

"It is that, your Highness."

"Will you take me back for a visit someday, should time permit?"

"It would be my greatest pleasure, your Highness, as time permits."

"I am your shieldbearer, I have to go, too," exclaimed Caradog.

"Lleu, you seem to have assignments for everyone else. What am I to do?" asked Cymri.

"Well, if you could arrange for the coronation when we return, I would appreciate it."

"When we return?"

"I want to have a look at some things, if possible, and the sooner the better. You can help me search."

Lleu stood, stretched, and then leaped into the air above the tower, becoming an eagle in mid-leap, rapidly winging his way upwards.

Cymri was as startled as any present but, a moment later, a second eagle rose to join him.

Chapter XLI

The Essence of Surprise

Four days later, the hours before sunrise were as any other. Light wispy clouds obscured some of the stars overhead, while the moon itself was notably absent. The fires of the great encampment had all burnt low. The lone Pict keeping watch at the camp nearest the gates to the walled town was bored, but he was not asleep. Thus he was the first to hear the loud noise from the direction of the gates. It was loud enough to wake many of his tribesmen. Even as they were rising to see what the commotion was, the sentry already had his eyes on the gate. The noise was not one he had ever heard before and he was unsure what it portended. Yet the gates, had not opened, so, he decided, whatever the cause of the disturbance, it was not an immediate threat but even so—

It was then that several dozen stones, each about the weight of a human head, angled into the camp at high speed. Most hit nothing important, not at first, but as they skipped along the ground many of them intercepted men, and one even went through the fire circle, scattering hot ash that sent an opaque cloud over everything. Within it, men died, and men were maimed by the careening stones. The attack was not just upon this camp either; through the screaming and chaos all around him, the sentry could hear similar sounds, further away and in both directions, along the wall.

The sentry could only know that the town was attacking with some cowardly new weapon; it was one that allowed them to kill without honor, striking against even the greatest of warriors, while giving them no opportunity to demonstrate their skill and bravery.

Whatever it was, it was killing and crippling many men and, as those closest to him constituted nearly all of the males of his immediate family, he knew this was a potential disaster the clan might never recover from! He pushed aside his panic, and it came to him that this new weapon had to have some sort of range. He opened his mouth to call for his clan to fall back, but no warning came forth. A six foot bolt, fired from a wall-mounted scorpion, had found him before that could happen.

Less than a minute after Caradog's siege engine first attacked, it fired again, targeting another camp. Caradog watched the slaughter and confusion amongst the unprepared Picts. It looked to be a full rout. Thousands of panicked warriors were fleeing backwards, away from the town and into their own forces. This was going to do nothing good for their ability to deal with what would come next.

In his own encampment, directly in the center of the great arc of encampments that swept around the walled town from river to river, Goll One-Eye scrambled out of his hut and glared out into the confusion towards the town. Some trick of these people, these grubs so soft that they hid themselves in stone boxes, was responsible for this. If he could just figure out what it was and, more importantly, what purpose it was meant to serve . . . .

From behind came a strange voice that spoke badly, and in a thick accent. "This bad for you, Goll, I am here for other eye now."

Goll whipped about, not believing what he saw. Here, in his own camp, was one of the soft men! A thought, driven by what the man had said, plucked at him. Eye? Could this be that one? The very one? If it was, he was bigger than Goll remembered, but he had been young, he could be growing. The Pict war chieftain scanned the intruder for some other familiar sign. Armor was not something Picts paid much attention to it, but he could recognize a distinctive suit of it when he thought to take notice. Only then did it register that this was the same armor."

"Little man," he cried in delight, "I would invite you to come take my eye but I would have to hurt you. I have better in mind for you. You like armor, like all cowards, we will put a nice wicker armor upon you, and then we will put you someplace warm."

"I learn not much Pictish yet," the Tetheran replied. "What you say I not all know, but you must fight or coward I call you."

Goll gave Lleu a look that was pure contempt. "Little man is stupid, too. I do not fight sacrifices and that is what you are. You will replace the sacrifice you stole."

"Goll wrong, Goll must fight."

Without even a glance in their direction, Goll gestured to the many ranks of Pictish warriors surrounding them. These were his closest kinsmen, and their closest kinsmen as well. "Goll thinks he will not. All of us think he will not."

"Lleu thinks must." Lleu nodded to the Pictish warriors surrounding them. "Lleu thinks they agree."

Goll turned his head to regard the many Picts surrounding them. The nearest ones he did not recognize. Looking about wildly, it came to him that he did not see any familiar faces amongst them. Still, they were Picts! They were his to command. He glanced to the blue woad patterns upon their faces and bodies to see just what clan they were from, and went suddenly cold. There were no clan markings, no stories of the wearer's deeds, just wretched, poorly drawn things meant to look somewhat like them. Even those drawings meant to please the gods were drawn strangely, as if by someone who had no idea what they were doing.

These were not real Pict warriors at all! They were just more of those sneaky, honorless, soft men, pretending to be warriors. Although, he granted, they had shown a little spirit in coming to fight without the armor they always hid within.

He was still taking this in, looking directly at them while he did, and so got to see them as they began to blur and grow larger, sprouting fur and fangs and claws until, within a just a few seconds, he was surrounded by dozens of wolf-like things that stood on two legs.

In his shock, it took Goll a moment to realize what must have happened to all of his close male relatives. When such a shape-shifting monster came upon an unsuspecting man in the dark, the outcome would never be in question. After a time, his gaze returned to Lleu. "Yes, we fight, you and me."

"Not me," Lleu corrected. "You say I thief? I stole man sacrifice and must replace? Agreement. I give him back. Here he is."

Racing footsteps approached, then something leaped to the top of a large log and vaulted over the line of encircling Pwacca. Helgar landed, knees bent, one leg slightly before the other, and a two-handed axe in each hand. He clanged them both together, twice, at speed, and gave Goll a huge smile that had no mirth in it.

"Here is your sacrifice, Goll," called Helgar, in Pictish. "Are you now ready to send me on with my brothers?"

It seemed even Goll One-Eye had a breaking point. He turned to flee, then hesitated at once when he saw the wall of Pwacca behind him. No living man of flesh and bone could hope to pass through that. Spear firmly in both hands, he spun back to Helgar, but it was too late. The Northman had already closed the distance between them. It was over in a second.

Helgar stood motionless over his fallen enemy, still breathing hard from his exertion. Despite the completeness of his victory, it seemed to Lleu that his friend was terribly unhappy. He put a hand to Helgar's shoulder as they regarded Goll One-Eye's still form, and tried to find some way to cheer him. "At the last he tried to run. What scary fellows we—"

Helgar blew a heavy sigh and said, "Not right now, please, Lleu. I am so much disappointed."

"I know. You wanted more of a fight from this monster that did such terrible things to your family, but do not be feeling sorry for yourself," Lleu remonstrated. "Look, there are more Picts out there, tens of thousands of them, any of them would happily burn a Tetheran or a Northman, and all of them are asking for it just by being here. It is up to you to give it to them. And you are so concerned about one? Go destroy the rest. Then you can be dissatisfied with the one that did not satisfy your sense of vengeance."

The Northman looked up, a thoughtful expression evident. "You know, Lleu, I think there is something to what you say."

"I am very glad to hear you say that," Lleu replied.

To Araf, the prince asked, "Is the tunnel mouth fully open now?"

"Aye, and it is, your Highness, most of Jarl Helgar's men that are coming here are already out and assembling. The warriors of Gwent and Clwyd are nearly ready as well, although a few are still exiting. Should I go ahead and collect the head now?"

Helgar and Lleu each raised a lone eyebrow at the Pwacca.

"We need to place their warleader's head on a pike and carry it before us," he explained. "The savages need to see he is gone. From what I know of Picts, the loss of their war chieftain should ensure they break, even if our own force of arms should run into difficulties,"

"Very well," replied Lleu, "then please make sure it is wearing the eye patch, so it will be even more recognizable to them. I will sound the horn as soon you tell me that is done."

It was not long before Araf got his attention and said, "Your Highness, we are all of us ready. I checked and the Ergynglings under your sister's command are all assembled just outside the town gates. In their haste to withdraw from the engines upon the walls, the Picts have paid them scant notice yet, but that will change. Unless—"

Lleu put the horn to his lips and blew a long note. From Llewellyn's forces came another in acknowledgment, and then, from the far periphery of the great encampment, came yet another. Northmen poured out of the tree line then, most on foot, but many were mounted, and Lleu knew that Afaggdu and other warriors of Gwent rode with them.

"They seem almost overeager," Lleu observed.

His pride evident, Helgar said, "They are eager to impress you, Lleu, also, they really do not like Picts. They also just like to fight, it is part of who we are," he confided. "Speaking of which?"

Lleu glanced toward Erg, dawn was beginning to show its first faintest traces to the East, beyond the town, and the Ergyng formations before it were charging into the disorganized and retreating Picts. The tribesmen would find it very difficult, if not impossible, to rally in the face of that, especially with what he and Helgar had just launched: a full attack right out of their own war chief's camp, carrying his head before them.

Even had the Picts been familiar with siege warfare and sappers, and tactics that involved tunneling under the enemy, they could never have anticipated a hundred Pwacca, shape-shifting into badgers, the greatest of all burrowers, and giant ones at that, digging a secret tunnel from the town to their war chief's camp, all in the span of just three days. Still, Lleu had delayed the attack one more day than he had originally intended for, when he and Cymri, flying overhead as giant eagles, had located the approaching Northmen, it had only made sense to wait the extra day so they could extend the tunnel to the tree line and bring some of the Northmen in to attack the center as well. First to emerge was Helgar. Lleu had promised Goll One-Eye to him back when they were still in Lindenjal.

"Let us get to it then," agreed Lleu. "We are only outnumbered nine to one, so I expect the Picts are already in serious trouble."

By early afternoon there was not a Pict to be found within five leagues of Erg.

Chapter XLII

Aftermath

Another encampment, not nearly so large as that of the Picts, but much more comfortable, was quickly taking shape under the city walls. From his temporary field headquarters, Lleu attempted to get a full understanding of where things now stood.

The nobles had wanted to bring out a throne for him to sit upon but he was having none of that. Instead, he sat upon a pile of empty boxes that had been carried forth from Erg, earlier, full of food. Just the feeding of the armies, now greatly augmented by the large number of Northmen, was no small undertaking in and of itself.

The boxes were uncomfortable, but he still had it soft. Everyone else had to stand, partly because there was no good place for them to sit, and partly because Lleu hoped that it would encourage them to make speedier, more concise reports.

"Per your directions, we allowed the families to flee without harassment, your Highness," Afaggdu told him.

"You disagree with that decision?" Lleu asked.

Afaggdu made a face, although on him it was harder to see than it would have been on most. "Your Highness, perhaps it was a little soft, but that is certainly your prerogative." The ugly warrior appeared to give it another thought, then said, "Actually, it is probably a good thing. We did not even have enough to properly pursue the men. As it was, at least two thirds of their number escaped us."

Lleu winced inwardly. That meant a third would never return to the wilderness from which they had come—and Picts did not surrender or allow themselves to be taken captive. A third of seventy-thousand was a depressingly large number.

"Any sign they may rally and return?"

"Nay, your Highness, as we have noted before, they are tribes people, and ill-suited to the losses of a war on this scale, where entire clans can easily wind up without a single man left. No doubt that has happened to many of them. It will be a generation or more before they are capable of another such invasion, if they are willing, even then."

"Yar," agreed Helgar. "They were running so fast we finally let them go. Most of us were on foot and the Picts may not stop running before they reach the eastern shores."

"What of our own losses?

Prince Ian looked up at that from a collection of parchments and hides spread before him on a makeshift table. "Very light, Prince Lleu, remarkably light. The Picts were in full retreat and unable to give back anything at all like what they were receiving. When Queen Llewellyn breaks off her own pursuit, and her forces return, we should have the final numbers but, as she only has about three hundred riders with her, it still will not overly change the totals."

"We were very fortunate," Lleu agreed.

"It was not luck," Afaggdu disagreed. "It was a superb plan and ably executed. Take credit where credit is due."

"And Araf?" Lleu asked, pointedly.

"Who?"

"Slow Tomos."

"Ah well, lad, that was just bad luck."

Lleu started to ask something else but the sound of dozens of horses returning would have drowned out his words. Llewellyn had returned.

Four servants came running to assist her as she made to dismount. She shooed them away and climbed down without aid. Turning around she found Helgar directly in front of her, both of them still liberally doused with the blood of their enemies. Lleu winced inwardly, waiting for some pithy remark about Helgar's big oafish self being in her way.

Instead, she just regarded him for a split second before leaping directly at him. He caught her with arms wide and lifted her up, spinning half about with the force of the impact. It was an impressive feat, all the same, for she was very tall and well-muscled, and wearing full armor as well. Their lips met and did not separate for an awkwardly long time. It gave Lleu time to realize his mouth was hanging open. He self-consciously closed it, hoping no one had noticed. He need not have worried; for a change, no one was watching him.

Eventually, the two of them seemed to become aware of the attention they had drawn. Although they remained embraced, they drew their faces apart to look about themselves and Lleu realized he had never before seen Llewellyn blush.

"Whoops," said Helgar.

Chapter XLIII

Look to the West

There were no prisoners taken from the Picts. They fought and fell, or else they ran. Of those that ran, many of the faster ones even escaped. So far as they were concerned, there were no other alternatives. The very idea of surrendering to anyone who was not a fellow Pict was, quite literally it seemed, unthinkable.

Despite this, on the day after the battle, a prisoner was brought before Lleu. The man was no Pict, that much was immediately obvious. More than that was hard to say, as he was so covered in ash and dirt it was difficult to see that there was a man underneath, only that he must be nearly half dead from whatever his recent travails had done to him.

"Well," said Lleu at last, "I am tempted to order that he be cleaned up a bit before we proceed, but the filth may be all that is holding him together."

The subaltern that had dragged the prisoner in reserved comment, saying only, "Your Highness, we found him digging himself out of a tunnel where all those siege engines were being constructed a few days ago."

"Really? Now that is passing strange. I suppose he must have managed to get deep enough to survive the fire—partially survive it, at any rate." A sudden thought came to him then and he gave the prisoner a sharp glance. Was it possible? The size was about right, and there was nothing about the rags he was wearing to invalidate the idea.

"Why, Garl," Lleu crooned, "imagine my surprise. Here I thought we had seen the last of you and yet, here you are. Alive and hale and looking as well as ever."

Largely unresponsive to his surroundings until then, that got the man's attention, and he slowly lifted his head to look at Lleu. A despairing groan was his only reply.

"Hmm," temporized Lleu, "perhaps you do look a tiny bit worse for the wear."

A long silence passed before Lleu broke it by saying, not unkindly, "Garl, you realize this is it for you? Do you understand me? I am not fond of ordering men to the block, but for you I will lose little sleep. Bran the Blessed himself told me how I must deal with such situations and you have earned nothing else.

"You never should have escaped from Hafgan. That was foolish. His plan for you was by far the more merciful, and mercy is something I cannot grant you, not for what you have done. I cannot even begin to imagine a situation where you could hope to merit any."

Garl tried to say something then, but only garbled rasping noises came forth from his soot smudged mouth.

Lleu held up his own bronze goblet, still half full with a pleasing red wine he had been slowly savoring, and gestured with it at Garl. A servant came and took it from him to the prisoner, holding it while Garl drank.

The goblet drained, it was removed.

"You were trying to say something, Garl?" Lleu inquired.

Garl's voice was never good at the best of times, and this was clearly not the best of times for him. "Your Highness, I can barter for my life, but you must promise not to kill me, and to keep me safe from Lord Arawen's wrath."

Lleu affected astonishment. "So you believe your future is now safer with us? That we may yet win out against the Lord of Annwyn?"

"No, my lord, I do not. He will triumph in the end, he always does, but you may yet have a few years left before that happens. Were I to return to him now I would not even have a few days left. I must take what I can get."

"And what information do you think might be sufficient for me to grant you any clemency whatsoever? Come, do not attempt to bargain. It is good enough or it is not."

"Then I will tell you, your Highness, he is has planted a great harvest. Soon he will reap what he has sown and he will draw forth more barrow warriors than all the kingdoms of Tethera can hope to stand against. It will wash over you all in a great wave and that will be an end to it. It will not be this year, or even the next, I think, but it will certainly be in fewer years than you have fingers on your hand."

Lleu was chilled to the bone by this, but managed to yawn and pat his mouth. "Yes, that is information I already have."

"You lie!" exclaimed Garl, "you seek to avoid your promise."

"Do not," Lleu cautioned, "make such an accusation again. That is your only warning. And yes, I know all about those many barrows he raised deep in Annwyn, each loaded with sixty lost souls, dug by armies of barrow warriors as they were overseen by his pet Cyhyraeth. Really, Garl, that news is over a century old. How uninformed do you think I am?"

Garl simply stared, his face, even through the filth, conveying a mix of complete astonishment, coupled with near total despondency.

Privately, Lleu was glad that no one standing near enough to overhear this was prone to crying out in despair at bad news. "Come Garl, give me fresher news or none at all. Last chance."

Garl nervously licked his lips, something he seemed to regret as soon as he tasted them, but he then spoke again. "Here is something you cannot possibly be aware of. Lord Arawen knows the prophecies as well as you. You have to unite all the kingdoms as their high king in order to fulfill them before you can pose even the least threat to him. He needs only to destroy one to make this impossible."

"I think we all know that, Garl."

"I am not finished. You denied him Clwyd, for the moment, but he is a nimble strategist. Thus he convinced the Picts that now was their time to destroy Ergyng."

"And he has failed here as well. Get to the point, Garl."

"Lord Arawen had no great faith in the savages—for good reason it seems. Had they succeeded, well and good for him but, even in failure, they were an adequate diversion."

Lleu rose from his throne of boxes. "What are you saying?"

"Now, while so much of your strength is here, as far away to the east as it can be, it is even at this moment that Dylan, Lord of the Sea, prepares to burst forth upon the shores of Dyfyd, with uncounted numbers of Fomorii. He will not stop until he has destroyed it utterly."

* * *

Everyone was called to the war room save, of course, for Slow Tomos.

"What is there left for us to do?" asked Caradog. "We are here, and Dyfyd is where it is. Lord Arawen has thoroughly foxed us this time. Yet King Govannon has his own warriors, he might yet rally and prevail."

"I do not believe that, and neither do you," said Afaggdu. "The smith king is a fine and dangerous warrior, and well skilled in war. What sort of war leader this Dylan is remains unknown but, with nothing unexpected to upset his carefully laid plans, I do not believe Lord Arawen would commit to a plan with much chance of failure. He would never have failed at either Clwyd, or here, had it not been for the occurrence of the completely unexpected in both cases. Meanwhile, he is attacking Dyfyd because it is an easy target, given his resources. Dylan is a force from the sea and Dyfyd, with two long coast lines, and split by a great inlet, is far more vulnerable than any other kingdom would be."

"There is no help for it," Lleu declared. "I must get myself to Dyfyd and do what I may or all is lost. Indeed, all might well be lost already."

Cymri shook her head, "It is too far, Lleu. Also, what could you do by yourself? And do not forget that the king of the Iron Throne is not precisely an ally at this point."

"On the former, you are wrong. I checked the maps and I know my own capabilities. It is not yet mid-afternoon. If I leave now I could be on the coast of Dyfyd come sunrise."

"It is too far. Exhaustion would claim you and, even if you did make it, you would be in no fit shape to help with anything, even if King Govannon did not immediately seek to take you hostage," she insisted.

"Again, no. I am no longer a novice at flying. I can rest at intervals and just soar during the day and the first part of the night. The land beneath will still be warm from the sun, and rising currents of air will support me without real effort."

"Then I am coming with you as well. I can change into any number of birds as easily as you can."

"Aye, maybe," Lleu admitted. "But you do not have Boudicca's torc to lend you strength and energy—yes, it does do that. Additionally, recall how sore you were after we went searching for Afaggdu and our Northmen reinforcements? Although Moriganna very well might, you do not yet have the muscles and tendons required to do this thing. That will take time and exercise and there is no substitute for either."

"You are saying I would slow you down," she accused.

"That is precisely what I am saying."

She scowled at that but said nothing.

"Gower and Slow Tomos are both injured and will be at least another month healing, else one or both of them could accompany me. Gower might even carry another. But these are not options at this time. Even Cilgwri will not be able to keep up. Once again, I find that I am destined to be an example of working royalty, and therefore I must do things myself.

It was Helgar's turn to object. "Lleu, you can do much, this I know. But there will be none to guard your side or watch your back against either this Dylan or King Govannon."

"Govannon is not a problem I will solve with the edge of my sword, but there are other ways. I will have time to think on this as I travel. As for what I may do about Dylan? It may be as you say. There may be little or nothing I can do to alter the outcome, yet I must make the attempt, for the outcome will alter my future—in truth, it will alter the futures for all of us.

"Do what you can for Ergyng, then send your armies home; doubtless there is much they can be doing there. Dyfyd will live or die without them and, with the enemy's every piece countered or already in play, I do not believe we will see any other great battles this year. When that is done, please assemble yourselves at Caerleon. Whichever way things go with Dyfyd, that is where you will need be when this is settled. Oh, and I only promised Garl his life, not his liberty. Have him delivered to Hafgan's people at Cas-Eiddew, and ask them to be more cautious this time. A century spent working for the Firvulag should be just what Garl needs."

"Lleu," said Llewellyn, "I must speak to you now, before you depart. If you are going to face Dylan, I am the only one here that has ever laid eyes on that monster, and there is something I must tell you about him. Something that, for the moment, must be for your ears alone."

Chapter XLIV

Oath of Fealty

Lleu passed over Pembroke at dawn. A great force of men had recently left the capital of Dyfyd and gone almost directly west. It was easy enough to follow the trail from there. No army could move and not leave a trail of empty containers, straggling reinforcements following, and supply wagons and messengers moving back and forth along that trail.

An hour more and he found the main force of Dyfyd, drawn up in battle array on a great, grassy slope overlooking a long, wide beach. It was a beach occupied by a vast force of creatures which had walked, and crawled, from the sea itself. More were still emerging every minute. A burned out town lay on the north end of that beach. It looked to have had a substantial number of docks before misfortune had overwhelmed it.

The Fomorii had no incentive to spare anything, not even for their own use, Lleu realized. This war was not being fought for land, goods, nor even glory. In this war, a scorched earth campaign would only serve the attacker's needs, not the defenders, for their goal was total destruction. They wanted nothing more than to deny the possibility of this kingdom, the last one that had not agreed to be ruled by a high king, any chance of doing so.

He landed in a rush right in front of the Dyfyd leader, changing back to a man as he did so. All around, the warriors of Dyfyd yelled in surprise and drew weapons, determined to defend their king.

"Stop!" ordered Lleu and Govannon simultaneously and, miraculously, they all did.

"Greetings, King Govannon," said Lleu. "I take it you know who I must be?"

The king allowed his stern features to assume a pained look, for a moment. "You do not look quite as I expected, but I would not be bright enough to rule here if I did not. Welcome, Prince Llew. We did not accede to your request to rule us and now we prepare to die. Have you come to gloat at our destruction?"

"Surprisingly enough, I have not. Know this: you are only singled out for destruction because the Lord of Death fears your joining me, even now. He would have Tethera face the coming might of Annwyn with as little strength as possible. He has engineered this entire invasion and you, in your pride, or for whatever other reason there may be for your denying the return of a high king, are why he saw profit in doing so."

Govannon gave him a look of appraisal. "So you are not here to watch our end, eh? If you mean to aid us, I hope you brought every warrior you can call on to aid us, for that is no less than it will take."

"I have brought myself. If that is not sufficient, then nothing else will be."

"Yourself?" The king gave a bitter laugh. "I have heard you are a talented warrior, and that ability of yours to shape-shift must be useful indeed, but do you really think that is enough to turn the tide here? Awkward as yon beasties might be out of the water, there are yet enough of them to bury us in the first wave."

"Then let us hope it does not come to that. First, however, there is a price for my assistance, and it is not one you should ever have been loath to give."

The king looked, if anything, more troubled. "Dyfyd is a proud and free kingdom, and I am its king. Why would I seek to declare fealty to any outsider?"

"I am no outsider, I am the rightful high king of all Tethera, and Dyfyd is a Tetheran kingdom."

"So you claim to be Pwyl's heir? That would be even more reason why none should follow you. The Mad King did these lands no good."

"I am not he. Possessed by Lord Arawen, he sundered these lands; I seek the reverse, and for a higher purpose. With the merger of Glywysing, Gwent has been restored to its full size. I have united Gwent, Gwynedd, and Ergyng under my reign and, with regard to Ceredigion, despite your claims to the contrary, I effectively have already done the same there, and I can say the same for Clwyd. Neither Clwyd nor Ergyng would even still exist, were it not for me. They made the right choices, as should you."

Govannon regarded him with frank skepticism. "You imply that I should swear fealty unto you because then you will save us from the terrible sea creatures?"

"You should swear fealty to me because it is the proper thing to do and every other course is less so. I will furnish whatever proofs you need when matters are less urgent but, if the only argument that can persuade you is the obvious one, then here it is. You stand alone when you need not do so. Acknowledge me as your high king and we shall see if the Fomorii can still be turned back.

"If you refuse to acknowledge me, the Fomorii will work Lord Arawen's will upon you, Dyfyd will join with fallen Powys and, in time, Annwyn will engulf and destroy all that remains. The hour is quite late, and what I have in mind may not save you but, then again, it might."

The king waved his hand dismissively, "I can argue with none of that, even were this the time or the place. For that reason I will not dither or delay but will simply say this: save this kingdom and I will pledge to you."

Lleu shook his head in refusal. "No, no more conditions. You cannot place conditions on me as I am already your rightful high king, and you will acknowledge that, here and now. Should I fail, both of us will be destroyed, and Dyfyd as well. In that event it will not matter to you, or to anyone, who is high king, or even if there is one. So I say to you, before we proceed even one step further, you will pledge to me now, without reservation. Do so and you may still fall but, then again, you may not, and you will not be alone if you do. Refuse to do so and you will most definitely fall . . . and all Dyfyd with you."

King Govannon made to reply, but stopped. For a long moment he stood there unmoving, then he took a long breath and appeared to grow relatively calmer. "I am a king, but I am also a smith—no, please, hear me out—working with the raw metal, forcing it to my will and producing something strong and useful, something to be desired, is, perhaps, an odd skill for a king, but I am what I am, and I am so skilled at it that the dwarves themselves sometimes come to swap secrets with me. I love working at the forge with my hammer, far more than sitting atop my throne with my scepter, but I must admit it colors my thinking."

Lleu wanted to ask how it did, but saw that King Govannon was not finished speaking.

"Whether I am on a throne, or at an anvil, my respect is earned only by strength and purity of purpose. I have no use for that which is not proven to be well-made and as strong as possible. For me, everything is forged for a purpose, and it must serve that purpose. I have no desire or need for anything, or anyone, that fails to meet my standards. Whatever fails to measure up I will destroy or discard. It is a harsh way, I know, but it is the way of a smith, and it is my way. I make no apologies, for I hold myself to the same standard. Over time, however, it makes me loath to allow anyone to take precedence over me, for I tend to distrust their capabilities, relative to my own. But there is something else that well-made steel must be, and that is flexible. Too much is a bad thing, but too little and the steel will be useless, so brittle it will surely shatter and break when tested. I know that I am frequently too inflexible and this may be one of those times."

Lleu opened his mouth to speak, and Govannon said, "Please, just a moment more. I want you to understand that I am not blindly arrogant, too proud and unbending, nor am I a coward who bends to the shape of whatever wind is blowing. I can see the steel in you, and I have heard you are flexible, but now I see you are not overly so. If you are properly tempered and prove strong enough, then perhaps we may somehow persevere and, if not, it is as you imply; whether I should pledge of not would be a moot point.

"This is why I now pledge to swear my fealty to you. It is not out of any fear of my own death, or even the destruction of Dyfyd, your Highness. I simply could not, in good faith, swear my fealty, and the fate of Dyfyd, to one who was not at least my equal. I declare you my liege and high king. We can formalize it later, perhaps, when you show me some of those proofs you speak of, for I am still a cautious man, and there is a line to be walked there as well. For the moment, it will be enough that you show me how we may save Dyfyd."

Lleu regarded his new subject wonderingly. "I confess when I heard of your resistance to my reign, and your refusal to acknowledge Taliesin's rights in Ceredigion, I assumed you must be a far different man than you now appear to be. I find I am pleased, not only by your acquiescence but, if not by your earlier resistance, then by your reasons for it. I will be proud to have you at my side when we face Dylan."

"We will face him then? Now?"

Lleu looked downslope at the massed army of strange beings below them, still constantly growing as ever more of them strode out of the sea. "Yes, although, if my thoughts are correct, perhaps it will only be him that we face."

* * *

"Why must we wait, your Highness? Govannon asked. "We are as ready as we shall ever be and his assembled forces only grow larger."

The two had eaten from common travel rations as they sat atop the rocks that offered them the best view of the enemy. They now sipped at watered wine and, to Govannon's mind, Lleu was showing no inclination to put whatever plan he had into effect."

"Patience, please," replied Lleu. "I have it from my sister, Llewellyn, who has personally encountered him, that this Dylan is, if a trifle grim, an extremely handsome fellow, well-proportioned and quite tall. Do you espy anyone below who meets those requirements?"

"Nay, I most certainly do not. Every individual there appears to be singularly disfigured in its own way."

"Therefore, he has not come yet," said Lleu. "The one that currently appears to be in charge is named Dux Sevasto. We have met before, and he would most definitely be subordinate to Dylan, were he there. I also imagine that there will be quite a stir amongst them when he does come."

"What makes you believe he will come?"

"If any of my conjectures upon which I have based my plan are correct, then he will surely come. Even if he does not care to accompany his own creatures into battle—and I think that he very much does—he knows we are here, or soon will, and that will draw him forth inexorably."

"May I ask why that would be the case, your Highness?"

"He hates men, especially royalty, beyond all measure. He hates them to the point where he will go far out of his way even to give insult, let alone harm. But please, you are sworn to me and we are about be comrades in arms against a terrible threat. This is not a formal setting and, for all that we are surrounded by many thousands, both friends and foe, it is not a public setting either; call me Lleu."

"Lleu? Not Llew? I fail to see—"

"Ho," called a voice from upslope. Both men looked up and saw several riders approaching. The foremost of these dismounted and left his horse to Govannon's men. Armored and accoutered as one of considerable station, he strode rapidly in their direction.

"Drat," said Govannon. "I had hoped to have this well underway before he arrived. I was counting on him to salvage what he could after I fell. Now he will insist on joining us and I cannot prevent that—not even you can, I expect."

"Who is he then?" Lleu inquired.

"My cousin, a fair warrior and a masterful spy. He has been away for some time, and only returned this summer, but he has already made himself invaluable again. If you thought I acceded rather easily to your demands for my fealty, he would be part of the reason. He has been urging me to see the error of my ways ever since he returned."

The man came through a group of warriors that parted like water to let him pass, and then he stood before the rocks on which they sat. Lleu stared. In a voice he was sure must sound weak, he croaked, "Addfwyn?"

Chapter XLV

On the Beach

Addfwyn's bravado fled and he looked more sheepish than anything. "Yes, my prince, for now I know you to be, despite your new appearance. I am so very sorry I did not accept your word as to who you were . . . and the things I said!"

"What," asked the still stunned Lleu. Then it came to him: the attack in his rooms at Caerleon. "Oh, think nothing of it. Please accept my own apologies; I hope being bound and shut into my wardrobe did you no harm? I really did not know what else I could do."

"Oh no, no harm at all. It would have been a trifle embarrassing perhaps, had anyone else managed it, but I would expect such treatment from you, my prince." Addfwyn's face contorted, "Ack, my lord, that is not how I meant that to sound. I mean given your general puissance and strength—"

He was unable to continue, due to the noise made by King Govannon clapping his sides and gasping in laughter. Lleu permitted himself a grin as well.

"So," gasped Govannon, as he calmed himself, "the two of you know each other, that is plain, but have you met?"

"Perhaps," said Lleu, speaking slowly, "not."

"Fine then, High King Lleu, I give you King Addfwyn. King Addfwyn, High King Lleu."

"King?" said Llew.

"Say rather king-in-exile," corrected Addfwyn, "for until Powys is restored, that is all I can lay claim to. Ah, and my kinsman called you high king." To Govannon: "You have finally sworn fealty, cousin? I am much gladdened to hear that."

"Yes, as I was telling him, I am somewhat like the metal I work. Getting me to change can take a lot of pounding, and often from more than one direction."

"It just dawned on me that I have lost the best man-servant any prince could ever hope for," remarked Lleu. To Addfwyn: "You do realize you have some serious explaining to do? What of the wife and children you told me you had buried on your croft?"

"They were real enough, your Highness, but they were not buried there. They died years earlier, when Powys fell before the forces of Annwyn."

"Ah, and I am sorry to hear that," Lleu sympathized. "Yet what were you doing on that croft in the first place?"

"Moriganna suggested I go there and establish a croft nearly a full year before you came. She said inserting myself into the coming high king's company, and doing my level best to assist him, was the best way in which I could contribute to paying back Lord Arawen. When the bandits came, I had to kill several of them, and join the remainder, because I could not leave until you arrived. Moriganna also said it is likely, when you defeat Lord Arawen, that you will be inclined to aid me in restoring Powys."

Lleu sighed. "I do wish she would stop doing that," he complained.

"Does that mean, even should we eventually win out over Lord Arawen, that you will not help me restore Powys?" asked

Addfwyn, his disappointment evident yet, for the most part, constrained.

"No, of course I would—will. Moriganna or no Moriganna, I cannot imagine myself doing anything else. I just wish she would stop doing that. Specifically, telling people what I will or will not do, even before I am aware there is a choice to be made, let alone before I have had a chance to make up my own mind. It sometimes makes me feel like I am some sort of clockwork mechanism, not unlike the jeweled birds I once gave to Queen Enid that, when they are sufficiently wound up, will always behave in a perfectly predictable manner."

"Your Highness," said Addfwyn, "before we can deal with Lord Arawen, there is still Dylan to contend with. May I ask how you intend to do this?"

"Certainly," replied Lleu. "I hope to get him sufficiently wound up such that he will behave in a perfectly predictable manner."

* * *

They did not have long to wait. At terce, Dylan rose from the sea. There was no way to miss it, it was impossible not to hear the chanting approbation of the Fomorii, although their garbled voices en masse made it impossible to understand what it was they were chanting.

With Addfwyn carrying a white pennant, the three kings walked forward from the warriors of Dyfyd, only stopping when they were fully a third of the way downslope to the masses of Fomorii forming up along the beach. Lleu was fairly certain that, even in full armor, the three of them could make it back to the forces of Dyfyd far ahead of any Fomorii sent to attack them.

There they waited. At length Govannon ventured, "I fail to see why Dylan will deign to meet with us at all, when there are no terms we could come to that we would all agree with. He is bent on a general extirpation of Dyfyd and, for us, everything depends on not letting him do that."

"He should take the offer of a meeting, all the same," responded Lleu. "While it is true we can offer him nothing in the way of his final objective, I judge, from what Llewellyn has told me, that his fury against us, or at least me, is so great that he will not pass up an opportunity to hear our pleading, or to inflict his cruel insults upon us. I believe that, for whatever reason, he has a deep-seated need to assure himself that he is better than anyone else, and he needs contact with others, especially his enemies, in order to facilitate this.

"He also may hope to make some assessment of us for the purpose of being able to gauge our leadership capabilities and predilections more accurately. He is, from what few accounts I have heard of him, sufficiently arrogant to believe he can do that without us being able to do at least as much in return."

"You were right, my prince," said Addfwyn. If we are the bait, then he has taken it, for here he comes. "Let us take care. He is flanked by two of his warriors, one of which appears to be our old friend, Dux Sevasto. They show no white pennant to indicate truce or parley, although that is implied by our own, yet all three bear weapons in hand."

"We cannot fault them for that. Dylan carries a great trident, and the other two have those bone harpoons they seem to favor. It would be a bit difficult to sheath them. Your own mace, I notice, though still depending from your belt, is not thonged on, while good King Govannon openly carries a spear so vicious-looking as to make Helgar envious, should he see it."

"It is of my own manufacture, of course," rumbled the smith king. "It is well tested, and will serve me best, should it come to that."

"Aye, well, let us take every possible precaution even though we should not need our weapons, nor they theirs. I hope to end this on a better note than that."

"You think they will just leave once you have spoken to them?" Govannon was frankly incredulous.

"It is my hope," admitted Lleu.

Dylan's party reached a point approximately as far away from his own army as they were from theirs. Then Dux Sevasto continued to the halfway point and stopped, apparently waiting.

"I think they expect one of us to meet him in the center. Being as Dylan is not there, and I am presumably his opposite, would you go, Addfwyn? I do not doubt you could put another lump on his head should he try anything untoward, but do your best not to let it come to that—then again, do not be caught unprepared should he attempt a rematch."

Addfwyn and Dux Sevasto spoke heatedly for a minute or two before both backed up several dozen paces, then spun about and headed back to their respective parties. Lleu had not been able to hear what was being said, the rumble of the opposing armies, and the waves on the beach below, and on the cliffs to either side, were just too loud for that.

Upon returning, Addfwyn wore a grim smile. "I do not think he has forgiven me for my rough handling when we met aboard the Wave-Strider, your Highness. He demands you come to the center to speak with Dylan directly. King Govannon and I may come also, as will the two with him, but both we and they must remain fifty paces back while the two of you meet."

"How odd," remarked Lleu, "it is almost as if they do not trust us. Let us proceed."

At fifty paces out from the mutual center point, Govannon and Addfwyn stopped while Lleu continued on. As the distance between them decreased by half, he called out, "Greetings, King

Dylan, I have come a long way to speak with you and am glad of the opportunity."

"Is that so?" called back Dylan, as the two continued to close the remaining distance. "I cannot imagine why that would be, there is only one outcome possible this day, and it is nothing you should be glad of."

Llewellyn had once described Dylan to him but, now faced with the real creature before him, he found her description accurate, but lacking. She had said he was tall and powerful, starkly handsome with long dark hair still wet from the sea, and without beard, wearing only the moustache that framed his mouth, after the custom of most men of Tethera. He was indeed wearing armor made from the shells of strange sea creatures. She had also described him as cold, desperately cold, with aloof and arrogant eyes. She had, Lleu thought to himself, considerably understated the staggering iciness his manner projected. The Prince of Gwent suddenly had good cause to wonder if his plan had been nothing more than a forlorn hope.

Still . . . with Fragaroc yet sheathed, he was free to reach up and remove his helm while they were still a good thirty paces apart.

Both men stopped then, Lleu because Dylan had, Dylan because he seemed overcome with shock. Then the words came, hard and bitter, heat mixing with the cold. "What insipid treachery is this? You dare? Did you really think wearing my face would earn you one bit of advantage? I am the son of the wave, the flood that recedes, the tide that returns, and the wave that floods over all. No puny trick of yours can change what will be!"

He started forward towards Lleu, intended violence on his face when, ten steps past what should have been the halfway point between the two armies, that same face blurred and he let forth an anguished moan. Dropping his trident, he seized his head in both hands, then staggered forward at an angle and fell, still moaning, upon the grass.

Everything started to happen then. Lleu moved toward the fallen Dylan while a pair of furious gurgling shouts came from downslope, matched by those of Addfwyn and Govannon from behind him. Running footsteps were coming in all directions, and then he and Dylan were surrounded.

"Take your hands off the son of the—" Dux Sevasto began, his harpoon held ready, then halted in apparent confusion upon seeing Lleu's face. "A thousand pardons, exalted one, I thought I saw you fall—hold, why are you wearing your foe's armor?"

Dylan, partially recovered, pushed himself up from the ground. "He is wearing it because he is my foe. Some foolish stratagem to replace me, no doubt, but it has failed. His enchantment was not strong enough to keep me down."

This brought a puzzled look from Dux Sevasto. "And who are you that wears the Sea Lord's armor but is not he? You wish me to believe the enemy has swapped faces with you, rather than just armor?"

Lleu turned his head enough to look at Addfwyn and Govannon without the Fomorii being able to see his face, then winked at their confused stares.

"My head still aches and you wish to play the ignorant lout, Sevasto?" Dylan roared. I was lord of the sea since long before your progenitor's own eggs were quickened, let alone your own. Ask yourself how our armor could have possibly been removed and donned again so quickly?"

The Fomorii warrior shrugged. "It still seems easier than swapping your entire face and body. You are not quite even as long—I mean tall—as he, and those things you call your ears seem a bit too pointed."

"I can answer both your questions," Lleu asserted. "We look quite similar because we are both sons of the same father, High King Pwyl. My brother's mother, however, was Queen Mab,

Mistress of the Unseelie Courts, hence the ears. My mother was High Queen Rhiannon."

"You lie!" said Dylan, in a voice somehow evoking both the coldest of ices and the hottest of fires. "I know who you are now! Lord Arawen told me all. I am the true heir of Tethera and you are but a mere usurper, worse, an usurper who is but the tool of others. In collusion with my own parents, they sought to murder me and put you in my place, but their mistake was in throwing me into the sea. The sea and I were made for each other, and I survived easily. My Fomorii saw this at once and declared me lord of the sea and son of the wave, belatedly at that, as the sea herself had already done so."

"No," declared Lleu, "the latter part of what you say may be true, but the fact is that you were taken by guile from Queen Mab by one she trusted, as much as she trusts anyone, enchanted as a changeling, and substituted in my place. When assassins came to throw me into the sea, and incriminate my mother for the awful deed, they found you instead. Ultimately, you may blame Lord Arawen for your travails as it was his proxies that made it all happen. Your mother wanted you badly, you could still go to her, and all could be as it should have been. I will freely cede you lands in Tethera and, together, we two, as brothers, shall destroy Lord Arawen utterly. Land, sea, and Fae shall all live in peace, and we will preside over a new golden age."

Dylan released a quick humorless laugh. "You seek to turn me against Lord Arawen? The only one who has treated fairly with me and made no attempt to use me? I think not, and I certainly have no use for anything Queen Mab may claim. She is no less deceitful than the Queen of Deceit herself, and far more capricious. You are a weak imitation and you have failed. I will have nothing less that my birthright, the High King's crown and, with it, the Torc of Tethera, which I see is already on your neck. How convenient; taking it will cost me only a single scheming brother."

He whipped up his trident, preparatory to bringing it down on Lleu, who had not yet even drawn his weapon.

Panicked, Dux Sevasto blurted, "No, not now, my Lord. We are under truce! The punishment will be swift and severe!"

Yet when Dylan gave no sign of even the slightest of hesitations, Dux Sevasto dropped his harpoon to seize one of the Sea Lord's arms, while the second Fomorii grappled with the other.

Dylan cried out in rage, "Traitors!" With a mighty surge of strength he flung off both the restraining Fomorii, his freed trident slashing the one that had not yet spoken such that it was dead before it hit the ground. Then, while Lleu was still drawing forth Fragaroc, the trident swung around towards Dux Sevasto, lying prone and helpless before the descending prongs.

Abruptly, the motion stopped and Dylan released an inhuman scream that went echoing over the slope, carrying itself to both outraged armies; each of which had many members already breaking ranks to run to the aid of their respective rulers.

Dylan, trident still raised, was looking downwards and all eyes followed his gaze. King Govannon's spear had struck him in the center of his chest, penetrating armor and sea lord alike. The spearhead stood out a full three feet from Dylan's back plate.

A great silence fell where no one of either race moved, or spoke, anywhere on the great slope. Govannon released hold of his spear and Dylan fell lifeless to the turf.

Yet Lleu was barely aware of any of this as grappled with his own emotions. Just like that, he had gained a brother and lost him. He had held everything he had ever wanted in the palm of his hand, even a new golden age, and it was all vanished now. All his recently raised hope, gone, another victim to the same madness that had claimed his only living relative.

The wind picked up and whistled past him, carrying his cloak fluttering as it did so. His attention returned to his surroundings and it all came to him at once. The wind was still rising and the sea was now crowned everywhere with whitecaps. Looking, and listening, to the very limit of his abilities, he took in what was happening, then realized why.

Ignoring Dylan for the moment, he strode to Dux Sevasto, still trapped by his own private horror at what had just taken place. He extended his hand to the Fomorii. "Rise, Dux Sevasto, there is no time to be lost."

Wonderingly, the Fomorii allowed himself to be pulled to his feet, then looked at Lleu, still partly entranced by his appearance, a perfect likeness for the son of the wave that was no more. "I should kill you," he murmured, "should I not?"

"Nay," replied Lleu, "my own brother has died here, and I am no less aggrieved than you are, yet others look to us and we have responsibilities that cannot be shirked, no matter how much we might wish to."

"What do you mean by this?"

"Look at the sea." Lleu swept his arms out to indicate the seaward horizon on three sides. "Whatever else he was, Dylan was truly lord of the sea. Now the sea mourns his passing. Each crashing wave grows higher than the last as its lamentations increase. We do not know how hard or how long they will last, but men will move inland and survive until, at last, even this passes. But a great number of your people, perhaps even the greater part of them, are on the beaches and in the shallows. I fear they will be destroyed if someone does not take charge, someone who knows what is going on, and gets them out to the deep waters where the depths may offer some protection for them."

Dux Sevasto looked out to the sea, and then at the legions of Fomorii lining the beaches and coastline, as the import of Lleu's words became understood.

"The waves build too quickly. I think you will still lose a great many of them," said Lleu, in his gravest tone. "But you must make the effort; you must save what you can. It is what good leaders do."

Still in considerable confusion, Dux Sevasto asked, "But what of you and us, the war?"

"I think the war is over if you will but let it be. Other than the Fae, there are only a very few, like my brother and myself, that could prosper equally well beneath the waves or above them. The people of the land and the people of the sea do not contest for the same things, and there is little point of contention between them, unless it is for the occasional fish. I think that, instead of fighting, we could help each other. There must be many trade opportunities at the very least and, as you rebuild from what my brother's hatred has done to you—and will do to you—so we will be rebuilding and preparing ourselves for Lord Arawen. For he will be coming and, should he triumph, then not even the depths of the seas will long be safe from him."

Lleu clapped Dux Sevasto on the back and pointed him to the Fomorii armies below, already being savaged by the enormous waves from the sea. "You have your work cut out for you. To continue my brother's war would be foolishly wasteful, and against both our interests. I hope you will come to agree."

"I already do, your Highness," replied Dux Sevasto. "Yes, I do. Thank you for helping me see that. I now even wonder if the sea, perhaps, mistook your brother for you."

Chapter XLVI

The High King Speaks

With a day's much needed rest, Lleu was confident he could have flown back to Caerleon, but the cousin kings, Addfwyn and Govannon, were having none of that. Nothing would do but that they accompany him, and with a huge honor guard as well.

It took a full week for the seaborne storms to abate before they could even begin. The trip itself took another week and a half, as there was nothing for it but that they go slowly through every village and town along the way while the citizenry flocked to cheer them. Although hazy on the details, word of their victory traveled far faster than they did.

Upon their arrival, they found Caerwent in full celebration. Word of Lleu's coming had not only preceded him, so had the news from all fronts, and the fields surrounding the town were full to bursting with tents of travelers from every corner of Tethera. There were even quite a few of some strange design which, after noting the people most prevalent among them, Lleu realized must be a large encampment of Northmen. It was rather shocking to see them there, right out in the open, and so close to Caerleon.

The streets of Caerwent itself were festooned with a vast variety of flowers, as well as brightly colored garlands, streamers, and banners, such that it was almost too much for the senses to look upon for too long.

It took his party nearly three hours to win free to the gates of Caerleon. There he was met and cheered by still more of his subjects including the castle staff. It dawned on Lleu that, with the addition of himself, Govannon, and Addfwyn, the royalty from every kingdom he ever heard of was present as well. Lindenjal, Gwynedd, Dyfyd, Powys, Ceredigion, Ergyng, Gwent, and even Vandwy, if one counted Araf as heir. That gave him pause and he glanced about for Moriganna. He did not see her but, of course, that meant nothing.

Jarl Helgar, King Caradog, King Govannon, King Addfwyn, King Taliesin, Queen Llewellyn, Prince Ian, and Araf. Privately, he marveled that he already knew all of them, either as traveling companions, comrades in arms, or both. And he knew in his heart it was beyond coincidence, even allowing that Moriganna had engineered his meeting with Addfwyn far in advance. She had surely been involved in some of the others, too.

Putting aside the unease this caused him, he accepted well wishes, congratulations and, in many cases, embraces, from nearly everyone he had ever met, and a few more besides. It was hard not to get dragged away by their excitement, yet there was never a moment when he could stop thinking of all those barrows, deep within the gloom of Annwyn, where Lord Arawen's horrendous harvest must now be nearly ready.

When he got to the courtyard and dismounted, he found an anxious Gower, nearly full-healed, waiting for him. As he ran his hands along the great horses mane, dodged his licks, and assured his Pwacca steed that he was a very good boy indeed, a singular question came to him and pushed all his other concerns away. Where was King Pendaran, Llewellyn's father and his own adoptive father?

* * *

"So he just up and left? By himself? How could he get away without a contingent of guards following him? I know he is the king, but even so, there are limits even on what a king may do. Traveling alone is beyond that limit."

With a bit of help from Taliesin, Lleu had managed to collar King Pendaran's seneschal and draw him into a side room off the great hall for some much needed answers.

The seneschal, one Dillie ap Winn by name, shrugged. "He did not go alone, nor is he the king. Either one of those would excuse him from your limits, my king."

"He—wait—why is he no longer a king, who went with him, and what did you just call me?"

"Your Highness, he left a document that was not to be opened until you rode through the gate. It his abdication, properly signed and witnessed, and naming you his successor."

Lleu paused for a moment, caught off balance as the world reeled about him. Pushing certain thoughts to the side, he said, "I doubt it worth the ink it is written with. I need to see that document at once."

"Yes, your Highness, I have it right here." Dillie opened an ivory tube and coaxed out a new vellum document.

All but snatching it away from the older man, Lleu ran his eyes over the proclamation. He did not doubt that the document was genuine, but he was certain it was not valid. King Pendaran, still hoping Lleu was not who he was, had almost certainly left his throne to his son, Llew, dead these past seventeen years, and thereby ineligible to reign. His reading ability was still sketchy, at best, but he ran his finger down the scroll until he came to a name that was familiar, despite the fact he had never seen it written before. King Pendaran had named his successor as Lleu ap Pwyl.

Feet frozen to the floor beneath shock-weakened knees, Lleu asked, "When last we met, even I did not know who I was. How could he have known my real identity? He could not have! Not unless—"

His forehead creased in thought. "Ah, I am suspicious but, tell me, Dillie. You said he did not leave alone. Who was with him?"

"My king, it was a beautiful red-haired woman, neither young nor old. She was richly attired, and her many fine mounts and ferocious guards were richly equipped. Even her servants lacked for nothing. She identified herself only as the Queen of Vandwy, a kingdom none here have ever heard of it, save in certain old tales. The king took her at her word and, at her request, they went to Math's Tower to privately discuss matters. Three days later, as soon as the unending storm quit, and the sea stopped trying to drown us, he left with her. He ordered his own guards to remain and told us the Queen of Vandwy had enough, and more, for the both of them. I do not believe he was gone a day before the first pigeons arrived with the news of your triumph in Dyfyd, and of your impending return."

"A question Dillie, would you, or anyone else here, have recognized Queen Moriganna were she to ride across the drawbridge and through the gates in broad daylight?"

Dillie looked at him blankly. "I must reply in the negative as I do not believe anyone in Gwent is likely to have ever had the, um, honor of meeting her in person, your Highness."

"I suspect the actual number of such individuals who could now so claim, would surprise you," muttered Lleu, before giving the steward a sharp look. "And what of all these royals that have descended upon us? When did they arrive?"

"King Taliesin returned from Ceredigion a few days later. King Helgar of Lindenjal, King Caradog of Gwynedd, Queen Llewellyn of Ergyng, as well as Prince Ian of Clwyd, all arrived together from Ergyng a week after that—and, of course, King Govannon of Dyfyd, and King Addfwyn of fallen Powys, arrived today with you. King Addfwyn—how amazing is it that we suspected so little while he posed as your man-servant?"

Lleu turned to the other person present and said, "I do not know why she took King Pendaran with her, or why he agreed to go, but it seems you just missed meeting Moriganna."

Taliesin regarded him calmly. "We have met before, and on more than one occasion, your Highness. Now please tell me of this strange Cymri that returned from Ergyng before I seek her out. My heart is heavy at the news that my daughter, whom I so dearly loved, was not my daughter at all but, instead, my nemesis in disguise."

"Moriganna is not so bad for all of that, I think," said Lleu, surprised, and then resentful, that he was now in a position where he was having to defend the Queen of Deceit.

"The new Cymri has never met you, although she does possess some memories of you. I think she regards you and Afaggdu quite fondly. Borrowed memories or not, from her point of view, you both helped her considerably," Lleu explained. A thought came to him at that and his eyes went wide. "What of Afaggdu? You must know now that he inserted Moriganna into your own household, even while he knew she was not actually your daughter?"

The older man raised one eyebrow. "You mean do I intend to inflict some gruesome revenge upon him for his treachery? No, Lleu, we have already talked and I have forgiven him, even though I wound up spending a few years as an oak tree. It is what brothers do."

Seeing Lleu's expression, he hastened to add, "Sane brothers, Lleu. Dylan's madness might have been hereditary—it is difficult to see how anyone of Queen Mab's blood could be entirely of whole mind. It could also be the deliberate machinations of Lord Arawen, over the course of a century, that twisted his mind to the point where he was unable to accept your overtures of peace."

Something Lleu had heard earlier had raised a warning in his mind. "Taliesin? What of King Baddon of Clwyd? Is he not coming?"

"Nay, your Highness, I am led to understand he has recently suffered a rather bad fall from a horse. Plans here will not be affected, despite this. He has sent his son, Prince Ian, and given him full credentials to act upon his behalf in all ways necessary."

"All ways necessary?"

"Impelled by King Pendaran's abdication, the nobles of Gwent intend to hold your coronation in the morning, two days hence. Having no one on the throne makes them understandably uneasy and they want it to be official. That afternoon a ceremony is planned where all the rulers of Tethera will formerly swear fealty to you. Immediately afterwards will be a second coronation, crowning you as high king."

Taliesin bided a moment to let that sink in.

Lleu gave him an appraising look. "It is something like what Moriganna said, so I am not completely surprised that there will be no difficulties in my no longer appearing as I did. What about the fact that the bigger secret is out of the sack? I was expecting at least some problems due to the fact that I am the rightful heir of the mad high king, the heir that would never be allowed near a throne, even if he actually did exist."

"You worry too much. They will just have to give up saying 'When the high king's heir takes up his crown' as an alternative way of saying 'never.' With the lands of Annwyn encroaching farther each day, no one cares about your father's misdeeds. You are the shining hero of the day, and the prime hope of all those desiring a world where their descendants may still be born and live, rather than one that will come to an abrupt end in fire and strife, relieved only by the eternal grip of the grave. Plus," Taliesin coughed gently, "I may have composed and released a few simple songs that my bards have carried both far and wide. They would be songs that encourage people not to look askance on you—quite the reverse, in fact."

"Somehow, I find what you say to be both cheering and disturbing."

The chief of all bards laughed at that. "You did it, Lleu. The great kingdom of Tethera is reborn. The old prophecies are either fulfilled or shattered, and the new ones are in contention with each other. We now have a chance, and at least a little time for a breather before the final horn is blown. What do you intend to do first after your coronation?"

"I have actually given some thought to that. I feel a short excursion is necessary. If, as I suspect, the Fomorii will no longer be sinking any ship that strays out of sight of the coast, I may even have Wave-Strider provisioned and make a little voyage. Yes, perhaps it will even be a peaceful cruise, on which I may relax and appreciate the sun and the wind and the stars."

Taliesin looked startled. "Are you serious? At this time?"

Lleu gave the chief of all bards a tight smile. "We have the time, and the kings and queens of Tethera can ready its full might without the High King looking over their shoulders at all times. Meanwhile, there is something I must do, and the sooner I take care of it, the better for us all."

"And after that?" Taliesin asked.

Lleu's face grew somber. "A time of horror will be nearly upon us, a fearful time. The endless barrows will be ready to open so the Lord of Death may reap his grisly harvest and come forth to visit destruction on all the world.

"Yet the world holds more dangerous things than barrow warriors. Consider it from my enemy's vantage point. We have turned his every scheme against him, shattered his every strategy, all while rebuilding the great kingdom and gaining in strength at every single step as we did so. We have found new friends and allies, and even potential allies, at every turn, while eliminating his own. Now he stands alone and, mad or no, his confidence must be badly shaken. He must also know we will come for him before he is ready, and prophecy is no longer on anyone's side. It will be a time of fear—but now it will be at least as much his fear as our own.

"He begins to question whether he can stop me."

About the Author

The author thinks it a bit silly to write about himself from a third person point of view and believes he will soon cease doing so. Before doing so, he would like to point out that it seems a bit early for a bio as he is quite certain he is still not even halfway done with providing content for it.

I've lived all over the world and worked in a large number of jobs ranging from lifeguard, appliance salesman, rifle range instructor, missile launch officer, assistant professor at the University of South Carolina, and captain in special ops. More recently, I have primarily worked as a contractor/consultant in fields pertaining to software development.

The Forged Prince was my first published work of fiction.

I live with my wife, Linda, in Westchester County, New York. Between us we have four grown children and expect that this may eventually lead to grandchildren (even though we are obviously much too young to be grandparents). Currently we are between dogs.

Please feel welcome to visit my site at: http://lairdmichael.com

I can also be twittered (what a word!) with @King_of_Tethera